SEARCHING
FOR
WALLENBERG

ALSO BY ALAN LELCHUK

American Mischief

Miriam at Thirty-Four

Shrinking: The Beginning of My Own Ending

Miriam in Her Forties

On Home Ground

Brooklyn Boy

Playing the Game

Ziff: A Life?

SEARCHING
FOR A NOVEL
WALLENBERG

ALAN
LELCHUK

Mandel Vilar Press

This book is typeset in Minion Pro. The paper used in this book meets the minimum requirements of ANSI/NISO Z39-48-1992 (R1997). ∞

Publisher's Cataloging-In-Publication Data
Lelchuk, Alan.
    Searching for Wallenberg : a novel / Alan Lelchuk.
        pages ; cm

    Issued also as an ebook.   978-1-942134-02-2 (Kindle)
                               1-942134-16-9 (ePub)
    Includes bibliographical references.
    ISBN (cloth)   978-1-942134-03-9
    ISBN (paper)   978-1-942134-04-6
    1. Wallenberg, Raoul, 1912–1947—Fiction.   2.   Diplomats—Sweden—Fiction.
3. Righteous Gentiles in the Holocaust—Hungary—Fiction.   4. Jews—Hungary—History—
20th century—Fiction.   5. College teachers—Fiction.   6. Mystery and detective stories.
7. Love stories.   I. Title.

PS3562.E464 S43 2015
813/.54

Image of Holocaust Memorial on the Danube River © Can Stock Photo Inc. / Jule Berlin
Designed by Barbara Werden

Printed in the United States of America

15 16 17 18 19 20 21 22 / 9 8 7 6 5 4 3 2 1

Mandel Vilar Press
19 Oxford Court, Simsbury, Connecticut 06070
www.americasforconservation.org | www.mvpress.org

To the memory of
Saul Bellow

I would like to acknowledge the generous help in Moscow of Nikita Petrov of Memorial House, and of Tatiana Lokis, my Russian translator and interpreter.

I would also like to thank the Wallenberg historian, Susanne Berger, for her gracious guidance.

The Making of Fiction, the Revising of History

A Prefatory Note

The world remembers Raoul Wallenberg as the Swedish diplomat who saved thousands of Jews in Budapest in 1944–45, and was then arrested by the Soviets in 1945, taken to Moscow where he disappeared until his apparent death in 1947. When I first began researching the life of Wallenberg, in Budapest 2001,while I was teaching there and lived near his impressive Buda statue, the most obvious items were the major mysteries still outstanding. There were several. First, how and when did he die, in Lybianka prison in Moscow in 1947? Or did he live on, in some Gulag camp or psychiatric hospital? Second, and just as significant, why did he languish in a Soviet prison for two whole years, from 1945–1947, without being exchanged by the Swedish government—as other political prisoners in Europe were—or rescued by his very wealthy, well-connected family in Stockholm? Even now, some 65 years after the events, these mysteries have remained into the 21st century. (Despite the two recent biographies.) Yet perhaps the deepest mystery was, *who was Raoul Wallenberg?* Who was the *living man* behind the legendary persona of noble diplomat and hero of Budapest Jews? The basic questions of his personal identity and motivation compelled me, as I studied the perplexing history.

Because of the above enduring mysteries, which existed as spaces or gaps to be meditated on and filled in, as plausibly as possible, I chose to look at my project from the perspective of fiction, and not history. (It helped that I was a novelist, yet I had been offered a chance to write it as history) This would enable the writer to imagine the scenes and characters with which to fill in those missing spaces. Especially since those mysteries had eluded the answers of historians and biographers for over half a century, it struck me that only within the realm of fiction would the writer have enough license and justification to imagine what might have really happened in the past. Hence the genre of the novel—the most flexible of the genres— seemed apt to suit the open-ended material. Yet, in order to give my poetic license and imagination a solid grounding, I knew I had to pursue the historical ground thoroughly. This meant homework by footwork, traveling to Stockholm, Budapest, Moscow, to interview witnesses and historians, read documents and archives, visit physical sites. In short, my grounding had to be firm enough for me to feel confident that I knew the material as well as any historian.

It turned out, surprisingly, that I was able to meet with several highly relevant figures still alive who had never before been visited or talked to. In Stockholm,I met Olof Selling, in his 70s, who had been in Officers training camp with young Raoul; this gentleman proved to be both frank and useful in revealing character traits already evident back then in the youthful Raoul, traits which would emerge in his mature life to help fill in the puzzle of his character. In Budapest I spoke with a survivor who knew Wallenberg as a 12 year old boy, a witness who explained how he and his fellow Jews saw and experienced, first hand, the Swedish savior. Also there I met with a Hungarian journalist who had specialized in the Wallenberg case, a gutsy lady who informed me of new, interesting information from the wartime years.

Most importantly in Moscow, I was lucky enough, by means of chance and timing, to meet with and interview the original KGB interrogator of Wallenberg in Lybianka Prison in 1945-47. Thanks to this octogenerian's son, who answered the front door of his father's apartment in central Moscow when my translator and I knocked unexpectedly on a Sunday afternoon—after he had told me *not* to come over—*I was fortunate to meet and talk with the reluctant Daniel Pagliansky, becoming the first and only Westerner ever to talk with this intentionally obscure and truculent agent.* (This meeting was witnessed by Daniel's son, Georgy, and by my interpreter.) One week later, Pagliansky died at age 88.

So while I was trying to learn the history, I was also making some history.

What might I do with these actual events? I had several choices, but the one I decided upon was to write those real meetings into the fiction as they had occurred, at the same time that I felt more able to invent freely from those meetings, and project imaginatively onto other scenes with the same characters, though at a different historical time or place. For example, I recorded the actual meeting (from my notes) I had with the KGB officer, in Moscow in 2006, and then, based on that actual meeting, try to imagine the scene of the original interrogation, back in 1947. In *SFW* I indicate clearly which meeting is real, which scene is invented, so that the reader can judge for himself the value and credibility of each. My final hybrid creation is a mingling of the three: the experienced real, the historical, and the fictionalized; thus my reasoning for thinking of the work as a kind of docu-novel. To some extent the genre has been approached before, in works like *Compulsion, In Cold Blood* or

The Executioner's Song, but in those books there was much more emphasis on simple re-enactments of past events, rather than what I was attempting—seeking to imagine and fill in gaps and mysteries in history by means of fictional scenes based on (my) actual meetings, which themselves are scenes in the novel. Far from playing tricks with the reader, my aim was to permit the reader more freedom and more authority to judge for him/herself the imagined realities and projected scenes by the author.

Since I had little interest in writing a conventional historical novel, I had also to figure out an overall scheme for my novel. To begin with, I brought in a chief co-protagonist—Manny Gellerman, a professor of history who grows interested in the topic of what happened to Wallenberg via a graduate student. By means of his professional curiosity, and his adventurous soul. Gellerman becomes part detective, part historian, gradually throwing in all his cards on a gamble that might lead him to a deeper understanding of the vanished mysterious Swede. The search leads him on unorthodox paths, which, in the end, allows him to travel as a kind of private alter ego to the lost Wallenberg, forming a comrade-ship marked by unusual intimacy and Secret-Sharer dialogues.

Any fictional work is of course judged by the qualities of invention and prose, and *SFW* is no different. This novel may present itself, however, with a larger burden upon the writer's historical judgment and the basis for that judgment. Here I accept full responsibility for those judgments, and do not fall back on a novelist's license of free imagination. My judgments on the history—or the missing history, the mysterious history— is fair game for the reader, be he an historian or a literary critic, a Wallenberg case follower or cult-fan. I can only hope that my rather unorthodox mapping of the old terrain is both compelling and revealing at the same time.

As the great English historian Thomas B..Macaulay wrote, in 1828, "History, at least in its state of ideal perfection, is a compound of poetry and philosophy." I would assume he meant here the realm of fiction, as we know it. I concur.

ALAN LELCHUK
Canaan, New Hampshire
September 2014

Where there's a man,
there's a problem.

STALIN

SEARCHING
FOR
WALLENBERG

CHAPTER 1

The university was like a national park, with protected land, preserved forests, a clean river, and, in place of RVs, red-brick and white clapboard buildings with pampered undergraduates instead of wild animals. Indeed, periodic safaris of new recruits and innocent parents were ushered through, persuaded to look agog at the newest sports fields or the high-tech library and science buildings. Important new buildings, not faculty, were on exhibition.

Gellerman surveyed the park from his third-floor office overlooking the Dartmouth Green, waiting for his grad student Angela to show up to report on her progress since her winter trip to Budapest. During the months since she began the project, Manny had done much reading up on her—or *his?*—new subject. He'd read three or four books, multiple articles, a slew of online information, and he had found it more and more intriguing. And bewildering. Was her thesis and his newfound interest setting up a new serious project for Gellerman?

He got up and went to the bookshelf, and pulled down his previous two books. The first, *Turning-Point*, concerned the dropping of the A-bomb. He had come down strongly on the side of the revisionist historians, such as Sherwin and Alperoff, who had argued that there was no pressing need to have dropped those bombs on civilian centers, and that the motives had much to do with displaying political and military power to the Russians. The second, on Vietnam, *The Spoils of Defeat*, was an examination of the dire consequences of ideological fervor, showing how Cold War policies had cost America thousands of unnecessary deaths and misguided policies. He looked again at the date of *Spoils* and winced, realizing that it came out over twenty years ago! Now, in his mid-sixties, Manny felt somewhat deflated. He set the two books down on his cluttered desk, and reflected that his Fulbright trip to Budapest and Prague, several years back, had been an attempt to start up the engines for a new work on the fall of Communism in those parts and the vacuum of

American policy. However, he had not written much, and had lost his initial thrust. But now, this Raoul W. had beckoned . . . a thin gleam on the horizon . . .

He heard the knock on the door, and there was Angela, in winter regalia: yellow down jacket, ski ticket hanging off the zipper, and blue sweater brightened by a smart scarf. "Hey Professor G.!" She sat down, fiddling with her attaché.

"Hi, Angie, how was your trip? Some progress on the thesis?" He added, "And did you get some skiing in?"

"Both," she beamed, and took a sheaf of papers out of her Lands' End case. "I think I hit it rich, sir! Really! Like you may not believe it, Professor."

He accepted the sheaf of forty-odd pages, and quietly observed this bright angel of a young student. Some of the best future researchers of our land would be these athletic Ivy League detectives, who left their skis temporarily for the archives, made major discoveries, and returned to the slopes.

"I'm listening, Angela. What won't I believe?"

"Well, Professor, I followed your 'rumor' lead, and I think I uncovered Hungarian members of his family, alive still, in Budapest. Can you believe it?"

Manny came around to the front of the desk and sat on it. "Go on, I'm all ears."

"Well, it turns out that Mr. Wallenberg was very connected to a Budapest woman, and maybe even married her, and had a child with her as well. And that child, now in her fifties or so, and her daughter are, like, alive and well in Budapest! I met and talked with them, briefly, and totally believe their story!"

Manny suppressed a large grin, and gave instead a small smile. "On what evidence are you basing your 'belief'? What records do you have in hand, or was it just the woman's words?"

"Yes, sir, the woman's words! And a promised journal!" Her face gleamed with triumph. "I tried to search for records in the city office, but that was inconclusive, in part because I have no Hungarian."

Manny nodded in appreciation of her attempted search. Would it have been that difficult to dig up a Hungarian translator? he wondered privately.

"So she talked freely with you?"

"Well, once she saw that I was serious, and doing my research for scholarly work, yes, she talked a bit."

Manny nodded. "Where did you ski?"

"In the Swiss Alps, on the way back. Nothing like it, 'cause the days are so mild and the snow so wonderful!"

Manny took the sheaf of papers and said he would read it, very soon.

"You should meet her yourself, Professor G. I gave her your name and your e-mail as well, which she had asked for, for corroboration. But I guess she was too shy to write you."

"I guess so."

"But she did check out the Dartmouth website, I know. So maybe that was enough for her, huh?"

"Could be." He paused. "So, if Wallenberg fathered this child, when did it happen? And how much did he see her, before he got caught by the Soviets?"

She sipped from her water bottle. "Good question. Not much, not much at all. But then, as I understand it—and this part was a bit cloudy—she was sneaked in somehow to Lybianka once, and he was sneaked in for a visit to see her and their child, in Budapest. A bribed few visits, of course, and highly controlled."

Gellerman scratched at his trim beard, smiled, and turned back to his seat.

"Highly unusual, what you describe, Angela. Almost, if not altogether, impossible. The Soviet Union was a closed, very closed society."

"Yeah, I know. That's why I didn't go all over that too much in my thesis. But for sure, you should chat with her yourself—I mean, to corroborate my research."

"And . . . instinct?"

"Yeah, sure. My instinct." She jumped up. "I *really* look forward to hearing what you think of it. But it's still a rough draft sort of, please remember."

Manny nodded. "I will remember, thanks."

The student left and, true to form, Manny removed his shoes, kicked his legs up onto the desk, and settled into his favorite reading-and-thinking cockpit. What a crazy, unbelievable tale! Well, he hoped she had a sense of humor. After all, much of what occurred in Communist society was so bizarre, so outlandish, that only big grim jokes could get at it. That's why Milan Kundera's and George Conrad's early fiction, the Czech films of the sixties, Bulgakov's *The Master and Margarita*, were so richly revelatory. Not to mention Solzhenitsyn's *The First Circle* or *One Day in the Life of Ivan Denisovich*. All those novelists filled out history—and documented it?—better than the historians . . .

A few hours later, when he had finished the quick reading and checked his e-mails, there appeared, almost on cue, a missive from a stranger in Budapest. Only it wasn't from the expected party, but from a professor:

> *Dear Professor Gellerman,*
> *I write for Zsuzsanna Frank Wallenberg, who wishes to confirm that one student of yours, Angela Robinson, visited her last 10 days ago, and*

took some notes, for a thesis she writes with you. Is this student's information factual? We will be happy to hear from you.
  Yours sincerely,
  Prof. Zoltan Gerevich

How very interesting, thought Manny, and answered:

Dear Prof. Gerevich,
  Yes, I can assure you that Angela Robinson is my student, and she is writing her thesis with me. And if your friend—or client?—Zsuzsanna Frank Wallenberg, wishes to write me directly, for any reason, I will be pleased to hear from her.

Just as he was about to hit the send button, Gellerman added: "I would be happy to visit ZFW myself sometime, in Budapest, if she welcomes me."

Gellerman sent the message on, but wondered, Was this his entry into History, or rather, and more probable, his entry into a private Fantasyland?

Teaching his seminar the next Tuesday, from 4 to 7 p.m., Manny felt at home, relaxed, purposeful, as he greeted his fourteen students seated around a long oval table in the modern Rockefeller building. His seminar was History through Literature, and he had already taught such novels as *History* by Elsa Morante, *Man's Fate* by André Malraux, *The Joke* by Milan Kundera, *Life and Fate* by Vasily Grossman, *The Secret Agent* by Joseph Conrad, and presently was doing *The Book of Daniel* by E. L. Doctorow. At home in the classroom, Manny always reminded himself of how the university existed right here, in this quiet room, with the students, the professor, and the text, far away from administrators, bureaucrats, new buildings, sporting fields, and public relations propaganda. Here, in this sacred sanctuary, each book presented a different problem about how history had entered fiction and, conversely, how fiction had shaped the history. The course was a new one for Gellerman, and he felt energized.

Teaching these seminars was always a question of knowing the text well, the historical context just as well, and presenting the right questions to be discussed. "So tell me," he began, "why does Doctorow choose to tell the story from the point of view of the son, Danny Isaacson? And does he make the son like the real-life Rosenberg boy? And if not, why not?" He paused. "Furthermore, how is history brought into the narrative? Through the characters, or otherwise? And is the writer redressing history, so to speak—at least history as it has been written by the historians? Does the fiction writer have such a right? You can answer any of those questions."

Matt Cheney, a thin fellow from Maine, spoke up first, "Well, Danny is not at all a saintly type. Quite the opposite. In fact he's portrayed at times as nasty and selfish, even brutal to his own wife. Clearly Doctorow doesn't paint the picture of a perfect sort of radical kid."

Carolyn Johnson, a smart, heavyset young woman from a poor black Roxbury background, opined, in her clear slow voice, "Well, history also comes in through those small essays that Danny enters into the narrative, like mini-lectures, you know like when he tells us about Stimson, the secretary of state, thinking maybe we should tell the Russians our secrets about the A-bomb, so we and they would have parity and trust each other, and maybe avoid the whole Cold War. And then he's shoved aside. Or when . . ."

These kids were good, Manny knew, when you gave them the opportunity, and when you trained them to think. They even taught him on occasion, if he listened closely to their semi-articulated views and cut through those to their true thoughts.

"Yeah, but I think he went too far and got it wrong," said Paul Olsen, a short-haired conservative who doubted all his peers' ideas. "They were guilty as hell, like the recent histories show, and the writer is merely trying to justify his own leftist interpretation."

"Well, actually, the recent histories show that Ethel was not guilty, just Julius," Gellerman corrected, "but perhaps the more important question is, Does the writer not have the right to put in his own interpretation? Especially if the particular case is not clear at all, but filled with an assortment of prejudices, mysteries, and inventions posing as facts?"

"Sure, here in a novel he can interpret as much as he wants," suggested Paul. "But if he were writing a real history—"

"What do you mean, a 'real' history?" said Matt. "Don't historians make their own interpretations as well? Is that what you mean by 'real' history?"

"And of course it's based on what they take to be 'the facts,'" said Caroline. "And maybe *their* facts?"

Country girl Jodie Reyes offered, "Maybe we should read some of the histories as fiction then? And some of the fictions as history?"

"Well, why not?" answered Matt. "We've had some good examples this term, haven't we?"

"Especially if people who have mostly written the histories have been those elites at the top?" Mike Reynolds put in. "Wasn't that what E. P. Thompson said, in his *Making of the English Working Class,* at the beginning of the term?"

"Well," Manny refereed, "let's look at what were the so-called facts in the trial itself. Take out the source book, and let's check out those documents."

As the class opened up their source books—which Manny had created for them, in the form of a thick scrapbook, with other documents for other cases, such as the Sacco-Venzetti letters and papers, English anarchist documents, and recent KGB file openings—he decided perhaps to make one for his own Wallenberg case. Weren't there as many prejudices and mysteries there as with these legendary cases?

Why, he might even bring that RW case in here, for the seminar to study and inquire about. Especially if there was a novel already written about it. He'd have to check up on that.

As the class proceeded to look at the sources for the Rosenberg trial and the histories written about it afterwards, with mocking scorn and disbelief, Manny felt proud of their newly-trained skepticism and newfound openness.

"This is really hard to believe," asserted Paul, who wanted to become a prosecuting attorney, "that they would allow such stuff to appear as evidence."

"Hey, you haven't been legally indoctrinated yet!" noted Matt good-naturedly. He said, "See us in a dozen years!" and got everyone laughing.

Manny spoke up, "So here we have a clear example of a country that wants to create its own patriotic history, using the legal system, so that it is willing to put into evidence in a federal trial untrustworthy and illegal material, not to mention bringing in a prejudicial judge. But soon thereafter, in the next years, equally as pernicious and maybe worse, we have historians who rush in to support the illegal trial and accuse the same victims, and thereby help create a patriotic narrative about the nation and its politics, which contributes of course to the Cold War theme and belief system. After all, in a nation that comes first in "selling," both its products and its ideas, this is not too surprising. Fortunately, however, we still have a counterhistory, which begins to kick in some years later, and we start to have a more balanced and fair perspective. Clearly, we should count *The Book of Daniel* as part of that counterhistory, one of the first and strongest documents to stir up rethinking about the whole issue, and despite—or because of?—its fictional package. For if it is merely a novel, it is not supposed to be as politically dangerous as a formal history, right? But actually it turns out to be just as dangerous, and maybe more so."

Some discussion ensued, while Manny considered his notion of creating a Wallenberg source book.

He paused and checked his watch. "Okay, that's it for today; we'll see each other on Thursday, and we will have several oral reports. Okay? See you then."

The class packed up, along with Manny, while several students came over to continue the discussion with their bearded, bespectacled professor.

One student uttered, "You know, sir, I've never quite taken a history course like this before. It's kinda . . . different. Not just the dates and years. Now, how long should my oral report be on Thursday? About ten or fifteen minutes?"

Afterwards, Manny looked toward his regular ritual—either playing tennis with his regular partner, or going to a movie at the local movie house up the street from the campus. With Peter not around, Gellerman deposited his brief-case in his car and walked up to the small theater, The Nugget. Once upon a time a fine art cinema with two large screens, it had succumbed to commercial pressures and reduced itself to four squeezed theaters with much smaller screens and louder speakers; instead of art films, it offered commercial fare. No matter; all Gellerman wanted was to escape from his classroom and his intense mental focus, see a movie, and later grab a quick bite when the restaurants were emptying out.

He got lucky. Sitting up close, he watched with interest *Good Night and Good Luck*, the semi-documentary film about Edward R. Murrow and Senator Joe McCarthy. Surprisingly, the movie was gripping, with fine acting, TV-like black and white scenes, the gloomy sense of the shadowy fifties, the intimidation of McCarthyism. Now, some sixty years after the fact, it was safe to make such a movie, and even make a hit. Murrow had become a kind of Radio God, though Manny recalled his broadcast about Buchenwald, and his glaring omission of the word "Jew" when speaking about the "victims." How come the moral icon of the radio had omitted "Jews" and substituted "Europeans?" Gellerman had never forgotten that.

Still the movie was a worthy effort, and he felt grateful that he could actually sit through an American flick and not be insulted or bored, on edge to leave.

After an avocado pizza at Molly's, he drove to his countryside home, twenty-eight miles, and settled into his living room. He built a fire in his Indian Room—his private name for the room, which had, on the wall between high bookcases, four of Edward Curtis's striking portraits—and read the newspaper and mail. Tomorrow, when he was fresh, he could read through Angela's draft a little more seriously. Meanwhile, his thoughts wandered to East Europe, its different cities and values, its culture of gray scarcity. So different from the native pot of overflowing Plenty. With a value system of what, nowadays? Power, gluttony, greed?

In the morning, he had his orange juice, a full bowl of mixed cereals and sliced banana, and freshly ground coffee. Having slept decently, he felt well, felt firm, and looked forward to his own work and to the thesis. All the sins and failures of his recent past—no book in a while, the divorce, certain friends lost—were now relegated to the back burner. The beauty of mornings, after real sleep, wiped all that away. Before getting to the work, he checked his e-mails and found a new one from the East.

> *Dear American Professor Gellerman,*
> *My friend Gerevich tells me of your interest in my dead father. Your student also was here. What is it you wish to know to work on, please tell me? I am open to your questions, and your interest.*
> *Sincerely,*
> *Zsuzsanna W.*

Intrigued, surprised, baffled, Gellerman absorbed the note and considered a possible response.

In the living room, he turned on the classical music station, took his second mug of coffee, and turned to the thesis. As he began reading, he found his attention engaged in both places—in the pages, and over yonder, in Budapest. Happily, Angela could write well, and so it was not unusual torture to go through her thesis more carefully. He read—while listening to Beethoven's Opus 59, the "Razumovsky" quartet—and was pleased to find her work competent: a reasonable amount of footnotes, a good bibliography, solidly written sentences. And when he came to the section describing the interview with the daughter, he observed that the temperature of the prose grow more heated. Angela had bought the cockeyed story, hook, line, and sinker, and spent nearly a half dozen pages on it, acknowledging that there was no hard evidence to back it up. So Manny marked it in red and made the suggestion that perhaps she should drop it into a long footnote. And treat it as a local myth that grew naturally from the unnatural facts, a sort of apocryphal legend . . . As Mozart took over, Gellerman moved on, getting through all sixty-eight pages in an hour and a half, and understood the kind of romantic hero she had portrayed. Yet he learned two things from it. One was the number of RW "sightings" that she had come up with—ex-prisoners of the Gulag who had claimed, in one way or another, that they had seen an old ailing Swedish prisoner in different work camps of the Soviet Union, after 1947. Second was the source where Angela had come up with this finding: a "Swedish-Russian Working Group that in the early 1990s had put out regular papers and reports, some very long, every few years." So the case had lingered, and remained of continuing, haunting interest. This meant that secrets remained, along with guilt and shame . . .

Manny rose, stretched, went for a walk in the woods, stepping over the crunchy snow-covered trail toward his old writing cabin. The smells and sights of the white branches, the glistening birch trees, the protected delicious air of the forest—all that refreshed the spirit. Footprints of a deer and droppings appeared. He walked up and down the looping trail, stopping by the huge shelter tree, of some two hundred years, admiring its vast girth. The state forester who had walked through with him had explained that deer and bear would huddle there, during bad weather or wind. (A good place for Manny one day?) Even now, here, in this season, he could hear some birds twittering. The forest was always alive with its own noises, creakings, silences. His loop took him through his sixty acres and out into a lower meadow . . .

Who was the *real Raoul*? And *why* did he go to bat, and sacrifice himself, for the Jews? (And not even Swedish Jews, but Hungarian ones.) Made little sense. But then, many of the best things often made little sense. Maybe like his own increasing pursuit of that curious Swedish diplomat turned noble man.

Manny watched the news: the latest surveillance scandal of the Bush administration; one minute and thirty seconds about the ongoing Iraq war; one minute for the latest rumor about the next likeliest anchor of the CBS news (a smiley talkshow host to replace cordial Uncle Schieffer, about twelve million bucks annually for reading the teleprompter for twenty minutes); a possible new drug for the arthritic, delivered by a pretty blonde (and the ads for drugs to aid the heart, the penis, the bladder). The celebrities and the distractions received as much time as the real news, if not more. The nation had become so bent out of shape, with anchors deemed newsworthy and celebrities thought to have "heft," it was no wonder that audiences could hardly tell the differences between the real, the illusory, and the irrelevant.

Sitting back in his study, he read a 1996 *U.S. News & World Report* essay on Wallenberg, making the claim that he was a double spy for both the Americans and the Germans. A conspiracy theory coauthored by a Russian émigré. Manny took a few notes on the melodramatic piece and then returned to the collection of RW's *Letters*. He read a half dozen of these letters, imagining the various sites—Haifa, Capetown, Ann Arbor—of Raoul's broad education, provided by his pragmatic grandfather. Next he read an interesting piece on a German prisoner, Rodel, who had been in prison with RW . . .

He opened his laptop and composed a little scene:

A gray misty day, typical for Budapest in February. The thin man in the dark suit sat at his small wooden desk, examining a sheaf of papers he had received that issued new rules and boundaries for the Swedish mission.

As he skimmed through the monotonous bureaucratic language, he looked up to see Vilmos, his husky secretary and driver, approaching. The large fellow motioned to the phone, and the diplomat lifted the receiver.

"Wallenberg here," he said cooly, and listened to the speaker at the other end. In a few seconds he nodded to Vilmos, motioned with his hand, and the secretary departed. The diplomat said a few more words, hung up, and stood. Getting on his overcoat, he made for the door, but, checking the inside pocket of his suit jacket, he returned to the desk and removed a small revolver from the drawer. Now he moved out quickly, grabbing his backpack, and, saying a word to a colleague in the hallway, he bounded down the stairs of the large three-story private house.

"How bad is it?" the driver asked.

"About two hundred fifty Jews, including children and grandparents, are at the Keleti Station, about to be deported in one hour. If you get us there in twenty minutes or so, that will give me approximately forty minutes to do something."

"Oh, you have plenty of time then."

Raoul lighted up, and said dryly, "Yes, plenty of time."

Vilmos knew the city like the palm of his Hungarian hand, having grown up there, and he slippped the car through the gray side streets like an eel through water. Once again Raoul was grateful for the sleek American car, which he had insisted on, having once driven one for over a year in Michigan. Whenever he felt deeply gloomy, he returned to those three golden years in Ann Arbor.

Driving about in that 1934 Studebaker was a delicious freedom. He recalled driving it the two and a half hours from Ann Arbor up to a small town, Ganges, on the banks of Lake Michigan, where a friend's family owned a cottage on the ravishing lake. An architecture colleague in Slusser's studio, Sof (for Sofield) had become a good pal who beat him regularly in tennis but educated him about the Midwestern laid back style. After staying with the genial family for a few nights, he'd go on a road trip way up north to the Upper Peninsula, a region wild and remote. It reminded him of the wild north of Sweden, where he had gone skiing as a young man, and where he had done his army training. An isolated wilderness for hunting and fishing, which he had tried once or twice. Oddly enough, he never felt lonely driving up there among the mountains and forests, but, rather, highly gratified, whole.

Sometimes he'd drive over to Chicago and view the soaring skyscrapers, created by his favorite architects. Harmony in steel, they shaped a powerhouse introduction to the city of rugged beauty and slaughterhouse crudeness. So appealing—and so very different from his tame, proper Stockholm.

At the Keleti Station in Buda, he alighted from the Studebaker, followed by Vilmos, and made his way into the station yard itself. The scene was half chaotic, half orderly, with two young sentries asking him for papers, in Hungarian, and Vilmos responding, and Raoul taking out his diplomat's papers. A crowd of families with luggage and children milled around each other, for warmth, comfort.

The guards called for their superior, and a middle-aged fellow in an Arrow Cross uniform came over and brusquely asked who they were, what they wanted.

Vilmos repeated his information, and the lieutenant shook his head, pointed to the exit. Immediately Wallenberg stepped into his face, took out a notebook, asked his name in German, and told him that if anything happened to any of these people, for whom he had safe house passes—which he waved in the man's face—he would be shot or hung. Or far worse, if the Russians arrived first.

The lieutenant's face changed from fury to bafflement, and Wallenberg stood right before him, not budging, blocking his way. The gray sky hung very low.

Wallenberg told him, if he was in doubt, to call the German high commissioner, whose number Raoul held out for him.

The lieutenant said something in disgust, waved his hand, and walked off. The sentries moved out of the way. Wallenberg and Vilmos walked into the yard.

The crowd moved in closer, very slowly, and an older woman wearing a large black hat pointed at Raoul and whispered to her husband, and presently the whisper circled through the crowd, creating a consensual hushed conversation. They moved closer toward Raoul. Two children were allowed to run up to him, chattering away in Hungarian. They fiddled with his trousers, reached for his hand, and held it.

A light sleet began to fall as Vilmos called out to the group to stand in queue, and he collected their Swedish safe house passes.

He remarked to Raoul, "I didn't know you had Wiesenmeyer's direct phone number."

Raoul smiled and made a face. "Oh, I thought *you* did." He began filling out the safe pass, or Schutz-Pass, cards, while asking the mulling families not to push forward. "Please, let's get this done orderly."

But the old lady, wearing lipstick and the odd hat, had stayed by his side and now handed him an old leather bag, a doctor's black bag, and set it furtively in his hand. In German she said, "You will hold this for us, yes? For the two families, Dr. Kornis and Mr. Marton. Please."

Raoul understood and nodded, and held onto the bag, knowing that inside would be a collection of family heirlooms and old jewelry, maybe some cash and a few bank books, and an important address book. A life in a bag. To be added to his collection.

The Arrow Cross lieutenant came up and said, "Get the scum out of here soon, or I will change my mind!"

Raoul allowed the fake sign of bravado, and observed a flock of pigeons flying overhead. He signaled Vilmos to hurry the Jews into the vans and rickety bus that had arrived.

"What is that smell?" he asked his friend.

"Coal, probably. There is a plant not far away."

"Awful."

"Yes, but it is good to be able to have the time for the smell."

Raoul smoked, noticed the cold wind whipping now, and walked a few steps back and forth. These minutes were always the most nerve-racking, waiting for everyone to line up and get out before there was a sudden change of mind for any reason, and more desperate measures had to be taken. How could he ever do this without his Vilmos? Well, he couldn't.

The ten minutes passed slowly, the crowd dwindled, the light went out from the short day.

"Perhaps we'll stop on the way to Pest and grab a few of those custards," proposed Vilmos, "to celebrate our little victory today."

"A charming idea—but I think we would do better to deliver our clients safely, and tonight, maybe at the Arizona Club, then celebrate with a few drinks."

"What about the bag?"

"Leave it in the trunk of the car. Until we can make the transfer, later tonight."

Vilmos nodded, a cigarette dangling from his thick sensuous lips, as he shepherded the remaining Jews into the last vehicles. "We can take the final three with us, yes?"

"Sure."

They got into the car and squeezed the three old souls into the back, setting their few bags into the trunk; Raoul kept the bag of valuables in the front, by his legs, alongside his backpack.

On the streets, driving, they viewed the pitted buildings and the sparse traffic, seeing armed groups of Arrow Cross on the way as they headed down through the hills of Buda. Occasionally Raoul or Vilmos motioned each other when passing a German military vehicle; up here the Germans were fortifying themselves for the oncoming Russians from the East.

With slow calm, Raoul inhaled and exhaled, enjoying the pleasure of the smoke and the drive, listening to the nervous chatter in the back. He took out his little notebook, wet the lead tip of his pencil, and wrote down the names of the two families . . . Should he put the bag in the vault or keep it with him? One day he'd have to transfer it all, back to Stockholm. But for tonight, he'd focus on drinks at the Arizona.

Manny looked up from his computer and thought about the scenario he had just composed. Had he written the railroad scene too smoothly, with Raoul a bit too competent, even though it was based upon research? Was there enough sense of imminent danger, personal risk? What about the times when RW had to use his revolver to threaten a guard? And what if an Iron Cross officer had indeed wanted to call Wiesenmeyer, the German commissioner? Well, the important thing, Manny decided, was to try to recover the visceral scene, the actual moment. But, he thought—playing devil's advocate—why would a historian go this indirect route, even exotic path? Was Gellerman risking his own career here? Well, he recalled one of his old professor's advice—was it Curti or Williams?—at Wisconsin: "Get to the heart of the matter, the truth however you can get to it. Sometimes fiction is a better route than the so-called facts." Said half in jest, but meant seriously. And wasn't Manny's scene based on his reading and research?

Manny gazed out at his meadow, with the rows of trees at the edge of the field, and sighted a hawk flying overhead, circling, hovering, and diving. A New England pastoral scene down there, while up here, in his head, he tried to insert himself back into the Hungarian scene of 1944. Quite a challenge. He wondered if he needed a touch of the real Budapest to continue the quest.

Doing his ablutions in the bathroom before bed, he washed his face thoroughly with the shea butter soap and studied his reflection. The skin was clear, the hair mostly gone except for silver wings and the slim beard, and the nose prominent. The look read? Determination, skepticism, openness, and . . . folly. What percentage of each, he wondered? And where was Belief in something beyond his boys? In history, for example? He smiled mockingly at his cynical view, and decided to close the windows in case of hard rain.

CHAPTER 2

Manny glanced out his tinted-glass window at the large green, on the Dartmouth College campus. It was March. Some kids were tossing a Frisbee, and others, strolling from classes. A twenty-first-century New England postcard scene down there, while up here, in his office, he tried to imagine Budapest of 1944. Quite a transport. Realistic? Or merely fanciful, hopeful? He set his feet up on the messy desk.

How did he get into this fix in the first place? Get involved with the long dead and long forgotten Swede? With the horror show of Budapest 1944? He had this easy, comfortable life, here on this protected campus oasis. Why go and tamper with it?

He recalled the beginning of the fall term, when the bright graduate student had come to see him, said she still hadn't a good idea for a thesis, and he offered, "Well, maybe I have a topic for you: Raoul Wallenberg. Ever hear of him? His case is full of problems and mysteries, just right for research and educated speculation. See what you think."

She immediately took notes as he gave her a few ideas and a few leads, and told her to see him in ten weeks at the end of the quarter. "And if you can find this rumored lady in Budapest . . ." And he gave her the name. The rest was history, as they say.

Manny had always wanted to figure out the mysterious Swede, as well as the mysterious circumstances, so here was a chance to start.

During her December trip, doing research, the student had e-mailed him, saying how excited she was, and her father also. ("He's half Swedish you know, and Lutheran too, so he was delighted at the project, and he's even supporting my trip to Budapest.") Later on, she had e-mailed him from Budapest, saying she was visiting the libraries, meeting people, getting the feel of the place, and making real "hands-on" progress.

When reading her ten-page proposal, sent via e-mail from Budapest, he had kept his doubts to himself, thinking, Let her get through it. Why not? So what if it produced not much new? Had the legions of experts done any better for the past half century? Not really. Besides, it might trigger his own detective work. Which it did. (But where had his own interest come from?)

When she called him from Budapest, he told her that the proposal was pretty decent, and cautioned, routinely, "There's been a lot of stuff written about him, so you will have to come up with some sort of real argument, you understand?"

"Yeah, for sure!" she responded. "But I just wanted to check with you, to make sure you'll go along with it, and me!"

"I'm not really an expert in the field," he said. "There is Michael Atworthy, who is the European World War II specialist, you realize, and—"

"Oh, no, sir, it's you I want to direct it, absolutely. You suggested it, and also, you're Jewish, not that that makes a great difference. But you're the one who knows me, and whom I trust totally!"

"Jewish? Who told you that?" he deadpanned in his voice. "And what difference would that make?" Then he said, "Okay, it looks good. You're on."

And maybe, he advised, the Budapest lady would be worth a footnote in the thesis, and maybe in history too.

A few days later, having done some more RW reading, Manny found an observation from C. Vann Woodward on Francis Parkman and tacked it up—"He sought by creative imagination to bring the past to life"—then proceeded with his own imagination to create a new scene for his small portfolio:

Raoul walked into the Adolph Fredricks Kyrkan in Stockholm, and when the pastor sighted him, he walked up the aisle to greet Raoul. "Well, it has been a while, Raoul," said the graying pastor, in his sixties. "Five years?"

"Probably more, Johann."

"Good of you to come in, Raoul. Your cousins will be pleased that you accepted my invitation. Let us go to my office. Your mother, she is well?"

"As well as can be expected, thank you."

"I don't see her often, you know." He smiled narrowly, showing forbearance. "And I was sorry to hear about grandfather. But you are looking fit and handsome. Please sit."

Raoul nodded, and sat, holding his hat on his lap.

"So, you must catch me up on so many things. You have been all over the map, haven't you? America, Palestine, South Africa." He laughed. "Where *haven't you been* is the better question!"

"Yes, I have been around, haven't I?" Raoul mused, to himself as well.

"And now I understand you are off again, to Budapest, yes?"

Raoul nodded.

"For the foreign ministry, yes?"

"Yes," he said, lighting up a cigarette.

"I know these are difficult days in Hungary, and I know too that the Jews are in particular trouble over there, so you will have your hands full, Raoul."

Raoul nodded. "I am glad you keep up with things, Pastor."

"We may be neutral politically, but morally we have to stand firm." The pastor smiled narrowly. "But I asked you in, to ask you, before you go, if you have thought more about your faith?"

Raoul took up his hat and twirled it, hiding his impatience. "'Thought more about it?' That is an odd way to put it."

"But you know what I mean, son."

"Did my cousins—" Raoul smiled. "Yes, I do. But I am not sure I have thought much more about it than I did when I was younger."

The pastor, his neck straining in his white collar, leaned forward. "Do you not believe, even now, that Jesus died for your sins?"

"Please, Pastor, I have not come for this sort of testing now."

"But Raoul, my son, this is crucial for you, as you are about to embark on this journey. It is a journey of danger as much as one of challenge."

Raoul nodded. "I think you are right."

"Please, then, you should come to terms with yourself, with your faith, with Christ, before you embark. This will be a comfort for you, in your trials ahead."

Raoul smoked, and said, rather casually, "You don't really think that that man named Jesus actually died for *my* personal sins, do you, Pastor? Don't you really think that that is an elaborate interpretation of that curious man's death?"

The pastor reddened. "Raoul, so you don't have faith, after all these years?" He paused. "At your confirmation, I was worried, and now . . . I am dismayed."

Raoul restrained himself. "Oh, I think that would be an exaggeration to say that. I do have faith, sir, but it is not quite in the form, or frame, of your belief. My faith is in the human side of things, rather than in the divine. Or, the divine is rather subsumed under the human."

"*Subsumed?* How strange a term to use here. What do you mean, Raoul?"

"Well, if we bring Jesus into the argument, that he died for our sins, does that include all human beings, or just Christians?"

"For all people, of course—once they are believers."

"But are Jews believers?"

The pastor stood and rubbed his hands together. "Not in their present form, no. But certainly once they become believers—"

"But supposing they don't wish to become believers of Jesus as a God?"

The pastor shook his head and spoke sternly, "You always were a rebel, Raoul, stubbornly rebellious. Rebellion for its own sake? I don't know . . ." He strolled up and down in the office. "You are so different from the rest of your family. Never in step, always out on your own. In everything, from what I hear, but especially here in our sacred place. Why, Raoul, why?"

Raoul smoked and eyed the leather chairs, the large crucifix, the framed documents of divinity degrees, a portrait of Luther, alongside one of Marcus Wallenberg, Bishop of Linköping, 1819, and was comforted by these hard in-animate objects. "I want to thank you, and my cousins, for their concern over my spiritual welfare, Pastor. I appreciate it."

The pastor pulled up into a chair opposite his pupil. "Do you not believe yourself a sinner, Raoul?" He paused. "All of us?"

"Tell me, Johann, are the Jews sinners too? And are they being punished by our Christ for not being believers yet? Is that why they are being persecuted and sent off to be murdered in Nazi camps now?"

The pastor swallowed visibly. "Are you being intentionally perverse?"

"No, not at all, sir."

"You are confusing current political struggles with essential spiritual truths and facts. Is this intentional?"

"I am simply trying to apply principles to realities and see what the out-come is, Pastor."

The pastor reached out for Raoul's hand, but Raoul refrained, and with-drew his hand, out of reach.

"What happens now, here, on this globe, is less important than what occurs afterward, to our eternal souls."

"Perhaps. But for now, before eternity, I have immediate situations to take into account."

The pastor shook his head. "I will only repeat, from 2 Corinthians 5:7, 'We walk by faith, not by sight.' And from Ephesians 2:8, 'By grace are ye saved through faith; and that not of yourselves; it is the gift of God.'"

Raoul had prepared, just in case, and chose a favorite essayist instead of Spinoza for his retort: "Let me quote to you from one of my bibles: 'How many things that were articles of faith yesterday are fables today.'" He stood up and put out his hand, and the pastor hesitated, then shook his hand. "Montaigne's *Essays*."

Dryly, the pastor said, "I wish you luck, Raoul. And God's blessing."

Raoul nodded, released the grip, and walked out of the office and back through the church. What had Johann meant, "from what I hear?"

Professor Gellerman sat and considered the scene. Had he put Raoul too much in charge? Was he too strong there at the end? . . . Raoul's rebelliousness against authority and against the church—that was fitting, in keeping. And maybe too he resented his cousins putting up the pastor to invite him over and gossiping about him? ("from what I hear . . .") . . . What about the pastor? Would—or should—he have been more openly anti-Semitic? Quite possibly. But perhaps, by 1944, something of a guilty conscience in a Christian minister was certainly realistic . . . So what Manny had presented in the end was a Raoul of his own personal faith, neither religious nor patriotic, but human and humanistic, standing for justice and for fairness. That indeed sounded a lot like the Raoul that Manny had learned about and come to believe in. Not a well-costumed saint, but a very good man and a brave soul . . . Not the Church, not the State, not the Family, with all of their bullying chauvinism and lip-service pieties, would deter him from following his high principles. Nor would the Swedes with their self-interested neutrality, or the Hungarians and Nazis with their brutality, deter him. Raoul was a man on a mission, a life mission, it may be said, shaped early on by his pragmatic and open-minded grandfather, and sustained by his own firm independence . . .

He went for a long walk, strolling briskly around the idyllic campus of huge trees, golf course, and oval pond, and onto the paths snaking around the red-brick buildings, and down along the boathouse and Dartmouth Canoe Club set alongside the Connecticut River; all the while, in the soft spring air, he passed joggers and walkers and bicyclists. So orderly, so bucolic, this site. Could he have imagined it as a boy in Brooklyn? And how many other green campuses and private oases were there, tucked away amidst the vast, busy, noisy, crazy country? Who ever dreamed, in history, of such a protected, lucky geography?

When he ambled on down the one main street of two or three blocks long, filled with spry shoppers, stores, banks, realtor offices, Manny again felt the presence of free and easy serenity, sanity. Just as God—or Private Property and well-heeled capitalism—had ordered, in His Intelligent Design, right? At the end he returned to the large oval green at the center of the campus, sat on a white rocking chair at the Hanover Inn, and read through the *New York Times* while sipping a bottle of water. A leisurely wait to pick up his son after school. Engulfed in this autumnal comfort, could he really project himself back into the gray world of East Europe, the unimaginable world of the Holocaust? A reach of the imagination, to be sure. And maybe even a world too far for the imagination to encompass? But how else to search for that RW mystery, now that his own past interest was re-ignited? . . .

As he basked in the spring sun, within the safe port of the campus, he remembered fondly his days in Madison, as a grad student, sitting in the student building overlooking the glorious lake, and waiting for one of his dynamic professors to join him for a coffee. It didn't really matter who it was—Hesseltine or Curti, Williams or Mosse or Goldberg. Each contributed a different intensity, a new idea, to stir him up for the month. (George Mosse, the transplanted German Jew, had first talked to him about Wallenberg, suggesting he was a perfect 'mystery study.') A vibrant history department, in the late 1960s, in one of the heated intellectual centers of the country. Activism—including a real blowup or two!—combined with the scholarly. But the scholarly always trumped activism, no matter how activist the prof, and it remained the password to accomplishment.

An exciting five years, all told. Launched Manny into the future. Toward his teaching, his writing. And toward the track of easy academic jogging. Staring at the green oval, he recalled those salad days, a superior graduate ride of post-pubescent pleasure, where serious learning mingled with stretches of Wisconsin Dells idleness; bursts of study and paper-writing interrupted days of lazy ping-pong indulgence. Grad school had become a native pastime, a middle-class pastoral not to be missed. A pastoral that had continued into the faculty present, into Manny's later teaching days.

He saw the clock hit ten to three on the white library tower, and knew it was time to go pick up the boy and drive him to his cello lesson. One of the unique pleasures of his adult life, having the boy, watching him turn into a little cellist, and listening to his music. (And the older boy, a budding literary fellow.) Manny stood up and moved off. Taking a pit stop in the inn's basement bathroom, he washed his face vigorously and took a quick view of himself in the wall mirror: a sixty-four-year-old gent with a glint in his eyes, still swinging. Perhaps a pale version of the "Trotsky" that was his nickname in his forties. Was he ready for a new nickname?

Manny figured he'd surprise the boy with an ice cream cone, and he found the Ben & Jerry's shop. As the aromas hit him, another memory wafted back, from his youth in Brooklyn. Al's Pizza and Italian Ices Shop on Rutland Road, the Sutter Ave. El subway stop rumbling overhead. He had worked there as a young teenager, selling pizza slices for twelve cents, and custard or soft ice cream. Al was a round, pink-faced, kindly boss in his thirties, whose white T-shirt and apron were always smeared with ices or pizza. His two Hungarian brothers, older and less jolly, owned the restaurant next door. Once Manny had repeated a nasty Hungarian curse, and the shorter fellow had slapped him across the face. Another time, the older mustached brother had shown him two photos of his parents eating ice cream on a Budapest square, several months before they were shot. The boys had survived because of a Swedish diplomat. And he recalled, roughly, words from brother Imre: "No one here knows about Budapest 1944. But you're a Jewish boy." He poked Manny's chest. "You should remember the name Wallenberg." And further, on a different track, when he watched Ernie Kovacs—the mad mustached Hungarian who opened his show with a machine gun rattling the screen—on TV, he thought of RW. So, thoughts on the man had been planted early in Manny.

His mind caught up, and he picked up the boy. Little Josh did school dutifully, here in the ninth grade, but he didn't enjoy the rules, the boring stretches. He was too singular a soul, his sensibility too musical. "Oh, nothing too much," Joshie responded when Manny asked him how it went. "School is school, Dad. You know that." While listening to Fournier's version of the Bach Cello Suites— the boy already had developed a special interest in the suites—they chatted about mundane school. The boy took an ironic pleasure in describing the hallway wanderings of the tough principal. "Really, Dad, that's what she does; she *prowls* the halls looking for trouble. You should see her!"

They drove down Route 89, carved through the mountains, Manny taking it easy at the windy five-mile stretch near Grantham, where, in winter, black ice frequently hid beneath the innocent snow covering. Alternating with his ex-wife on these journeys of thirty miles down the road, Manny enjoyed the drive, with the boy putting on his favorite CDs, commenting on the orchestra and conductor, and chomping on his chips. Presently they were turning off the ramp at the Springfield exit. Another ten minutes, and they proceeded up the steep dirt driveway of Constance Logan's log house, a driveway that could be hazardous, and where they once got terribly stuck in the thick muck of snow and mud. The boy at ten or so had been an ardent little helper.

In the small music room, Manny sat in the rocking chair in the corner, a privileged witness to the lesson. The room was wood paneled, with photos of several of Connie's students and her own chamber groups on the walls; and alongside some bookshelves sat a small chest of open files with musical scores.

Connie was a heavyset woman who felt most comfortable with her young pupils; she had been teaching Josh since he was four and three quarters. Frequently she would still call him "Baby" or "Honey" when correcting him. "All right, what do we have for today? What have you worked on?" He answered her, sitting on his wooden chair with his cello, and she asked him to start with some warm-up études from his Schroder booklet.

As he played, the late afternoon sun slanting through the one window, Manny observed the boy's small fingers handling the strings adroitly on his full-sized cello, and recalled the earlier quarter- and half-sized cellos. Connie eyed him from her chair a few feet away. For Manny, this was his enchantment hour, as he was transported by the boy's deft hands and perfect pitch—though Manny himself was tone-deaf. How had the boy come to this passion, this talent? Not from the parents' genes certainly. His wife had taken the boy to hear a quartet play in the local Monsthire Museum, and afterward the musicians had invited the children up to meet the players and view the instruments. Little Josh, age two and a half, rubbed his cheek against the cello wood, fingered the strings, and that was it. The passion commenced and never wavered.

And Manny, starting in his late fifties and still going strong, was converted, as the boy had opened him up to this new realm of listening—the cello and classical music, seen and felt from a (little) musician's sensibility. These hours of weekly practice with the teacher, or those when the boy practiced alone, carved out time-units of new beauty in his late life. It was a startling discovery, like finding a new planet. Just now, Connie was correcting something in Josh's bow grip, leaning over him and showing him, and next asking him to play the Bach he had rehearsed. Now the boy played the Prelude to the fifth Bach suite, and Manny tried his best to follow the meticulous intricacies and labyrinthian harmonies (with their variations), of this precise and amazing piece. Like reading a few pages of Proust. Periodically Manny closed his eyes and listened, seeking to discern the difference between the Prelude as played by the boy and by a professional. He found it difficult to tell. Even though he was a rank amateur, he took satisfaction in this.

And for some reason the music led him to another forgotten Wallenberg memory, a television movie from the 1980s starring Richard Chamberlain as the Swedish hero. Very long, and filled with the usual TV emphasis on the obvious melodramatics, Manny recalled, but played credibly by the actor. The show had prodded Manny to wonder about the case at the time. Thus, another subtle marker had been planted quietly in his brain . . .

"That was good! Really expressive!" approved his teacher, gleaming. "Only in those middle notes I think you could go a bit more slowly, for emphasis, okay?" Josh nodded. "And I definitely think you can use that for one of your audition pieces, yes?"

At this the boy's broad little face beamed. She asked him to go over a few of the scales before finishing up, and he restarted . . .

Later, in the rambling country house, Gellerman, after dropping the boy off with his mother in town, made a scotch and water, glanced through the mail, took some cheese and sat in the book-filled living room, putting on the radio. He loved radios almost as much as books, and kept a radio in every room. He was especially fond of an old KLH and a Grundig. (He still preferred those to iPods and earbuds.) The late afternoon filled with the darkening sky, hanging low over the meadow and the forest. The house needed decluttering, for sure— as his ex-wife always complained—but so what? The mounds of books were piled everywhere, but he knew where to find any book, and the wild ménage seemed finer to his eye than the clarity of orderliness. Sitting in his Swedish leather chair, he looked through the new books he had borrowed from the library on Raoul, and drank the scotch. Quietly, he read. After two hours he was stirred, and, acting on an urge, walked to his far corner study to give his new project a little twilight surge. He took out a notebook and scribbled a few notes to add to his gathered pages. Vermont Public Radio 89.5 delivered classical music through his old Emerson radio.

From his old knowledge of the case and the new studies, he saw that the obvious problems with the case remained. Had Raoul been killed by the Russians in 1947? (Originally they said they knew nothing; years later, they claimed heart failure; and in the 1980s, they said he had been shot, but that no records existed—no interrogation or criminal case file, no documentation of the killing or a death certificate.) Had he lived on somewhere in the Gulag? More significantly, why hadn't he been traded out, or exchanged, by the Swedish government, during those two years in Soviet imprisonment? Or purchased into freedom by the very wealthy and prominent Wallenberg family in Stockholm? Wouldn't the Rockefellers, for example, have rescued one of their own, by hook or by crook (money, threats, influence)? Manny read a few dozen of the letters between Raoul and his paternal grandfather who had replaced, with affection, the naval father who had died when Raoul was less than a year old. He had tutored the young man well, sending him all over, from Haifa to Capetown, including three years at Ann Arbor for his architecture education. The grandfather's letters hardly ever mentioned the rich cousins, let alone suggested that Raoul join up with them. In other words, the grandfather and Raoul were on the same page, the same axis of feelings and values regarding money and power.

Gradually Manny began to get a clearer sense of things, a sharper angle: Raoul was the outsider within the conservative and iron-fisted Wallenberg family and its vast banking and business empire. But an outsider with what qualities? Manny wondered and jotted. Was he a threat? If so, what sort?

He took a hike through the long rambling house—a kind of three-part Lego creation of an old house, a barn, a 1930s wing, put together in different decades—arriving in the kitchen and cutting a few slices of cheese and apple, and setting them on a plate with stoned wheat crackers. In the large living room he searched through a few piles of books and found several old black and white postcards from Budapest, of the charming Lancid and Elisabeth Bridges, and of the tree-lined Andrássy Street boulevard. Manny recalled his days there, a few years back, as a visiting professor at the Eötvös Loránd University; his friends Lazslo, Tibor, Loke, Julia, Andras; and the bronze statue of RW near his apartment in the second district of Buda. The bronze Raoul had seemed to eye him daily as he had walked up the Szilágyi Erzsébet Fasor to shop at Budagyöngye. (He learned that his Salgo Professorship was named after the same man, Nicolas Salgo, who had commissioned the sculpture.)

Revved up, Gellerman opened his laptop and began writing a scene:

At the grand mansion of Marcus Wallenberg in Stockholm, in the salon with family portraits in gilded frames on the walls, a red-jacketed servant appeared with drinks on a silver tray.

"I don't really see how we should arrange anything, Marcus, without putting ourselves and our firm at some risk," said Jacob.

Marcus nodded. "Maybe great risk, I concur."

"Also," Jacob went on, "it's not like he's one of us really. His father was part of our inner circle, to be sure, but when Raoul Oscar died, the connection grew much thinner. His mother—well, she didn't count. As for that disagreeable grandfather . . ."

"Yes, I understand, and quite agree." Marcus drank his aquavit.

"And Raoul's personality . . . arrogant, skeptical, not a family player. I never trusted him, or even liked him. Far too independent. And stubbornly so. Even when we gave him those few handout jobs to perform, he had to go around poking his nose everywhere."

"And not really interested in Enskilda or any of our business ventures, no matter—"

"Or very interested in females, from what we have observed. Just the one so-called girlfriend and ten-minute 'engagement' perhaps, but that ended quickly enough. Who knew if that was even *real*? Or a clever camouflage, like all of them? And since then? Never a steady woman, definitely strange. And we will not permit *queers* in our family."

Marcus nodded. "Too much risk all around. Practically speaking, he knows a little too much about our business. Our dealings with the Germans. And remember, he looks at matters from a very different angle. I cautioned you a long time ago"—he accepted a new round of drinks—"we never should have let him get so near to our private arrangements and our international dealings."

"He cannot *prove* anything, of course."

"True enough. Still, when I go off to the states to clean up things and try to get us off that nuisance FBI Blacklist, it would be most unfortunate if there were any 'entanglements' dangling whatsoever. And Raoul, let us face it, could create a few if he wished to."

"I don't think—"

"He is a purist ethically, isn't he? The naïve fool!"

They sipped their aquavits, in their monogrammed glasses.

"Then we will do nothing on the Lybianka matter, agreed?"

"Agreed."

"And if the shrewd PM or the king should ask our advice, our counsel?"

"Sympathy from a distance, neutrality from up close. Whatever the government wishes to do, we will respect that wish, but not push them in any way, of course."

"Of course."

"Will it look . . . odd? Or cold-blooded?"

"Oh, I think it will look *patriotic*, first and foremost. Our family and Enskilda Bank have always sought to look like, and act like, true Swedish patriots."

A pause, while the grandfather clock ticked loudly.

"Poor fellow, though—Soviet prisons are not exactly a tea party."

"He brought it all on himself. The kind of headstrong and stubborn fellow he was, and remained. Helping Jews! Imagine! Why? What business was it of his anyway?"

"Well," Marcus considered, "his side of the family did have some Jewish blood, ages ago, before the conversion. And his aim may have been . . . idealistic."

"In our day and age," Jacob declared, "there is only room for aims that are realistic, determinedly realistic."

"Come, let us take our drinks in to dinner, and not let the ladies complain of our usual lateness."

The two gentlemen stood up.

Gellerman stopped, leaned back, read his pages. Too exaggerated? A *convenient* scene? Was there enough evidence to support this psychological picture, this 1945–46 "situation" of these tough Wallenbergs scheming for their self-protection and abandoning Raoul? Well, yes, there was, and if some of it was only circumstantial as yet, it was strongly circumstantial. Verify, only verify, Moritz Schlick had said, in Manny's college reading. He recalled the aphoristic wisdom of the Austrian philosopher. Not an easy task, he told himself. Would he need Stockholm, Budapest, Moscow, to fill in the gaps, test his ideas? Or would Google do the job—well, fill in parts at least? . . . His imagination would do the rest.

He looked out at the Japanese crabapple tree, whose pink May blossoms made the month burst with delicate beauty.

Why was he getting involved this way, drawn in to Raoul's ordeal and mysteries? The thesis may have sharpened Manny's probe, and the surprising hidden memories unfolded to enhance the interest, true enough; and yet, was there more? Something deeper, which he didn't know of? Was there something about Raoul and his situation(s), his outsider status, his sense of family exile, his apparent aloneness, that appealed especially to Manny? Well, he'd have to wait and see it through, work it through, and then understand, judge. Wallenberg was a personal conundrum wrapped in a mystery of history, which in itself drew in Manny the historian.

"Wallenberg and Gellerman," he murmured to himself. "What a strange pairing."

CHAPTER 3

The next day Manny played tennis at the indoor courts with his regular partner, Peter Harrison of the English department. They were a good match: roughly the same age of mid- sixties, the same sturdy five-foot-eight build, and had the same hearty stamina and competitive desire. Peter was a steady player, a crafty southpaw, and the two battled to a close match for an hour. Manny loved the sport, which he'd learned relatively late in life at age twenty-nine, and continued to absorb new aspects of strategy. Against this player, for example, he had to cope with high lobs from his backhand side, to his own backhand, and he had two choices: either to hit the ball with his weak backhand or to run around it and smash it with his stronger forehand, either cross-court, or down the line. Today the tendonitis in his forearm felt well enough to hit through, so Manny ran around the lob for his firm forehand hits and did well. They played a 6–6 set, and then ran to 8–6 in the tiebreaker, with Manny losing. They shook hands, chatted, arranged another match, and showered. Afterward, Peter asked what he was working on, and Manny found himself answering, "Oh, I think I'm onto a new project, something over in East Europe, but it's a little too early to talk about it just yet."

In a few minutes he was driving over to the college, body relaxed, spirit lifted—as from yoga—and he grew conscious of the taken-for-granted pleasures of this little town, the ease of daily acts, the rounds of sporting pleasures. Something like what Raoul had said about his life in Ann Arbor, in letters to his grandfather, including tennis. Immediately Manny's sunny feeling diminished as he thought of that faraway young man wasting away in the Soviet prison, his harrowing two years there, and uncertain ending . . . Gripped by a darker feeling, Manny felt that faraway hand for the next few hours, before he came up again.

He sat in his office and read through the thesis draft once more, for Angela was coming to see him later. There was not much new in this reading, as he had expected. Raoul was still a great savior of Jews, etc., except for the brief few pages on that fanciful Budapest lady and her mad fantasy; and something else, buried in a long footnote: the sightings by those other prisoners. These were cited in a Swedish-Russian Working Group paper. Well, he'd have to check into that—maybe have Angela "research" it on Google, where "research" of fifteen minutes equalled fifteen hours of the old ways of pursuing a subject—and probably missed crucial tucked-away items. Also mentioned was an unpublished manuscript suggesting again that RW may have been that double spy working for the Germans and Americans, this one written by a Soviet émigré living in New York. He recalled that the *U.S. News* article was cowritten by a Hungarian émigré, and realized that conspiracy theory was an East European specialty, like one of their rich strudels or thick custards. Manny jotted down the information, and would check up on that as well.

Meanwhile, there was that weird woman of Budapest—a version of the Madwoman of Chaillot? He had to answer her, and maybe check her out too? Was it worth it, or was she just another crackpot?

On an urge, he opened his e-mail and wrote to her:

> *Dear Zsuzsanna W.,*
> *Thank you for contacting me last week. Yes, I would like to be in*
> *touch with you. Perhaps on the telephone, or if I should get to Budapest,*
> *in person? I am growing interested in the lost or disappeared life of Raoul*
> *Wallenberg, well, the whole case, and understand from my graduate stu-*
> *dent that you may have some useful information.*
> *Yours sincerely,*
> *Prof. Emmanuel Gellerman*

Be careful, he warned himself; you know your penchant for foolish goose chases, for winding up looking like a clown. It's always been your Achilles' heel. But still . . . it was an adventure, wasn't it? And think back to your youth, when you cut out for Africa on a Norwegian freighter and everyone in the Brooklyn neighborhood thought you were out of your mind, looney. But it turned out be a great adventure, one that changed and broadened you, causing you to move into the adventure trade whenever the opportunity arose. Furthermore, Manny knew from grad school days that every lead needed to be followed, no matter how silly it seemed or where it led. Yes, let's see what the lady says. Besides, going to Budapest, which he knew from having taught there, was essential anyway. Too bad Prof. Mosse was not around. He always spoke highly of that "Little Paris."

Later in the afternoon, Angela showed up. He sat down with her and went through the draft, making sure his scribbled markings were clear. And after telling her to try to check out that unpublished manuscript from the Russian down in New York, he remarked that her Budapest lady had now answered him and invited him to meet with her. Angela beamed and said, "Believe me Professor G., it will be worth it!" She threw her blonde hair back from her eyes. "And I'm so glad you liked my pages. That pumps me. I really will work to lengthen and polish it for the next draft." As she packed her Lands' End attaché, Manny was glad he had put her onto the project—American youth serving Swedish memory.

Manny went for his constitutional, walking across campus and down along the river and across the bridge over to Vermont, squinting at the bright sun sparkling upon the water. The air was nippy but felt energizing, especially after he had warmed up. He walked all the way up to the general store in Norwich, maybe two miles, bought himself a newspaper, and retraced his steps, from commonsense Vermont to melodramatic "Live Free or Die" New Hampshire. What a comic pair. Well, one got used to anything, even the *meshugenah*. Legs still strong, he marched all the way back up to the inn and sat in the charming old-world lounge, relaxing and reading in a red leather chair, drinking his water . . .

"We should eat, sleep, and dream history," Prof. Hesseltine had proclaimed, in Madison, and it had been a long while since he had lived according to that credo. His two books were from long ago, and since then, he had fooled around with history more than engaged it. Cold War America and McCarthyism were old hat—one was a revised thesis—and though he had written on those subjects, they had not really excited him—grabbed him and not let go, a long-term obsession. It was not that he had lost the necessary discipline, but rather, the riveting passion; and without that, history might have been any subject, just another career choice. God, he hated that path, and those types that trekked it. In academia, they littered and ruled the place. Now, with Wallenberg in his focus . . .

An older couple sat down near the fireplace and bookshelves, and a younger power pair, here for an interview perhaps, walked through the spacious lounge. He saw that the room was now bustling with salesmen, academics, alumni.

He couldn't wait till the boy showed up, so that he might be regaled with the tales and woes of the school day. Nothing merrier than a lively boy with his own passion and school laments. This boy, and the other one away in college, had lifted him up in these past half-dozen years of being bogged down. Losing his interest in the profession, his old idealism, maybe his own powers . . . Was Raoul brought to him then as a kind of gift, a surprise lighthouse for his drifting ship? Could be. Once upon a time Oppenheimer had done that for him—given him a fine wind at his back, a sail with direction, with purposefulness. Was he feeling this surge again now? A breezy illusion, or a firm reality?

"Hi, Dad. Have you been waiting long? I had to stay and talk to Mr. Soames again, about the history paper . . ."

At the college he attended a department meeting of several hours, akin to an army inspection. This, despite the fact that Manny liked his liberal arts graduate department very much, in theory anyway, and also enjoyed the good-hearted lion-leader, Richard Mackie, who ruled the department with magnanimity, power and crusader passion. An intellectual dynamo, he had built an autonomous and furtive empire from this marginalized graduate department, a closet hideaway in the undergraduate college. Every now and then, maybe once every year or two, Mackie called a faculty meeting, attended by a wide variety of professors from various disciplines, most of whom hardly knew each other. Richard seemed to prefer it that way. A few were even lively creatures.

"Well I still don't know why we aren't pursuing a fifth track in the department," began Marsha Kepler, a slender lady in her late fifties who had just entered the department several months ago. "A graduate degree in gender studies would seem to be essential in today's world. Especially since we have an undergraduate major now . . ."

As she proceeded on in her casual dogmatic fashion, Manny recalled an incident many years ago, when she had first come to the college, and Manny, who had met her briefly at a conference, had invited her for a dinner at his country place. She arrived with a newly baked challah for him, and he was touched, and the evening was pleasant enough, though Manny felt she was interested in a romance. But Manny was not, not in the least. And soon thereafter, she began to snub him publicly, and in the next year or two, she instigated rumors and became his open enemy. No good deed goes unpunished, he learned first-hand. Too bad, as the challah was tasty.

Why in the world had Mackie invited her into the department? "Well, she asked to teach a course," he told Manny, "and she can be useful to us."

That phrase summed up Mackie's weak spot: it was hard for him to say no even to those he scorned (the vulnerability of a political animal). Again, as she prattled on, Manny stared out the window, across the green to the redbrick administration building . . . and realized that this could go on and on, with the parrying, and the underlying politics of personal egos playing their part, on top of the ideological politics. Such was the petty nature of academic meetings too often, if they weren't strongly monitored, and why Manny had avoided them at all costs. The humming of the overhead fluorescent eased him to day-dreaming, starting with playing baseball as a twelve-year-old in the sandlots of Lincoln Terrace Park in Brooklyn . . . Moving on, for no clear reason, to an incident when he was a boy of sixteen, and traveling in the South, selling magazines in Texas. One of a group of four, he had pedaled *Collier's*, *Ladies Home Companion*, *Saturday Evening Post*, and there had been a problem with a contract, and a woman complained, and the police showed up and put the four of them against a wall. When Manny gave his name and address, the policeman drawled, "Oh, so you're from New York, and a Jewboy to boot, I'll bet. Right? And I'll bet you've come down here to show us Southerners how dumb we rednecks are? And maybe take a few extra dollars from the lady of the house? Yeah, son, you New York kikes are one clever bunch, aren't you? Well, boy, maybe we can surprise you, but first let's see some identification." As Manny carefully handed over his wallet, the bulky policeman with the high black boots stood right before him, less than a foot away from his face, and Manny felt himself shaking, anticipating a slap, a punch in the gut . . . Manny stood frozen from the open anti-Semitism, as the policeman eyed him like a biologist eyeing a microbe, waiting for him to move. . .

Why had he thought of this now? Was Wallenberg already operating in his unconscious, roaming through his life? Arousing wounds and insults of his past, small incidents of anti-Semitism buried in obscure niches . . . Gentile pressures making him feel more Jewish . . .

The politics of gender and ego rattled on exhaustingly, a sharp contrast from the real politics of Budapest 1944, Manny figured, feeling trapped in this academic version of Sartre's *No Exit*. He let his mind wander, and furtively jotted down notes for a new scene to explore and speculate on. Interesting how he seemed to be composing a sort of fictional historical narrative, reinventing a mystery character from the past, in an attempt to find out what had happened and how RW had acted. A narrative running counter in time to his own life. Were they meant to intersect, somehow?

Much later, at home, he opened his mailbox and found two messages of interest, among the many, one from an old friend inviting him to a conference in Moscow, and the other from the Budapest lady again. Setting Bach on the hi-fi—Gould playing the Goldberg Variations—he sat down with a glass of red wine, and took up Macauley's long John Milton essay in the eleventh edition of the *Encylopedia Britannica*, where he read with pleasure a few pages of the master's formal, translucent prose. (He had the original edition, with the very fine India paper and several columns per page.) His head still filled with that famous prose style, he skimmed again the nefarious article in *U.S. News &*

World Report, composed by the two journalists. He appreciated the irony: the man who had saved Jews in Budapest, the diplomat captured by the Soviets, the prisoner abandoned by the Swedish family and state, now being turned, via yellow journalism, into a spy! A good example of how history, even this cheap history, could become the final and most exquisite executioner.

(Or was it true somehow? Gellerman wondered. Could he have been a double agent? Anything was possible, right?)

At his computer, he read through the two e-mail messages. From Budapest he heard from the familiar lady again, asking if he was soon planning a trip. And from Prof. Eli Kushner at SUNY Albany, he read an invitation to a May conference on "Recent Responses in East Europe to the End of Communism." How serendipitous. Might the two converge?

He meandered among his books, piled up everywhere on tables, chairs, the floor. He knew where to find each: Hegel and Kierkegaard and Gibbon in old Modern Library editions; assorted paperback histories by DeVoto, C. Vann Woodward, Foner, Hofstader, Orwell; favorite fiction by Bellow, Svevo, Euclides da Cunha, Stendhal. Sometimes he wondered if he shouldn't have gone into the literary trade, not the history profession. It seemed so much more fun, inventing things, rather than researching them. In the next life, he would try it.

He built a fire, sat down, and wrote notes to the lady in Budapest and the inquiring professor over in Albany, and considered plans for a trip next spring to Budapest and Moscow, to see what was going on over there, in the eastern region. Maybe there were green shoots growing in that former wilderness that were worth noting?

Now he went back to his valuable note-taking from the department meeting, and setting his drink down, began to compose:

They were driving on the road to Debrecen, followed by their Russian Army escort. Props of the war zone passed on the sides of the road: rolled over cars, burned jeeps, patches of black ground. Occasionally refugees wandered, in small groups, gazing up bleakly at the passing car.

"What will happen to them?" asked Vilmos, his driver. "They're like packs of stray, hungry dogs."

Raoul nodded, patted his friend's large arm. "It will take a while, yes."

"Poor devils. Now they are all Jews . . ."

A pause, as Raoul checked the glove compartment. "It will be sad to give up our old Studebaker, if we are forced to. She has served us well."

Vilmos nodded.

"I still am not sure whether we're going to be taken as guests or prisoners."

"Well, we will know soon enough; but with the Russians, I would not be optimistic."

"Yes, I should know better. Still . . ."

They smoked, and drove, the two Russian motorcycles tailing them closely. Raoul had always enjoyed the driving with his trusty friend, the hefty fellow being an excellent driver and chauffeur. And though Raoul was used to uncertainty, this was a little different, driving to Soviet military headquarters.

"I had no time to get rid of my bag, and there is a good deal of cash in it. Plus my black book. This could be a problem."

"Or a blessing. They are not unknown to accept cash for favors."

Raoul smiled wanly.

They drove.

"Look, Willy," he patted the friend's wrist, calling him by his private nickname, and trying to say something, but not sure what. "Whatever happens, you have been a great comfort. Always there when I needed you, no matter what the circumstances. So, thank you, Willy."

Vilmos glanced over at him, his dark face staring, half-embarrassed. He uttered, "Have you forgotten that you rescued me from a forced labor camp? Among other small favors."

Raoul nodded. He was thinking of something else, but still couldn't get the proper words out. Did he even know them? He stared out the window, saw someone waving a white flag, and said, "You've been a good friend, a close friend, and that's meant a lot. Personally, I mean, as well as professionally."

Vilmos tapped Raoul's leg with the back of his hand. "No need. I know."

Did he know, really know? wondered Raoul. He pondered *whether he himself knew. And knew what?* Who understood anything about personal relations? He knew how to save Jews, how to stay calm in difficult and tense situations, how to stand up to authority. But about his own personal or intimate relations, what did he know or really understand? Very little—maybe nothing?

"They will probably try to turn us into spies, if we are not made honorary colonels—in the NKVD."

"I will be happy enough to be a simple engineer again," Vilmos remarked.

"And I, an ex-diplomat with architectural ambitions."

They drove through the bleak landscape, Raoul catching fleeting images of his mother in Stockholm, and half-brother Guy, half-sister Nina. They hadn't been in his thoughts in a long time. When would he see them again?

"There is the landmark, less than a dozen kilometers now."

"If we should be split apart," Raoul offered, "we must find a way to stay in touch. If it is prison for a while, we will use that same knocking system as we used for our entrances in Pest, yes?"

"Perfect. Yes."

They drove, and Raoul said, "You must survive, Willy, that is the most important thing."

Vilmos looked over at him, with his dark grin beneath his longish nose, and replied, "Oh, I know how to do that. It is you I am worried about, Raoul. They may want to press you for information, which . . ."

"Which I may or may not know, I understand. But remember, I have important friends, both in Budapest and in Sweden, so they will probably go easy on me. And besides, I am sure our cells will be airier than our home in the Hazai Bank vault."

Vilmos laughed and nodded, remembering.

"Well, the motorcylist friends are signaling us, so we are almost there."

Almost there—but where? thought Raoul—and still he had not gotten to say what he wanted to say. Better left unsaid anyway, he figured; not a good time or space for the intimate. There were more pressing matters at hand. Like where to hide that bag if possible . . ."

Was there enough evidence to warrant the subtext of baffling intimacy here? Was Manny making certain emotions too obvious for the evidence? Well, he'd have to continue his investigating and research for sure, but from what he understood now, it seemed to fit. At least the basic material facts were real enough: the trip down to Debrecen under the Soviet overseers, the uncertainty of what awaited them; all that he had added was an interpretation. And the personal was as important as the historical.

Again, what sort of hybrid genre was he seeking to create with these little scenes? A shadow history, a docu-fiction, a what-if narrative? Well, who cared for now? Manny thought, getting out his workout mat for his yoga exercises. Just proceed ahead and figure things out later, especially when he had more to go on. If the whole thing blew up in a comedy of smoke and illusion, a fog of wishful thinking, so be it. It wouldn't be the first time, he thought, bending forward in Sun Salutation, neck and back stretching, feeling familiar body-joy.

CHAPTER 4

For the next several months Manny taught, read, researched, walked, saw his son, and listened to him play regularly. He learned a bit about pizzicato and pitch and intonation, and about three classical cellists, Feuermann, Fournier, Piatigorsky. (Josh had put a photo of Feuerman, his favorite, inside his cello, the way Manny used to collect cards of baseball heroes.) The weather was better than in the old days, when minus twenty degrees at night would last for two weeks; freezing pipes and snowstorms would arrive late in spring, weighing down flat roofs and blocking walkways. Now, there were milder temperatures, less snow, and reports of disasters elsewhere. Apart from his class work and the newspapers—for the news, the sports, the obits—he read all he could about Raoul and tried to absorb the many parts, the odd gaps, the accepted information, conventional wisdom, attempts at interpretation. The mysteries remained, even deepened, it seemed to Manny.

Yet, when he brought the matter up to a British colleague at a local restaurant one day, the fellow said, "Forget it; it's ancient history. The Rooskies knocked him off; so where's the mystery? Standard operating procedure—you know what Stalin said, 'Where there's a man, there's a problem.'" Coughlin smiled, drank his beer. "So they got rid of him."

"But what about the other problems, the more serious ones, like why didn't someone get him out? Or trade for him? The family, the country?"

Tom said, "Hmmm. Hadn't thought much about that. You have a point. What'd the Soviets have him locked up for, two years or so? Yeah," he nodded, "that is strange, and may be worth looking into. I don't know much about him personally, actually. Was he an interesting fellow?"

As Manny went on to explain a little about Raoul, he understood how much he had taken in, in recent months, about the man, and yet how much there was left to know. Yes, he was interesting, but exactly how? His identity was still a mystery.

"Was he Jewish?" Tom asked. "I always wondered that, because of what he did."

"Oh, he was one sixteenth or so Jewish on his mother's side, from way back. But he wasn't raised Jewish and didn't feel that way."

Tom circled the rim of his glass. "Gelly, you always were skeptical of the conventional lines given on stories, so maybe you are sniffing up a trail that will lead you somewhere interesting. So, let's see what you turn up."

Soon, driving home, listening to the frustrating three- or four-minute news segments on frustrating NPR, Manny replayed the conversation with Tom and felt a certain stirring. What was it? Did Manny himself, a totally secular fellow, *feel Jewish*? Well, he had always felt culturally Jewish, but was that a polite defense mechanism of sorts? And in recent years, hadn't he felt, more and more—maybe subconsciously?—the hangover wounds of the Holocaust? Wounds that had been transformed into certain emotions, attitudes, that were complex and undifferentiated. Had these now been raised more to the surface, like an injury causing blood vessels to discolor the skin, by his Wallenberg reading? . . . Manny bounced along his dirt road, bumpy with early frost heaves, and tried to understand these inchoate feelings.

How interesting was this legendary Swede? Who knew, who really knew? But certainly it was a real and intriguing question. And how many of those big figures in history were truly interesting, rather than standing out by means of an important circumstance? . . . In other words, History carried so many pipsqueak figures on its shoulders, and made them seem like little giants.

On an impulse, Manny hopped on a plane to Ann Arbor, where Raoul had gone to the School of Architecture for three years, in the early 1930s. There on the campus Manny moseyed around, walked into the outdated Lorch Hall, with its wonderful staircase and its studios, where Raoul had done his drafting. Found the old architecture library in the West Engineering Building, and visited the large skylighted room on the fourth floor of the north end, where the freehand drawing and projection drawing was done. (It had been cited by Raoul.) He walked to the pleasant house on tree-lined Madison Street, where Raoul had lived for his three years. Visited the archives and found several items of interest, including a small notebook with his clear handwriting and a humorous photo of Raoul kidding around at the Architects' Ball, wearing pantaloons and holding his hand over his face in feigned shame. (One note of interest in the notebook: how he wanted to visit the Southwest and see the Frank Lloyd Wright Taliesin West project, and also one of the Indian reservations. Did he ever get there?) Raoul graduated with honors in 1935, and received a silver medal from the American Institute of Architects, given to the student with the highest scholastic standing. (Manny saw the citation.) Finally, he came across a later clipping from the *Detroit Jewish News*, of all places, from his professor, Jean Paul Slusser, describing Raoul as one of his brightest students in his thirty years of teaching there. (Had Raoul known that his favorite professor was Jewish?)

Manny had taken along the *Letters and Dispatches* volume and the letters to the grandfather, and he put a few relevant letters together with bits and pieces from the archive to get a fuller picture of the young man: how popular a student he was among his peers; how much he preferred the students here to the snobbish Swedish kids; how he loved wearing his sneakers and eating hot dogs and wouldn't join a fraternity because it would isolate him from other student strata; and how he loved hitchhiking all around the country on school holidays. As he explained to his grandfather, "When you travel like a hobo, everything's different. You have to be on the alert the whole time. You're in close contact with new people every day. Hitchiking gives you training in diplomacy and tact." What a perfect training for his later role as diplomat.

So Raoul got a full robust education in America, just as his grandfather had hoped when he sent him here and not to Swedish or European architecture schools. (And he sent him to a public and not an Ivy school.) Here he learned up close about the land, about democracy, about different ethnicities, and maybe about *who he was,* at heart. For Manny perceived quickly that all his best pals were male; when he traveled about, to Chicago or Mexico, it was always with his male friends. Nary a woman was mentioned in his three-year sojourn here, let alone one dated on a regular basis—circumstantial evidence, to be sure.

In his honor, now there was a plaque and a distinguished lecture series, by architects, some of whom, it turned out, hardly knew who he was. Well, that was about par for the course. In fact, it seemed that no one at the school, or the university, knew much about RW (including a humanities dean, who had never heard of him). Several faculty were skeptical that he had ever attended Michigan. ("Are you sure it was the *same Wallenberg*?") Well, why not? After all, he had made his mark in the world beyond Michigan, beyond architecture. And beyond the classrooms in the streets of humanity.

One memorable incident stood out, when Raoul was hitchhiking and was kidnapped and in real danger, taken into in the back of the car of three young gangsters, who brandished a loaded revolver. He gave them his wallet, made a casual joke, and convinced them to leave him in a deserted ground—not bad for the young lad. Raoul tossed off the whole thing, to his grandfather, as nothing to fret over. He had escaped any real injury, and exhibited supreme cool and calm—perhaps preparing him for his future adventures with larger gangsters: the Arrow Cross Nazis of Budapest. Manny came to realize how playful and witty was this Raoul, how adaptable, brave and dedicated, back in his late twenties. And how highly talented. He was a figure in the making, to himself, to Grandfather perhaps, and later, to the world. A singular soul. *Was it Manny's job to complete the making of that unfinished identity, with his own vision and the facts as they were given? Well, he surmised, let that be part of my task, my mission. Help him out, in history at least. Though that was a long way off, just yet.*

Manny returned home, strangely fortified, feeling he had been in touch with the real man behind the legend, the thin, darkly-complected figure hidden within the clouds of history. Even Raoul's small but clear handwriting, in the one notebook there, gave Manny a surge of intimacy. Oh, he knew, driving back from the Manchester airport, that he had only scratched the surface of who Raoul was, but that was enough. A modest breakthrough. Maybe he'd try to stop in Sweden sometime during the spring trip? He had a friend in Lindingö, a suburb of Stockholm, and he'd write him. A young architect no less. Perfect.

At home he took care of all the immediate needs—his part-time handyman, Russ, had done a good job of house-watching—and then went through the snail mail and the few dozen e-mails. He wanted to get to sleep early, but his head was still filled with the trip, with thoughts, impressions. So he sat down by his computer, checked some of his notes, and got ready to compose a new little scenario. As he felt a bit sleepy, however, he put on an Ella Fitzgerald CD and sat back with a drink listening to the velvety smoothness of her voice.

But a stranger came in silently, a gentleman in a dark suit; he nodded, as though familiar, and sat down on the leather chair in Gellerman's study. He removed his fedora, and spoke in a quiet, slightly accented voice:

"Ella and Louis, my favorites, and no one had her wonderful clarity," he began, and crossed his leg. "But now, Professor, here with me, do you really think there is a point in this pursuit? What's done is done. The past is the past. What happened to me will never really be found out, or completely understood. I was alone through it all, please remember. Well, almost alone; my driver was with me for a time. Suffice it to say, I managed to help a good number of Jews, and they in turn gave me a sudden sense of purpose. So we each benefitted from the other." He gazed at Manny. "Isn't that enough of a story?"

Gellerman responded calmly. "I understand your views, sir, but I am determined to push forward and find out the truth. Well, if not the whole truth, a piece of it, or perhaps several truths."

The gentleman fiddled with his hat. "I see you are one of these 'stubborn' Americans that I used to know back in Ann Arbor—stubborn in their pursuit of any adventure of interest. Even off-limits." He flickered a smile. "Well, do me one small favor then. If you should find out anything too dark in my 'case,' don't be afraid of exposing it. Even if it might hurt me personally."

"Why do you say this, or rather, sir, think this way?"

"You should call me Raoul." A pause. "I lived so long with truth as my only bedfellow, that I became devoted to it; it was the only thing I had, you see. So, if you should by accident find out anything resembling it, feel free to reveal or expose it."

"Sounds a bit dangerous, sir."

"Dangerous? Well, the real truth always is, I suppose, to one or another. But in my case, it would be something like Sicilian revenge, served up nice and cold."

Gellerman was quietly stunned, and also somewhat confused over what was being said. *And who was saying it.* He felt the heat from the fire.

"Let me caution you, if I may, about certain things. You will find in your path false leads, varieties of disguise, appearances of truth that are in fact untruths or semi-truths. Are you prepared?"

Gellerman opened his palms in uncertainty.

"And beware the Swedes—their government dispatches, subsequent covering statements. And beware my family. They both have an interest in concealing the past, brushing it clean, leaving no marks, protecting it from outsiders, whom they view as unpleasant intruders. All of this will pose a problem for you, Professor, an obstacle. Not to mention the usual zealots and cult followers, harmless though most of them are, in Stockholm, Budapest, maybe Moscow. They also will cloud your vision."

Manny felt uncomfortably chided, and nodded. "Why are you telling me all this, sir?"

The stranger crossed and recrossed his leg. "To prepare you, to warn you, so you do not waste months or years on this pursuit."

Manny stared at the strange, formal figure.

"Please remember, Professor Gellerman, what I said earlier: that if you come upon something of importance, or if you are avenging me in some way, you must not worry about my personal feelings, but 'go full steam ahead!' as my Michigan friends used to say"—he smiled—"and reveal it to the world."

■

Presently, as the gentleman departed, Ella also finished. Manny poured himself a scotch and reflected. Did that chat really happen? Or, if not, why had he conjured it up? "Avenge him" in some way, Raoul had said. Like Hamlet's old man, eh? Go forward then, and full steam ahead! Just watch out for the pitfalls, disguises, traps. Paradoxical wisdom . . .

The strange conversation lingered in Manny's head for weeks, and haunted him with its words, its hallucinatory credibility. And the closeness he felt with the presence of that ghost. Was this the way the real RW had to be discovered, he mused, by invention? Like his true history?

Spring came, and suddenly all the outdoor fields sprang up—not merely with flowers, but with sports. The little college town suddenly was blooming with tennis matches, track runners, jousting lacrosse battlers, joggers with headbands, Frisbee tossers, baseball players, fierce bicyclists, canoeists and kayakers— sports players popping up like Dutch tulips. The town waited to play, to rise up from winter interiors and gray weather and enter into the sunlight and soft winds. Yet, through all this sudden spring sprouting, Gellerman tried to keep his concentration focused back there and then: Budapest 1944 and Moscow 1945. A bit difficult, sure. But soon he would be heading over there—and it would be easier to enter into memory and history, while walking around amidst the dour streets of scarcity—instead of staying here, amidst the fields and greens of pastel plenty.

"Why do you have to go there now? Why not wait till June and take me, Dad?"

"Well, first of all, you have school, my boy, and secondly, if I have a successful trip, I return in June or July, and then you could be freer to perhaps accompany me."

The boy shook his head in sharp disappointment. He exaggerated all the gestures of an adult, and the result was the fondest (for Dad) comic mimicry.

"Now, why don't you practice, okay?"

"All right," he muttered, and picked up his cello and began to tune up.

"What's on for today?"

"Oh, some Schroder and then a Bach prelude." He practiced with his back to the windows in the living room.

Gellerman nodded, and soon felt the boy's cello pleasing his senses. How had he been ignorant for so long of this form of beauty?

Now, looking out through the windows, he saw what looked like a wild turkey out by the far end of the oval pond, and he wished he had his binoculars right there. The sun went in and out. He pointed to the outside, and the boy turned about and stared.

"What is it, Dad, a turkey?"

"Actually, I think a wild peacock. Look—see the fantastic tail with those iridescent feathers?"

"Wow!" Josh stared. "Amazing!"

"You're right, and wait till you hear the mating call sometime. Fierce! But now go back to Bach. Remember, you have math homework as well."

So the boy played, and a pair of swallows flew by, and Manny wondered why he would ever want to leave this place, this sanctuary of boy, cello, and birds? Wasn't it comfortable to the point of perfection?

As the musical intricacies developed, Gellerman read through the revised pages of Angela's competent thesis, and considered the pale tenacious Swede. Manny felt he was getting to know him, from the inside, not from the pages of historical material after the fact. Partly from his own words in his *Letters and Dispatches*, partly from his footprints at Ann Arbor, and lastly from Manny's own inquiry and imagination. Who was he? A private soul. A subtle man. An outsider, both within his conservative family and his country. And maybe a lost soul too, until he received the commission from K. Lauer, the Hungarian businessman in Stockholm, to help the Jews of Budapest, an offer augmented privately by Iver Olsen, who worked for the US War Refugee Board. The commisson that evolved into a life mission. And the little office in the Swedish legation building in Buda—with Vilmos on hand—became an ideal sanctuary. Where saving Jews became *his calling*, not a job.

To the world at large he was a figure of political turbulence and heroism; to Manny, he was becoming a personal puzzle, and probably a puzzle to himself!

"Dad, the phone's ringing. Don't you want to get it?"

Manny answered it—a local nursing charity asking for his annual contribution. Afterward, he was back in his living room chair, with a glass of red wine, listening, contemplating. This boy had come to Manny when he was fifty, and he had been a mighty bundle of work, and a little human blessing. All that high maintenance had been channeled into his curved wooden instrument of energy and devotion. In a similar way, Manny, in his middle age, had channeled his devotion and energy toward the boy. You needed something serious in your fifties to lift you up from complacency or melancholy for the final few decades. But maybe now, a dozen years later, he needed a new channel and a new challenge—like RW. One with as much unpredictability as the boy, but with high risk, professionally. Was this turning into *his mission*?

"Hey, Dad, how long have I been practicing? What's for dinner?"

"Well, lamb chops with potatoes."

"Can I make mashed, please? I'll use the Cuisinart, but I won't make a mess, I promise! It won't be like last time."

He remembered the last time, with bits of mashed potatoes shooting out from the whirring machine over pots pans and dishes onto kitchen shelves and walls, like a July 4 shower of potato stars. Manny winced, smiled, and gave in. Spoiling the boy had become second nature, and he felt fine with it, just fine.

On the river, on a sixty-degree sunny day that felt like eighty after winter, Gellerman canoed with Jack Littletree, a graduate student and pal, carrying sandwiches and coffee. They canoed upriver, the current light and the sun glinting off the greenish-blue water. A single sailboat was out, and a pair of kayakers.

"Out here spring is different from back home."

"Yes, I imagine."

"We sure could use a river like this."

"I'll bet."

They headed upriver about forty minutes, and chose a small island on the New Hampshire side to have their lunch. They pulled the canoe onto the shore, tied it to a rock, and found a flat patch to sit on, by the shade of a maple.

"I read on Yahoo that the Danube's flooding right now," Jack observed.

"Yeah, that happens over there periodically, and it can be pretty bad."

Jack smiled, revealing yellowing teeth. "Still, we'd take a river anyway."

Manny nodded, remembering his several visits out to Hopi land in southern Arizona, where the land was dusty, arid, a moonscape without rivers or lakes breaking up the monotonous brown landscape.

"Warmer than last year, remember?" Jack said. "And do you remember that wind, going back?"

"Yeah, I do, actually." Manny laughed. "Almost turned us over!"

Shielded from the high sun, they opened their co-op tuna salad sandwiches and began eating, watching the smooth water.

"So, how did you do this quarter, tell me? How was the work?"

"Not too bad," Jack replied. "A couple of high passes in Globalization, Oral History."

"Hey, what's going on? Sucking up to the profs?"

The young man in his early thirties with the jet-black hair broke into a warm smile. "Yeah, you got me pegged."

Gellerman enjoyed this mature student, who was one of a series of Hopi Indians that he had mentored through the years, here at Dartmouth, a college whose original charter was devoted to educating Native Americans (and making them over into Christian gentlemen). And now he was devoted to pampering young Caucasian natives. Years ago, he had met a colleague in anthropology, an expert on Native Americans, with a focus on Hopis, and he had recruited young men from the tribe to come to this rural Ivy League college, first setting them in local private schools for a year of prepping. And when that prof retired, he asked Manny to continue the tradition, which he did, making annual trips to the reservation and recruiting one student every few years for his graduate interdisciplinary department. He had seen Jack Littletree three or four times a year, over lunch or dinner, for a fall or spring day trip, either on a mountain trail or out here on the river, which Jack delighted in.

"How's the family doing?"

"Pretty well, thanks. Kids miss me, but I talk to them at least once a week."

"I hope some of the family will come for your graduation."

Jack shook his head. "Too expensive, man, the travel from there to here."

Manny made a mental note to seek some travel money for the wife at least, or maybe the parents.

"Yeah, if we had some water out there, there's no telling what we could do."

Manny nodded, and marveled at how they had sustained themselves for hundreds of years in that high desert plateau, through all the adversities of arid landscape, disease, and predatory Navajo.

"How's the job going, with that timber framer?" It was a job that Manny had arranged.

"Oh, he's a good guy, and when he has work, I really learn things. And earn some money. We put up two trusses a few weeks back, and that was good. He says he has a whole timber-frame house scheduled for this May, so I look forward to that."

"Don't shortchange the school work, when you're so close to finishing."

Oh, I won't Professor G., I won't."

"How about your thesis? What do you want to do?"

"I think an oral history of the family. You know, with my grandfather still alive, I can gather some good stories. Real or imagined." He winked. "And the prof is very keen on the idea."

"Sounds good."

"And what about you? When are you going to head out west again and visit the res?"

"First I have to go the other direction, to East Europe, and then maybe later on, maybe in the late summer or September, I can make it out there."

"Well, do it when I'm around."

"Will do. Meanwhile, keep up the good work!" He patted John's arm. "But for now, we should head back. I have a meeting."

"Oh, yeah. I got you a little something."

"What? Why? I told you, there's never a need for that."

Jack gestured with his head, and handed Manny a small stiff package wrapped in a brown paper bag.

Carefully Manny took it, slipped out the inside packet and unwrapped an item tucked into bubble wrap. Using his penknife, he slit the masking tape, felt inside, and pulled out a license plate. Baffled, Gellerman shook his head.

Jack pointed to the face, and Manny read, "AY 152" beneath the "Live Free or Die" New Hampshire state motto! Manny was dumbfounded. Jack gestured to something else, and Manny discovered a framed photo of a 1940s blue Studebaker. Wallenberg's old car and license plate!

Manny broke into a smile, took Jack into his arms and hugged him, and nodded, "Are you kidding?! How'd you do this, how'd you find out?"

"You know I've been getting trained in research, sir. Grad school. You have a good trip to Hungary, but maybe leave this at home, right?"

"Right."

"Too bad Mr. Wallenberg never made it out to the Southwest, huh?"

Manny got up. "He wanted to, actually, according to a note in his notebook. And his professor had also suggested it. To study the Frank Lloyd Wright project and the different local architecture."

Jack stood too. "Well, you'll have to be his surrogate."

Manny smiled at the thought. "Hey, Jack, maybe we should buy an old Studebaker on eBay, attach the plate, and cruise around?"

Jack lit up at that.

CHAPTER 5

Before leaving for Budapest, Manny alerted a few friends there, found a small hotel in Pest, and took some notes for his conference talk in Moscow. He armed himself like a schoolboy, with separate notebooks, small soft-sided ones, one blue and the other orange, for each city. (One of his favorite things was visiting a local stationary store.) Researching, he wrote down three to four names to look up in Moscow, just in case he got lucky, and arranged for a translator through a Moscow State colleague. He then took a long walk through the small college town of Hanover, winding through its neat streets and orderly lawns, in preparation for East Europe. On the Internet he had ordered a new cello score for his son, an old Berenreiter Bach edition. Always, he left him with a small present, and would return with another one. He surprised his son now with a photograph of the youthful Feuerman, cut out from a music text, to paste alongside his others inside his cello case, where he kept his private gallery of Cellist Gods, just as Manny had kept baseball cards of the Brooklyn Dodgers in an old scrapbook.

"Dad, where'd you find these? On eBay?"

"My secret! Now take care of Mom, and I'll see you in about three weeks, okay?"

"Okay. Though I am sorry you are leaving me here," he shook his head, as though being left in a ravine.

"Yeah, it's a tough life."

Manny hugged the little charmer, who hugged back as hard as he could.

Inside the plane, in the first hour when he was still alert enough, he read over sections of Angela's thesis, and read closely one long footnote:

"It is perhaps the case that Wallenberg got involved in the Jewish situation in the first place because of an affair the nobleman may have had with a young Jewess in Budapest whose parents he had placed in his safe houses. This affair was kept secret for several obvious reasons: protection for the young woman, and fear for his own diplomatic position. It is also a strong possibility that he kept quiet in Lybianka Prison because of fear of further endangering the young woman and the child she was bearing of Raoul. This could explain much about the mysteries surrounding RW. [Manny noted, "Kept quiet? About what?"]

Now what evidence do I base these suppositions on? First and foremost, on the statement in December 2005, of Zsuzsanna Frank (Wallenberg), a vibrant woman in her late fifties currently living in Budapest, who claimed, to this writer, that she is the grown-up child of that affair and eventual marriage between her mother, Klara Frank, and RW. To substantiate this declaration, Ms. Frank produced for me a series of documents and some photographs, including a birth certificate copy, original safe house passes of her parents, a sheaf of personal letters (some smuggled from Moscow) between RW and her mother, an old photograph of RW in Sweden as a boy, and other old items. When I questioned why Ms. Frank suddenly would acknowledge this important past, she claims she was never asked by anyone else . . .

I came upon this curious "missing" lady in the first place through the good guidance of my professor, E. Gellerman, who first mentioned the rumor of her existence. On my research trip to Budapest, I was scoping out the Jewish community, asking if anyone was still around who might remember RW, some old witnesses, and came across a middle-aged woman in the old Yiddish restaurant, Hannah's, who claimed she knew his daughter, and she lived not far away, in the old ghetto. She accompanied me to the street, off Wychensky, and there, after waiting a few hours, I met Zsuzsa Frank Wallenberg. A gray-eyed, intelligent woman with reasonable English, she invited me in, and in her modest living room, asked me some questions and then proceeded to talk and answer my queries. To my astonishment, she made no bones about the familial connection, but rather was surprised that no one had come looking for her before. "The world seems very interested still in the whereabouts of my dead father," she put in awkwardly, "but doesn't seem to care too much about his living daughter."

"Sir, what drink would you like?" the airline hostess asked, breaking his focus.

Manny took a ginger ale, scribbled some notes on the thesis, and wrote other notes regarding the important news about the self-declared Hungarian daughter. He settled back in with his reading and music. No, it would be impossible now to try to concentrate on the project, what with a child crying and the plane's hectic activity taking over. That was all right, he figured, gazing out at the high lofty clouds below, a floating comforter of white down. His future ground had been laid in that buried footnote of possibility and conjecture. Get to the bottom of that and he'd maybe have something. Something original. The jet seemed hardly to be moving, but levitating, stopped in an illusion of cloud stillness. His hour of homework was over; the rest would be on the ground. Illusions there too, he figured. Well, he had chased many of those before; he was an old pro at that.

Thoughts of Budapest soon turned into streets of Budapest, which, by contrast, reinforced the truths of the little town in New Hampshire: its piety, provincialism, Puritanism. How sexless those little towns in America were, with no bordellos allowed, only repressive sublimation and illicit affairs, and torrents of gossip. So boring, so corny too. You purchased your safe and tame streets at the high price of noisy interest, thrilling variety, rich vulgarity. Here, this East European city was a kind of battered Paris, filled with old bridges, potholed streets, eroded trees, stunning women. And living scars from World War II: shrapnel holes still decorated the walls of Pest buildings. Is that how Kovacs got the idea, decades ago, to open his television show with a make-believe machine gun spraying holes across the brick walls of the set? In other words, transferring his Hungarian youth into his scary black comedy?

He found the phone number of Zsuzsanna W., and she asked to meet in a coffee shop on Dob utca, in the old ghetto district. Inside Freuhlich's, a small coffee and pastry shop of two rooms, he found a seat at a formica table and waited. Presently, he was joined by a broad-shouldered woman in her fifties with long dark hair, fine smooth skin, a prominent nose. She was handsome in a fatigued way. Dressed simply in a beige cardigan sweater and brown slacks, she introduced herself, put out her hand, and advised him, in accented English, to have the vegetable salad: "They do that well here." He accepted; she ordered at the counter and returned to their small round table in the second room.

He really didn't know what to say, so he began by explaining the nature of his responsibility as Angie's thesis director, and that he wanted to confirm some of the facts in her thesis. "But also, I want to learn more about the subject for myself," he explained. She responded, in fairly good English, that she had heard much about him from that "appealing young student," but still it was "surprising" that he should journey all the way here to see her, Zsuzsanna. "So far for so little," she offered, and he was surprised by the deft phrase. Uncertain how to proceed, he asked if she lived in the neighborhood, and she said yes. The food was brought, two cold salads, a beer for him, a coffee for her.

"What is it actually you've come over for, Professor Gellerman?"

"Well, to be frank, to meet you, to see . . ."

"If I exist?" she smiled. "Yes?"

"Well, yes. That."

She held out her hands and turned them. "What do you think?"

He paused. "They look real, and maybe you play the piano." He smiled. "So, yes, I think you do exist."

"Good. We are in agreement about this."

He took a bite, following her, and it was surprisingly tasty.

"And also, for what else you have made the journey?"

"Well, to see if . . . if you are who my student claims you are."

"Or, who I claim I am?" Her look was an unblinking stare. "You mean, am I related to Mr. Wallenberg?"

"Yes, to put it simply."

She took another bite, using both utensils, and offered, "I believe I am. I have always been told so, and thought so. My mother was his lover and wife, though discreet, secret." Again, no smile, just a look of interest in the gray-green eyes, and in the firm chin jutted forward slightly, a touch of defiance. "I remember my father well, or vivid, I think you say, the little I saw him."

The cold salad was filled with small potatoes, carrots, broccoli, and had a lively sauce. "Where did you learn your good English, if I may ask?"

"Oh, it is not so good really, not anymore." The face softened now. "I learned it in the schools, of course, but then I went to Michigan for nearly a year, re-membering my father's love of the place as a youth." She wiped her mouth and nodded. "I agree with his estimate very much."

Her words brought me up short; she had studied the biography well! And learned her part in the script perfectly.

"Yes, Ann Arbor is very nice. Perhaps you'll return one day?"

"Oh, I don't think so. I stay here now, and enjoy my daughter, and my friends. Budapest is always melancholic, of course, but it is always . . . full of intrigue too."

He made small talk with her, seeking to earn her trust, while noticing the observant Jewish folk coming and going. Now and then he glanced at her face, observing the fine angles, the high forehead, semi-almond eyes, the pale complexion. Did he see a resemblance to RW in that nose, forehead, eyes? Hard to tell, really; he only had old newspaper and magazine photographs to go on.

"By the way," he said, inspired by these thoughts, "do you have any old pho-tographs I might see? Out of curiosity."

She restrained her laugh, and set down her coffee. "I am sure, 'out of curios-ity.' Let me think about it. Where are you staying? Do you have a phone?"

He explained where and gave her the number from the hotel card.

"You should try the Café Central; it's not far from you and it's very pleasant."

In the next twenty-four hours he walked about the city, finding the busy noisy streets and small shops altogether agreeable, despite the semi-grubby streets and ill-maintained buildings. It reminded him of his home turf, Brooklyn, in the late forties and fifties. Would he hear from her again, or was the mystery lady too cagey, too shrewd not to keep herself elusive? Keeping her invented identity alive for herself and maybe for grad students alone? Oh, well. He'd give her a little more time for the fantasy to unfold.

He remembered her suggestion, found the Central Café, took his morning coffee and a thick cheese omelet for lunch. The café was a pair of large rooms, high-ceilinged and darkly wooded, with two crystal chandeliers and a formidable literary history recorded on the inside of the menu. The waiters wore formal black outfits and served with obvious pride; he especially liked one who spoke English and was a David Niven look-alike. Over a second cup of superb coffee, he read the *International Herald Tribune*, and wondered just how far the full fantasy extended? (And, where might it lead? . . .)

That night, after three hours of sitting inside waiting for the lady to call, and making his own call to Moscow to check on his translator there—she had located several persons of interest, including an aged KGB interrogator!—he again walked the streets, alive with pedestrians, tourists, trams, buses, and ambled all the way across the old-fashioned Liberty Bridge, admiring the green ironwork and the view of the auspicious Hotel Gellért coming closer on the Buda side. In the evening glow, the choppy Danube curved up and around the bend, and reflected the shimmering lights from the castle area and the newer hotels. The darkening sky started to blink with stars, and he thought how memorializing if a new constellation were to be named for RW. The late April weather was cool, but wafts of spring were blowing. A soft landscape with little trace of the area's dark history. Later, back in his room, no message beeped on his message machine. Well, maybe it was time to leave?

The next morning he was back at the Central Café for his juice, coffee, and sweet roll, served by the knowledgeable waiter, who nodded. The small tables were occupied by morning clients, and the air was aromatic with a strong coffee smell. He felt down, disappointed, and began to make plans to depart soon—maybe even that evening?

"So you did find the place. How do you like it?"

Zsuzsanna had discovered him, and asked permission to join him. He said, yes, it was his pleasure, and she sat, wearing a beige blouse and yellow pullover and cloche hat. Her pale face looked fresher in the morning, less fatigued, more mobile. She ordered an espresso from the waiter, Peter.

"What a pleasant surprise," he uttered.

"I thought it would be rude for you to be alone too often."

"How thoughtful," he said. How old was she? Approaching sixty? He wanted to ask, When and how did she pick up this curious RW obsession? But how could he put it?

He asked about the history of the café, and while she told him of its artistic history, he tried to think of a strategy. Finally, at a break, he said, "It would be very useful if at some point I could see some of those old photos you mentioned the other night."

"I'm sure you would. And," she smiled mirthfully, for the first time, "should I ask to see what your student has written about me?"

"Touché," he retorted, "Ask her; you should. If she wishes it, you will be delighted. She admired you very much. And trusted you totally."

She gestured with her mouth. "Unlike you, you mean. Yes, I will be happy to show you some of the old photos, and memories. First, you must tell me, however, what you want to do with all this . . . information gathering." Her tone changed, and she teased, "You are writing your own book perhaps?"

"Oh, no, I'm not in that neighborhood," he decided to say. "My student has gotten me interested in the subject, made me aware of my ignorance, actually. And I am wanting to check her own historical . . . digging."

"What is this 'digging?'"

"Her investigative research."

She smiled, more fully, not unlike an Ingrid Bergman smile. "Into me?"

"Oh, well, you're part of it, yes."

"And you are checking on other facts in her thesis?"

"Well, yes, I am, or will be."

She had placed him squarely on the defensive, and he felt uncertain of his ground, actually. But he sipped his coffee and persevered, hearing the tinkling of glasses, low chatter.

"So, I will show you a few things if you wish, and you can check up on Angela's work. She is very thorough, I will tell you, though."

They took one of the trams, Zsuzsanna decrying his taxi suggestion, and in ten minutes they had wound their way to a stop near her apartment. They walked another six or eight minutes, past the impressive Parliament building by the river, and soon were climbing the stairs of an old shabby apartment building.

Her apartment was large, old, high-ceilinged, and fitted out with 1930s furniture. No upscaling or modernizing here. She escorted him through a dark vestibule into a kind of sitting room/salon, and through that to a large living room where she sat him down at a round wooden table. He was growing faintly excited. She asked if he wanted a tea or coffee, and he said sure. While she put it up, he looked around: a daybed in one corner covered with old brocade, a large dreary armoire, a desk and study chair and several bulging bookcases, a maroon upholstered reading chair. He stood and walked to one of the two large mullioned windows, and to his surprise was able to spot the river at the end of a long street between buildings. He checked out one of the pictures on the wall, an old family photograph, entirely foreign.

He sat back down and waited, staring at a bookcase protected by glass, and thinking how preposterous this whole thing was, this Hungarian woman inventing a life for herself, and blurring the line between the fictitious and the real. Well, that was fine for her, but not for history or Wallenberg. And for his student, well, he'd have to educate her gently in the way of hard investigating into original sources and hard documents.

"So, here we are. Can you move that notebook? Thanks." And she set down a tray of small cakes and tea. Rather formal, with decorated porcelain teapot and cups and saucers; but why not? She was European. "Let's let it settle for a few minutes, yes?"

"Are these ruglach?" he asked.

"Yes, they are." She smiled at his recognition—a lovely smile, tarnished, he saw now, by yellowing teeth. She got up, walked to the old Winthrop-like secretary, removed from a drawer an old scrapbook, and brought it over.

"Here, some photos of my mother and her parents: as you can see, I look a good bit like her. And this is the same apartment, before they moved her."

The enchantment of old photographs pasted on a scrapbook page, each held by four white corners, recalled his childhood scrapbooks.

Early on, small photos of the grandparents, a tall doctor with a goatee and a plump grandmother, with their only daughter, Zsuzsanna's mom, Klara. Patience, he told himself, as they went through those nostalgic worn photos from the 1930s and '40s. His host turned each ancient page as though it were a rare jewel, reminding him, because of the thick paper, of leafing through those old thick pages of the book catalogues at the British Museum. Zsuzsanna looked with an attached but restrained emotion, and her long fingers suggested the upright piano in the room. He was slowly drawn in to the atmosphere before and during the Great War, though the figures could have been his own mother and father, Russian immigrants.

"You do this often?" he asked.

A wry smile. "Some months yes, some no. Depends on my inside life. And also on Dora, my daughter, whenever she wishes to look through them."

"Oh, your daughter. How old is she?"

"Twenty-nine. Perhaps you'll meet her one day, if you stay long enough."

She leafed through several more pages of these three-by-five black and white photos. Next came an enlargement of several photos of ID cards, one each of the mother and father, and a third of the daughter, Zsuzsanna's mother. Each bore a stamp of the Swedish delegation, and a signature. "This is signed by Carl-Ivan Danielsson, the head of the diplomatic office; the other two by my father . . . Immediately afterward, we were taken to this apartment house, one of the first of the safety houses, you see? A plain, nondescript six-story apartment building, with corner balconies." She had pulled her chair closer to his, and spoke in a small quiet voice, showing and telling him her family history. "Here," and she turned to a photo of Wallenberg himself, the pale narrow face, the solemn stare; and alongside, a handwritten card of his phone numbers. Manny realized he was gradually getting hooked on this strange stuff, like a whiff of opium, and cautioned himself to take it easy.

A photograph of a railway station, a crowd of a few hundred Jews, several Arrow Cross soldiers and authorities. "Look, I show you something," she gestured, taking up a magnifying glass, and holding it in position for him to gaze through. "There is my mother, you see? And here is my father, speaking with the local commandant." Well, yes, it did look to be whom Zsuzsanna claimed it was. But so what? "He already knew her, you understand, originally from the orphanage, but pretended not to."

Stay skeptical, he counseled himself; no real proof here. But she was performing well.

Zsuzsanna smoothed her hand over the next two crinkled pages, proudly displaying photographs of her young mother, a pretty woman of eighteen or so, with flowing dark hair and a lovely smile, a good looking Jewish *maidela*. "She was active in the resistance already as a teenager, in late 1943, and then became a helper to the woman who became Raoul's secretary, Elizabeth Nako, once he realized his true mission in Budapest."

"Oh," he said, going along with the story.

"And here you will see, the two of them together . . ."

Well, what he saw was what appeared to be Wallenberg and the same young woman in several photos, with the faces ambiguous, though, and the figures in rooms or outdoors in parks, also too shadowy for clear identification. What was he seeing?

"You may say it was a great *mitzvah*, you realize, this union," she explained, leaning back, exalted at the photos, the thought, "A young Hungarian Jewish girl and this older Swedish diplomat who was turning into a demigod. I believe that it was his love for my mother which truly inspired his great mission."

"Oh," he murmured, not wanting just now to break her spell. He couldn't resist saying, "He did have a task assigned to him in Stockholm, though, by the Hungarian businessman and by—"

"A task assigned is not the same as *inspiration*, Professor," she corrected, taking his wrist for just a moment. "It is inspiration that drives great missions, not the assignment of tasks."

He nodded, drained his cup, and felt the room to be losing all its light somehow.

"And here you can see the true union." She shifted course and smiled radiantly, and pointed to a strange photo, again shadowy and hard to read, of a man and woman and a rabbi with tallis holding a book, in the outdoors, with overhead boughs crossing. "You know what this is?" she asked.

What could he say? What the hell was she getting at?

"You are not Jewish, are you?"

Did he redden from shame or anger? "Yes, I am, actually."

"And you don't know what a *chupah* is?"

Looking hard at the odd, ambiguous photo, he kept his doubts private. "Yes, I do know what a *chupah* is—what Jews get married under."

She shot him a look. Then, "Naturally. And there it is, on the outskirts of Budapest. A miracle, no?"

"A miracle," he repeated dumbly. But, he wondered, how might he crash this miracle politely, without injuring feelings, and yet preserve trust? "You are sure that this is what it is, are you?"

Her face tightened, and the pale skin got color. "*Bist du meshuggah*? You are asking me about the most sacred photograph, most important memory, in my life, whether I am sure it is what it is? Yes, Professor, I am sure it is what it looks like," she noted derisively, "a marriage ceremony according to Jewish law and tradition." She shut tightly the scrapbook and checked her wristwatch.

"Wait, please," he pleaded, "you mustn't misunderstand me, Zsuzsanna. I was only asking, you realize. Of course, I don't doubt you or your veracity, but the photograph, well, it is a little vague or shadowy, you will admit, as to its participants. Not," he reassured her, sounding somewhat foolish in his imploring, "its underlying meaning."

"Enough for one day at least." She relented slightly in her stiffness. "More tea, this time with some milk or lemon?"

"Lemon," he said, resting easier.

She poured a second cup, spooned him a wedge on his saucer, and said, "Please be honest with me. What is it you want to know about my father?"

He felt he had to get back on the right track now, in order to explore further those pictures and the curious madness of this invented biography. Did it have a medical name? "Well, I want to know how come he was so special? I mean there were others who saved Jews, right? The wonderful Swiss diplomat Carl

Lutz, for example, and the Spanish ambassador, and even the Vatican's man, Antonio Rotto—I forget their exact names. So what made your father"—he used the noun easily—"so different, so unique?"

She relaxed more fully, the lines of the face softening, and she brushed her hair from her forehead. "Do you know the word 'tikkun?'"

"Well, I know the word, but not really the meaning."

"It is a word that means healing, restoration. That is what my father brought to the Hungarian Jews in 1944. The sense of healing, recovery, in the middle of catastrophe; that is very special. And for that they loved him, you see. Not merely admired him, but loved him." Her face grew luminous. "Wanted to touch him like touching the Torah itself, you understand? Others may have helped Jews, but from afar, and with letters and papers; my father stood with them bodily on the ground, at the railway stations, on the streets, at warehouses or on the forced marches, always." She stared at, scrutinized, him, to see if he was understanding the depth of her words. He followed her eyes closely. "I would not call him their zaddik, you know; he wasn't quite that; he was their mentor, their tikkun; their on-the-ground *living* moshiach, you may say, though that is blasphemy for our people. But the Soviets, later on, knew what they were doing when they took him away and kept him locked up, in isolation; their vengeance was Stalinist anti-Semitism. But he tricked them, even then." Her smile was filled with furtive pleasures.

"How do you mean?"

"Never mind, Professor, never mind. And please, it is late, I must do my errands."

Had she somehow gone too far? In any case, he was escorted out and returned to the busy streets and his hotel room and his swirling thoughts. He took notes. What did she mean by that last remark about tricking the Soviets after all? More tantalizing but fraudulent leads? He felt annoyed with himself for putting up with the charade for so long and not getting tougher with Madame Frank. Oh, well, that was not really needed. Let her be. A cultish nut? A self-styled mystic? A would-be astrologer? Whatever. The main point was, after two hours plus in that dark room of her strange fantasy, he was delighted to be out and connected again to the real world.

Should he leave early for Moscow? he pondered. And rid himself, for now anyway, of that haunted lady? That would be best, he thought, glancing at CNN and packing. After a bit, he went for a walk, hit up a travel agent, and boarded Trolley 64, bumping along and remembering the old electric trolleys at Ralph Avenue in Brooklyn. He headed over to Margaret Island, a recreation park situated on the Danube between Pest and Buda, a ten-minute ride away.

Presently he was wandering in that wonderful park, opened in May for the season, enjoying the warm sunshine and the parade of citizens out walking, bicycling, sunbathing, picnicking. What a relief after that room of dark memories and Madame's fantasies! He decided to rent a motorized golf cart and ride leisurely through the strip of island, a few miles in length.

He was feeling at loose ends; what was he doing here now? What was this mad lady's relation to Raoul? Was there one, in some bizarre way? In Moscow would he be able to dig up some hard facts, a counter to this mystical adventure? Who could have imagined such a scene? Here in the broad sunshine, in his little cart, he felt himself driven, heading somewhere. But where? Toward further mystery, further illusion, or toward real explanation, a surprising truth? . . .

And should he not try for a pit stop in Stockholm—he thought, darting around and heading back—and try to meet with the living Wallenbergs? To ask some hard questions about the dead one, and their family's role in Raoul's ordeal? What did those rich uncles and powerful cousins know, or remember and lock away? And how in the world might Detective Gellerman pursue those secrets? Clearly, whatever "scenes" the professor/scriptwriter had invented, or would invent, were to be equaled or eclipsed by the dark actualities, if they could be unearthed . . . Just consider the fantastical Zsuzsanna Wallenberg here in Budapest, and go from there . . .

Before heading back, he stopped for an ice cream at a stall, and realized there were more parts to this plot, and maybe more surprising characters, than he could have imagined . . .

CHAPTER 6

Picked up at Sheremetyevo airport by an appointed driver who held up a placard with his name on it, he had an immediate impression of Moscow as he rode away from the airport and slowly passed a huge truck on fire, blazing away, the heat visceral, creating a massive traffic jam on the incoming road. Where were the fire engines to pour water on the spectacular blaze? he wondered aloud, and his driver shrugged, smiled wanly, and said, "Russia."

At the hotel he was too exhausted to go outside; he dove into bed, woke up in the middle of the night, read for an hour and a half, and returned to sleep.

In the morning, after a full breakfast, he was picked up, along with two other conference participants from Prague and Paris, and driven through the gray vast city to Moscow State University, a huge place. Soon, on the podium before about 150 people, he waited his turn along with four colleagues, and gave his little speech. He explained how Hungary's coming entrance into the EU might help erase the heavy stain of recent history and politics, its self-betrayals and its persecutions, especially if the economy was prodded upward. He spoke about the literary and musical culture in the old Central and East Europe, especially during its years of Communist oppression, and emphasized how cultural expression was probably the best outlet for politically oppressed people. Did culture flourish as well in democratic societies? he asked rhetorically.

He listened to the next two speakers drone on about contemporary politics, and prayed for lunch. The last lecturer was a hefty Russian, and, speaking in a thick émigré accent, he jolted Manny alert with his talk. Concerning the Cold War, his talk also touched upon the case of Raoul Wallenberg; this Vladimir R. made the argument that RW was a rich dandy in his normal life, but in Budapest in 1944 was most probably a double spy who was at the center of the East-West political game. As he lumbered on, pumped by his conspiratorial theories, Manny came to understand that this was the fellow who had written the long unpublished essay that he had heard about, early on. Though he provided certain circumstantial notes for evidence, Manny remained skeptical but interested. Finally, after running fifteen minutes over his time, he was shut down by the moderator, and the call for lunch intermission was given.

As they moved toward the cafeteria, Manny sidled up alongside him, introduced himself, and said he'd love to read the unpublished manuscript.

"Of course, of course," he said, taking Manny's arm, enthused. "Where are you, England?"

"No, in New Hampshire."

"Oh, well, that makes it very easy indeed. I will send it to you as an e-mail attachment when we return, all right? And you must give me your opinion on it please." He paused and took out a pack of cigarettes. "I still need to complete the last section, but don't worry, it will be worth it! I am hoping Harvard will publish it as a monograph. And now I must step outside for my smoke—American ways are sneaking into the Soviet—rather, Russian—state, sad to say." Before departing he added, "I hope I didn't offend you with my interpretation. But, you see, a lot of people think otherwise about Wallenberg; but what can you expect from a charming Swedish playboy?"

He smiled and shook his head. That last phrase played in his head.

In the cafeteria, an impoverished wood-paneled room, he took soup and a cheese and ham-style sandwich, and found a table.

A brown-haired middle-aged woman appeared, introduced herself, and said, "Please, I am Natasha Davidoff, you recall, yes?" and she handed him a card.

"Oh, yes," he said to the would-be interpreter he had hired through e-mail. "Please join me."

As they proceeded to chat, he was impressed by her English, her soft manner. He asked, "Have you had any luck with any of the names I gave you?"

"Not yet," she acknowledged, "but I am still trying. You will be here longer than the conference, yes?"

"For a few days, that's right."

"Good. Maybe I can come up with someone of interest before you leave. Meanwhile, perhaps you would like to see a few of the relevant sites later today and tomorrow?"

They agreed to meet after the afternoon session, and he returned to the conference.

Fortunately, it ended about 3:15 p.m., and he was able to sidestep Vladimir and meet up with Natasha, who was waiting.

"Do you mind the metro? Much faster at this hour."

They walked the ten minutes from the outsized university to the red-line stop, passing cheap kiosks selling sodas, chips, and chocolates, and rode down on the old escalator into the deep recess to catch their train. ("The Moscow subway system was built much farther down than the Western ones because of the fear of Nazi attacks," she explained.) Within a minute it rumbled in, and they were whisked off.

In a half hour they were alighting from the red-line Lybianka metro stop, and in the cool gray air, Natasha headed them across the wide street. "Here is the monster itself, Lybianka Prison, home of the old KGB, where all the best secrets—and acts—of Soviet horror have been kept and preserved." A huge fortress of a building, a large square block of cement and stone, with small windows peering out over the square.

"What is it now?"

"Home of the new security force, the FSB."

As they ambled by, a Russian guard eyed them beneath his absurd thick cap, and Manny felt the first chill of the legendary infamy.

"So this is where Wallenberg was kept," he observed. "And killed."

She nodded. "Or perhaps they transferred him at the very end to Vladimir Prison, a few hours away, for his finish."

They strolled around the mountainous fortress in the somber light, and he was gripped by the Stalinist force of the architecture, an authoritarian block of death.

"No file was ever found on the case. Do you think it still exists somewhere?"

She gave him a skeptical look, and indicated the lower part of the building. "Down there, in the basement, there remain files locked away, but it's so off-limits that most of today's officials have no access, and they don't even know what they have. That 'lost' file may very well be there, and probably is. No file is ever lost, just conveniently misplaced."

They walked up the street a few blocks, found a café, and sat for a coffee. Moscow was no Budapest for elegant cafés. He checked the list of four or five names he had given her and told her the priorities, and she explained her progress with each.

"Come, at 6 p.m. I am introducing you to a friend of mine who works at night at a very interesting place. He is an archivist and historian, and knows a good deal about all sorts of Soviet matters."

Memorial House, later, was in another part of town, but the efficient crowded subway got them there in a half hour. They alighted at Pushkinskaya, walked fifteen minutes to an undistinguished side street, and halted at a modest three-story house. If Lybianka Prison was a lethal Mount Rushmore in the city, this Memorial House was a small, shabby triple-decker that belonged in South Boston. They entered, walked up to the first floor, saw posters on the walls of various Soviet political prisoners and noble dissenters, and rang at the door. They were buzzed in, and met a fellow who said to follow him down a small narrow corridor, off of which were pigeonhole rooms attended by researchers invariably smoking and poring over papers and computers.

"Ah, there you are," Natasha said, finding her man. "This is Nikita, Nikita Petrov."

Manny shook the man's firm grip, gave him his name, and Nikita asked if he wanted tea or coffee. He chose tea, and Nikita went to make it. The room was not more than a cubbyhole, with a few computers on small desks. A man in shirtsleeves worked at one. On the walls were portraits of Gulag survivors and Soviet dissidents. In a minute Nikita returned, with tea in teacups for them, and he asked if Manny wanted to look around. Nikita was a black-haired man, handsome, in his late forties, and wore a Levi jacket and dungarees. Not exactly your Western historian dress code. Manny nodded and they proceeded. The house was divided into small rooms, mostly filled with research scholars working.

"Everything to do with Stalin's murders we try to document here. Letters about missing people, records of deaths, camp names, family inquiries, unknown victims, everything." There seemed to be plenty of work to occupy this many people, as they walked about, finally entering a small room of odd objects in cases and bookshelves.

Nikita explained their presence to the librarian, and said, "Our museum and library."

Manny walked amidst the windowed cases, noting a wooden nameplate from Perm, a pair of old shoes, a homemade knife, a deck of cards, a striped prisoner's uniform, an abstract wooden sculpture made from twigs, pages from a tattered diary, a lined torn notebook, an old rusted wristwatch . . . These everyday objects were the poignant remains that had been retrieved and saved from the long horror show. Their simplicity moved him.

"And once a year we have a contest for high school students across Russia, asking them to write an essay on some aspect of the Stalin years. Then we bring the winner and his parents for a week to Moscow, where they have never been. You see, many or most of them have never learned anything in the high schools about the Gulag. Or the truths about Stalin."

Presently they sat in his office and chatted some more. It was amazing to Manny that the entire building of researchers was devoted to the One Great Ordeal: Stalin's purges, prisons, and murders. It turned out that it was the Germans and Americans who supported Memorial House. "The present regime tolerates us, since we don't go after them; but for how long?"

Before leaving, Manny showed Nikita the list of people he would like to see. He nodded at one, said he'd never get to see that one (RW's interrogator), crossed off another as useless propaganda, and said another was of dubious use; he added a name, in case Manny went to Vladimir Prison. "And please forget all the nonsense about those later witnesses of Wallenberg, who claimed to see him in the Gulag somewhere; none has ever been verified or documented." At the end of another forty-five minutes they said good-bye to the amiable fellow, who rose and said that if he could be of help, Manny should e-mail or call him.

"Quite a place," he commented.

"Yes, it is very special. Most citizens do not know of it, even Muscovites."

Following the local tradition, they hailed a citizen taxi in the street—several cars immediately pulled over when they put out their hands—and went back to his hotel. Natasha and he parted, agreeing to see each other the next day, or else talk on the phone if she couldn't make the conference. "I may be busy trying to find one of your spies to talk to," she said. He nodded and went inside. He read the *Moscow Times*, thought about that Budapest woman, and took notes before falling off.

The next day at the conference he drank coffee and tried to concentrate on the next set of speakers, realizing why he hardly ever attended such meetings. Too many speakers, too much to hold in your head at one time. At the intermission he was found and collared by the Soviet émigré bear and conspiracy specialist of the day before, who took him to the cafeteria and proceeded once again to play the same tune. RW was a Swedish playboy and dandy, and worked for the American OSS as well as probably the Germans. He said this with unassailable authority, no doubts or qualms. "I am trying to publish my long essay at Harvard. Do you happen to know Rick Lansing there? He has held my paper for over a year now, and I need to get him nudged a little!" I told him, happily, that I didn't know Rick, and couldn't help. Sagging perceptibly, he said, no matter, he'd send Manny the piece and he might be able to suggest another place to send it. When the afternoon session began, he felt relieved.

In the evening he found Natasha at his hotel, waiting in the lobby. "I have found out that this one fellow, the KGB interrogator Daniel Pagliansky, is still alive and lives not far away from here, a short walk from Pushkinskaya, and I have found his phone number and called him; but his wife, who is actually alert and nice, says he is ill and doesn't really want to speak with anyone. As for the others, this Dmitri is off somewhere, and . . ."

He nodded, realized it was pretty futile, and invited her to dinner to reward her for her trouble. They went to a classy restaurant, The Pushkin, a fifteen-minute walk; and inside, over some superb borscht with sour cream and a wild boar entrée, they chatted more. This Nastasha was truly civilized, and had spent a few years at Indiana University, where she had honed her English. "I even taught two summers at Middlebury, a charming college and town." She added, "Well, we still have two days before you leave, so maybe we can turn up something."

Two days later, his last day in town, he and Natasha decided to give it a shot, and simply go show up and knock on the door of the Pagliansky apartment. After asking their identity through the closed door, a bulky gentleman of about sixty opened the door, asked them in cordially, and took their jackets. He inquired what they wanted. Natasha explained that Manny was an American writer who was working on a novel about World War II and the old days in Moscow in the 1940s. Just then there was a calling out from the other room, in Russian; the son smiled, used to such screaming, and said it was his father, who was angry that they had come after he and his wife had clearly refused Natasha's requests twice on the phone!

Gyorgi, the son, ushered them into a study, explaining, using Russian and body gestures, that they should take it easy, and asked specifically what Manny wanted to ask his father. He cited the Soviet and Moscow atmosphere in the forties, and perhaps a few questions about Wallenberg, the KGB . . .

Gyorgi shook his head, told Natasha he could not ask about the latter two subjects—the old man would throw them out—and said to wait; Father was finishing lunch with Mother. He went to the adjoining room to see them, and perhaps pacify them.

In the book-lined study, maybe nine by fourteen feet, Natasha and Manny stood and waited. He looked about at the bookshelves, the large glass-top desk, the numerous small photos on the shelves and desk. Voices came from the other room. On the wall bookshelf, he was startled to see a few books in Yiddish, and focused on the nineteenth-century novel by Mendele, which he had read decades ago in his old Hebrew school in Brownsville. He glanced through it, trying to recall his Yiddish reading. So this Daniel got around. Next, Manny saw a small photograph of a Soviet officer, handsome and vital. Was this the Daniel Pagliansky that was in the next room? He had an inclination to slip it into his pocket, as evidence of the meeting . . . On the desk, he viewed other old photos, the mother and father and small son in the playground . . . other military and personal photos . . . That youthful Daniel had been rugged, good-looking, energetic.

The door opened from the adjoining room, and Gyorgi, escorting in a very old man, introducing his father, who proceeded slowly. The father sat down opposite Manny, in the guest chair, while he sat in his, at the son's gesture. He was blind in one eye, his white hair was thin as a baby's, the bones of his face were pushing forward from the taut covering of skin, and his visage was the mask of Death.

"Why did you come here?!" he suddenly proclaimed in loud English, "after we had told her on the phone not to come!" He pounded the desk with his frail hand, shouting now. "Why do you Americans think you can come wherever you want, whether you are invited or not?!"

Manny was shocked, by the English, by the declarations, by the death mask.

"Well, it was my last opportunity to see you, as I am leaving very soon," he said, surprisingly calm. "And to try to chat with you."

The old man looked at him savagely, and turned to his son for the full translation—even though he may have understood the words—who in turn waited to hear from Natasha.

On an impulse, Manny said quietly, "You see, even though I am trained as a historian, I am writing a novel, and I wanted to get the atmosphere of the old days in Moscow, during the war years."

The old man eyed Manny skeptically, from beneath bushy eyebrows, and waited for the translators to finish their transaction.

He waited a moment, considering Manny, who faced him squarely; he believed the old man was asking him to face his frightening face without flinching or turning away. Fair enough. Finally he said, in Russian, "The climate was special, despite the danger. We were all united against the Nazi threat." He paused and added, "It was a great time in Russia."

Manny took in that Stalinist accolade, and cautioned himself about approaching the two taboo subjects. "And you were studying at the time—what? Where?"

His hands had moved to the table, and one began to fidget, tremble. Parkinson's? He offered, "Of course, I studied, at the gymnasium. Poetry. Mathematics. Architecture. Excellent school in those days. I am a trained architect, as is my wife."

"I see," Manny said, nodding, exhaling, and remembering Wallenberg's desires and training in the field of architecture.

"So you studied poetry too in the gymnasium?"

"Yes, of course. Especially German poetry I read, and enjoyed."

"Your German was fluent then?"

Manny waited for the translations to go through.

"Of course, one had to learn a language well. German was my second language, after English."

So that was how he and Raoul conversed, in German. "Oh, you studied English that early?"

Pagliansky sneered at him. "Soviet education demanded high standards. Not like these days. I studied English in the first school."

Manny paused in appreciation, staring at him; his rage had receded as he had entered into the conversation. Manny got up and found the Mendele book and brought it to the desk. "I read this in my Hebrew school in Brooklyn, a Sholem Aleichem Bund school. It was good."

The old man looked at him with new interest. "You can read Yiddish?"

"Well, I did then, but probably not now. But Mendele was pretty good, as I recall."

He nodded, and continued in English, "In Brooklyn? You came from there? I used to read the writers from Brooklyn from the 1930s—Michael Gold, Daniel Fuchs."

Manny stared at this amazing, ghostly bag of bones, who was startling him with his memory, his education, his precision.

"Why?"

"To learn the idiom, of course. Reading those novels was the easiest way to obtain the idiom."

No wonder they had picked this fellow for Raoul! he thought. A multipurpose brilliant talent.

"I didn't know they had Bund schools over there," Pagliansky murmured in Russian to his son. "So you are Jewish yourself?"

"Yes," I acknowledged. "Like yourself."

He shrugged. "Religion played no part in our education, you understand."

"I understand. I am not religious either."

"So tell me," he said in Russian, "what sort of book are you writing?"

"A novel."

"Fiction?"

"Yes, fiction."

Pagliansky nodded, half dismissing it, he thought, half relieved.

"But you have written histories before this?"

"Yes. Would you like to see one?"

"Why not?" he said in English, before speaking in Russian to his son, who then said to him, "Father is tired. He should go rest now. You must leave."

Manny stood up as the old man did, and put out his hand; he put out his limp one. He was very small. Age had shrunk him to less than five feet. "Thank you, I enjoyed our chat."

He nodded, and they went into the adjoining hallway, where their coats were hung on a clothes tree. The son Gyorgi handed the coats to them, and as Manny was getting his on, the old man suddenly spit out something in Russian.

"What did he say?"

The son smiled sheepishly, while Natasha raised her eyes. "Fuck off!" Gyorgi added in Russian, apologetically. "He says that to me quite frequently too, so please don't take it too personally. His mind . . ."

Manny didn't know how to take it, but thought it half-comical, half-serious.

"If you can bring a book next time, that would be good," said Gyorgi.

"Next time?" Manny repeated low. But he was leaving the next day . . .

As they turned, the old man again offered his fierce cry of fuck off! (in Russian). Nashasha smiled as they shook Gyorgi's hand and thanked him. He told Natasha to call him in the next day or two.

Outside the apartment, walking down the large renovated staircase, Natasha said, "Quite a meeting. You may have to stay on a few days now . . ."

Several hours later, they returned to Memorial House, and indeed were able to catch their friendly mentor, Nikita Petrov. They told him of their lucky meeting with Pagliansky.

"What? Are you sure it was him? No one has been able to see him from the West, at all, ever. In 1991 the KGB called him in, here in Moscow, and tried to put questions to him about that period, without judging him, and he said, 'I remember nothing.' And that was it; they never bothered with him again. And a few years ago, Guy von Dardel, Wallenberg's half brother, came from Switzerland to meet him, but Paglainsky never opened the door. So this is quite extraordinary. Did he tell you anything of value?"

"Nothing direct, but indirectly it was of great value, I believe."

"He even agreed to see us again," said Natasha. "But the professor is scheduled to leave in a day."

"Well, maybe you should think about it? . . ."

"Yes, maybe I should." Manny considered his great good luck and asked, "Do you think he also did actually torture Wallenberg? Or participate?"

Nikita shook his head. "No, no. The KGB had professional medical persons who were trained specifically in torture; they knew all the methods and devices. They were a separate branch from the regular interrogators like Daniel."

"I see," Manny said, comforted somewhat, as he looked at one of those dissident meeting posters from post-Stalinist days on a bulletin board.

"You must write up your interview; it is a first," Nikita urged.

Walking back to Pushkinskaya with Natasha, he felt a certain quiet glow at their small victory, which Nikita had verified. "You did well," he told her.

"You mean we did well," she replied, "Will it be of real use for your work?"

"I don't know yet," he said, "but when I think it over, and maybe start to figure it out, I will let you know."

They reached the black marble statue of Pushkin, surrounded by people waiting for friends. He thought it best to walk alone to his hotel, to gather and digest the information unto himself. He explained this to Natasha, and she said, "I will call Gyorgy in a few hours and see how the father reacted afterward, and when he might be free again to see you. Then you can make up your own mind about leaving tomorrow afternoon or not."

"Thanks, and you've been super." He pecked her on her cheeks, and departed in the cool air, down their Fifth Avenue, Tverskaya. Stores sparkled with all sorts of expensive goods, along with Nite Flite, the infamous Swedish nightclub. Russian consumers were on the march, shopping, walking, chatting. He came upon the huge store of the nineteenth-century merchant Eliseevsky, which Natasha had cited; he entered, trying to clear his head, and picked up an item or two. It was an elegant shop of two large rooms, and carried an array of gourmet groceries, from cheeses to pastas to croissants, and fancy vodkas under lock and key (some $200 per bottle), with ceilings like those in a cathedral and the high stained-glass windows. Nearly destroyed in World War II, and languishing in Stalin's days, Eliseevsky's had been renovated in the past decade. He moseyed about, found fresh bread, and investigated the huge array of vodkas, including expensive ones in a locked glass case, settling for a small bottle for ten bucks, and went on his way.

Soon, he was back in his hotel room, sitting at the small desk and taking notes on his extraordinary meeting. Had it really happened? (It was a little like the ghost of Wallenberg appearing in his New Hampshire study.) He was glad for the witnesses, the son, and his translator. He pondered how Daniel had actually interrogated Raoul, with what instruments of persuasion, and with what results?

The phone rang, and Natasha said, "The father was very angry, it seems, that he spoke with us at all. And Gyorgy says it will probably be best to wait a week before seeing him again. He will calm down and forget it all anyway; he is very old, you know, eighty-eight next weekend. In fact, they are having a birthday party for him."

He took that in. "Sure, I understand. So, why don't you come over for a coffee in the late morning and we can finish up our conversation and plans for the future? My taxi is picking me up at 2:30."

They arranged the time, he made a note to take out enough cash to pay Natasha, and he returned to his notes and thoughts. So the old boy was going to be eighty-eight? A well-rounded figure. Too bad he wouldn't be around for the birthday, as a few of the invited guests might be interesting people! (Maybe he could bring him a token from Memorial House?)

He flicked on the TV, found CNN, listened to more dreadful news about Baghdad, and tried to tunnel back into that Lybianka Prison cell in late June and July 1945. He was sorry now that he hadn't snatched that small photo of the KGB Daniel; he had many others. That youthful Russian officer's face haunted him, in a montage superimposed over that savage death mask he had just encountered. *Had he been present at the final stage, the execution?*

How far flung was this puzzle? he wondered, stepping into one of those un-American showers, with the hot and cold positions reversed and no shower curtains. How deeply into a strange middle of the case was he plunging? He knew he was getting a long way away from that graduate thesis and his early clues.

Back in Budapest, he went to his favorite library, the law library of Eötvös Loránd University downtown, and sat at a small desk in an empty wood-paneled room. He opened his charged laptop, and waited for all operating systems to kick in. Shifting from his historian role to the growing, more fragile, role of imaginative scenewriter, he felt stronger just now, armed with the evidence of the recent interview. His challenge was how to turn that recent preternaturally real hour into the distant faraway hours of the powerfully imagined? He proceeded:

Lybianka Prison; late June 1945. The interrogation room, approximately fourteen by sixteen feet. The thick walls and floor were made of cement blocks whitewashed over; a rectangular wooden table and three chairs were set in the center. The lighting: an overhead bare bulb and a pair of bright strobe lights off to the side.

Raoul was brought in by two Soviet guards, and sat down; a glass of water was at his place. He was wearing a prisoner's uniform, and his regular dark visage was now pale.

After a few minutes the young, handsome KGB officer, with a thick mop of dark curly hair, entered, nodded to the guards, who departed, and nodded to Raoul. Carrying a sheaf of papers, wearing his uniform informally, open at the collar, he sat down opposite the prisoner and offered him a cigarette. Raoul accepted, and lit up. The interrogator opened the manila folder, searched through it, and took out a long white pad.

In German, Pagliansky asked Raoul if he had been treated well thus far. Raoul nodded and asked when he would be released.

"I don't know how much longer you will be treated well, with our full courtesy," Daniel said, with reluctance. "I am doing all I can to keep it this way, but there are others, including my bosses, who are growing impatient."

"I still don't understand. What am I doing here? Why are you keeping me here this way? I am a Swedish diplomat, with full international immunity. You have seen my official papers."

Daniel inhaled and blew the smoke out to the side.

"And what about my driver, Vilmos, who has a family back in Budapest? Is he being provided for?"

"I believe so."

"I will appreciate it if you keep your eye on his situation."

"I will do my best."

Another officer entered, came over, leaned down to Daniel, and whispered something. Then he departed.

"Mr. Wallenberg," Daniel began, "have you been working with the American secret service, the OSS? Please consider your answers carefully this time."

"But you have asked me this twice already, and I explained my situation. I knew only Mr. Olsen, of the War Refugee Board. I accepted a modest amount of money to help save the Jews of Budapest, and knew nothing else about any OSS organization."

"But then why did we find such a large sum of cash, over two hundred thousand, in your possession when we stopped you?"

Raoul shook his head in frustration. "Some of the Jewish victims gave me the money to hold, knowing that their lives and property were in severe danger. I could use it for bribes, to save people, or put it in a Swedish bank when I returned to Stockholm."

Daniel jotted down a note on his pad. "Did you cooperate with the German Nazis or Hungarian Arrow Cross?"

"Of course not."

"Did you make any deals with the Nazis?"

"No."

"Not with Veesenmayer, or Eichmann?"

"No."

"Did you work for the Nazis?"

"Of course not. I was their staunchest enemy."

"But you spoke with them constantly? And you did manage to save those thousands of Jews through some of these conversations? How?"

"Various means, as I've told you: various sorts of bribes, and threats for when the German occupation would end. I've already explained this to you."

Daniel P., whose head was bent slightly forward in pursuing these questions, leaned back now. "But, Raoul, we both know that the Wallenberg family and bank and businesses in Stockholm were very friendly with the Nazis."

Raoul shrugged.

"So why would you be any different?"

"You are merely trying to provoke me."

A pause. Daniel smoked. Raoul drank water.

"Did you stay in touch with your family while you were in Budapest at the Enskilde Bank?"

"No."

"Were they in touch with the Nazi officials in Budapest, concerning you there?"

"Not that I knew of."

"But that was possible, to make things easier for you?"

Raoul shook his head. "Possible, but highly unlikely, since they did not know—that I know of—German officials in Budapest."

Daniel got up, circled around the table and the seated Wallenberg, and when he returned, asked, "So tell me, whom do you prefer? Goethe or Schiller?"

A slow smile emerged from Raoul. "Goethe."

"And why?"

He considered his words. "His use of the language, his cadences, his feelings."

"You know," Daniel nodded, "I'm afraid I agree."

Raoul squeezed out the butt of one cigarette, gestured permission for another, and said, "Actually, I probably prefer Rilke to both of them. He seems to speak more deeply, to me anyway."

Daniel lifted his glass of water. "We agree again! Yes, Rilke is special, a German with a noble soul."

Raoul smiled, "You are rather educated."

"So are you."

"A humanist, beneath it all?"

"Of course."

"Then why . . . why this?"

Daniel smiled wryly. "It is not a contradiction to be a patriot and a humanist, Mr. Wallenberg. In fact, quite the contrary. This Great War has been fought on behalf of both principles, don't you think?'

Raoul nodded, almost reluctantly.

"Now tell me, these Jews, what did they mean to you? Why did they come to compel your attention so much? Was it purely . . . idealistic?"

Raoul clasped his hands and faced Daniel intently. "Sir, though I am a Christian of a sort, I am a humanist too, as you are; when people are being deported and murdered in front of your eyes, you try to do something."

"Did you want to be a hero, do you think?"

Raoul shook his head slowly. "Not a hero, just a man doing what needs to be done. Or doing what he can do, in the face of extreme circumstances."

"Let us go back to the subject of the money these wealthy Jews gave you. Did they also give you other assets, such as paintings, gold, jewelry?"

"Well, a few gave me addresses of where their paintings or other art works might be in hiding, yes; but I never was able to check on the authenticity of those."

"A few families, or many?"

Wallenberg craned his neck in a circle. "Several families did, yes."

"Where are those names and addresses?"

"They might have been in my small black address book."

"Might have been? Well, where is that?"

"I believe in my diplomatic pouch, confiscated by the soldiers who stopped me."

Daniel made a note on his pad. "Did you happen to sneak out any of those art works, to Switzerland, for example? Or give the Nazis any of those secret addresses?"

"No, absolutely not. And I wouldn't."

"Do you happen to remember the soldiers' names or even the uniforms of those who initially stopped you on the road to Debrecen?"

Raoul shook his head. "Standard Red Army uniforms, from what I recall. One was an officer, a colonel I think. My driver, Vilmos, may remember more details."

Daniel put down his pencil and drank water.

"Naturally I will check on the whereabouts of this little book. And I imagine that there were more than a few wealthy bourgeois Jews who wanted to protect their art works from the Nazis—or the Russians!" He smiled at his irony. "Raoul, let me speak to you now as a . . . *friendly* interrogator; there are those who are worse than me, far worse. Do you understand?"

Raoul shook his head. "I'm afraid I don't."

"There are other interrogators who are less lenient, less delicate, less patient, than myself; and *their methods will not be with words alone.*"

Raoul stared.

"That is what I am trying to make clear to you, Mr. Wallenberg. We seem to be *on the same cultural plane, share a common understanding,* though we come from very different backgrounds. But some of these others who may question you, they may not be . . . And things could get difficult, even painful."

"You wouldn't dare; you are simply trying to intimidate me."

Daniel shook his head. "I am afraid I am telling you the truth."

Raoul stood up, walked to the wall, smoked, returned. "Am I through now?"

"No, I wanted to share one other thing with you. Your drawings, those architectural drawings you have made, I admire them very much, especially the one for the new quay—very impressive!"

Raoul looked anew at his inquisitor. "When did you—I didn't know you had taken those drawings from my cell."

"Oh, I didn't, not at all. I simply looked through them. You see, I too am an architect," he confessed modestly. "That's what I was trained for. Another coincidence."

Raoul shook his head, dumbfounded.

"Yes, it is true. Here in Moscow. When all this business is over, I shall return to my profession, my passion. Therefore, my compliments are not those of an amateur. I speak to you as one professional to another. They are very fine drawings, perspectives, both in scale and in vision."

Daniel put out his hand in congratulation, and Raoul fixed him, staring.

"I assume you will be wanting to go back to Stockholm to hand them in and see them realized, so please, do cooperate with us."

Daniel called out in Russian. The two guards appeared and escorted the bewildered Wallenberg out. The interrogator sat back down and wrote copious notes in his long white pad.

Gellerman sat back, rolled his head, and read through his pages, noting here and there a mistaken phrase, a nuance missed. Were the sensibilities and cultural affinities between the two men too close to be believed? Was the KGB that precise? Thank god for actuality, for his real interview with the old man, so Manny could have imagined it the way he did. And what about the threat made to Raoul? Real or strategic? Why not both? The torturer's track was a separate track from the interrogator's track, Petrov had advised, so it could very well be that Daniel was trying to "protect" his charge. But was all this to be "allowed" in, if he were to do a semi-documentary fiction? His colleagues in the profession would smile in disdain, mock his attempt at "inventiveness," and write it off as amateurism. And maybe they were right. Sure they were. But how else to get at what possibly happened, without sources, documents, witnesses? . . . So he'd play the fool, the history clown, the adventurer in the speculation trade, and see what he came up with. After all, he already came up with something real and important . . . (He would call Natasha and check on Gyorgi and the father's availability for another meeting.)

Just now, he'd have to return to playing the fool with the madwoman of Budapest . . . Pulling the chain on the small desk lamp, Manny was reminded of the old New York Public Library reading room, where he periodically read, in college, and the other two libraries he had been nourished by: the Brooklyn Public as a youth, and later on, as a grad student, the womb-like British Museum Reading Room. Libraries were as cherished as playing fields, and even this small one in downtown Budapest served as an honorable field for work, memory, invention.

CHAPTER 7

He called the lady Zsuzsa, and said he was back in town for a few days, and she replied with cordiality and warmth. Yes, she wanted very much to continue their discussion, and arranged a date for the late afternoon.

Manny then called Moscow, and Natasha immediately reported, "I have some bad news, Professor Gellerman. I spoke to the son Gyorgi last night, and his father had a bad fall at his birthday party on the weekend and is in a coma. At eighty-eight, who knows if Daniel will recover?"

"My god!" Manny exclaimed, and added, only half kidding, "I hope it wasn't the interview that 'induced' the fall and the coma."

"Oh, I doubt that, Professor. You saw how frail he was at the interview. I will check back with him in a day or two, and see if there is any news."

Manny thanked her and hung up. How awful, he thought.

He went outside, found a kiosk with an *International Tribune*, and went to the Central Café, a few blocks away, where he ordered a coffee and tried to relax reading about the home sports and dismal Baghdad news. Through the years, playing tennis or watching good football or baseball had relaxed him. America concealed its true business—power, money, wars—by means of such diversions as playoffs, clever articles, flicks. Here in the *Trib* there was a huge piece on three new Hollywood movies, featuring the sons and daughters of famous movie stars. These were not the kids of Hepburn, Cagney, Bogart. Not only did the country produce mountains of moronic movies—for budgets that equaled the GNP of many small countries—but it produced endless waves of movie talk that floated all through the nation, via every newspaper, journal, college classroom, and blogger, plus NPR of course, swamping the brain power of the citizenry in a tsunami of endless celebrity, chat, and public gossip. The average citizen knew far more about Tom Cruise than Mark Twain, cared far more about Hanks or Nicholson than Melville or Bellow. The nation had become Certified Dumbed Down.

An older well-dressed group of four sat nearby. While observing the varied crowd, he awaited his new friend, whom he dubbed his "Madwoman of Budapest" (after the Giraudoux play).

But instead there appeared a young woman, maybe in her late twenties, who smiled modestly and asked, "Are you the American Professor?"

He nodded in bewilderment.

"My mother asked me to come and meet you, as she had a sudden appointment to reach. May I sit?"

"Please," and he stood up to hold her chair, ridiculously. She was trim, smallish, curly-haired, and darkly beautiful. As she sat opposite him, he took notice of her vivid brown eyes and sensuous lips, as well as the cheekbones of the mother.

The waiter came by; she ordered jasmine tea and sat quietly, looking a bit afraid.

Gellerman, who himself didn't quite know what to say, offered, "And what do you do, if I may ask?"

"I am a graduate student, going for a PhD in psychology."

"Oh. What area?"

"I work with children, handicapped children."

"I see." A porcelain pot and cup arrived on a silver tray. "Where?"

"Well, I work with the children here, but started my thesis at Debrecen. But now, I have moved to Eötvös Loránd University, where the new referee of my thesis teaches."

Was everyone writing a thesis? he wondered, observing her small earrings, her full lips, her shy demeanor. Or mentoring one?

"Well," he began, not knowing how to approach the subject, "Your mother seems to think, or truly believes, that she is the daughter of Raoul Wallenberg. I assume you know this?"

"But of course," she said, sipping. Her eyes stayed down.

"Do you believe this?"

She gazed up at him, cheeks reddening slightly. "What do you mean? This is what I was brought up on—why should I think otherwise?"

"That would make you the granddaughter. His."

"I suppose so, yes."

"And you know who he was?"

"Of course. I have learned."

The waiter approached. Manny asked, "A cake or sandwich?"

She shook her head. She wore a white blouse, and around her neck, a gold pendant, actually a locket.

He took a chance and put out a question like putting out a risky pawn. "Do you think that perhaps she could be wrong—your mother, I mean? That maybe she has *imagined* this relationship?"

To Manny's surprise, the daughter took this proposition calmly. "Perhaps. But I don't bother about it too much, you may say."

"You mean . . . what?"

"I live my life, and my mother lives hers. She is a bit strange, but wonderful. I respect her, and her memories, and her directions, or wishes."

Manny finished his coffee, digesting her sentences, with their ambiguities.

He nodded, pretending to understand, and not wanting to push his luck now.

"And you live here, in town?"

"Yes, I do."

"I like your city."

She shrugged. "I prefer the countryside."

In all of this she had hardly faced him, glancing at his eyes only now and then.

Finally, she looked up, above her teacup, and asked, "Would you tell me what you want with my mother?"

What a perfect retort to his questioning! Was that the real reason for her coming? "Well, that is a fair question. I am not really sure, actually. A student at my university is writing a graduate thesis on Wallenberg, and has interviewed your mother, and I am here to verify what my student has written, and to learn more about the interesting man." He paused. "Forgive me, I haven't asked your name?"

"Dora."

He put out his hand awkwardly. "I am Emmanuel, or Manny, Gellerman."

She shook his limply. "So have you confirmed this knowledge already?"

"Well, sort of, yes."

"Then why do you stay on?"

He wanted to ask her what was inside the locket. "I am not staying on; I am leaving in two days."

"And you are writing your own book on the subject of Mr. Wallenberg?"

Another question in perfect pitch, this one maybe a curve. "I don't think so, but actually I don't quite know. I am learning about the subject, you might say, as I go on. And the more I get into it, the more I am intrigued. He was a great puzzle, this Wallenberg. And what happened to him was also puzzling."

The waiter appeared, asked if there was anything else desired, and they declined.

"So you believe that my mother is one part of this puzzle for you?"

He didn't really know the motive for this line of questioning, and he proffered delicately, "Do you think I am, in some way, invading her privacy? Or using her for my purposes?"

Her face looked troubled, maybe confused. "My mother is . . . I am interested in protecting her, yes. She has, as I said, her own way of looking at things. She has had a hard life. And is very . . . vulnerable, you say? But I don't think you are here to injure her, if that is what you are asking."

The waiter brought the check; Manny was grateful, and took out Hungarian forints to pay.

"I assure you I am not here to take advantage of her, at all." He leaned over and added, "Maybe I am here for her to take advantage of me?" And that prompted a smile, a sudden wide smile, in the young woman's small beautiful face.

The dinner was the next night, his last in Budapest, at Zsuzsanna's apartment, and he was pleased to hear that Dora would be there too, not just the two of them. Manny had become increasingly baffled by what he was doing there, and by his relationship to the odd woman, and her daughter. He had come to his resolute conclusions, and this last evening was for courtesy and politeness, he advised himself. He sat awkwardly in the sitting room, looking aimlessly at the old furniture and mahogany piano and old photos on the walls, while dinner was being prepared. He heard some conversation, and knew that the daughter had come in. He sipped from a glass of wine in his stuffed chair. His eye wandered to a small Menorah set on a mantelpiece, and he got up and went to inspect it. It was small, old—made from iron? Probably a family heirloom. He was about to leave the area, when he noticed a small black and white photo showing the same candelabra, set on a Passover table, with a family portrait of a youngish mother, her small child, and a darkly complected man. They were dressed formally, standing by a shining challah and a decanter of wine, set on the white lace holiday table. He lifted the small, framed photograph, and began to realize, almost painfully, that the man seemed to be Wallenberg! (Or a close facsimile?) Manny's chest thumped as he had a strong urge to steal the picture—just as he had wanted to take the KGB photo of Daniel P. from the Moscow bookcase—but just then heard the ladies coming and set the framed photo back in its resting place. He walked back toward his chair, his head spinning, and wondering what was going on here.

At the dinner, over a savory paprika chicken and superb red cabbage, Gellerman quietly asked about the menorah, and Zsuzsanna explained how it had been in the family from the early forties, obtained from a small synagogue in Pecs, and how much her mother and father cherished it. Gellerman listened, and at dessert stood up, went to the mantelpiece, and brought back the framed photograph. Was this the same menorah? When Zsuzsa replied yes, Manny said, "And is that your family—you the baby, your mother, and Mr. Wallenberg?" She responded, "Why, yes, of course. It's one of my old photos from the family scrapbook." Taking the news in stride, Gellerman accepted a slice of home-made strudel and offered, "Oh, a whole album of pictures? I would like to see that one day." To which the lady replied, "Yes, one day I will be pleased to show them to you. May I pour you some tea?"

Throughout the dessert and aftermath, Manny was careful not to seem too zealous, but was eager enough to find out any more details or facts about her family that Mrs. W. was willing to disclose. While she answered everything politely, she volunteered little; meanwhile, the daughter Dora sat quietly, attending to her mom's needs—helping to clear and move the dessert trolley to the kitchen—but also, privately, it seemed to him, observing Gellerman, to make sure he was acting with the requisite amount of respect for her vulnerable mother. It certainly was an odd arrangement, he thought, a configuration layered with mystery and intrigue—and maybe deceit?

As he sat in the sitting room afterward, with Dvorak's cello concerto playing, Dora sat knitting, and Mrs. W., speaking slowly, answered his questions, often wandering, sometimes asking her daughter for the right word. Gradually he became immersed in the heavy-lidded room, the thick drapes, the 1930s stuffed furniture, the black and white photographs, the huge mysterious armoire or wardrobe. Manny felt himself encased in some sort of time warp, not here in 2006, but back, back in time, maybe fifty, sixty years, in old Budapest. Was this a weird tale by E. T. A. Hoffmann or a drama by Schnitzler?

Mrs W. smiled so broadly, so warmly, to many of his queries, treating him as though he were a young innocent nephew asking his wise old aunt family questions whose answers were patently obvious. Did she grow up Jewish? Of course. Religious Jewish? We observed the religious holidays, yes. We observed many of the simple traditions, such as Friday night shabbat, yes. What about Mr. Wallenberg's wartime efforts and obligations, and the family? Oh, we were sent to the countryside, of course, to the north, and he visited periodically. It was very difficult. Was he a good father? She was too small to really remember. And when he was detained by the Russians and imprisoned, did her mother know about it? Yes, actually, yes. How so? Oh, there were ways, with bribes, that you could find out most things. Any direct communication? There were a few letters, yes. Do you still have those? Yes. Dare he ask if he might see them?

She smiled. "Why not? Later on. When I know you better, *trust you more, see that you are serious about us,* not merely a journalist intruder. So there is hope for me? he half joked. "Yes, why not?" And on and on played János Starker and next Chopin, while the mother sat in her chair wearing that half smile and looking to be in perfect rapture, and the young daughter said nothing in a corner chair, but knitted and eyed everything. At one point, he asked how Raoul first met her mother, and she explained how he rescued her grandparents and her mother from the orphanage, and then began to know her more intimately. Aloud he speculated, "Was that how he got his inspiration to make it his mission to save the Jews?" and she reacted with such a modest smile, such an embarrassed sideways nod of her head, that he couldn't push the speculation any further.

After an hour and a half of this melancholic atmosphere, played out in this scene of cat and mouse fragility and moral uncertainty, Gellerman wanted out and didn't want out, wanted to lift himself away from the spell, and also felt that the spell had its real and specific attractions. Could he open that huge wardrobe and enter a door into another world, like that Narnia beloved by his son as a boy? Or was he already inside that world of pure fantasy? Yes, of course, and he needed to escape back to the real.

"Thank you so much for your hospitality tonight, and for the past meetings, and I shall stay in good touch with you," he said, standing at the door with both ladies.

"I hope you got what you came for, Professor," she offered, slightly embarrassed at taking any credit, "but you are always welcome back, to learn more."

He nodded, didn't know if he was supposed to kiss her hand or cheeks, performed the latter, and, looking over at Dora, standing just behind her mother, reached over and took her hands in both of his, thanking her too. She stared back at him with those small brown eyes, and he wasn't sure if he was being inspected, or invited . . .

Departing down the three flights of concrete steps, in the dim light, he felt unsteady, and gripped the banister tightly, since a fall could be disastrous. This old 1920s Budapest apartment house was darker, more dilapidated, than his old Brooklyn one, and was clearly more dangerous with its secrets.

Before leaving town, Gellerman had made contact with two historians, and finally found one in: Professor László Borhi. In Borhi's fourth-floor apartment in Buda, Gellerman sat over a cup of coffee and put to the fiftyish gentleman questions, speculations. A trim fellow whose Jewish father had been persecuted, and later a well-known reformer and historian in Hungary after the war,

Borhi was responsive and alert, speaking fine English, and showing considerable knowledge of Wallenberg and what had occurred. After explaining about the Arrow Cross and their vicious campaign—including killing three thousand Jews alongside the Danube in winter and tossing them into the river, where some bodies were recovered in the spring floating down river—Borhi gave his opinion that, yes, RW had been a genuine hero, and had been helped by various organizations, including the Americans, but that he doubted very much that he was a double spy.

Leaning over the low coffee table, Manny said, "Tell me, personally, do you think—as I do—that Raoul was probably gay? Or do you think I am over the top?" (No need to mention here the other bizarre story, a few miles away.) "You see, I know of no document, not any letters or notes, indicating any girlfriend in his life; and when he writes his grandfather from places like Haifa or Capetown, or especially Michigan, where he was for three years, it's always about his buddies, never girls. Even when he takes trips to Mexico or Chicago, he never mentions a young woman."

Surprisingly, Borhi nodded. "I think I agree. All the evidence I have seen would suggest you are right."

Relieved, Manny added, "Which would make him even more of an outlaw or outcast in the Wallenberg family's eyes. I mean Marcus and Jacob."

Borhi nodded again, picked up a small piece of paper and pen, and jotted something down. "You should call Mária Ember. She is an older journalist, a serious one, who has followed Wallenberg and his case for years, and she may offer you some valuable information. But do it soon, as she is ill, and I think it is cancer."

Manny took the paper, chatted for another hour, learned more about the opposition to Raoul from some of the other delegations, especially the Swiss, and departed. As soon as he got back to his hotel, he called the number of this journalist, found her in and most receptive to a meeting. He asked if it could be tomorrow, as he was leaving soon.

"Yes, do come over," she said, after consulting her husband, "but please call me in the early afternoon to hear about my energy. Sometimes I have it, sometimes not. I am receiving strong medicines."

Manny thanked her, and the next day, after checking with her, he took a taxi back to Buda, to a different side of town, and was greeted by the husband upstairs at her front door. He brought Manny into the living room, where a short plump woman in her sixties stood up, greeted him warmly, invited him to sit down. Maria was pale but welcoming; her hair was clearly dyed red, and she seemed of a piece with the formal Victorian decoration. The husband excused himself to get drinks. Mária Ember coughed a bit and explained, with a thick accent, how happy she was to hear of his interest in RW, and praised Borhi, "a moral historian, not just a fact-recorder." Gellerman smiled, took note of the distinction, and asked about her interest in RW. By way of answer, she handed him two paperbacks, one a museum catalogue, and the other a small booklet on RW, authored by herself; the latter was in Hungarian, the former, a mix of English and Hungarian. "I organized the first and only museum show about Wallenberg, in the 1960s, and this is the catalogue revealing everything in it. Please, you can keep this one." He thanked her and continued to glance through the two books, filled with pictures of the man and the various artifacts of his life.

The husband brought in a tea cart, with coffee, tea, and cakes as well, and poured a cup of tea each for Maria and Manny.

He asked her some questions about Budapest in 1944, and she suggested an important book on the subject, *The Siege of Budapest,* by Ungváry, which she believed was in translation, and continued for another half hour on elements of his arrest and Soviet deportation. Manny, sensing he had only a limited amount of time with the brave lady, then put out his gambit: "My strong feeling or opinion is that he was gay, a closet sort of gay probably, if you understand what I mean. This is based on the evidence I have seen. Do you think I am mistaken?"

She smiled wryly, coughed, excused herself as she brought a handkerchief to her mouth, before she was finally was able to speak. "Yes, I do think you are mistaken. He was not a 'closet gay,' as you put it, but an active gay!" She looked at him for a reaction. "I spoke with several German officers from the war, who had seen him in the several known gay bars of Budapest of the time, openly with men. Also, there were Hungarian witnesses who knew about this and kept it quiet, of course. I even have some written letters. So it is not a mystery, or even a well-kept secret, but rather, *a closed open secret.*"

Manny almost fell back, as though he had taken a punch. "But why, why has this never been mentioned or cited?"

As she leaned over to put down her cup, she revealed a Hebrew *chai* around her neck. "Why do you think? It was his private life, and what he did with that private life was his business, especially since his public life was so important, so necessary. It was not a big deal, in the light of the whole context."

Gellerman scratched his head, returned to drinking tea, and took a slice of cake. He asked, "Have you spoken to anyone else about this?"

"Only Borhi, whom I trust, as I informed you."

"No Americans or Western historians?"

"Who comes to see an old lady?" She smiled, even beamed, at her self-description. "Or wants to see an insignificant journalist."

Manny wanted to ask to see those letters, but Maria began coughing; the husband came to her aid, and nodded to Manny in a signal to depart. Manny stood up, waited several minutes until the coughing spell diminished, then took Maria's hand. "Please, no need to get up. Thank you so much. I will be in touch. Here is my card with e-mail. Do you use e-mailing?"

She shook her head. "But you have my telephone and can call me always. Also, you may write my husband, who checks his e-mail at the university."

As Manny turned to leave, he realized he might never see her again. "I think Mr. Wallenberg would have appreciated knowing you, for many reasons."

She smiled, clearly exhausted. "The feeling is common, you say?"

He nodded, understanding her intended meaning, and left. Rather than take a taxi back, he decided on a tram; and as it zigzagged and rattled through the streets, it felt like his old Ralph Avenue trolley ride in Brownsville. His head was buzzing, and he tried to connect up the many thoughts racing through his brain. This new information was stunning, and upsetting to his view of the man. (If only he could see actual evidence!) But Borhi had vouched for this Maria; Manny had met and found her totally credible and sincere, and he held in his hands her two booklets. As the tram rocked, he tried to absorb his recent findings. While passing over the Danube on the Margaret Bridge—no Jews floating now—Manny contemplated the sharp careening passage from Budapest family fantasy to sudden real history. It was dizzying. This new piece of the puzzle—did it change the overall picture, or just add some invaluable if oddly-shaped pieces? . . . *Maybe Raoul needed Manny the historian more than either of them had suspected?*

CHAPTER 8

Walking through his country house in New Hampshire, he felt comforted to be back amidst his orderly disorder: mounds of papers and books, clothes strewn everywhere, notes upon notes of things to take care of, people to call. Surrounded by the photos of old friends and the boys when they were little. This fond past had provided nutrition for his rather thin present. Outside, the green meadows of June were already high, and he spotted the monarch butterflies back again, flitting among the clumps of milkweeds. Three radios were going in his daily rooms, one classical, one country, one NPR talk. He had made arrangements for his son to come over later and mow the lawns on the riding tractor, a task the boy adored and did rather well, if somewhat dangerously. In the two weeks since he had been home he had gradually caught up with the piled-up e-mails, attending first to the more urgent ones from the students, his son in New York, his ex-wife, his CPA. And just yesterday a note arrived from Angela, telling him that her final draft was done. Should they meet so she could deposit it with him?

In the stacks of mail from the post office, he found the long one-hundred-page essay from Vladimir, the Russian exile in New York, asking him to read it through carefully and help find a place for it perhaps, if Harvard didn't want it.

Several e-mails arrived from Budapest, one from the intriguing lady herself, which said how much she had enjoyed their meetings, and when did he plan on returning, "to continue their discussions?" Another came from the historian Borhi, reporting that Mária Ember had been taken to the hospital, very ill, and had he had a chance to meet with her? (Manny scolded himself for not informing the good fellow!) Also, he cited a conference coming up on RW in the fall; did Manny want to submit a paper? And a third, from daughter Dora who wondered if it was really "in Mother's best interests, your visiting again?" So, demure Dora was quietly shrewd and protective. Maybe she was right?

Where was Gellerman in all this? he asked himself, sitting at his desk and gazing out at the nearby mountains, the foothills of the Whites. He felt in the middle of things, between the long ordeal of Raoul and the gray pall of the past, and this America the Easy; where kids tossed their Frisbees and were wired to iPods, where a student's education often signified a brand name ticket to his future, and sports stadiums had come to replace churches for millions, with sports stars and movie celebrities their true ministers. Where was moral insight or understanding to be found—in CNN or PBS or NPR wisdom, corporate bottom lines? The society as a whole had been so deluged by Internet culture and cable journalism that real thought was hard to discover, limited to a few journals and a few thousand souls. On top of all that mass thinning down, so much of current "thought"—especially in the universities—had been traduced, mutilated by political correctness, in all areas. In this mess, Manny felt somewhere in the middle, in a peculiar cultural exile. Journals that used to mean a lot to him, such as the *New Republic* or even *The Nation*, he now barely looked at.

In the *Times* he glanced through articles on the brutal Iraq war, a new damning report on the environmental oil disaster, more European fury at Israel—all surrounded by the big ads for wristwatches, leather goods, jewelry. No, this was not tabloid reality, but, rather, advertising chic, with an emphasis on stylishness for its readers. Or consider the latest journalist star, whose op-ed columns were bejeweled with "witty" references from pop culture, TV sitcoms, and whose moral judgments were straight out of Sunday school. Was the *Times* serious? Style ruled the day here; thus you had the intermingling of the important with the cute, the important flattened out by the glamorous. The New Decadence was displayed everywhere. When had all this happened? In the nineties? Turn of the century?

But now, here, Manny wondered, why serve the long lost cause of trying to find out the truth about the elusive Swede? And what would Manny do with it, once figured out? Was he on a journey of self-discovery as well as a historical pursuit? Would he be contributing any serious revision of history? Or was its chief impact to be felt by the present Wallenberg dynasty in Stockholm, and maybe the state memory, part of contemporary history? As for the personal journey, did Manny really need Raoul for that? Was there an unknown connection? At this, something in him stirred, an odd emotional wave, but what was it? . . .

The next day he sat on a bench on the large college green, looking out at the white-steepled Baker Library, waiting to meet with Angela. The air was soft, and the green was filled with students reading in the grass, hooked up to their iPods, tossing balls, and sunning with friends. Here and there a mother with a toddler passed by, letting the child run free. Cars moved slowly, pausing to stop for any pedestrian who showed any sign of crossing the street.

"Here you are," Angela announced, smiling brightly, "and here it is, sir, my final words of wisdom about the man." She sat down alongside, opened her canvas briefcase, and took out her thesis. "One hundred-forty-two pages. I hope it works for you!"

Charmed by her turn of phrase, "working" for him, he nodded and thanked her. "I look forward to reading it, of course."

"And how was your trip to Budapest? Did you meet with Mrs. W.?"

"Yes, I did."

"What did you think? Was she real?" she gushed. "I mean, did you buy her story, as I did?"

Taking note of her new headband, shorts, and running shoes, he asked, "Are you jogging today?"

"Oh, this?" she smiled animatedly, "Yeah, I'm training for the marathon. First, a local charity one, and then down in Boston. Do you run?"

He shook his head. "I do all I can to walk, regularly."

She nodded. "It's a blast; you should try it, really."

"Well, I may be a bit too old for a marathon."

She hit his arm. "Don't pretend you're too old! You look in shape; you can still do it, with some training. C'mon, get into a program. I can start you up, and before you know it, you'll really be with it."

He was impressed with Angela's enthusiasm for him, and smiled at the kindly young woman. He'd remember to tuck in his belly when he stood up.

"So, sir, what did you think? I know she's a bit weird, but . . ."

"Yes, I think your catch-all word is a good one here. To tell you the truth, I don't quite know what to think. How to take her. And you?"

She angled her head, shrugged. "If it's a fantasy, it's a great one. But her tale may be too strange to be fictitious."

"You put the matter well. On the other hand," he smiled, reflecting on the matter, "*her fiction may be her life.*"

Angela paused, and she said, "Well, I never thought of it that way, sir."

He stood up, said he'd read the thesis with interest, and they hugged.

"My dad is taking me out for graduation, to Simon Pearce, and he asked if you wanted to join us."

"A nice invitation, thanks. Let's see where I am, both in geography and in the thesis. But the food is good there, I understand. I've only visited the glass-blowing shop."

"Oh, Dad says it's the best around, and worth the pricy-ness. And he'd love to chat with you about your views on RW. Being half-Swedish himself, and from that generation."

"It's a bit warm for running, so take care."

"Oh, I'm prepared, thanks!" She displayed her hip bottles of water.

Left alone, Manny went for his regular walk, striding first across the green and then over to Occom Pond and around to the golf course, and back again. The area was surrounded by trees, pond, lawns, fine homes. He began feeling firmer, walking quickly, checking his wristwatch to make it real exercise. When he read the thesis, he'd pay attention to the documentation, and the writing, since the content would be familiar and predictable; but maybe she'd have picked up a clue or two of some use. Young energy could do that. And maybe the father would supply a fact of interest. . . . Should he indeed get into his own long-distance training, as Angela had suggested? But wasn't he already in some sort of training, though he wasn't sure what its nature was, just yet? . . . A wired-up jogger ran past, oblivious, and a group of youngsters emerged from the golf course with clubs and bags. Maybe heading to the river now? College had been different for Manny, back in Brooklyn. Classes, library, study, and then work. Hard to figure this world of sports leisure at the college, even here. Yet, just last year the college had hired a new football coach (ex-quarterback), who declared that the old stadium needed a facelift to attract new recruits and crowds; so ten million was raised to remove one half of the stands, build a new field house, and lay down new turf. How did this happen so swiftly, so easily? Especially when the college was proclaiming huge cutbacks in humanities departments, secretaries and janitors were laid off, and adjuncts dropped. And Dartmouth was Ivy League, not a juco or state U. football factory.

On his return route, Manny recalled, out of the blue, the great Holocaust historian up in Vermont, who, curiously enough, had almost the same first name as RW. Amidst the tall maples, he made a mental note to contact the fellow.

He finished up the hearty walk, feeling heady in the wonderful sunshine, and met his son on the green. They drove over to The Jewel of India for their ritual dinner. Over their standard fare—curried lamb and tikka masala chicken, vegetable pakora and garlic nan—Manny listened to the brown-eyed boy describe, with bubbly excitement, his desire to try out for a Young Artist Orchestra in Tanglewood, where he might play for six weeks. "And, Dad, we would get to go *free to all* of the BSO performances. Can you believe it?!" I reminded him he was still a bit young for that. No matter. His fervent emotion was matched by his anticipation of the music to be played—Sibelius, Mozart,

Beethoven—and the fact that he would get to see his regular teacher, the third cellist in the BSO, throughout the summer. As the boy wolfed the lavish dishes with familiar gusto and spoke about Mozart's deceptive surface simplicity and underlying intricacy, Manny attended with interest and amazement—how had the boy turned out this way? How had this meteorite of talent and energy descended upon him? (From trying to match his older brother?) Manny wrote down the dates of the three orchestral performances and promised to go to every one. "But you have to be there on time, remember!" the son warned, knowing the father's terrible habit of tardiness.

Four days later, on a cloudy Tuesday morning, Manny was knocking on the door of a small white cape in a town twenty minutes north of Burlington, sent there by Raul Hilberg, the historian, who said, "If you want to know what Wallenberg meant, go visit Sándor, a survivor." An elderly man, in his late seventies with a curling mustache, opened the door, and after hearing Hilberg's name, Sándor Torok welcomed Manny in. After lemonade, served by the wife, and some introductory chat, Manny asked what he remembered about the great Swede.

Torok shrugged his shoulders, gave a small smile, and spoke slowly, with a heavy accent. "*Remember him*? Well, he saved my life, so, yes, I do remember him. I was nearly fifteen, had lost my parents and my sister, and was hiding out wherever I could, when one evening he ran into me in an apartment building in Pest. I had made myself a little nest under the stairwell, and somehow we met, as he used that apartment building sometimes to sleep in, and when he understood that I was a Jewish boy, he asked me, in German, about myself. Soon, he asked if I wanted to work for him, and when I said, yes, of course, he brought me upstairs, created a safe pass for me, and"—he got up now and went to a bureau, brought back a small wooden box—"and he handed me a small crucifix and told me to wear it around my neck, not to take it off, until the war was over." He opened the box and lifted out a silver crucifix along with the safe pass. "My souvenirs from the war. And from Mr. Wallenberg." I handled the simple cross, and looked at the teenager in the photo. (Not too different from Manny's Joshua at that age.) He sat back down and went on. "I worked for him, sometimes for the legation, sometimes for the agency, doing errands of all sorts, mostly as a messenger boy on a bicycle. And whenever I was stopped, I made sure my crucifix showed, first thing. For the Arrow Cross, this was an important sign." He shrugged, meaning it wasn't much. "So, what else would you like to know, sir?"

Manny noted two small black and white photos of Budapest bridges in frames on the mantelpiece. "Did you know anything about him personally? For example, did you know his driver, Langfelder?"

"Oh, yes, I saw him quite often. A big fellow, witty, and very decent. Always brought me a licorice twist or a chocolate."

"Ever see him with any of his women friends?"

Drinking his lemonade, Sándor shook his head. "Except for his female secretaries, like Countess Nako or Hedda Kattai, I don't recall any . . . But, remember, I didn't socialize with him in the evenings, and mostly saw him if he came to sleep in our apartment building; you know he changed places to sleep every night or two, as a precaution."

Manny got up and went to the mantelpiece and held up the bridge photos, old postcards, trying to find a new avenue of interest, or a new path of chance.

"If you are asking did he 'womanize,' no, I don't think so." He smiled kindly. "For example, I do remember that once I had to deliver a message to him at night in a nightclub, of all places, and even there he was not womanizing. There were only men at his table, in fact. So you see," he shook his head, "you are going up the wrong tree."

Manny nodded, and looked at the old man with the grand mustache and full memories.

"No one could really imagine what it meant to be with him in those days. He was like a god, or a *moshiach*, if you know what that is, a real *moshiach*."

"Yes, I do know," Manny said, more interested in what the old man, a graying walrus, had given me inadvertently. I nodded and said, yes, I understood, and we chatted for another twenty minutes or so. Then he walked me out to the car, in the driveway of his cape.

"Looks like a nice little neighborhood," Manny remarked, seeing the row of well-kept houses and suburban lawns.

"Oh, yes," he smiled broadly, "Nice and dull, just the way I like things nowadays."

"So your past life is unknown to all your neighbors?"

"Of course!" he said, rather proudly. "Why bother them, or burden them, with my unpleasant past?" He hit me in the shoulder. "Why bother myself?"

Manny asked him to call or write if he remembered anything else of interest, and he said he would, most definitely.

Manny added, "There's a woman in Budapest who claims her mother was Wallenberg's lover or mistress, maybe even wife, and she was the product of that union. What do you think? Can this be true?"

He tugged at his mustache. "Could be. But please remember, people idolized him then; his name was whispered on all Jewish lips; he was the *moshiach*, a real savior, as I said. Probably now he has become a sort of celebrity, you may say, and people may develop fantasies about him, I don't know. But you know what? I've learned one thing in my life: *anything is possible.*" He looked around, held out his hands wide, "Look, Sándor Torok—a boy hiding in Budapest, now a man alive and well in Vermont!" His smile was large, and somewhat mirthful. "So, to me, anything is possible, my friend."

Driving back south through the wonderful green hills on empty Highway 89, Manny retraced the interview and recalled Hilberg's words: "Yes, see this Torok; he's trustworthy."

Back home in his study, Manny felt stirred, his imagination revved up:

The scene was an evening at the Arizona Mulatto, a cabaret nightclub on Nagymezo utca in 1944 during the siege of Budapest, where German SS and Wehrmacht officers mingled with British spies, counterintelligence agents, Hungarian VKF2 (military intelligence). The place was packed, tables full, clients two deep at the bar. At a corner table four men sat, one in military uniform, and Wallenberg, in jacket and tie. A band was playing, waiters were scurrying back and forth, and the smoke from cigarettes and cigars was billowing upward to the high ceiling. The noise was deafening, but it did little to quiet the rumors, spreading all over the restaurant, of the Russians landing, or the Allies bombing, or the SS coming. A burlesque show was onstage.

"Perhaps this is what Dante meant by hell," mused a young man, in German.

"But which circle, do you think?" inquired a second.

The young man, in German uniform, looked at him. "Ninth?"

"My god, no," Raoul retorted, "closer to the third or fourth, no more."

A hearty laugh.

"So tell me, what will happen when the Russians come in?"

"Oh, I don't think anything unusual—for them," the fourth man, Gábor, said. "Rapes, pillage, theft, lawlessness. The usual delicacies offered by the Red Army—each man for himself, whatever he can take, grab, or steal."

"And if the Americans should come first?"

"Oh, they won't, don't worry. Their bombs, yes, but not their tanks or soldiers."

"And it's better that way, for my side," put in Raoul. "Trials and lawful procedures are not for the Soviets. Which means, if I were a German officer, I would worry seriously." He smiled amiably.

A waiter came by, bringing more drinks.

"So what is new with your highbrow reading?" asked the military officer, Klaus. "Is it still Musil, or another degenerate?"

"Arthur Schnitzler, his novellas."

The German smiled. "Schnitzler? I understand he is rich—richly perverse!"

Everyone smiled. "Actually, he is rather interesting," observed Raoul. "Especially if you know the old Vienna."

"Do you?"

"Not really. But I have a good imagination!"

Lean Gábor gripped Raoul's forearm playfully, "For the perverse, do you mean?"

"For old Vienna," Raoul responded, to the jocularity of his group.

The waiter brought over a new round of beers.

"Everything is watered down, though they charge you the same," noted Klaus.

"No, no, they charge you more, now, for the delivery service under stress!"

Wallenberg leaned in, "Tell me frankly, Klaus, did they hunt down and prosecute homosexuals in Germany as hard as they did Jews?"

"Why, Raoul, what do you think? Our Führer was an egalitarian when it came to his killing—once you made his favorite lists. Jews, homos, gypsies— they were all highly and *equally* deserving!"

"Excuse me, gentlemen," said Gábor, "it is time to drain out my beer," and he stood.

"Make sure you don't get detained unnecessarily in there," advised Klaus. "Those restrooms are gaining a reputation as high—or low—as the baths!"

As he departed, Miklós offered, "So tell me, are we to be forgiven for our sins because of this special time of chaos?"

"Oh, I thought we would be charged doubly for our current immorality, until I met a few priests the other evening, with their collars, and pants, off!"

Everyone laughed and toasted that quip, though Raoul barely smiled.

Gellerman got up, walked from his study, came back, read through his pages. Was he being too blunt, too coarse? Was he overreaching, moving beyond what his evidence had suggested? After all, *what and where was his hard evidence?* . . . Yes, he had surmised something of that gayness himself, and built on that supposition with the confirmation from the historian and the words of the trusted journalist Mária E. But still, nothing hard existed . . . He pondered his text, his imagined scenario. Supposing it were true, more or less, what he was inventing. Would Manny want to go on record with it? If he were writing a shadow thesis or drama like the one he was perhaps creating in this series of invented scenes, would he choose to go public with these radical findings, unsettling conclusions? Probably not. After all, which world did Raoul W. deserve? That vulgar, amoral, sensation-crazed media world that dominated the masses, or that hypocritical government and family world that had abandoned him in the first place? Which Raoul? The idealized Raoul who was pure and saintly, or the truer Raoul who was flawed and tainted? (Both existed.) The choice was hardly a choice; for Manny had grown steadily closer to Wallenberg, as he understood him more, climbed inside his skin. No, he would not really want to betray him to that larger world. But in doing that, would he not be betraying *the historian Gellerman?* And going against the request of the intrepid ghost?

The interpretation of Raoul through that franker lens gave him even more of an outsider status, Manny realized, which in turn fit in well with his abandonment in Soviet prison by the Wallenberg family; after all, he was more useful tucked away in Lybianka than alive and well in Sweden. Through his reading and research, Gellerman had learned a good deal about the family dynasty of that time. It wasn't a pretty story. The Enskilda Bank in Stockholm, a Wallenberg institution for centuries, had been the main banking institution in Scandanavia for the Nazis; there they were free to to use their various accounts, transfer monies, etc. Their European laundering machine. From the Wallenberg SKF mines in the north, the Nazis were able to purchase coal and iron ore, and from their factories, wheel bearings for their airplanes and tanks. In other words, the Nazis and the Wallenbergs were intertwined and mutually dependent, financially and practically. Without them and their resources, the Nazi war machine would have had a much more difficult time proceeding across Europe. Unfortunately for Raoul, he knew a good deal about that murky activity, which was borderline legal, brazenly unethical.

And later after the war, that wartime marriage of convenience, in "neutral" Sweden, created a practical problem for the Wallenbergs in the Allied countries. In America, they were put on the FBI list of about fifty banned companies that were off-limits to do business here. This occurred in 1945, just when Raoul was taken to Lybianka by the Soviets, and it was decided by cousins Marcus and Jacob that one of them had to go to the States and make a lobbying pitch, which would include a bribe, to get the Wallenbergs off of that list. It would not help much if Raoul—a loose canon, a man of morality and a family outlaw, as well as a figure of growing international reputation—were around and available to be called upon as a witness, to speak to the FBI, the media, American political leaders. On the outside, Raoul might be a dangerous figure for the Wallenberg dynasty. On the inside, in a Soviet prison, however, without voice or presence, armed only with a noble reputation for the family name, Raoul could be very helpful. So if he were to linger there, invisible, unheard, until his end, Marcus and Jacob would not mind too much, and could lament his misfortune.

And as for the Swedish government? There too the family could have played a strong influence. Yes, the government had its own business interests and military fears relating to the Soviets, and they were also feeling pressured by their own "neutral" stance amidst their angry Norwegian and Danish friends. Cowardice, pragmatism—and maybe guilt?—were built in to their 1945 diplomatic decision making. Plus they had an incompetent and stubborn foreign minister. Still and all, if they had they been pushed hard by the Wallenbergs— the Swedish Rockefellers in money, power, and prominence—the government would have been hard pressed not to seek an exchange for Raoul (as the Swiss, the Italians, and the Spanish had done). All the more so since the Swedes had discovered an important Russian mole high up in their military, whom the Soviets badly wanted back (and received, for the asking!). But the government did nothing, made no exchange, voiced no public outrage, made no fuss, and received no prodding from Marcus and Jacob, or from the King, who might have acted if he had gotten a signal from the Wallenbergs.

Thus, Raoul, a family member, a nation's diplomat, a distinguished gentleman, was sacrificed, left to rot in Lybianka. This was not a pretty chapter in Swedish history.

Nor would it be an easy dilemma for Gellerman, if the dilemma came to its point of no return, to have to choose between the intellectual historian (in himself) and the personal gatekeeper of Raoul. To choose between the obligations of his history profession and the personal ethics of biographical protection? How would this play out in himself? Manny wondered . . .

CHAPTER 9

When you entered the ballpark in the evening, at twilight, and walked up the grandstand ramp and first viewed the oval of grassy green, it was a return to the countryside and a return to childhood for Gellerman. The crowd was still settling in, the blue-gray sky was pink striped, and the ballplayers were just finishing up their infield practice, with fungo hits to the outfielders, infielders fielding ground balls, the sounds of balls hitting wood and smacking leather.

"Hey, these seats are pretty good," Manny complimented Norm, whose brother had given him the four company seats, and whose son was a pal of Josh's. "Maybe we should have brought our gloves just in case of a line drive foul."

"Do you really think we have a chance, Dad?" Josh asked, excited.

"Why not?" Manny answered.

The lower grandstand seats were behind third; the two boys were sitting next to each other, and the fathers, alongside. "Yeah, we might just get a ball here."

Fenway Park was much like the old Ebbets Field, a small bandstand of a park where the stands were very close to the field, and the fans had an intimacy with the players. (Always surprising, how young the players looked!) For Manny, it was a return to his boyhood in Brooklyn, 1947, where he had gone to many Dodgers games as a young boy, courtesy of his older friend, a kind of big brother, who had been wounded in the war and thus got in free to the games, wearing his uniform. And in 1947 he had gotten to see Jackie Robinson in his first season, when he played first base, and Manny and Burt, his big brother friend with the Purple Heart, sat behind first, mostly in empty boxes during the weekday games. It had been exciting for nine-year-old Manny to see Jackie play baseball, his style so daring, his skills so unusual—apart from his being the only ebony player in a sea of white faces.

"I actually prefer sitting behind third for foul balls," Norm said, "because there are more right-handed pitchers, and therefore you have many left-handed hitters in the lineup, who will foul balls over here. Only they can come hard."

"Yeah, I see what you mean; you have a point."

Manny enjoyed Norm, an emergency room doctor at the college hospital, because he knew his baseball, and was laid back, not one of the crazy driven Jews. And his son, Dan Y., was easygoing too, and a great friend of Josh's.

The Red Sox were playing arch-rival Yankees, and for Manny it was a return to the old Dodgers-Giant games or Dodgers-Yankee World Series games. Any kid who had rooted in those days, and gotten to see any of those games, had had a rare treat, a memory not to be forgotten. That was baseball played at the highest level, a game of native excellence and unusual subtleties.

"No matter how much big money, TV, and agents have ruined this game," Manny said, "when you see the players out on the field for the actual game, it's a dream."

"Yeah, it's still the best, no doubt."

The instant the boys spotted a vendor in white, they asked for hot dogs and soda, and Manny got them for the fathers too.

The heat from youth rose in his adult bones, and Gellerman felt strongly present in the here and now, a passionate moment, amidst the filling crowd and sparkling baseball diamond. And as the crowd stood and roared in unison as the home team took the field, Manny felt at home, nestled and easy, and oddly free. If he closed his eyes he could actually see Jackie and Pee Wee in their soft white and blues down around second, waiting for the final practice throw from the catcher. He wondered, What did all this have to do with his life now?

The pitcher threw the first pitch; you could hear the spinning ball thwack in the catcher's mitt, and Josh said, "Wow, Dad, he's fast!"

He was right too; this young gunner was fast, and when the batter actually made contact with the fourth pitch, it was indeed a foul, toward them over third! Over their heads, fortunately, as it landed with a quick thud!

Presently, Manny saw in his memory Jackie tormenting Ewell "The Whip" Blackwell, who was thirty feet down from third base, arms wide out, body ready to spring; he sensed the vivid presence of the ebony outsider, daring the pitcher to throw to third to try to keep him from stealing home. Not merely an outsider, but a black outlaw too. And Manny sensed Raoul in Budapest the same way—not merely an outsider but a daring outlaw as well, threatening the Arrow Cross, the Nazis, even the conventional Swedes, with his will, his gutsy mission, his intimate ways. Oh, Manny knew *how crazy* this comparison was, *how personal*, but he *felt* its truthfulness. There was something untamed in both, a passionate gene of individual will. Implacable will.

The batter cracked the ball, and Manny could tell immediately that it was a line drive. Everyone stood, hoping it was going out of the park, but the center fielder was in perfect position. The crowd sighed and sat.

Even the sound of their names, Robinson and Wallenberg, suggested some association, albeit a mysterious one. And Gellerman had come to know, or believe, that certain sounds, certain truths resided deep down in himself, and they had little to do with logic or external reality. They simply emerged from his central nervous system, crisscrossing out of the past, and waited for him to recognize and accept them. His truths. And here was one: this curious affinity between the gutsy Swedish diplomat and the daring American ballplayer; 1945 Budapest and 1947 Brooklyn. A most unlikely pairing of persons and towns.

The crowd grew suddenly, terribly hushed, as a Yankee hitter smacked a three-run homer over the Green Monster. A perfect gloom settled over the large crowd, which slowly turned into a kind of mourning as the Yankees began pounding the ball and running up the score . . . Just like the old days, when the old Yankees pounded the ball against all opponents . . . Many found himself staying back in youth, with Robinson and the Dodgers, and that 1947 Brooklyn of small shops and cozy neighborhoods and electric trolleys. Not very different from the current Budapest of zigzagging trams and small pastry shops and cracked sidewalks . . .

While Manny meandered in his thoughts, the lights came on, and the green diamond had a bright sheen to it. Norm was talking about the pitcher, and Manny nodded, trying to catch up. "He loses his fastball after a few innings, right?" Manny responded, "Yeah, I think so." How odd, that here at the ballpark at night, he should notice such unlikely symmetries; and that he should yield himself up to this one. Jackie and Raoul stirred him, and he felt he understood the Swede in a new way now, via his own native youthful hero.

"Tell me, Dad," Josh said on the drive back, "Was Ebbets Field really like Fenway Park?"

How did his sports-innocent Josh know about that old field? "Certain similarities, yes. Both small and intimate parks, with the fans up close. But how did you know about Ebbets Field?"

Josh shook his head in dismay. "Daad!"

Driving home to New Hampshire in the soft but now drizzly night, Manny felt a kind of surge from his new feeling, and odd insight. Cultures and families had their outsiders, and those outsiders or outlaws made little sense outside those spheres. So too, through his pairing of Jackie and Raoul Manny understood Wallenberg better. The wiper blades slapped back and forth, the rain droplets appeared and vanished, the boys were chattering, and Norm was saying something, but Manny was elsewhere, far away. Where was this journey taking him? he wondered anew . . .

During the next few days he was in a quandary about what to do next, especially as the woman from Budapest had written him an e-mail asking when he was returning. A good question, along with the other questions swarming in his head. So he did what he usually did when he was baffled and excited: he walked over to the small redbrick Hood Museum of Art on the campus, a rectangular gem squeezed between a residence hall and the Hopkins Center for the Arts. There, in the large central viewing room on the ground floor, he walked amidst the huge Assyrian reliefs, contemplating their origins. Six of those ten- to twelve-foot-high reliefs were on permanent display, thanks to a Dartmouth alum who had been a missionary in Iraq in 1856, who reportedly cut the reliefs down from one-foot to three-inch thickness and arranged for them to be packed and shipped across the Syrian desert by camel caravan to Alexandria and then by sea to America. Another six reliefs were part of a visiting show. These panels served as decorations for walls of palaces and monumental buildings. He stopped and studied the details from *Genie with Pail and Date-Palm Spathe and King*, a relief from the Northwest Palace of Ashurnasirpal II (883–859 BC). Manny was taken by the serenity of the pose, the lines of detail on the armor, the austere beard and stylized hair, the smooth bronze terra-cotta finish. A calm and sure king. In another he observed the hunting and battle scenes, created with meticulous detail, and yet affording the same serene impression. Now, here, the long distance of ancient history seemed closer, and those Assyrian figures, behind the masks, much more human . . . Manny felt calmer, surer.

Manny had an impulse, a travel whim, but first he decided to view at home a Wallenberg video that he had once seen, early on in his inquiry, and forgotten about. It was a European documentary about Raoul, in which Lars Berg, a colleague in the Swedish legation, spoke of a meeting between Wallenberg and Eichmann, something Manny had wondered about. And there was Berg, about sixty, recalling the meeting that he had set up at his apartment in Budapest. Manny watched it with interest, and still had his doubts . . . No one else had ever witnessed such a meeting, or even mentioned it. In it, Lars Berg says little about what transpired. Had it in fact happened? Could he have made it up? . . . Why? Afterward, Gellerman went into the living room, sat down in his leather chair, leaned back, and pictured a scene between the pair. But he found that he was not yet ready to write the scene, not sure yet how to imagine Raoul negotiating over the "banality of evil." He got onto the Internet and searched for flights. Budapest beckoned.

Before taking off, however, Manny attended a party for the graduates of the master's program. This included, of course, Angela, who was accompanied by her dad to the graduation. Her thesis had turned out just fine: well written, well reasoned, a good accounting of RW and his achievements; the more eccentric aspects of the history, like the dubious lady of Budapest, were set down in footnotes. After the graduation ceremony, the pious talks and inflated honorary degrees (one given to a corporate mogul and donor who had contributed to the partial financial meltdown), the party was held in the faculty room of the Hopkins Center, the performing arts center of Dartmouth.

Taking a beer and avocado dip outside to the sunshiney terrace, he immediately was met by Angela, looking like a tulip blooming in her pink suit and broad hat, and with her was Jonas Anderson, her father.

After introductions, the tall, angular, white-haired lawyer, dressed smartly in a cord suit and yellow tie, thanked Gellerman for all he had done for his daughter. He draped his arm around her. "You were a great guide for her."

For some reason Manny thought of the movie *Chinatown*, but only said, "Well, she did the work, and a good deal of research, interesting research."

"I know. I paid for those trips." He laughed cordially. "I am half Swedish, you know. And so I had my own interest in Mr. Wallenberg."

"Yes, she mentioned your original enthusiasm and encouragement."

"Well," he said, drinking white wine, "We all wondered what had happened to the poor soul. Still no satisfying answer, I gather. Maybe one day the Swedes will open up—when we are all safely tucked away in our graves."

Angela inserted, "Or maybe there will come along a trustworthy Russian defector, who can supply some more definite answers."

As if on cue, we all paused, as though to drink in the pastoral scene, the summery June air, the view of the green with rows of white folding chairs and the large striped tent, the steepled Baker Library in the far end, and perched on the hillside, the three oldest white academic buildings, like Ivy judges.

"Did you ever think he lived on beyond his prison years?" Jonas asked.

"Oh, I don't think so; at least it's highly doubtful. But who really knows?"

"Yes," he agreed, "who knows?"

"So many different sightings, by so many different prisoners," Angela mused. "Maybe one of them was onto something."

"Could very well be."

"An old man Wallenberg living on somewhere, off in some remote region," Manny smiled. "It's an interesting fantasy. Or reality."

"With the Swedish government paying him a handsome pension to stay put!" said Jonas.

"Or his family paying him a handsome bribe to stay put," Manny added, to everyone's mirth.

"Say," Jonas offered, "would you like to join us for dinner? Angela's half brother is coming up, and her aunt, a stern character, and we would love to have you along."

I finished my beer. "Thanks, but I have so much to take care of immediately after this, at home, as I'll be traveling for a bit. Besides, this is a good time for a family to celebrate off by itself."

"Maybe not this family with Aunt Anitra coming!" half joked Angela.

"I understand," Jonas acknowledged, "But if you should change your mind, please come along. Simon Pearce over in Quechee."

"Where are you going, sir?"

"Oh, a little bit of this and that, over in Europe."

"Ah, I wish I were going back, but I have to earn some money this summer and pay Dad back a bit." She took his arm.

"Good idea. Duty first, pleasure second," Manny said. "But let me hear from you about your plans."

"Oh, for sure, Professor. You won't be getting rid of me that easily."

Jonas put out his firm hand and Manny took it.

Some friends came up to greet Angela, and Manny said good-bye.

He made his way out of the terrace, down the stairs, and back into the street, where parents were helping kids pack up their cars, some profs were still strolling in their university robes, and the sense of the serene was still palpable. A grand day, brimming with future possibilitiy and promise.

Manny had his own more questionable possibilities in mind.

On the overseas flight, away from telephones and e-mails, students and responsibilities, he felt freer, easier, up above the clouds in the wild blue yonder. The woman next to him, a petite Vermont librarian, was happily quiet, so Manny could wander in his thoughts, reflect upon things. This might be it, he thought, this current crazy mission; this might be his last chance for having a mission in life, for going forward intellectually with a passion, not as an exercise, not as an academic formula. Where was this leading, this wild pursuit, this imaginative journey back into history? Was it to recover a life as well as a history? Well, he figured—helping the librarian Mary Jo Edwards fix her movie channel sound—even if it didn't give him all the answers, it would energize him anew, fill him with a youthfulness that might propel him toward his new work. And give him a New Life, now in his sixties, like some new romance— only maybe better because it wouldn't leave him high, dry, and exhausted if and when she were to shift her affection. Here, the affection was his to sustain, and his alone. (Though he might need some help from his subject, the elusive, abandoned Raoul.) This pleased him, and he jotted down a few addresses to visit on his spiral pad.

CHAPTER 10

In two days he was walking about the cool windy streets of Stockholm. It was an austere city, with its blue archipelago sea and harbor, the narrow cobblestone streets, the well dressed, unsmiling citizens. All in all, an elegant quiet town. He found his two research sites, the City Municipal Building and the Archives of the Foreign Ministry, where he sought any new open files about the RW case. The library and reading room in each was stylish and impressive, with high ceilings, comfortable chairs, modern tables, light pouring through the high windows. There wasn't much on file, however, that he hadn't seen before; the government still had not opened key diplomatic notes from the 1945–50 period. The Swedes in power had stayed secretive and protective of those years of strategic mistakes, hidden calumnies, cowardly betrayals.

So Manny proceeded, in the cool June air, to the famed Enskilda Bank, still run by the Wallenbergs, as it had been for hundreds of years, but he was given the polite brush-off, first by an assistant manager, and then one of the main managers. In a small office he was told that there had been a full report written on the subject of Raoul at the bank, and that he could find that online. When Manny responded that he had read that report, found it filled with huge gaps and censored pages, and carefully managed materials, the pale-faced manager shrugged, and said he could be of no further help. Just as he had imagined, Manny figured, departing the bank.

At an old wood-paneled coffee house, he sat at a table and opened the *International Tribune*. Presently his coffee was delivered on a silver tray, and he felt a sense of having been taken around, or in, once again, in a goose chase.

A slender tall fellow appeared, well dressed, and asked, in good English, if he might join him. Surprised, Manny invited him to sit down. The fellow ordered a coffee and a small cake.

"My name is Peter. My last name is not important. I work in Enskilda, you should know. And I have seen you in there, a little while ago."

"Yes, I was . . . I didn't notice you."

"Why would you? I work in the back. Investments, acquisitions. But I overheard your request."

"Oh, I see. But . . . I don't quite . . ."

"I know, you were given little information, and then you were 'asked' out. Or at least left alone, to leave."

Manny nodded, noting the regal cufflinks on the shirtsleeves. A gaunt man with a pale face, Peter resembled the knight in Bergman's *The Seventh Seal*.

"I believe you should probably desist from your search here."

"What?!"

"Yes, for your own good I mean. It will not work out well if you persist on this particular path of inquiry."

Manny sipped his coffee, taken aback by the words, but the face opposite him was cool composed. *Was he being threatened, or protected?* He had already decided to forego the inquiry, and now, abruptly, was tempted or provoked to dive back into it.

He set down his porcelain cup and said, "Oh, I think the story goes deeper than what I have gotten thus far."

"It probably does, Professor, but the risks may not be worth it. I offer this as a friend, or at least, as a friend of the memory of Mr. Wallenberg, whom I have admired tremendously." He sliced his fruitcake and smiled. "He and Björn Borg were the heroes of my youth."

Manny removed his eyeglasses and wiped the lenses with the linen napkin. "Well, thank you for the cautionary words. Are you saying, though, that I could be in some danger if I continue on?"

"Oh, I didn't, and wouldn't, use such words. But you should know there is a boundary line, drawn somewhere, and if you cross that, even unawares, the other side is a territory unfamiliar."

What an odd way to put the matter! thought Manny. "Your English is very good."

"I studied in the states, at the Wharton School, where I took my MBA. And I traveled around a good bit. I liked the states very much: its freedoms, its wilderness, its freaks." He smiled narrowly, his blue eyes narrowing too. "We are a more uniform, conformist people. That's why I admired Mr. Wallenberg so much. He went his own way, always, and stubbornly so."

"Have others tried to inquire about him at the bank?"

"Let us say they have been discouraged earlier, before they arrive at it."

"Oh, really."

"Discouraged, or charmed, I might add."

"Wined and dined? By the two cousins themselves?"

A wan smile. "It depends on the name, the power, the pedigree."

"And you know Marcus or Jacob personally?"

The waiter came, asked if anything else was desired, and went for the bill.

"Oh, I know them by face, yes, and greet them formally, if I should see them, but I do not know them. In fact, no one really *knows* them, you understand. Unless you are perhaps the prime minister or the king."

"I see," said Manny, taking the bill. "Please. And I appreciate it. May I call you sometime?"

"I think not, if you will forgive me. But if you give me your e-mail, perhaps I can reach you if I have something more to add."

Manny gave him a university card with his e-mail, and observed the tall stranger stand, nod, and depart.

Manny stood up, walked over to a wall of wood panels and mirrors, and tried to catch up to the turn of events. What sort of warning was this? Was he really treading into perilous waters? Heart pounding, he observed himself, a middle-aged bearded fellow, a kind of New Hampshire bear with spectacles, peaked cap, and sport jacket. Set down in this elegant coffee house . . . But who could tell the clown or fool beneath? . . .

Who was that stranger, and had someone provoked him into that act? Might the bosses of Enskilda, those Wallenberg cousins, act that reckless? Or was it he, Manny, who was being reckless?

On the side street to his hotel, he came across some graffiti: "Down with Zionist State! Yids To The Ovens Again!" This was plastered in black spray paint across a long bulletin board with posters of upcoming theater shows and stars. What was going on over here in Europe? Such filth—even here, in sedate Stockholm? . . .

Upstairs in his bed-and-breakfast bedroom, he sat by the small desk, took out his laptop, and drank peach tea. The view outside revealed small shops, brick buildings and thatched roofs, citizens passing. Everything in order, solid Swedish order. He began to write:

Lars Berg has told us, in memoir and video, that he arranged a meeting between Raoul and Eichmann, at Berg's flat in Budapest in 1944. Did this take place? The only witness, according to Berg, was Göte Carlsson, an aide, who, however, never mentioned the meeting, either confirming or denying it. Did it happen? We don't really know. We do know it was on RW's calendar at one point; but he never discussed it or referred to it. Per Anger, his good friend in the embassy, never referenced this in his memoir, nor did any other friend. Would Berg have made this up? Why? For attention to himself and his prowess in arranging the meeting? Perhaps. In that supposed meeting, Berg claims that Wallenberg argued with the SS killer, and actually convinced him, to the point where Eichmann said, "I admit you're right, Mr. Wallenberg. I actually never believed in Nazism as such but it has given me power and wealth. I know that this pleasant life will be over soon . . ." Oh? Are we really supposed to take these "heroic" words as the real thing, part of a real meeting? Or as a wished-for fantasy? Or was the meeting private? If it occurred, did it go in another direction? So we have this problem in history: Did it occur and, if so, what transpired? My old U. of W. prof, William Appleman Williams, comes to mind; he once suggested to a student in the 1960s to write a history of the 1930s based wholly on the films of the period. Always creative. Well, here was Gellerman getting creative, shaping his version of that ephemeral meeting, given Budapest 1944, Raoul's personality, and Eichmann's interests.

The Berg house in Hunfalvy utca in Buda was well appointed, and included six servants and a superb cook. The large dining room was fitted with a large oval dining table, and set out were fine china and crystalware. A grand dinner had been prepared, so that when Eichmann showed up with two aides, he was duly impressed. "The best Rosenthal china as well, here in lowly Budapest. Well, this is an occasion. Now, where is your other guest?"

The problem was that that other guest had not yet arrived, and Eichmann, growing restive, was almost ready to leave when, nearly a half hour later, Wallenberg finally showed, with Vilmos, his personal chauffeur, in tow. Raoul wore his familiar wool overcoat and dark suit. Eichmann was in his black uniform, adorned by the SS band.

After a few formal introductions, Raoul took over. "Come, Eichmann, let us have a private little chat in the salon there."

Eichmann, taken aback—he was usually addressed as "Obersturmbannführer"—smiled narrowly, and signaled for an aide to accompany him. But Raoul signaled to forget him, and join him alone.

In the small salon, Raoul took a club chair, and Eichmann sat on the small divan. Drinks were brought; Raoul chose a Belgian beer, and Eichmann a Beck, and he chastised, "You are either recklessly bold or foolish, you realize."

"Yes, I have been told that before."

"Tell me, Wallenberg, why are you not friendlier to us Germans? Have we done something against your country, or comrades?"

Raoul continued to pour his beer into a glass. "Now, what is it you'd like to see me about?"

Eichmann took off his black horn rim glasses and massaged the bridge of his nose. "I usually don't tolerate that sort of tone, but I will forget about that for now. And speak to our purposes."

"Good." Raoul observed his adversary's small brown eyes, interpreting narrow greed and furtive cunning. What else was there? he wondered.

"Let me put the question in a different way: Why do you insist on saving these Jews? They are not your people, they are not from your country, and they are Europe's scum. So, why should you continue to serve them?"

Raoul drank his beer, savoring the tartness. He paused and looked at this man, with the half smile lingering on his small face, and wondered, for a moment, what was his childhood and youth like, before he was recruited into the army of savagery? Treated how by other boys? The schoolmasters? He spoke neutrally, "I think about the Jews the way I think about the Christians: many are good, some are less so, and there are even some beneath that. I try not to judge general categories, however."

"Oh, what noble bullshit! You know human nature is never so peaceful or accepting. Your Jews must be paying you very well, Wallenberg, and," he leaned closer, "for that motive, I secretly respect you."

Eichmann smiled slightly and took from his jacket pocket an envelope, and set it on the table. "You know, Mr. Wallenberg, I can have you killed later tonight, by Colonel Ferenczy, or tomorrow, by one of the Njilas boys, or right now, by me." And here he took out a small revolver and set it on the table. "And nothing would change, with your Jews or with our countries. Oh, some complaints, some diplomatic troubles for a while, but then it will be forgotten as the larger troubles descend."

Wallenberg took out a pencil and doodled on his napkin. "Yes, you may be right, Eichmann, but you may also be wrong. In which case you would be hanged soon enough."

Eichmann looked startled for a moment, ceased all motion, broke into a small laugh. "You have a sense of humor, and you stay cool in the face of a threat. Also, your German is excellent. I see now how you got your reputation."

"My reputation, Eichmann, is also of little importance to me."

The Nazi scraped his lips with his tongue and drank his drink. "Wallenberg, let me get to the point, although I thought we would chat after our dinner. I believe, no I know, that you have a little black book that contains the names and bank accounts of many of the rich Jews, and if you are truly interested in saving some of the poor scum, right here in Budapest before the Njilas boys gets their hands on them, deliver me that account book and we shall make a negotiation." He paused and looked at his Swedish rival. "Furthermore, my friend, I can also assure you that you shall receive your share of the funds, a percentage of one or two, say, on every account, which, in the long run, would make a tidy sum, and allow you after the war to retire very early and nicely."

Wallenberg continued to scribble, sketching a skyline of Lake Erie by Detroit, as he recalled it, from his drawing project at Ann Arbor. Could he somehow get it to Professor Slusser?

"I am very glad you are taking this offer most seriously," Eichmann remarked, sitting back, "and jotting notes to yourself. Please, go ahead, take your time in your figuring."

Raoul shaded in the large lake, recalling his class in landscape architecture and that challenging Michigan professor. Looking up he said, "Oh, I have no such book, I'm afraid."

Eichmann moved closer. "You are taking me lightly, Wallenberg, and that is very dangerous. Everyone knows that you are not in the business of saving Jews for the moral pleasure of sainthood. And as an American spy, which you may very well be, there are other projects of more importance. So stop toying with me."

A noise from the doorway, and Berg asked, uncomfortably, "Will you be finished soon? . . . The cook, dinner . . . And another incident occurred at the New York Club . . ."

Eichmann continued, to Raoul, "You see, those Njilas boys can smell a Jew from a long way off. Just as I can smell a Jew-lover from up close. And believe me, Wallenberg, you are not such a dumbass. You are a practical Swede from what I can make out. From *a very practical family, as we Germans know.* And, therefore, you are hurting yourself when you help out the Yids. So give it up."

"You know, Eichmann, those sorts of incidents will be remembered when the time comes, and the perpetrators punished. And that time is closing fast."

Eichmann's small face tightened, his mouth twisting. "Maybe you are not as practical as your family, or as I thought."

"And I've told Wiesenmeyer that what the Arrow Cross does will also be the German responsibility."

Eichmann grew visibly livid. "So you try to cover all your fronts! Well let me tell you something. Wiesenmeyer and all the polite diplomats will soon become obsolete, and then you will have to face the Gestapo without any protection. It will not be pretty."

"Shall I pass that along to the ambassador?"

Eichmann took up his pearl handled revolver. "I can shoot you dead right now, declaring you have insulted the Führer, and no one will lift a hand."

"Maybe. Maybe not." He gestured toward the other room. "My friends will not like that much. You may earn an equal reward. Besides, you have not let me make *my* offer."

After a tense moment, and pause, Eichmann relaxed his hold, smiled narrowly. "Well, go ahead, make it."

Wallenberg suspended his drawing and said, "Get rid of Krumey. We both know that beneath his apparent charm, he's a vicious fellow. Get a written order on the Njilas thugs, so that the German commanders run things. And finally, you will let me have the approximate 7,500 Jewish children who are currently warehoused for eventual deportation to Auschwitz. In return, I shall get you the shipment of trucks and food that you are looking for."

"How do you know this?" Eichmann stared, surprised. "How many trucks?"

"I can get you a dozen trucks immediately. For cargo and for armed personnel. And once the children and women are released to me personally, and given my safe passage out, I shall get you twelve more. Plus, five hundred barrels of petrol."

Eichmann drew back, in awe and reflection. He adjusted his glasses and, drinking his beer, eyed this surprising adversary.

"You are practical, then, as I imagined. Good. Only one thing is missing. Cash. How much will you give me for the Jewish bodies? Ten thousand a body?"

Wallenberg turned over the doodled napkin, wrote down figures, and said, "I can probably get you $50,000, half up front and half upon delivery."

"That's not very much." A half smile. "Aren't those children worth more?"

"If you allow me to put the cash into a Swiss account, I can get you seventy-five."

"One hundred, with suitable guarantees?"

Wallenberg leaned back. "All right, yes."

Eichmann nodded. "I will take that. After this fucking war is over, I have my sights on a South American retirement home, and access to Swiss accounts from there should be easy enough. Deliver the account and the guarantees beforehand—"

"Half beforehand, Eichmann."

He gave a little laugh. "All right, half before. But remember, any attempt to cheat me, and they will be shot immediately, right here in Budapest."

"You will have it. By the end of the week, Friday afternoon. If we can get wires through to Zurich and back by then . . ."

"You are a man of business, after all, as I thought. I don't like you, Wallenberg, but business doesn't require friendship, does it?" He put out his hand.

Wallenberg nodded, stood up, started to walk out,—

"Besides," said Eichmann, standing too, following, "all of this will be forgotten in generations to come, or denied, or so twisted, that what has really happened here will be subject to debate, and historians will have a field day revising and—hey, Wallenberg don't you believe me?"

But Wallenberg didn't turn around and walked out of the room into the dining room.

"So, you are still walking?" put in Berg, "You had a successful meeting?"

Raoul smiled wearily. "Sorry to have kept you from your dinner . . ."

"Is he yet another Nazi psychopath?" queried Göte Carlsson.

Raoul took out his napkin and unfolded it neatly. "Oh, I believe he combines what you might call an entrepreneurial urge along with his other 'urges.' Money for his personal retirement plans seems as important as deporting Jewish bodies. Not much difference to him. A different sort of Nazi specimen, let us say." He checked his notes on the napkin and turned it over to the other side.

"Have you been drawing again?" put in Elizabeth Nako, a late arrival. "One day we may publish these drawings?"

Raoul smiled weakly. "One day I'll collect them and send them on to Professor Slusser, my architecture professor, and ask him to revisit my old project grade." He turned to Langfelder, the mini-giant chauffeur who was standing aside, arms folded. "Come, Vilmos, we should get going now."

"What?! What about our dinner?" implored Lars Berg. " The chef has managed to find your favorite fowl!"

"Oh, another time," offered Raoul. "In some other company perhaps."

Vilmos held out his overcoat and Raoul got into it, and he bid farewell to his Swedish friends, just as Eichmann returned into the room, with his aides.

"Wallenberg, where are you going?"

"Oh, we have much work to do, Colonel, more tasks to perform than when we first came tonight. We will meet again, I am sure."

Berg and Elizabeth and Carlsson looked at each other, shook their heads in disbelief, as the prominent guest left the dinner party before it had actually begun.

What could Manny say, or think, about such a scene? Had he shaped the material too generously toward RW, gone too easy on him? Was the scene altogether too sensational? (Or not sensational enough?) Again, there was no hard evidence that the meeting ever took place, outside of Berg's claims. But many curious things happen that have no hard evidence, and they count for a lot.

Not everything that goes on in life gets recorded, and leaks sometimes take decades . . . But if Eichmann didn't meet Raoul, he certainly wished to; that much is clear from the history. So call Manny the historical facilitator of that hoped-for meeting, a scene-maker of tacit desires . . .

He settled back in his little room, poured a shot of cognac from his leather flask, and checked out the few old black and white photographs on the wall. Old Stockholm. Not too much different from today's city. Then, he opened his e-mail. Three from the college, one from family, another from the lady in Budapest, and a curious unknown one, which, when he opened it, turned out to be from the banker at Enskilda:

> *Do not put your life in any danger. What you seek is at the bottom of a well-preserved mystery, an intrigue. Sir, you will never get at the whole truth. That is buried under layers of paperwork obfuscation, discarded notes, lost files. It will take many years or decades before they are cleared away, and the truth about the circumstances of RW will be allowed to surface. Please enjoy our city, and do take a sailboat excursion in the archipelago; it is the best way to experience it.*
> *Peter S.*

Was this a written exclamation point on their meeting in the coffee house? Was the fellow a friend of the truth, offering Manny a STOP sign of caution? Was he a freak of some sort, or a paid servant of the current Wallenbergs? How to react? Manny had to figure out a next move, a plan of attack, or a retreat . . .

He went over his notes on the actual history.

What was America up to in 1945, when they learned that RW had been grabbed by the Soviets in Hungary and transferred to Lybianka Prison, never to get out? Did they try hard to get him out? Well, actually, the evidence of the diplomatic notes suggests strongly yes, starting with the American ambassador in Stockholm, Minister Johnson, who cabled the State Department (April 4) urging them to alert his counterpart in Moscow, Averell Harriman, to help the Swedish legation there in any way, since "we had a special interest in Wallenberg's mission to Hungary." And on April 9, Secretary of State Edward Stettinius cabled Harriman to "give all possible support to the Swedes." And even the secretary of the Treasury, Robert Morganthau Jr., having received a copy of the April 4 cable from Johnson via the War Refugee Board and its new director, Brigadier General William O'Dwyer, scribbled on the bottom, "Let Stettinius know that I am personally interested in this man." So everyone was on line, wanting to help the Swedes recover their famous diplomat. Moreoover, by then, even the Swedish population was alerted to the heroics of RW via a front-page story in March in their daily newspaper *Dagens Nyheter*, which carried an interview with a Hungarian Jew who gave an account of RW's heroic rescue operations.

But hold on: the Swedish ambassador in Moscow, Staffan Söderblom, re-buffed the American offer of help, and was quite satisfied to accept the Soviet explanation, that they knew nothing of this Wallenberg. This curious decision and feeble judgment was discovered only some twenty years later; also later discovered was that his telegrams on the issue were censored for the public by other diplomats in Stockholm. Furthermore, that mistake and cover-up was compounded by an act of direct cowardice, when Ambassador Söderblum was granted a surprising audience with Marshal Stalin, on June 15, 1946. In awe of Stalin, Söderblom brought up the name of Wallenberg only at the end of the meeting, and Stalin said that he never heard of the man; he wrote his name down and promised to look into the matter. Stalin reminded the ambassador that all Swedish citizens and diplomats in Budapest at the time were under the "protection" of the Soviet army. "Yes," Söderblom replied, "and I am personally convinced that Wallenberg fell victim either to a road accident or bandits."

"Have you not had any definite information on the matter from our side?" asked the dictator politely.

"No," said Söderblom, "but I assume that the Soviet military authorities do not have any further reliable information about what happened after that."

After that astonishing exchange, Söderblom went on to ask for an official statement from the Soviets, asserting that all possible action had been taken to find Wallenberg, though without success, and offering assurance that if they were to find out anything, it would be passed on.

"I promise you," Stalin replied, "that the matter will be investigated and cleared up. I shall see to it personally."

Documentation of the above Söderblom-Stalin exchange was released in 1980. One year before, Söderblom, in retirement in Uppsala, told his questioners that he had done all he could under the circumstances. "I didn't want to make a direct accusation to the Russians that they had killed Wallenberg or something of that kind," he said. "It would have made the whole situation more difficult if such an unsuitable suggestion had been made."

True, Gellerman knew, since those old days, the Swedes had become more and more critical of their ambassador and their diplomacy of that time. But where was the Wallenberg family, the powerful Marcus and Jacob, during all of that? Where was Swedish skepticism and inquiry about that famous family?

Why were they let off the hook, so conveniently, till this day, and the full blame placed on the politicians? . . .

Through a young Swedish friend who had once been a student of his ex-wife's at the college and was now an architect living in a suburb, Gellerman had a lead on a local gentleman who claimed some personal knowledge of Wallenberg.

A short older gentleman, paunchy in a suit, arrived at the house in Lindingö with boxes of files, and a shy smile and handshake. He introduced himself as Olaf Selling and sat in a chair; and, after introductory words, he explained who he was and how he had come to save all the clippings in the Swedish newspapers that had come out about RW. Politely Manny interrupted him and asked him to talk first about his relationship with Raoul. In a basic English, Olaf told of meeting Raoul when they were both drafted for their two-year service in the Swedish army. Their basic training was up north, for several months, and while he never came to know Raoul intimately—nobody did—it was a very small group of recruits that were housed together, several of them heading for officer school. In the training camp, RW proved himself to be a good soldier in every way, dutiful, respectful, modest, never relying on his famous name for any special privileges or preferences. Except for one time.

"A few things stood out."

"Like what?" inquired Manny.

"Well, Mr. Wallenberg was always a great practical joker, you see, never to really hurt anyone, but just to be sort of . . . playful."

"Mischief, you mean?"

"Yes, small mischief. Like creating a letter to a young man from a made-up admirer. Everyone liked him for this, very much. It made everyone laugh, and loosen up, you say?"

"Interesting. One wouldn't have known that. What else?"

"Well, I remember one situation very clearly to this day, which showed a different side. Our platoon sergeant grew very angry one day at one of us, a lower-class brat, and he called him out front and criticized him very severely, humiliating the fellow in front of all of of us. Suddenly, Mr. Wallenberg stepped forward, saying the sergeant was going out too far in his denunciations, and he had no right to do this! Everyone waited for the sergeant in command, who had total power to reprimand anyone, including Mr. W., and probably restrict his chances for making it into officer school. He challenged Raoul, who had taken two steps forward, standing at attention, to think about what he was doing, and I always remember Mr. W.'s words back: "I have thought about what I am doing. You may criticize and chastise any of us, but not humiliate us." This was amazing, a true challenge to army authority! And Mr. Wallenberg, despite his familiar name, was clearly endangering his status. That made no difference. He faced the tough sergeant who, after a very a tense minute or two, sent the first soldier back to the group, and he proceeded on with the next drills. We were all shocked at this rebellious act by our young comrade. And for the rest of our time there, we all admired Mr. Wallenberg very much, and he returned to being a well-behaved soldier. And, yes, Mr. Wallenberg made his officer school, and became a lieutenant, though he didn't stay in the army."

I thanked Olaf for these memories, adding that the same character traits he recalled had shown up both in graduate school in America and in service in Budapest.

"You see, though he stayed to himself," Olaf continued, "he was the favorite of our group, because we could rely on him, because he did not try to use the power of his name, and because he used his humor well. The army, and patriotism, were to be taken seriously, but not *that* seriously. We as individual human beings came first, always. It never mattered what class we came from."

I nodded, charting more of Raoul, and accepting the boxes of files, which Olaf had collected ever since those army days with his old training comrade.

Before leaving Stockholm, Manny did some more checking around and research. With the aid of historian Susanne Berger's work, he discovered that in 1943 the Enskilda Bank alone controlled resources of $647, 794, and 917 millions, and by 1947 Wallenberg firms world-wide employed 150,000 workers. (In 1999 the number of workers had grown to 600,000 and the Wallenberg business assets were valued at about 900 billion Swedish kroner, or about $90 billion.) Furthermore, he learned that during the war the Wallenberg firms had not only been the main supplier of ball bearings to the Nazis—to keep their tanks and planes running—but also to the Soviet Union, and in late 1944 Marcus Wallenberg was crucial in bringing about the Soviet-Finish Armistice Agreement. In other words, the power of the Wallenberg family was enormous, both financially and politically, and it was emphatically clear to Manny that, had the family exerted any pressure on the Swedish government, or even worked with the Russians (who needed the trade badly), Raoul would have had a far better fate. He would have been exchanged, and lived.

Manny went to the bank to try to see his source, Peter, but no luck; he was given the runaround. When he wrote Peter from his laptop, he heard back only a cryptic note, saying that, when it was time to contact Prof. G. again, he would. Shades of Deep Throat.

He tried to see Nina Lagergren, the half sister of Raoul, but she said she was just leaving town to visit a friend and was unsure of her return. A two-sentence note. So he ambled about the modest-sized cozy city, regal with order, charming with narrow streets, small elegant shops, thatched roofs, and church steeples. The sky hung low and was gray. The citizens were polite, orderly, cosmopolitan; they went about their business efficiently; and there was no big traffic noise or bustle like in New York. At the Stockholm Public Library, he admired the inside architecture, the beautiful circular shape and dark woods, the curving mahogany bookshelves, the cordiality of the librarians and students. Manny came to realize that, beneath all that, the city disguised its past, and the government, its secrets. All that order and civility was hiding deep dark truths of Wallenberg family power and betrayal, and of government cowardice. Beneath the handsome architecture, and the high moral declarations, ran Bergmanesque truths of cover-up and evil; the soul of its recent political history was rotten.

A pedestrian in the SoFo district recommended the Café Cinema coffee shop, where Manny ordered an open-faced sandwich of herring and onion and a cream sauce, reminiscent of his sailing days with Norwegian freighters. A superb dark coffee was brought first. The café was small, maybe ten tables, with film photos and posters on the walls, DVDs, and a cozy atmosphere.

A gentleman asked if he might sit across from him, as the other tables seemed filled up or private. The familiar stranger wore a dark sport jacket and patterned blue shirt, set down his fedora and asked how he was enjoying his visit.

Above him Manny noticed an old movie poster of Leslie Howard, with Myrna Loy, in *The Scarlet Pimpernel*. He remembered it from the Pitkin Theater in Brooklyn, years ago. "The visit has been fine."

"Have you learned anything new on this mission?"

Manny held back his surprise. "New? Not particularly, I guess."

"It's a cool sober city, as you can see. I had some good plans for modernizing it a bit more, in my small ways; even made some drawings. Did you get to the quay or dock?"

Manny shook his head.

The waiter came and brought over the sandwich, which was set on a large plate with sliced tomato and onions on the side.

"How about the Wallenbergs? Any luck there, with my cousins? Or my half sister?"

Manny shook his head.

A wan half smile. "I didn't think so. But you did try; so now, do you wish to give up the journey?"

A pause to take it all in. "Of course not, my friend."

The waiter asked if he needed anything else? "I heard you say something."

Manny motioned him away.

He spoke again, to Raoul. "I am in this for keeps."

The gentleman nodded. A gesture of understanding and sympathy. "But you did hear a danger signal, I imagine. Pay attention to it, Professor. My cousins are very strong people in this town. And elsewhere. All over Europe."

"I shall pay attention to it."

"Europe is not America, you know. Things have happened here that got covered over, for years sometimes. This is our history."

Manny nodded, thinking of all the American things "covered over"—the Dred Scott case, the Leo Frank lynching, Sacco and Vanzetti, the Rosenbergs, on and on, and the anonymous lynchings, killings, injustices. "Ours too."

"Ah, but Europe is a bit different. As is my family and its unique history, especially during the war."

"Did you know 'too much' for your own good, if I may ask?"

"Maybe. But regardless, I would have said nothing to injure my cousins."

"But they wouldn't or couldn't take any chances."

The gentleman shrugged. "Who knows? But finally it wasn't up to them to find or free me; that was the government's responsibility."

"But the family could have helped."

"We should avoid 'could haves' as much as possible. And pursue instead, well, what you wish to pursue."

The waiter was standing there, bowing slightly, asking if everything was in order? Smiling sympathetically.

"Oh, yes, perfectly in order. Thank you."

The bill was presented; Manny paid it and departed.

On the evening flight to Budapest, he sat in the window seat looking out at the lines of blue and white horizon, and felt himself to be like a constant commuter, flying back and forth without a final destination. Where he was going now, he knew; but later on?

Just then the man next to him removed his hat and asked if Gellerman might lower the porthole shade a bit.

Manny nodded and complied.

He put on his CD player and listened to his son's CD, playing the gavotte movement of the fifth Bach suite. The notes were clearly and surely played, and the repetitions and variations seemed nuanced and rather exquisite. In his mind, he saw the boy's bowing hand, with the elbow in its correct position, and the fingers moving quickly over the strings. Each year he took more and more control of the instrument. Soon he would go to music camp in Maine, and in a few weeks he would be playing a small chamber concert there, which Manny would attend. Recently, the boy had even begun taking an interest in composing! This stirred the father.

For some reason that movie poster of Leslie Howard as the Scarlet Pimpernel floated before him, and Manny remembered that handsome hero who led the double life during the French revolution, the undergound hero and the effete aristocrat. If he were alive and was playing in this current film, should he be cast as Manny, the professor/detective, or as RW, the noble hero? Easy choice. No question about it.

A woman next to him asked why he was going to Budapest.

Gellerman was taken aback, couldn't quite answer at first. "Well, I'm trying to find someone actually."

"Who?"

Manny stared at this curious woman, with the prominent-featured face, asking these oddly nosey questions.

"Well, he's dead now. The man I'm looking for. A Swedish fellow who lived in Budapest in 1944."

The woman took her eyeglasses from her chest and put them on; she nodded and opened her Swedish newspaper. "Why are you hunting down a dead man?"

Manny was bewildered both by the question and by the line of questioning. It was not the woman's business! And yet Manny didn't feel as though the stranger was being impertinent; it was something else—seriously inquisitive, even intimate. He couldn't quite find the right words to answer.

She refolded her newspaper and took out a laptop.

Manny felt perspiration. Why? The plane dipped. What was going on here?

"Do dead men really have that much to say to you? Unless they are family, of course." The lilt of her accent was Swedish, modified by expert English.

"No, he's not family. A stranger, actually, but one I have come to know."

"Know? How so?"

"Through letters, witnesses, research, bits and pages of history . . ."

The woman looked out over her bifocals. "You can't really know a man that way, can you?" She shook her head, skeptically. "That's hearsay. Other men's views and illusions. Then there is the distance of many years, and faulty, selective memories. No, not the same as the real person, living, acting, having to make difficult choices in a sudden moment."

Manny wondered about this woman, berating him this way.

"Besides, how do you ever know a man, unless you've been with him a long time and observed him under various circumstances?" A pause. "Most men hardly know themselves! Or can admit truths to themselves."

Manny closed his eyes for a minute, baffled, just as the jet was jarred suddenly by a wave of turbulence.

When he opened his eyes again, the woman was absent, replaced by a ruddy fellow in a suit, who jovially apologized for having taken the armrest!

CHAPTER 11

        In Budapest Manny called his cello boy in New Hampshire, got an update on his music plans, and told him to be prepared: Dad would be in the other Sweden, in Maine, to see his August performance. Next he read an e-mail from his other son, Seth, who was sending on a small piece he had written for a college course in essay writing. With force and clarity, the essay depicted the death of his uncle at a young age, twenty-one. Manny admired the boy's superior prose and his insights. He had secretly felt ashamed that he had never felt "authentic" grief like that of his mother and the other mourners, but only followed the protocol of the event. But the real success of the essay was the strategy of describing, and using as a metaphor, the Lego monorail that the young uncle had created and kept in his room while he was dying of cancer; such a creation had always been the highest aspiration of young Seth, whose passion for Lego building had started at age three, when he made his first piece, a green tractor, while on a plane ride to Jerusalem with his parents. The boy had it in him to be a writer, a real writer, not a journalist or advertising jingle man. Imagine that, one boy a cellist, the other a literary man. Where was the young historian? Well, no need; the world had enough of those.

        Could Manny find a clue to solving his present puzzle from those Lego creations? He recalled the child's patient, meticulous work on these ingenious innovations—miniature masterpieces. Sometimes, when Seth was not happy with a packaged result—too dull or too ordinary—he'd invent his own model, mix and match and come up with something original. And that result was unfailingly better than the packet's picture. So now, as Manny proceeded toward the Budapest lady of fantastic imagination, he'd observe her as some sort of new invention or creation, one that might shed light on the original order of things. In other words, mix and match her intimate fantasy with solid reality, her wish fulfillment with the grimmer truth. (Who was kidding whom here?)

        Budapest, he figured, with its series of painted bridges and its old castles and hills, cut through by the curving Danube, seemed built for a world of dreams and phantasmagoria, creating a convenient stage for Zsuzsa Frank Wallenberg to perform her lifework/act here.

But before seeing the lady, Manny took a little trip by train down along the river, about an hour and a half, to a small village. In Kismaros ("Keesh-marrosh") lived one József Nemeth, a man in his eighties now, who claimed to have seen Wallenberg back in his prisoner days. One of several dozen witnesses who provided annual "sightings" of the legendary man, in the years since the reputed death in 1947. Like birders sighting rare species, these Wallenberg watchers had turned up everywhere, in all countries, never able to provide enough evidence to make their sightings verifiable.

This Nemeth, who met him at the train station, was a small stocky man, with a rich skein of white hair. Walking with a cane, he took Manny to the local tavern, a ten-minute walk, where he ordered a couple of local beers; they were seated in the patio area by a plastic round table. He thanked Manny for coming down to see him, and they made some small talk.

József wore an open-necked shirt and a light windbreaker, and he was soon answering Manny's questions. "Well, you see I first heard about him when we were at Vladimir Prison—you know that place? The cleaner woman mentioned a Swedish prisoner to me, someone of importance, because he played chess, and so did I. I meet him several times to play. You could see a nobleman from his manner, polite ways, and he was a good player too. We didn't talk much, but when we did, in German, it was not about much."

"How long did you stay at Vladimir?" And how long did he stay?"

"Maybe some months?"

"And then?"

"Then? If you lived through Vladimir, you got your opportunity to serve in the Gulag. I was sent to a place called Vörkuta." He smiled. "Cold, and a long distance from all things."

"I have heard of it, yes. Up north somewhere. Not open to foreigners. Or Russians."

He shrugged. "But you should visit it now since it's been opened. To see the geography, ways of life, what's left of the place." He drank his beer. "Then I got sick and was sent to a psychiatric hospital, somewhere in Siberia. You see?" he pointed to a number on his wrist. "Out there, I heard again about this old Swedish prisoner who was there, and very sick."

Gellerman gestured for József to continue. "I saw this old shriveled man, wearing a small beard," he motioned his chin, "and we met a few times."

"But what makes you think, years later, this was Wallenberg?"

"Well, we realized we both played chess, and we played a few games, and you know what, he made the same moves he had made years before! Always with the same queen pawn opening and bishop threat! And then he made a few moves, to control the center. Years ago he explained that he was a follower of Nimzovitch!"

Manny eyed this curious fellow, who was anything but strange. "Still, what you knew was that he had played chess with you years ago at Vladimir; but why did you think this was Wallenberg?"

"Yes, I understand your question. First, that cleaner woman told me his name, years before. And second, he knew certain things, bits of news, which maybe only he could have known. We had no newspapers there."

Manny gazed at half-drunk men a few tables away, and at this firm lively octogenerian. "No proof, though? No other witnesses have you?"

"Maybe a German fellow, prisoner number? . . ." He shrugged. "It was him all right, I truly believe."

"Any name for the German? And the date, do you recall?"

"No name. The date? Oh, late seventies, early eighties maybe." He produced an apple and polished it with a handkerchief. "Who knows, he could still be alive! Look, I am," he said and he bit into the apple. "But he was sick; that was clear. Coughing a lot." He leaned forward. "But he was a good chess player, I can tell you, because I am not bad myself." A wonderful smile.

Presently, on the train ride back, Manny considered the hearty fellow, his secret sighting and firm belief. Sure, he could be right, like maybe trying hard to sight a true English nightingale in the New Hampshire woods and mistaking it for a wood thrush. Same song, different bird. Yes, it was possible, but improbable. Yet to cite it would bestow an immediate honor upon the sighter. (Like the German prisoner?) And didn't József have a right to imagine, speculate, exaggerate, after his years of deprivation and anonymity in Vladimir, Vörkuta? Out there, in the land beyond the Hungarian village, existed other sighters—in Russia, Israel, Germany, Poland—people who swore to have seen RW in one hospital or prison, or the Gulag. Hundreds. And why not? If you squinted real hard, pressed your temples, remembered your suffering and saw a photograph of a legend, a man of history, wouldn't he turn up in the flesh, in some sort of human replica? To make all those years suddenly worthwhile, have a meaning? . . .

Now, he read the *International Herald Tribune*: how the Iraq war dragged on, bodies torn open, a country torn apart, and a president still using phrases like "winning a victory" and "spreading democracy." Was there a connection between the words and the reality? Did anyone know how dangerous the preppie pipsqueek could be! In *USA Today* Manny read that *American Idol* was the top TV show, watched by forty million. So while the republic went down the tubes, the pop world assisted in dumbing down its young citizens. Further, our political culture of wars and violence was distracted and covered over by the newly expanded culture of fame, everyone encouraged to get in on the publicity, forget the talent. Crime would do just as well as merit. True crime stories, novels, movies, sold mightily. More, from the *Wall Street Journal*, yet another corporate head was forced to resign, this time a bankrupt airline, taking with him, for his failures, a golden parachute of sixty-seven million bucks, plus a hefty pension. Was all this really happening in one era? In all of Manny's adult four decades, the society never seemed this shallow, arrogant, or reckless. Was this descent part of a historical destiny, like that of any ruling empire—as Ferguson or Kennedy wrote—or was it a temporary fall due to the current inept and dangerous gang running things?

Before meeting the lady illusionist—or shrewd strategist?—later in the afternoon, he chose to take a walk and tram ride around the town, glimpsing the old way of life. The small shops of superb cakes and strudels, the narrow messy streets and bustling gloomy citizens, the snaking, rattling tram/trolley—all this stirred Manny. Took him back again five decades to his venerable Borough of Kings. He stopped and found a shop for a custard, something like a Charlotte Russe, with the soggy sponge cake at the bottom and the whipped cream on top. Too bad his own sons missed out on that delight, along with chocolate egg creams, Lime Rickeys on hot summer days, corner candy stores, and the green oval of Ebbets Field—all the grand treats of the 1940s and 1950s. At the same time that the Soviets were capturing and imprisoning Raoul, Manny was a boy coasting in childhood wonders amidst Brooklyn comforts. Well, maybe it was time to make up for it now?

In Buda he walked halfway up Gellert Hill, found Gyopar Street, and soon came upon the large four-story mansion, surrounded by trees, that served as the old Swedish legation. In his mind's eye he saw the Studebaker outside, with Vilmos standing by the car, perhaps with one of the Swedish girls, Margareta Bauer or Birgit Brulin, waiting with urgency for their boss, Raoul, to emerge. Then he wandered back down and took a taxi across the Margaret Bridge and over to the Pest area in the vicinity of the Wallenberg safe houses. Here he walked along the river, and found a small area where the Njilas thugs used to line up Jews, shoot them, and toss them into the river. It was noted here by a small marker in the stones. In the cool afternoon he walked along and asked a few people if they knew where Wallenberg utca was, but no one knew, or even knew the name. So much for history. He turned east and walked among small streets and apartment buildings, arrived at a bookstore, and asking again, learned from the woman assistant that he was headed in the right direction, just up the street a little until he hit the cross street. There, on the corner, he discovered a modest bronze sculpture set into the building, maybe ten or twelve feet high. A portrait of a handsome young man, in overcoat and hat, carrying a page in one hand, and with the other, holding up his palm to indicate *stop*, transformed the real into romance! The building was an ordinary one with many flats, hiding well the extraordinary tale within it.

This was the Budapest of Raoul in 1944–45, and Manny was experiencing it with a rising feeling in his chest that he couldn't quite name. Was this what the madwoman of Budapest was experiencing all the time? . . . A constant stir of emotion, tied to the thirty-three-year-old Swede of fifty years ago? No wonder she lived in that other world, the imagined, the delirious; it was richer, more intense.

Did these stucco buildings and brick tenements serve as fortresses of locked memory, guideposts to the scarred past? Keeping their secrets well hidden? The trick was to get the key to unlock them.

A fellow stepped out, lit a cigarette, motioned Manny inside, and led him to a long iron staircase and, behind it, to a dark crawl area.

The familiar fellow spoke:

I used to sleep there, every so often, on a thick blanket with a sweater covering my backpack for my pillow. For precaution, and only Vilmos knew my whereabouts at night. And it wasn't bad, once you got used to it. Others had it much worse, my American professor.

Now let me say a few words to answer your basic question, of a while ago. Why did I do this, subject myself to such inconveniences and trials? I shall tell you what I think, my interpretation. It may be true; it may not. As you know, Grandfather was my tutor and mentor, and he trained me, in his open-minded way, for some mission. I didn't really understand that then, as I moved around from place to place—Ann Arbor, Haifa, Capetown—and witnessed various situations and peoples. When Lauer gave me money to take care of his Jewish family in Budapest, and then the American Olsen added some funding, it seemed a good job, a good coincidence. But when I landed in Budapest, and saw up close what the Arrow Cross and Nazis were doing, I was shocked; I found my driver, Vilmos, and met his fearful Jewish family; and he took me around to see a few more of the Jews, awaiting deportation and death. Witnessing my first deportation at Keleti Railway Station, the moment seized me and I felt it much stronger. I understood what Grandfather had wanted for me, to fulfull myself through a great mission, not merely a job. I understood what was required and what I needed to do. And I felt comfortable doing it, not at all heroic, providing the Jews with whatever assistance they might need to stay alive. This was the mission that Grandfather had trained me for, I realized.

I will acknowledge, as well, that my Wallenberg family and their activities and beliefs added to my beliefs and determination. I knew how they had acted with the Nazis for business reasons, helping them in many key areas. Capitalists do many pragmatic things, but rich capitalists may have to do unethical things. But I didn't think they would not aid Jews, for many reasons. Even my "neutral" country helped Jews; did you know that Sweden took in five thousand Jewish women from East Europe, mainly Poland, and saved them in monasteries and religious sanctuaries until the war was over when they released them to Palestine? But my cousins, well they used Enskilde to serve the Nazis, also sold them iron ore for necessary wheel bearings, made much profit from them. Yet they looked away when it came to the Jews. And to me.

For them to stand aside when it came to my being in Lybianka, that was no surprise. It was a disappointment, yes, but not a big surprise. I did feel very badly for my mother, who suffered from their indifference, and my half brother, who genuinely liked me, but for myself, I knew I had done what Grandfather had intended for me all along. And what I had wanted. So I did not mind too much paying for it in Lybianka.

The gentleman nodded, adjusted his coat lapels, and departed.

Madame Zsuzsanna Frank Wallenberg looked as grave and austere as ever, when she opened the door and invited him in.

"I am very glad to see you again; I thought you would return," she said, taking his two hands in hers and surprising him with a real smile. She showed him into the living room, into the same wing chair as earlier.

He felt like a time traveler, going back to the 1940s and '50s as he awaited her tea cart. Restraining an impulse to get up, leave, and escape the mystifying spell that approached, he sat like a good schoolboy, hands clasped.

Presently he heard the sound of the wheels of the rolling cart. She wore an apron over her blouse and skirt while serving the cakes, pouring the tea.

"I have this for you," she said, placing a large book in his lap. "It's in Hungarian, unfortunately. But you can glance through it, for the pictures. What is interesting is that it is a series of personal articles, all by Christians, about Raoul, but there is no mention of Jews, no memoirs by Jews. In other words, they are doing their best to change his acts and steal his true identity, for them, for the Christians. Can you imagine this?"

Gellerman glanced through the well-made book, checked the familiar pictures, and looked up at Madame. "Why?"

She furrowed her brow. "This is the way it is, in Hungary. Jews don't count, especially dead Jews. And if you have saved them, then what is to be remembered is that *you are a great Christian*. And mention will be made *only* of the Christians you have saved." She sipped tea. "This is the way history is revised here, always."

"So anti-Semitism is creeping back again?"

She gave a little laugh. "You are innocent. It has never left. Not here. It is in the blood or DNA of the citizens."

"I see." He looked over the familiar interior, the flowery wallpaper coming apart at the seams, the faded upholstered chairs, the ancient daybed, and the black and white photographs bunched into corners. There was a musty odor too, and he made a note to send her sometime an air purifier. He felt oddly gripped, and estranged at the same time.

Zsuzsa smiled sympathetically. "You are seeing something you don't like, or understand?"

He gave a little uncomfortable smile. "Oh, it's nothing. Maybe something I don't understand. Or can't quite . . . believe."

She arranged her linen napkin on her lap. "Of course, I understand. You shouldn't feel the need to believe." She fingered the cameo locket hanging on a gold chain around her neck. "Belief and faith are the hardest things to achieve, in human relationships or religion."

Her modesty, or lack of defensiveness, touched him. He sipped the rich tea.

"Tell me, how did that young lady's thesis progress? Is it finished?"

"Yes, that's done. And it turned out well, I would say. If you'd like to see it, when I return, I will send you a copy."

She smiled narrowly, revealing yellowing teeth. "Not necessary. I am glad it went well. I simply never heard from her again."

They paused, and heard the cars whisking by below.

"And please tell me, are you writing something yourself?"

Was he? Well, yes, but he still wasn't sure of what that form was, his "Scenes from a Shadow History," but he did know that it was private, for now, anyway. "Oh, not really, not now."

"But you will tell me when you do write something, I hope."

"Absolutely."

The phone rang, and she excused herself to go to a corner of the room to answer the black phone. He admired her well-kept figure, her well-kept calm; he had never seen obsession in the midst of such calm, actually.

"So, Professor, how long will you stay this time?" she said, upon returning. "And tell me, if you would, why did you come this time?"

He pondered an answer. "I have returned because a part of me does believe there is something in your story, something important, but I am not sure if I can put my finger on it."

"Well, at least that is some progress, no?" she teased him.

He smiled, feeling more relaxed. "I've even had a private conversation or two with Raoul, if you must know; so therefore, I must have some sort of *faith* in me, in him!"

She eyed him. "Another piece of cake?"

"No, thank you."

"What sort of conversation?"

"A private one, in which he wondered what was I doing, still searching for him. He counseled me that his time was long ago, and that nobody was interested, then or certainly not now."

She laughed. "Well, I am not sure I knew you were 'searching for him,' but I am glad to hear the news! But of course he was mistaken, thinking he was forgotten. Deeply mistaken. In fact, it may be said that he is remembered more now, by a devoted circle, than when he was living."

"Oh, really? A more devoted circle? I must meet them one day."

"Maybe you will." She eyed him. "When next we meet."

Gellerman saw she wasn't kidding. A devoted circle . . . He kept learning from this smooth-faced mystery woman. But learning what?

She rose to remove the tea cups and saucers onto the cart, and he went to help her, but she waved him back. "This is my job, please."

"Tell me," he said, "is that locket a family heirloom?"

A soft smile. "Yes, it is actually. Raoul gave it to my mother." She fingered it and then put it forward. "She put a family photograph in it. Would you like to see it?"

"Why, yes."

She set down the cups, wiped her hands on a napkin, and flicked it open, then leaned forward so he could see the small photograph.

He peered at a small black and white photograph, heart shaped, that had been fit inside. A young mother holding a baby, accompanied by a young handsome man who indeed looked a bit like Wallenberg. The photograph was so small, however, that Manny couldn't quite tell; and he did not want to ask for a magnifying glass.

"I am impressed. She, you, the family, are really very beautiful."

She laughed, easily. "Of course! Why would you think otherwise? We were all younger then! And remember, we are Hungarian!"

"Good point, I am beginning to understand that."

She started pushing the cart. "So you like my photograph? Perhaps I will show you more later. You will stay for dinner, I hope?"

"Oh, I hadn't planned on that . . ."

"But Dora is expecting to see you."

"I didn't realize she was coming over."

Zsuzsa wagged her finger. "You do not come to visit us that often, you know; and you made an impression on her. Truly."

Manny felt a sensation in his chest. "She made an impression on me too."

"Good, then that is settled."

She left the room for the kitchen, and he was alone to think, to plan, to figure things out . . . He cleaned his eyeglasses, using a cotton cloth, stood up and wandered across the room. Feeling alone, he took a few steps into the adjoining room, a small study. Her "father's 'sanctuary,'" she had called it, and the cramped room did have a safe feel; it was a twelve-by-fourteen-foot room with oak desk, pictures, a file. Feeling like the intruder that he was, he took a step to leave, but stopped, just at the doorway. He viewed the small photos set in a tripartite frame, one of Raoul, one of her mother, one of a baby. And next to it, a kind of sketch for—?"

"I see you have found Father's private room," she smiled, forgivingly. "And you like his drawing? It was meant to describe the site of a new skyline off of Lake St. Clair, by Detroit."

He shook his head, in bafflement.

"An assignment from his graduate days in Ann Arbor," she smiled warmly, and observed him for his reaction. "It is not too bad, yes?"

Gellerman nodded. "Yes, not bad at all."

She took his arm and guided him out of the room. "He had this idea for creating a grouping of similar skylines all around the Great Lakes; those interested him very much as one geographical unity. It's in his notebooks, which fortunately I have kept." She squeezed his wrist. "Perhaps when you *trust me more*, I can show it to you!" She flirted like a teenager.

He nodded, dumbfounded, and followed her back into the dining area.

Standing there was Dora, the daughter. In a white blouse with ruffled sleeves and short tartan skirt, she looked fourteen. So the stage was set, he felt, for the next scene; what was that to be? This was brilliant theater, filled with surprise, changes of pace, and incongruous happenings. Touches of Ionesco?

Dora put her hand forward and greeted him, and he took her hand cordially. Actually, she resembled neither the mother nor the grandmother. Curly hair, small nose, pink skin, trim figure, short. What role was she to play in this? he pondered. He knew his role, at least: the intellectual fool, the country-bumpkin believer. Curiously, "Gimpel the Fool" by I. B. Singer struck him; he had a model to follow, if he wished—that perennial fool whose total belief is honed and tested by outrageous lies and fabulous acts, only to eventually become saintly. Saintly Gellerman, yes.

Now, as they moved around, arranging the dining table (adjusting the extra leaf), the women seating him with a cognac in the salon, he wondered what the remaining scenes of this play would portray? Tonight, and later on? He was open to conjecture, to a script of surprise and manipulation. You had to give them credit; they were a super team, crazy Mother and quiet sane daughter, and the spirit of Raoul hovering in the background, infusing the apartment, inspiring the play. Schubert seemed to be playing, hauntingly.

So was it all fantasy, or was it part real? Which part was which? Some of those photos perhaps, but how? Easy enough to cut and paste, as they did on the Internet, and/or have a photographer touch up. What about the notebooks that Madame had proclaimed? Might he read that, and then be able to get a copy and check that out, verify in some way, especially back home? . . . A long shot. How about DNA? But that seemed impossible, given the absence of RW. But let's say it was all fantasy, he mused as the cognac coursed through his blood. What did that suggest? A single woman's mad obsession with Wallenberg? Wouldn't it be more significant if there was indeed that group of worshippers, believing in RW like some ancient Greek or Jewish religious cult?

Over the three-course dinner of bean soup, a paprika meat stew, cucumber salad, he went through the motions of a conversation, listening to the mother and daughter chat about Dora's work on her thesis (on childhood trauma), the new scandal of the socialist government, the recent novel of Kertész. During the talk, he observed the young woman eating like a bird, her tiny adam's apple barely moving with her small bites, and every now and then looking over at Manny, checking on his interest. She seemed to be trying hard, in her body language, to restrain her impatience with the mother's focus on her. Zsuzsa meanwhile laughed heartily, scooped food onto Manny's plate at every opportunity, teased her daughter, and hosted the dinner with cool ease. She had put on a little jacket for the dinner table, and on her lapel wore a small golden band.

"What is that?" he asked.

"This hamsa?" she responded, shaking her head at his ignorance.

What was most strange, however, was that he didn't feel like an intruder here, an American stranger, but one of them, a family member. Yes, it was boring and unfamiliar (deeply) and the characters were odd, but he was made to feel at home, a natural part of unnatural things. So, once again, the course of the play had turned slightly, this time more subtly.

After dinner, he was escorted into the heavy salon, where he waited until the ladies cleaned up. He listened to the music—now Mozart?—and picked up a book.

An old edition of the work of Louis Henry Sullivan, the "pioneer of sky-scrapers." He sat on the pale green Chesterfield sofa, decorated with a white lace shawl, and looked through the book. Yes, a Mozart clarinet concerto. A bit of sweetness to lighten the somber room. What was next for him? Some magical trap, a central European seduction? If he were taking opium in a Shanghai den, would it be any stranger than this? Not by much. He waited, heard a clatter of cups and saucers, a car whisking by. Odors sweet and strange wafted by. What did all this have to do with his mission, to search for the truth about Raoul? Thank god, his colleagues were not there to witness this sort of "research." They'd laugh him out of the profession!

Well, there could be more curious hands-on research resources. He stood and went to the framed photograph corner, and there, bending closer, read the text of one, which was in Hungarian, Swedish, English:

> The Royal Swedish Legation in Budapest confirms that the aforementioned [a pass-port photo of an older couple] will travel to Sweden in accordance with the scheme of repatriation as authorized by the Swedish Ministry for Foreign Affairs. The afore-mentioned is also included in a collective passport. Until his repatriation the holder and his domicile are under the protection of the Royal Swedish Legation.
>
> Validity: Expires 14 days after entry into Sweden.

"Oh, you've discovered how my grandmother was saved," murmured Dora. "'The Protective Passport,' or 'letter of protection.' We've brought the dessert and tea."

She set it down on the small footstool, asked if that was all right, and sat across from him in a wing chair. She took up her knitting and looked like a little princess, feet swinging off the floor, in the huge chair.

"Mother is becoming more comfortable with you, more trusting," she observed, attending to her wool and needles. "She believes, I think, that your interest is genuine."

"There seems to be this question of authenticity around here," he retorted, "whether I am who I appear to be." And whether your mother is who she says she is, he might have added.

She smiled, her teeth a bit crooked. "Maybe I can hear what you are thinking."

His turn to smile.

"And you are satisfied with your student's thesis work?"

He nodded. "Yes, it is fine."

"Does it add anything to the 'controversy?'"

A new admiration rose in him for her. "Oh, I think it is a solid work. It's not a PhD thesis, you understand. But there is much that remains . . . unaccountable for, unexplained. Unknown."

"Lots of 'uns,'" noted Dora dryly.

Gellerman smiled.

"And tell me this, Professor," asked the sharp daughter, "are we also part of the 'unaccountable' facts?"

Just then the mother came in, rubbing her hands with lotion, he saw, and she took a seat across from them, in another chair.

"So you have been having a good chat? Have I interrupted?" Her look was eager, greedy even.

Dora shook her head, and Gellerman followed, adding, "I have been getting quietly tested."

Zsuzsanna laughed, "Have you passed?"

"You will have to ask the teacher."

Dora made a face. She helped serve the dessert, fresh fruit in small dishes, to both her mother and Manny. And then she said quietly that she had to depart; she had an appointment. Her mother was surprised, but then half giggled, hugged the girl, and said to Manny, as he stood up too, that she certainly hoped he was going to stay on; it was still very early. More of a declaration than an inquiry.

He avoided hugging little Dora, who without her heels would have been under five feet. She moved off into the foyer, for her coat and the door.

"I think she is rather special," Manny offered, "full of a quiet poise, and . . . intuition."

The mother clapped. "Yes, you have hit it on the head. Sometimes she knows things way before I can understand them."

Oh, and what had she intuited about me? he wanted to ask, when Zsuzsa beckoned him toward the large oak desk.

"Come, I will read to you a letter her grandfather, my father, wrote to me, which will be of interest perhaps."

At the desk she pulled open the second drawer on the right side, took out a green folder with a sheaf of letters, and, setting him down in a straight-backed chair, put on her reading glasses and searched through the letters. She proceeded to read in English:

> *My Dear Daughter,*
> *Although you are only a little child now, and do not understand all of my words, I want to tell you that your father loves you very much, that you are and will be a special girl, and that, along with common sense and a good heart, you must always rely on your intuition. This will tell you what to do in different and difficult situations, when you are at a loss for logic or past history. You must decide swiftly, about a person, a situation, a friend or enemy, and the best you can do is to allow your intuition to have its say, and to follow its way. This has always worked for me, whether in a difficult situation in Chicago, or in Haifa, or in Budapest. So once you learn the meaning of the word, and learn to listen to or consult your intuition, see if it works for you, as it has for me. I know that you will have a powerful one.*

She looked up at Manny, her face blissful as if she had just been spoken to by God.

All he could do was to nod, and stay silent, and listen to the sounds of the grandfather clock ticking, and the cars going by.

"Would you mind if I looked at the letter?"

She gave him a look as though he were a thief, about to steal something from her!

And then she handed over the page.

Manny stared at the legible handwriting, felt the thin quality of the paper, looked up at her, with the green folder beside her on the desk. "But this is in English?"

"Of course, why not? He never learned Hungarian to write it well, as he did with German. You knew that he wrote to Grandfather Gustaf in English as well as Swedish, didn't you? Besides, he wanted me to know English, the language of the future, he believed. He was right, wasn't he?"

"And those are all in English?"

She smiled, took the green folder into her arms like holding a child, shook her head. "Some are in English, some in German, but what difference? They are all magical." She rocked with it in her arms, his "inspired" lady.

He was bemused by her maternal pose, thought it best to say little of his avid interest in those letters, and said it was getting late; perhaps he should go now.

"No, no, please, you must stay on for a while anyway. Here, sit, and while I bathe, I will give you another letter to read." She giggled, "I must take my therapy bath, always at 10:30; so you will excuse me for a while?" A glance of girlish glory on her oval face.

What was she up to now? And this tempting offer?

She set him down, by his shoulders, and rummaged in her letters, selected one, and handed it to him, slowly letting go of it. What variation of cat and mouse was she playing? Smiling, she went to her disc player, made a selection, put it on, and took her leave. In a moment the jazzy rhythms of *Rhapsody in Blue* by Gershwin came on, for Manny's lullaby.

He sat, baffled, like a buffalo longing for the range, struck with a Valium dart. The letter from Raoul was addressed to his wife:

> *Dearest Klara,*
>
> *By now you will have received the papers documenting my arrangements with Kurt Becher, the German administrator, with whom I have had successful dealings. If anything were to happen to me, he will be able to provide for you. Though he is a Nazi, and a special representative for Himmler, I have found him to be reliable in past situations. He used to work with my cousins in Stockholm in banking, because of his own connections with German banks. And in Budapest on several occasions he has helped me stop a deportation of Jews by the Arrow Cross, and on two occasions he also aided me in preventing Eichmann from performing his own deportations. He has known of our family's existence, and has never betrayed the trust here. Naturally, there are strong reasons for his remaining true to his word while I am away, both financial and political. He understands that I will support him with the Americans, if they should capture him and try him for war crimes. He also understands that there are payments awaiting him in Geneva, once certain conditions are met. Now you should take my arrangement papers with Becher, composed in German, and send them along with Per Anger in a sealed envelope—or with Lars Berg—when they return to Sweden. They are both reliable, and they will have instructions of where to keep the envelopes in a safety deposit box. In fact they will be put into the same safe bank—not Enskilda—that our own papers are kept, should anything happen to me. They will provide insurance for you, as well as other papers for future safety.*

Some will protest my connection and arrangements with a Nazi like Becher. But in this era, this confusing day and terrible age, you must sleep with strange bedfellows, a little like Ishmael when he finds himself in bed with a very strange, tattooed Indian gentleman, Queequeg, in my favorite American novel, Moby Dick. *Thus I have had to deal with Becher and other unsavory sorts, even an occasional SS man, for me to get my work done effectively. Exquisite moral distinctions I must disregard for now, when I have a larger moral focus, namely, the saving of the Hungarian Jews. Toward that end, I have sacrificed many of my own moral niceties, and still feel clean. Early on, in Stockholm, before even departing for Budapest, Olson, the American chief of the OSS, a good man, warned me that I was not entering an academic school room or philosophy class, but a dangerous situation where Jewish lives were at stake, and whoever could help in that mission was worth dealing with.* Whoever. *There is no doubt that I shall be blamed for such dealings, now, and maybe later in short-term history, but I will not feel my hands dirty or my conscience guilty. I take some solace in this position, and I want you to know this.*

Please take care of our little prize, and yourself, until I see you again.

Yours faithfully, R.

Manny sat there, stunned, staring at the handwriting, and trying to make sense of all this. If he could perhaps make a copy of this letter and match up the handwriting with samples in the RW archive . . .

Gershwin played on, scenting the room with those American bluesy rhythms, and Manny wished he were back there, in his native land, walking past the green, watching the kids toss their Frisbees and the headbanded joggers with attached iPods looking like playful aliens, and be enfolded again within the easy zone of native playland. But instead he was sitting here, interned, in a stuffy apartment, suffocating in history. And his warden was a few rooms away, taking her bath! How ludicrous could this get! And who was she? And how'd she acquire or invent these letters? . . .

His heart palpitated, as he contemplated the possibility that these letters were authentic . . . Absurd! Probably some shrewd amateur imitations. Still, a copy for handwriting analysis would be very helpful indeed.

Switching up from this eerie situation, his mind wandered back to home turf . . . Playing baseball as a high school boy in Prospect Park, and hitting line drives in the parade grounds . . . in Madison, playing a shallow center field for the history department graduate team, in softball, and challenging the batters to hit straightaway over his head . . . in Hanover, playing tennis against his regular partner and figuring out how to hit the high lob to his backhand . . . These sporting memories calmed him, drawing him back to the familiar . . . Suddenly crossing his memory was Jackie Robinson, taking his provocative lead off third base, daring the pitcher to throw over, waiting to dart for home . . .

"So, I see, you have finished your homework?" she teased him, in her white faded bathrobe, looking like Garbo half sprawled on her thick divan. "What do you think?"

Gellerman shook his head. "How was your bath?"

"Ah, wonderful, always, though I stayed a shorter duration so you wouldn't be alone." She brushed her hair vigorously.

"Tell me, do you have that other letter, the arrangements with that Becher?"

"Of course, but that is in German, and I wasn't sure how well you knew German. Do you?"

"Not really. But I would like to see it anyway."

She laughed, her teeth gleaming. "I am sure you would. And I will show it to you, not just now perhaps. But I am glad you have found this one of interest. Now, join me with a little cognac I hope?"

Reluctantly—as he wanted to leave—he permitted this offering, and she poured two shots in cognac glasses.

"*L'chaim!*" she toasted. "To our future union."

He nodded, sipped, and wondered which union she had in mind?

"I have much to share with you," she offered, rubbing her white cheeks with a lotion, "the more I trust you, your sincerity."

"Yes," he said.

"Not merely letters, but a Moscow diary, and thoughts, memories, feelings. Maybe some secrets . . ."

He drained the remaining cognac. Best to hear her rich nonsense with this rich liquor flowing through him and Gershwin serenading.

"You have read some Kabbalah?" she asked.

He shook his head.

"That's a pity, really. There is much wisdom there. I study it."

"I see."

"You would do well to read some Zohar. And other texts of Rabbis Hayyim Vital or Dov Baer, or the visions by Ba'al Shem Tov. They are magical."

"I'm afraid not."

"I understand, a rationalist and a skeptic, all the way through. Why not? You are a historian." She smiled, sympathetically. "But I must tell you that my father was comforted very much by reading some of these materials in

Lybianka. You know that the usual name for the Kabbalah is in fact *hommah nistarah*, or 'the hidden science.' So it is not altogether fuzzy and foolish thinking, you realize."

He nodded, again not understanding. He blurted out, "But how in the world did your father get a hold of a Zohar sitting in a Lybianka cell?"

She smiled, put lotion on her cheeks, carefully. "Do you think we were not able to reach him there? Do you think that we left him alone, the way everyone else did? No, my dear professor, it was not like that. We did what we had to do to keep hope alive in him and to nourish him through the hard times. The concrete walls of Stalinism could not keep his loved ones from reaching him, loving him."

He waited patiently, and then stood to go. "I think it's time, you know; it is rather late, and—"

"I won't hear of it. Don't be silly. The bed is already made up for you. You can check on it. It is actually in my father's study."

This news jolted Manny, just as she had planned, the perfect bait.

He took it and moved into the study, where the single bed was turned down, fresh sheets crisp, hospital corners. Astonishing, this carefully prepared plan, or trap. He used the adjoining half bathroom to do his ablutions, aided by the fresh toothbrush sitting on the washbasin. He slipped on the bathrobe, folded neatly for him, returned to the small room, and got into the bed. A small bedside lamp was lit, and he looked around, like a mouse carefully assessing its chances for escape. Except he felt more like a cat, an alley cat that had been taken in from the streets and was being converted into a house pet. He scratched at his narrow beard.

He lay there listening to the whispering sounds of the streets, and a clock ticking on the desk. And waited. Was he supposed to get up and investigate? . . . He lay there, making out the framed photographs on the walls, the desk. He wondered, What if? What if the whole thing, this crazy fairytale, had an element or two of truth in it? Just one, or two? Like the mother had in fact known Raoul, through the parents who were saved by him? Or Raoul had kept up a friendship, even perhaps a correspondence, with the family? Maybe Zsuzsa had indeed recovered a letter or two? Any of that would be interesting enough, without all the other facts and details. Much could be mined from a single vein. As for the rest, well, let her have her embellishments, her strong fantasy; what was wrong with that?

The sound of someone walking about, lightly. He stiffened, wondering what to do if the lady appeared at the door, with that beckoning look? . . . He lay there, perfectly still, sorry he hadn't turned out the lamp.

But the footsteps passed on by, through the adjoining living room, and no one appeared . . . Maybe it was the ghost of Raoul walking about? Could be, he mused in his drowsy state. Maybe this was the residence where the ghost lived part-time? And walked about in the night, like in a Poe tale? . . .

Well, whatever it was, it set his nerves on edge, and he used that phrase again, *What if?* A First Alert warning beeped in his brain, whenever he got too complacent about things here . . .

Throughout the night, he seemed to hear more muted footsteps, several times sitting up, bolt upright, even pulling the light on, since the room was black due to the closed shutters . . . Was it the madwoman creeping around, checking on him? Or, more probable, the ghost of Raoul, wandering up and down, unnerved by the stranger in his room, on his daybed? . . .

Seeking sleep, he focused on Jackie taking his lead from first base, leaning low, arms dangling, ready to go! . . . and next on his little cellist, practicing his vibrato, playing the Bach prelude . . .

In the morning, he was a proper guest, sitting at the breakfast table, dutifully accepting the soft-boiled eggs and toast with jam from Zsuzsa, and nodding or answering politely whenever a question was put to him ("How did you sleep? Did you have to get up during the night? Was it quiet enough?") The sunlight was filtering through the white lace curtains; Mrs. Frank (or W.) was busy pampering him, and he accepted his role.

"Tell me," she said at their second cup of coffee, "do you think, if we continue to trust each other, that you will want to help me with a project?"

He held his espresso cup, just before it reached his lips.

"And what do you have in mind?"

"Well," she said, leaning forward demurely, "I believe that many people will want to know my story, or my father's story with the family. And since I am not a writer," she laughed girlishly, "perhaps you would want to help me?"

He slowly raised the cup again, eyeing her and trying to absorb her words. "You mean, a memoir of sorts?"

"Why, I suppose you can call it that." Her face was glowing, translucent.

He drank, savoring the taste, and wondered which bridge he would go for a walk on, the Lancet or the Chain? "That may be interesting, yes. When were you thinking of this?"

Her shoulders shrugged, and she smiled. "I have been patient; I can be patient further. If you would help me, however, I know that I can get to the materials much quicker."

Oh, he liked that noun; it rang up his historian's register! "Yes, it would take time to gather and examine the materials."

"I think I have many of the materials here, but some are hidden away, in the countryside. But it wouldn't take too long to gather them all up."

He restrained his heart from fluttering. "Fair enough. When you think you are ready, we will consider the matter very seriously."

"And how long do you think the actual writing would take?"

"Oh, I don't quite know, maybe six months? A year? . . ."

She nodded, soberly.

Patiently, Gellerman wiped his eyeglass lenses. "I better get going now; I have some work to do, and my plane leaves very early morning, you realize."

"No, I didn't realize."

He got up and she escorted him to the foyer, where she helped him with his raincoat.

"You will call me later, of course?"

He thanked her for all her hospitality, thought better of kissing her cheek, and shook her hand. "Yes, I will."

Outside the air was thin and clear, and though it was cloudy, the city never looked finer. Or was it rather the sense of escape that filled his lungs? Escape back to the real, the solid.

He walked toward the river and the first bridge, along the busy streets, but when he came across a used bookstore, he wandered in.

Finding a section on English books, he browsed. A mix of real books and incidental items. He came upon a book he had read many years ago, *The Varieties of Religious Experience* by William James. He skimmed through it, stopping at the chapter called "The Sick Soul," read a few of the interesting quotes on failure from Goethe and Robert Louis Stevenson, and moved on to passages about melancholy and the neurotic condition. He blew the dust away, took the surprise volume to the shopkeeper, paid, and walked outside again, grateful that he had reading for the evening and the plane ride.

Oh, it was quite wonderful to be free and easy on these streets, away from neurosis, fantasy, and madness, and back out into the world of normalcy. Soon, he came to the Chain bridge and began walking across it, toward the Buda hills, passing pedestrians. The steel-gray Danube ran below, choppy, and he looked toward the upward bend of the river, leading toward Prague. The wind blew, and at one point snatched his cap away! But a couple retrieved it, and he thanked them. His cell phone rang, startling him.

"Yes?"

"Will you say good-bye to me?"

Who? "Yes, of course."

"This afternoon at five, we can meet in the Central Café?"

"It's a date, thank you."

CHAPTER 12

On the Malév Airline morning flight to Stockholm he read through his notes, which he had worked on all through the evening and next day, after his tea with Dora, the skeptical daughter. The Zsuzsanna tale was an extraordinary one, no doubt—worthy of an Isaac B. Singer story, filled with miraculous faith and fairytale myth. Meticulously, Manny had written down everything about the meetings, from sepia photographs to sensational claims, not knowing what was important and what was dross; at home he would have much to digest. And at the tea Dora was once again sizing him up, to see whether he was remaining honest and trustworthy. (With her short skirt and pretty smile, was there also a seductive subtext?) In turn, Manny asked the small dark-haired beauty to check up on her mother, and see if she was truly serious in writing a memoir, and if so, to help her gather her "materials." Dora smiled, her thick lips and shining eyes mobile— mocking him or her mother? Or both? ("Yes, Mum does have a small desk locked up in the country cottage," she acknowledged, "and it's remained a secret even from me.") At the end he left with her his copy of William James, saying, "This may interest Mom." Now, riding smoothly above the white clouds, he felt satisfied, having come through a challenge, and now heading back to Sweden to check out his mole in the bank.

Back in his B and B in Stockholm, he wrote an e-mail note to Peter, and when he heard nothing by the next morning, he walked over to the Enskilda and asked for him. A gray-haired gentleman emerged from the barred-off area, escorted Manny to a private chair, and asked what was his business with "this Peter?" Manny explained it was a personal matter. And what was his last name? Manny was taken aback and tried to recall a name. The young banker nodded politely, and rejoined that there had been "a Peter" who had been transferred to another branch, beyond the city, and that if Manny wished to leave a note for him, he would send it on. Helpless, Manny scribbled a note and departed.

Gathering his thoughts, he walked around the town, past the tidy shops and the seaside yachts, took a coffee, and spent an hour and a half in a pocket-sized museum of Swedish interior designs, observing a new robotic vacuum cleaner and new automatic coffee machine and flat wall-mounted stereo, and assorted other elegant inventions dating back to the 1950s. After, he walked back to the street of the bank just near the five o'clock close, and waited across the street alongside a busy cheese shop. Soon, the employees began filing out steadily; no sign of him. After a half hour of standing there in the fine June weather, he moved off, found out the listed time of the next morning's opening, and meandered about again. He took a dinner in a small restaurant, observing the well-dressed patrons and thought about what it might mean if no Peter turned up.

The next morning, after another useless e-mail, he was back at his observation post at seven thirty, watching the trickling of employees enter the bank, and then a fuller stream near nine o'clock, but there was no Peter. Manny was perplexed, anxious, shocked. What should or could he do? Go to the police? Hire a private detective? He held onto his cap in the wind and took a taxi over to the Municipal Building holding the archivist records. He hunted about and found the archivist who had been kindly to him on his previous research expedition. He invited the archivist to lunch, and told his tale. "Weird, isn't it?" he asked. The fellow, Bengt, continued to eat his open-faced sandwich, and responded, "Perhaps not so weird, considering the family. The Wallenbergs are notorious for their secrecy and privacy. It is as if they are behind a high wall, powerful and private, and it is not easy to break through."

"Any suggestions for what I might do?"

"Not really," he shrugged. "They are very powerful, almost like a state within a state, with its own ministers and rules of governance. Moreover, nothing can be proved. Where is the evidence for any wrongdoing? Just the e-mail caution? That is not enough."

"So, am I supposed to . . . forget the whole matter?"

Bengt nodded slowly. "I am afraid, unless you happen to know the king, or the major editors of the big newspapers, and even then . . ."—he held his palms out—"there is not much to do."

Manny tried to absorb all that; he excused himself to go to the bathroom, on the way passing a wall of half mirrors. On his way back, he stopped by those mirrors and witnessed a rather helpless soul in a frayed sport jacket with a wearied look on his face. Defeat in the eyes. Is this where his goose chase was leading him?

At the table Manny thanked Bengt and said he'd be in touch.

"Please do not judge all of us by the Enskilda Wallenbergs," he said, standing. "By the standards and values of Raoul, yes, but not the others. Raoul was a courageous soul, and more and more we Swedes look up to him, and what he accomplished in his young life. So, please keep up your search; it is a worthy one."

Manny nodded, and felt the need to get out—of Sweden, and of Europe; the sudden real-life detective story, coming on top of his Hungarian theater of the absurd, was too unreal, too unsettling.

Back home on the hillside in New Hampshire, he wandered about, reflecting upon all that had occurred over there, surrounded now by his old environment, where country life and class schedules and boring routines were the principal matters at hand. Plus the usual Iraq war declarations by elected liars, crooks, and cowards, and yet a new shooting in a high school. Freedom, USA-style, meant shooting guns . . . No dark history hovering here, no odd fantasies, no unfathomable puzzles; reality here appeared easier and clearer, especially at the campus oasis. The psyche could stay cool and resilient, and not be subject to flights of fancy and fantasy. Let the heated memories and dementia of Budapest remain over there, along with the covered-up secrets of Stockholm. We here would go about our business of seeing movies, tossing Frisbees, throwing baseballs, bombing distant countries and shooting up the school kids.

As for written history and RW, the old scripts and traditional perspectives would hold their ground. A memoir by the bizarre woman might be written for her daughter and grandchildren, not for the public. The Swedish-Russian Working Group could renew itself and go on digging, and come up against the stone wall created by Putin's Russia, and Swedish cowardice. And maybe one day even Angela's thesis could become a university monograph, or better yet, an alternative narrative from that of Prof. Gellerman, which would focus up front and center on the lingering doubts and cloudy coverup. The biographies now—and those in the future—suffered from lack of concrete evidence, important and huge gaps, speculation parading as fact.

Driving over to Maine to hear the boy play and see the music camp, he passed through vast areas of open space and mountains, while listening to NPR (before it cut out). The usual fair-mindedness, giving both sides of the Iraq situation—did it have two sides?—delivered by the melodious voices. At one point the reporter was interviewing a Baghdad family about the implosion of their neighborhood in the past six months, a tale that proved to be informative and moving about daily life for Iraqis, not the headlines; but abruptly the studio announcer cut them off, thanking them and moving on. The "segment" was finished, its time allotment of three to four minutes used up. The melodious voice jumped from the really interesting family to a cute songwriter from Nashville! Manny was taken aback, angry. Is that where his dues went, for such stupidity? NPR, seeking increased "marketshare" like any commercial station, had become milk toast mainstream, its old liberal bite gone. Imagine them doing the RW story, giving it a full four-minute segment, providing both sides, of course, both Gromyko and the Swedish ambassador, for *fairness*.

A few hours of green hills later, he found the boy messy-haired, bushy-tailed, and excited. He gave him the visiting presents: two musical scores, a few DVDs (of conductors) and CDs of cellists, and a leather pouch for his music. "Wow, Dad, these are great!" He hugged his father warmly. In return, Manny asked him to play a little, before dinner, and they found an empty studio in the woods. Josh played a prelude of Bach, slow and lovely, and Manny applauded his rich sound. Smiling puckishly, he said, "Want to hear something else a little different, Dad?"

"Sure," he told him.

He commenced to play a new piece, strange and unfamiliar, odd sounds mingling with felt melodies, and the whole thing mixed and surprising. After five or six minutes, he was finished, and looked up, "What do you think?"

"Well, I don't really know. But it's interesting. Who wrote it?"

His face glowing, he said, "I did."

"Really?"

"Really."

"Hey," he uttered, "that's wonderful!"

"Thanks a lot. It's not finished yet."

Manny paused. "Do you have a name yet?"

He nodded, shyly, and said, "I call it the Wallenberg Suite."

Taken aback, he didn't know what to do, but he was so moved by his impulse that he got up and gave him a tight hug and kiss.

"That's special, my sweet composer, just very special."

"I am really glad you like it, Dad, 'cause I wrote it for you. I mean for your work on him."

Manny kneeled in front of him and stared at his hazel eyes. "You are a great boy. So thoughtful and so talented. Let's take you for a real treat over at that restaurant in Bridgeton, the one you've wanted to go to, okay?"

Growing excited, he said, "Oh, yes, that'll be a real treat all right!" And he stood up and began putting away his cello, his bow, the endpin. "Can I get whatever I want?"

"Whatever."

Outside in the early evening the large trees were swaying in the light wind; they had never looked stronger or finer, and you could smell the delicious forest aromas. If Maine in summer was a piece of heaven, he mused as they walked to his cabin to put away the cello, what was it when you just had a suite composed and played in your honor?

Over their dinner of lobsters and baked potatoes, they discussed the suite and the music he was aiming for . . . He explained how you "can't really try, Dad, to give exact sounds you know to match the feelings or meanings," and he nodded in agreement. "But I did want it to sound sad, like melancholy . . . that's how I understand his situation, so I also tried to play it with more vibrato wherever I could . . . Did you hear it?"

"Well, yeah, I think I did," he answered.

"Can we get more sour cream for the potato, Dad? The lobster's great!"

Later, at twilight, leaving Camp Encore Coda, he felt renewed by the boy, renewed and refreshed. His youth, his talent, his ebullience, seemed to be of a piece with the thick aromatic forest of the camp, maybe a little more magical. Sweden, Maine, and the Wallenberg Suite had washed away Budapest and that other Sweden.

On the way back, driving across empty western Maine, Manny was again taken aback by the vast space of open lands and low mountains for miles and miles. Could they have dumped Raoul, after Lybianka, in some forsaken land like this, over in Siberia? Simple disposal of the body. Manny pulled up at the side of the empty road, took out his laptop, and began to scribble notes.

Back at the college the next day, Manny looked up Sven Nagstrom, a semi-retired engineer who had come from Sweden as a student years ago, earned a PhD, and stayed on to teach here, with his lively eccentric wife. They sat in Rosey Jekes coffee shop, and he discussed the problem of the Wallenberg bank situation. How he had been cautioned and stonewalled, and then the whistleblower had suddenly disappeared.

He raised his eyebrows, sipped his espresso, and said, "It sounds strange all right, but not unexpected. They are a difficult family, from everything I know. Very difficult and very private, even secretive."

"But do you think they could dare be 'criminal' now?"

Sven smiled narrowly. "Isn't the line always thin between criminal and cautiously immoral for powerful people?"

Manny stared at his blue eyes and nodded.

"I don't think it's any different here in America. When you get that rich and that powerful, you can do what you want, and maybe adjust that thin line around a bit as well."

He had a point. "Still, I wished I knew a good Stockholm detective," Manny replied, which caused him to laugh aloud. "They probably own their own firm of detectives."

Later at home Manny scribbled down a few paragraphs about that thin line, with thoughts of following it up later on:

In America in the late forties, just after the war, how interested were we really in saving a Swedish life? Especially if that life was somehow invested in the OSS, our CIA of the time? No matter how much Iver Olsen, who recruited Raoul for the OSS and his special "Pond" project, might have fought to rescue RW, our government was already engaged in the Cold War with the Soviet Union. The last thing the US needed was to show support for someone who worked for our Secret Service in Hungary and who might have been in some cooperation with the Germans there. No, our government would be happy to put pressure on weak Sweden to try to save Wallenberg, but we weren't interested in doing the same to our forceful enemy who held him. Cowardice, or expediency? A bit of both?

It was more important for us to save the German rocket scientists who were or worked for the Nazis, and other scientists, but not a gutsy Swedish diplomat who had served the War Refugee Board and saved Jews. Fighting our newly declared foe, the Soviets, was far more crucial than rescuing a single noble soul who had worked for Good. (Or was it that, just as we had failed to bomb Auschwitz when we had the knowledge and the opportunity—one bombing would have destroyed the train tracks, and the Nazis were not going to rebuild those in 1943–44—the Jews, or their Swedish savior, were simply not worth our precious time?)

Manny scheduled a full day on Monday to see several students, check the library for two interlibrary loan research books, play a tennis match, have a dinner date. A sunny summer day in green New Hampshire, where the air was clear, the sky wide and blue, the worries few. (Intruded upon only by the occasional e-mail that might come shooting through, presenting a problem or challenge.) From May to October, rural New England was the place to be, a native version of Tuscany, only with more lakes, fewer tourists, better English.

Gellerman felt his routine was too cozy and easy for his project, so he decided to make a point of imprinting Raoul amidst his daily doings, reading about him, writing notes, imagining him. This focus on RW worked like a dark point on the day's lily-white surface, a Rorshach smudge to be interpreted in a variety of ways. Manny in New Hampshire 2006 sought daily contact with RW in Budapest 1944 and in Lybianka Prison 1945, and this smudge stood for mystery and remembrance. Searching for Raoul daily signaled to Manny's interior self his desire to be in constant touch with the forgotten soul.

Why? For living memory? For truth in history? For their developing, strange friendship?

And whenever Manny would read the periodic news article about the sincere Christian faith of the current president, he smiled to himself, sitting at the hotel inn, and recalled that other Christian. Why did Raoul do all that, really? Manny wondered again, Why endanger his life when he was so young? Was it because of the appointed mission given to him by the Hungarian businessman Lauer and then by the American OSS and Olsen? Was it because of the crazy woman's Jewish grandparents in the Budapest orphanage, and his affection for the Jewish mother? Was it because he had always been the black sheep Outsider, with a touch of Jewish blood, in the Wallenberg family? Or was it simply in his blood to resist, to stand up against brutal authority and overwhelming odds, as he had done as a young officer in Swedish basic training? There were Christians and there were Christians, and maybe the best, or most courageous, were the least religious.

In the summer air, looking out on the green of the college from the inn's white rocking chair, Manny reflected, and tried to fathom the truth.

At home he found new e-mails awaiting him, including one from the lady in Budapest:

> Dear Professor,
> I hope you will take seriously my request for you to help me compose my Life Story. It will surely make for interesting reading, don't you think? I have already started to "gather my private materials" from the country house, for us to work with. And naturally I will soon have to reveal to you a few of my long-cherished secrets, once we are working together on the project. I have waited patiently for the right person to trust to help me with this, and I now believe you are the one to put my full faith into. May I only add that Dora, who has excellent judgment about people, fully agrees.

So the carrot was laid out there for him—but carrot or bait? Manny smiled inwardly and decided to wait a day or two before answering her, as he turned to other messages. A few from college students and colleagues, another from a DC friend, nothing urgent. After reading them, he adjourned to his study and turned to his new focus. From reading the materials of Per Anger and Berg, and actual notes from RW, he compressed them and wrote:

On Nov. 13, 1944, the German head in Budapest, Veesenmayer, reported this to Berlin: "The deportation of the Budapest Jewry is going according to plan, despite the technical difficulties. According to SS Obersturmbannführer Eichmann's report, up to this day 27,000 Jews of both sexes who are able to march and work have left for imperial grounds. We can count on a further 40,000 able bodied Jews who will be transported daily in groups of 2,000–4,000."

In Nov. 1944, on the road from Budapest to Hegyeshalom in western Hungary, thousands of Jews, old and young, were being forced to walk the 240-kilometer route, an eight-day walk in bitter cold, biting winds, wet conditions. The strong ones who made it were sent to work camps in Austria; the weaker ones were sent to concentrations camps; others fell and died on the way. The forced Death March was started on Nov. 9 by the ruling Hungarian Nazis, the Arrow Cross. When Wallenberg learned about it, he alerted his driver, Vilmos Langerfeld, the young Jew, and, loading up their Studebaker coupe with food and water, they drove out on the road to see for themselves the grim march. What he saw shocked him, and he wrote notes to make an immediate report. On Nov. 23–24 he delivered a brief "Reminder" report personally to Kemény Gábor's Ministry for Foreign Affairs, and later, receiving little satisfaction from the Arrow Cross, he turned to the German overseer of Hungarian affairs, Edmund Veesenmayer. Here are RW's own words, factual, restrained, diplomatic, in his "Reminder."

The Jews transported to Germany fit the following categories: Jews who had been sent to forced labor, Jews who had been gathered together through police raids and taken to a Budapest location like the brick factory at Újpest, Jews who were gathered for trench digging; and after digging the trenches around Budapest, they were sent to Germany on foot.

The forced-labor people came in quite warm clothing and good shoes. They carry their belongings in a backpack or in a sack. The military commanders put in charge of them try to provide them with appropriate places to sleep.

The above-mentioned categories of Jewish persons carry their belongings usually in a sack, or simply under their arms. The women do not usually have shoes suitable for a longer march. Most of them do not have gloves.

The road from the brick factory to the border is 240 km. They mostly do it in eight days. During this time, the Jews are not given heated places to sleep.

Most overnight stops do not have appropriate facilities.

Most of the Jews get hot soup only once or twice during the journey to the border. The reason for this inappropriate provision is partly the lack of kitchen items, so if, for example. 2,500 people arrive at such a place at one time, only half of them can get food.

The horrible sufferings and the inappropriate treatment result in some of them dying of digestion problems.

Those having protection from abroad are treated badly, because neither at the Budapest locations (like the Újpest brick factory), nor at Hegyeshalom are foreign documents respected 100 percent.

On Nov. 23 and 24, both secretaries of the Royal Swedish Embassy traveled to Hegyeshalom to check the originality of the protecting passports there. The above report is an accurate account of the experiences during that trip. In addition, the following perceptions were made:

Among the marchers, there is a large number of people aged 60–70, and severely ill ones, paralyzed ones, etc.; 10- to 14-year-olds; an Aryan woman; people without shoes; people whose belongings had been taken away by the Arrow Cross in the brick factory; and finally, people whose documents or passports have been destroyed in the brick factory or elsewhere.

Many of the marchers claimed they did not eat normally or did not sleep normally and they could not wash themselves during the whole time.

In Gönyű, there are a couple hundred severely ill people lying in a towboat without sufficient food, medicine, or medical care, in the most appalling situation in all respects.

In Hegyeshalom, the people were given over to the German transportation section. The German SS officers were hitting and kicking them.

In Mosonmagyaróvár, seven people died on Nov. 24, and another seven on Nov. 23. Another diplomat had counted 42 corpses on the road two days before.

The people are so exhausted that they are barely human. Men and women are relieving themselves without leaving the road, and without minding the others around them. As the committee wanted to distribute some food from its own supply, they were attacked by the masses; people got in a fight in order to get the little sandwich packs.

As a summary, it should be noted that the happenings on the Viennese highway are not in the least in accordance with the often-mentioned "humane and just" solution to the Jewish question. The Swedish Embassy has raised the issue at meetings with his Excellence, the Deputy Prime Minister (Szöllősi Jenő), the Minister of Foreign Affairs (Kemény Gábor), the Minister of Internal Affairs (Vajna Gábor), and higher-ranking officers in the party, but nothing has changed whatsoever. Moreover, the Embassy had been denied the permission to send trucks with food there; it has become officially possible only in the last two days.

Budapest, Nov. 25, 1944.

Manny commented:

> This situation was changed, however, when Raoul visited Veesenmayer later in No-
> vember, and told him that he, and not the Arrow Cross leaders, would be held ac-
> countable for these crimes by the Russians and Americans when they took control
> of Hungary, if the German governor did not immediately put a halt to the forced
> marches now that he held in his hands the formal report by Wallenberg. The next
> day, the intelligent but frightened German chief, aware that the Russians were clos-
> ing in on one side and that it was likely the Allies were soon going to take the coun-
> try, gave an order to the Arrow Cross to stop the daily marches immediately.
>
> Once again, Wallenberg had found a way to stop the brutal torture and killing
> of Jews, this time making an end run around the (vicious) Hungarian Nazis, and
> again defeating Eichmann's will.

The gentleman was very clever in his tactics, his strategies, marveled Manny,
and very bold.

CHAPTER 13

In the heat of the day, the terrace of the Hanover Inn was a pleasant meeting place, especially in the twilight. Maybe twenty tables covered by linen tablecloths, with big green umbrellas providing shade, gave the place an old-world atmosphere. Before a larger dinner meeting, Manny met with his old buddy Richard Mackie, the chair of his department. A robust fellow with short hair and ruddy cheeks who loved boxing and movies as much as literary criticism, Mackie was hosting a small group to meet and discuss the summer's program of institutes and conferences focusing on American cultures. Richard and Manny met to chat privately, to discuss what Manny would teach in the coming year, and his salary, which they got through quickly; and then Richard asked about the Wallenberg project. Mackie, whose intelligence when focused was acute, probed Manny with several sharp questions, and he answered with voluminous answers. At one point Manny noted something humorous, and Richard erupted with his patented raucous laugh, causing many diners at nearby tables to turn and stare. As he went on, Mackie nodded and said, "I got it now—it's an ongoing mystery, isn't it? With a series of traps along the way. Well, if I can dig up any more research and travel money, and you need it, let me know. Maybe you'll come up with some original interpretation, or something new, eh? Sounds like you have already . . . But"—and he leaned over with his cranberry soda drink—"just be careful you don't get lost in the chase, know what I mean? Leave that part for the FSB and CIA hounds."

"You mean I should watch out for polonium-210 in my tea, huh?"

Another raucous laugh! Mackie was at his best when letting loose.

He asked, "How was that student's thesis, by the way—was it Angela?"

"Yeah, it was hers. And not bad."

"So are you writing an article, a book? Academic or trade publisher?"

Manny shook his head. "Just notes right now, a few scenes . . . I'm not sure what it is, maybe a shadow thesis."

A broad smile. "I like that. Sounds like the subject deserves a 'shadow' argument or thesis." He laughed again, this large and generous human volcano of Irish wit with a touch of Native American rebelliousness mixed in.

"Hey, here's our group," Mackie said and waved for them to come over. "Let's see if we can make headway on defining that new track . . ."

Yet, all through his braised venison dinner, in that polite and elegant setting, Manny replayed Richard Mackie's cautionary words, tossed at him as an aside. Don't get lost in the chase.

Later, at home in the country house, Manny put on his basic (three) radios and took up his current reading, Hofstadter's *Anti-Intellectualism in American Life*. Wonderful book, which he always enjoyed rereading a chapter or two from. Here, amidst the chaotic piles of books and notebooks, amidst the wonderful photos of the boys when they were little, he felt at home, yet also, paradoxically, in exile. An outsider. A good distance away from events—and people—in spoiled, rich, Teflon-America. (Well, two and three Americas.) A country more violent, more decadent, more packaged than when Hofstadter was writing about it. An empire now, a dark one too, run by Texan clowns and neocon goons. What a state of affairs! Oh, well, he figured, reading part 2, "The Religion of the Heart," let the empire have its fun with its chest-pounding wars and excessive rhetoric and pretend feel-good humanism. Manny preferred to stay with his old favorites—his historians, his memories, his mysterious Raoul. Enough pleasures and labors to fill his remaining years.

From the cyberuniverse of e-mails, he received one from Stockholm, a friend who alerted him to the National Archives and Intelligence at Riksarkivet. And another from a lost soul in Ektarinburg, Russia, who had heard about Manny's search and claimed he knew something of the Gulag whereabouts of Raoul in the 1970s. But how had he heard about Manny? Was he, or his project, on the Internet now? Circling through cyberspace with dizzying speed, and reaching all portals around the world? Manny going viral?

And another from Budapest, from the intriguing daughter:

> *When will you return, Professor? Do you have a definite date yet? Mother has been crazy, running to the countryside always, finding and preparing her papers for your project together. She is very excited, I may say.*
> *Your friend, Dora*

A stirring tapped in his chest, but he wasn't sure what it signified . . . Manny found his old vinyl set of János Starker, which his son had rediscovered, set a record on his turntable, listened, and read. The wind blew slightly outside, fluttering the trees at the end of the meadow, and the sky soon darkened into a bluish violet. A subtle purplish light, to be sure, but one that also suggested a possible thunderstorm. Manny recalled when there had been animals on the property, two horses and a cow, and the horses always stayed apart from the cow—enemies, save when a T-storm hit, and they would band together in a small circle, twenty feet apart, sudden friends in the midst of fear and doubt. While the rain poured and lightning struck wildly, they stayed right there, in a new union, three strange bedfellows waiting it out. When it passed over, they returned to their former roles, two horses and an outsider cow.

When three of the Bach suites were finished, he shifted to Dylan. Now reading the chapter "The Evangelical Spirit," he listened to Dylan's "Positively 4th Street" and "Queen Jane." Unlike many others, Manny thought fondly of the sixties. A time of agitation, social urgency, and visceral alertness. The country was alive, the citizens bewildered but excited, and democracy opening up. The nightly news counted. Those daily protests in college towns like Madison, Berkeley, Cambridge, created vibrant street theater, filled with new actors, kids working on improvised acts of revolt. And in the background—or forefront?— was the music of the minstrels and the rockers, the folksingers and the bluesy southerners. Dylan, The Band, Joe Cocker, The Stones, Richie Havens, Judy Collins, Joan Baez, and Joni Mitchell—those were the poets of the era. (Not the high poets, but the folk poets for the aspiring rebels.) An ongoing jam session of the national consciousness, with Dylan in the front marking the new roads. An American-style revolution, in which kids played mischievously and public theater mingled with ideas of the New Left. It had the effect of shaking up the nation, every which way, from bodies to body politic. Inexorably, in the years since, the fires of the sixties had been tamped down, and the citizenry had been steadily tranquilized, Valium-ed, furtively turned into willing sheep, by the political Right and frightened media servants, including the popular PBS culture. And many of the new historians (and journalists) had gone to work, helping all that along, rescripting a new narrative about how dangerous those times were, how immoral, how un-American!

Ah, history, as it is remade by the mainstream historians.

Record over, Manny set the vinyl Dylan and Starker back into their sleeves. In the Indian Room, named for his Curtis photographs, he turned on the television to see the Red Sox score. Winning, once again; but there was still plenty of time in the season to fall apart. Without sports, the country had little to offer him now. Except for his sons, of course, and some of the students. A phone call came, and it was Jack, his Hopi pal, who said he was returning home to Arizona for a while, and maybe they could have a coffee or lunch before he went? "Sure," Manny responded, and they made a date. He watched the ballgame, read Hofstadter, and set Raoul on the back burner. Made a note to answer the lost Russian soul and the Budapest lady.

The next morning he drove over to the adjacent town, Lyme. On the back way, he followed the narrow tree-lined dirt road that wound eight miles or so past the Skiway and through the small town itself, with a manicured green in the middle; then he headed down on Route 10 to the River Road, driving on the winding macadam and passing through rolling fields of green, with houses dotting the landscape every few miles. Adorning the pastoral scene were cows grazing. *And at the same time, he saw Raoul with Vilmos on the road to Hegyeshalom, driving slowly and tossing some chocolates and socks to the rows of Jews marching.* This running montage was bizarre . . . On the road, alongside the Connecticut River, Manny stopped at the Mill Gardens greenhouses to pick out flowers for his departing department secretary. The place was mostly empty, only a few shoppers and a young grower/salesman; he meandered among the several greenhouses and open rows of flowers—bright colors, aromas, plumages—and thought how the greenhouse business would be a good one for an ex-historian to hide out in. Read and write amidst the orchids, zinnias, gladiolas, African lilies. He settled on a pink fuscia hanging basket and two geranium pots, and went on his way.

On Route 10 again to town, he listened to the Vermont FM station, where they were playing Puccini. A selection of opera music. He recalled when the boy used to sing in the local opera company, over in the next town, Lebanon . . . Yes, opera was the music that should accompany his own personal journey, the music of high melodrama, unexpected comedy. Was he playing in his own version now? Perhaps what he thought noble was really comic?

Passing the golf course, sighting a group of men in Bermuda shorts alongside their carts practicing their swings, Gellerman stirred with a thought, envisioned a scene, and suddenly felt a direction. He drove over to the classic Baker Library, one of the oldest Ivy libraries, and parked.

Presently he was sitting on the third floor of the library, at a small desk near the old American Indian sculpture overlooking the green. A formidable figure. Manny had his laptop, which warmed itself up with little beeping sounds. Stretching inside.

He began writing an inspired scene:

Ambassador Söderblom, a tall well-dressed man in his fifties wearing a wide-brimmed hat and charcoal-gray suit, shook hands with Tage Erlander, and said, "Thank you for calling me in, Mr. Prime Minister."

"Please sit, Ambassador. Will you have a drink or sandwich?"

"Perhaps a coffee, yes. Thanks."

Tage called to his secretary, who brought in a pair of coffees on a tray.

"So, tell me, you saw this chief of security fellow, yes? How was it? And will you get to see the 'Great Leader' himself, do you think?"

Söderblom nodded. "I did see Abramov, the chief of counterintelligence, called SMERSH, as I wrote you. They are the ones who supposedly would be in charge of Wallenberg, if he were there, and considered a spy."

"*If,* you said. They are still claiming ignorance?"

"Yes. Abramov says he knows of no Wallenberg in their prison. Or his whereabouts."

"Tell me, is this Abramov as bad as the other monster, Beria?"

"They are in a competition, I believe."

The prime minister smiled wryly. "Did you press him on this issue?"

Söderblom considered. "I did, yes, as much as an ambassador can in such a case. Remember, I do not want to make them hostile toward us, as we have much business to complete with them."

The prime minister nodded. He stood up, and walked around his desk to an easy chair, carrying a notepad, to sit opposite from Söderblom. "I am very concerned about Mr. Wallenberg, and I fear if we don't find out something very soon, it will be too late." He paused and lit a cigarette.

"Well, there is some news; I will get to see Stalin himself very soon."

Tage Erlander leaned forward. "How do you know this?"

"I pressed Abramov, and he agreed to set up a meeting in a few weeks."

Erlander relaxed. "Well, that is something."

"Of course, this meeting will be in the context of larger issues, you know."

"Larger issues? Like business and economics and politics? Yes, they are larger issues, but not more important. The more I learn about this Wallenberg situation, the more disturbed I am. I take my responsibility in this too, believe me. I should have paid closer attention."

The ambassador pursed his thin lips. "We cannot attend to everything, Prime Minister. There are many issues and many problems on the table with the Soviets. Our immediate business dealings, for example, and their desire for a large line of credit."

"I accept that—and the fact that, on top of being a very difficult group to deal with, they don't trust us too much. Not after our position of neutrality." He paused. "They must not be too pleasant to deal with?"

"Oh, they have been polite enough with me."

"If I may say," said Erlander, "you don't seem too perturbed by the unknown whereabouts of Raoul Wallenberg."

"That is not true, Prime Minister. It's just that, so far, we have very little evidence to suggest where he is, or that the Soviets may be holding him."

Erlander checked his pad. "What about the Americans? They are asking if we want their help in pushing the Russian Bear on this case. What is your opinion?"

"I think we Swedes can and should take care of our own affairs, sir, without any help from others, especially the Americans. If you recall, Wallenberg was given aid by the OSS, a secret service organization of the Americans."

Erlander peered at his ambassador, whom he found reluctant and unhelpful, and increasingly unpleasant. "As I understand the matter, it was the War Refugee Board that gave financial aid to Mr. Wallenberg, in pursuit of helping the Jews of Budapest."

"No need to quibble, sir. The point is that I am in the midst of an ongoing discussion with them, and so far, I have not encountered any major obstacles."

The prime minister tapped his pad, the secretary knocked and entered, and announced that the expected guests had arrived.

"I have asked the Wallenbergs to come in and meet you, Ambassador."

For a fleeting moment, Söderblom looked miffed, before his face returned to its imperturbable mask. He stood and waited for the surprise guests to enter.

After the initial introductions and shaking of hands, Marcus and Jacob took their chairs. The prime minister brought them up to date on what had occurred.

"Now, would you like to inquire of the ambassador?" he invited. "Please ask anything. Or even, make any suggestions concerning your cousin."

Marcus spoke up. "I am sure that the ambassador is doing all he can on Raoul's behalf."

"Thank you, Mr. Wallenberg. I will try my best."

"And that it must not be easy dealing with the Bolsheviks."

"Not so easy, true. But I believe they have been searching for him."

The two cousins nodded and looked sympathetic.

Erlander spoke. "The ambassador's meeting with Stalin will likely be in a few weeks, and he'll be bringing the matter up with him personally. Do you have any suggestions for Ambassador Söderblom?"

Jacob played with the golden chain of his pocket watch on his black vest. "That is very good of you, Ambassador. Our entire family appreciates that, since we know you have much more significant dealings to talk over."

The prime minister waited for something more to be said, something stronger. But Jacob and Marcus only looked on quietly.

Prime Minister Erlander was puzzled; maybe they thought they had been asked there pro forma? "Naturally, I have asked the ambasador to press for urgency, as much as he can."

"Thank you, Prime Minister," said Marcus. "That is much appreciated. We realize how difficult this must be, to press for urgency on a single individual. Any news at all will be welcomed by us, by his mother, and by his two half siblings."

Söderblom nodded sympathetically.

"Naturally, if there is anything we can do to help, we are at your service."

"I will remember that," offered the ambassador. "I am sure your name and your high business affiliations will mean something to the Field Marshall."

The ambassador finished his cup of coffee; Jacob fingered his gold chain; Marcus sat quietly, staring ahead.

The prime minister, baffled, looked around at his group of guests, jotted a few notes down, and finally stood up and thanked the Wallenbergs for coming in; his heart was stirring. They shook hands all around, and the two men departed.

"You can see what gentlemen they are," offered Erlander. "They are not presuming to put too big a burden on you and your discussion with Stalin."

"Yes, I can see that. They are most definitely gentlemen of honor." He paused. "They are converted Christians, yes?"

"Born Christians. Conversion happened in the last century."

"And Raoul too?"

"I don't know his religious convictions."

With that, the prime minister went back around to his side of the large oak desk, thanked the ambassador for coming, and advised him to keep him posted on any development in this case.

Söderblom assured him he would.

After the ambassador departed, Erlander sat disappointed at his desk, not quite understanding what had gone on. He jotted a reminder to himself to check on the diplomatic notes that had been passed in the year since Wallenberg's disappearance, including those from Foreign Minister Günther, and to check on Söderblom's background: what sort of man he was, his origins, his diplomatic biography. He seemed oddly *undiplomatic,* the prime minister judged; and the Wallenbergs, noted for their business aggressiveness, seemed strangely unaggressive. Was it politeness, timidity, fear? Why hadn't they pushed harder? Everything was upside down in this case, Erlander decided; he half wished to meet the Stalin monster himself, to deliver a few straightforward messages regarding the return of Raoul.

■

Gellerman set down his laptop and began printing out the scene.

Was this good history, or good fiction? Manny wondered. (Or bad history, and bad fiction?) There was enough evidence, for sure, to draw the scene this way—Söderblom's indifference, cowardice, hypocrisy, maybe even some furtive political ambition. We do know that Söderblom came back from his meetings with both Abramov and Stalin and proclaimed that the Soviets knew nothing of the whereabouts of Raoul. The ambassador accepted this as fact, and said that Wallenberg was probably lost or dead. (Killed in an auto accident, he opined, at some point.) Why did he go along so easily with the Soviet feigned ignorance? Did he imagine Raoul as a part-Jew whose family conversion meant little, and quietly resent that? Did he resent that Raoul was saving Jews, and this was beyond his job description for a Swedish diplomat? After all, anti-Semitism among Swedish Lutherans, furtive or open, was not a new revelation. The chief fact was that Söderblom was totally ineffective, maybe intentionally so; and he went on to reject outright all American offers for help.

As for the brothers, Marcus and Jacob, was their passivity a matter of family greed, or fear? Was their neglect intentional—saving their own Enskilda necks, if Raoul were free to tell all he knew about their Nazi connections?

It came as no surprise that the Söderblom meeting with Stalin on June 15, 1946, produced no results. The meeting was infamous for its supine acquiescence, a missed opportunity. So Manny's scene, to be sure—as he analyzed it—actually set the stage for the real meeting.

The historian knew he had enough evidence, circumstantial and otherwise, to support the above creative scene. So fiction here could dramatize a piece of obscure history, complete the dotted lines, fill in a missing scene, and help to make clear what had been clouded, camouflaged. Those were not the best days in Swedish diplomatic history, and Söderblom was a prime exemplar of those black days (as the Swedes acknowledged, years later).

He closed his laptop, bid good-bye to the Indian statue, and went out onto the green to meet Jack, his real Indian (or Native American).

Jack was looking good, in a bright sport shirt and shorts, his dark face and jet black hair in sharp contrast to his clothes. "Hey, how goes it, Prof?"

"Not too bad. And yourself?"

"Good, man, good. I'm headed home for a month. Gonna see the family!"

"Sounds good. Hey, let's walk down around the pond, and we can have our sandwiches sitting on the golf course."

Jack smiled. "Why not?

Jack had a fine easy gait, and they began walking across the green and down behind the library and onto Rope Ferry Road. Students strolled or bicycled past, most white-wired to their iPods, others talking on cell phones.

"So, has the term gone well?"

"Yeah, pretty well. And guess what? I've begun a long essay on Samson Occom, at last!"

"Hey, bravo! But what about Crazy Horse?"

"Oh, yeah, that's going along, but remember, that's gonna be my thesis."

Manny gestured. "So what's your angle on Occom? You know there's been a lot of stuff written on him."

"Yeah, I knew you'd put on me something like that—well, he was a 'wild Injun' right there in the midst of those white Christian gentlemen! Isn't that enough of an angle?" A restrained smile. "And beating them at their own game—learning. The art of learning. He did that better than all of them!"

"Yeah, I think I did know something of that."

"Man, that cat knew Hebrew and Latin! Could read and write it, taught those langusges here at the college, can you believe it?"

"I am impressed."

"He was kinda like your Wallenberg," Jack said, with a gleaming smile, "an odd man out."

Gellerman looked over at his young friend. "You're getting to be a bit dangerous, know that?"

Jack nodded in delight and walked on. They passed the oval pond on the left—"That's what Samson got for his troubles, a pond named after him!"—strolled up the narrow sidewalk past the hefty houses, and turned left, passing the golf clubhouse on the right. They walked down the small hill, and found a hillock of green to sit on.

"This looks good. We can see a hole or two."

"Boy, what we would do with this green! Where we live it's brown most of the year—well, brown all the year!" He hit Gellerman's arm good-naturedly. "Just throw some seeds down here, come back in a month, and you have plants growing, grass growing!"

"Eat your sandwich. And remember, I've visited you out there."

"Recruiting me, I remember. But you didn't bring any New England rain!"

"You forgot to e-mail me."

They ate, observing some golfers lining up a shot, while swallows dived.

"The thing is, Occom reminded me a little of your Wallenberg, the way he always seemed a little finer than others, more Christian than the Christians!"

"Or maybe more essentially Christian, even though he was a Native!"

Jack nodded and laughed.

"That's a good analogy, Jack. An unusual pair, to be sure. Except my Raoul never learned Hebrew. At least that I knew of!"

"Well, there's always more to learn."

"True enough. Hey, look at the arc on that shot. A beauty, huh?"

"Now, this," observed Jack, moving his palm out, "is what I call the real graduate school life, right? Taking our lunch here and watching the golfers play a round. Who would want to do anything else?"

"Not anyone sensible, of course." He brushed off an insect. "Remember, last time we had to canoe for our lunch, so I tried to make it easier this time."

They ate, and breathed in the soft air, the aroma of freshly cut grass. Manny said, "Hard to believe a little white ball could torment so many."

Jack laughed. "So, are you going ahead with the book, or what?"

"Yeah, maybe so, if I ever get the time, the space."

They ate, listened, watched, swatted away bugs.

"Hey, I have an idea for you, Prof. Why don't you trek out to Hopi and write the book there? Really. I can get you a private space in a pottery studio, pretty spare, but it's quiet; my aunt makes pottery and dolls in one room, and you'd have the other. What d'ya think? And if you need inspiration, there is the grand mountain right in front of you. You'd write it there, believe me!"

Manny looked over at his friend, his dark eyes brimming with his new idea, and he squeezed his arm. "Maybe you're onto something."

"I know I am. And for breaks, we can play hoops. You're a shooter, right?"

"Centuries ago, I had a set shot." Manny smiled. "But, it's a thought."

"Think it over, Professor, really. It'll be great fun to have you out there! You'd probably get more work done in a Hopi month than in three months here! Away from papers, meetings, students—yeah, it's perfect!"

Manny pondered the surprise notion, recalling the unique aura of that small rectangle of arid land squeezed within the huge Navajo territory.

"Sir, if you finish up RW on our turf, you can become an honorary Hopi!"

"Oh, I think it'd be truer if you made Wallenberg an honorary Hopi."

"Hey, that's a thought. I'll talk to our chief."

"Too bad we didn't think of this before *our* chief, President Reagan, made him an honorary American, back in '81. Hopi citizen first, American second."

CHAPTER 14

A few days later Manny flew down to New York, was picked up at LaGuardia by a private town car, brought to his hotel (Affinia, across the street from Madison Square Garden), and, after showering and getting settled, was met in the lobby by a young woman, Cary, an assistant producer whom he had spoken with earlier. She had a cab waiting, which whisked them downtown to a private apartment in Tribeka, and inside that plush place, he met the director, whom he had talked with at length on the telephone, several times, before he had been invited down to do an interview for the HBO documentary.

"Good to meet you in person, Professor," said Bobby Jenkins, a tall young African American who was making a documentary on the Brooklyn Dodgers on the fiftieth anniversary of their departure from Brooklyn for Los Angeles. "I enjoyed our long phone calls very much. Look, we're still setting up here with the lighting and the sound crews, so if you don't mind waiting a bit, over in that room, we will let you know when to come in. It won't be too long. Meanwhile, either Cary or Joy can get you a coffee or cold drink, or whatever you want."

Manny walked into the adjoining room, darkened by the drawn drapes, sat on a cozy couch, and asked for a ginger ale. From the deep countryside and the birds singing in the morning to this hip apartment with the hustling crews and video cameras in a few hours was a leap of faith, not just a leap of geography.

Sitting there, in the shadowy darkness, he recalled his childhood of watching Jackie play, in his first year with the Dodgers, in 1947, and tried to pinpoint specifics. (That's why he had been asked down here, after all.) Ginger ale was brought, and he returned to boyhood . . . to the friendship with Burt, his boyhood hero who was shot down over Germany in his B-17 and put in a POW camp; he escaped and finally made it home, wounded badly. A series of surgeries ensued, and because of his US Air Force uniform and Purple Heart, he was let in free, along with his eight-year-old buddy, little Manny, and waved down to the box seats behind first base, where Jackie played that first year . . . Memories of Robinson flooded him now, clear and vivid, taking a big lead off of third base, daring the pitcher provocatively . . . Manny could hear the Philly and Cardinal curses and slurs slung out to Jackie, at bat or in the field . . .

A charmed boyhood, in old cozy Brooklyn . . . He knew well that whatever happened inside the shooting room, it would be a far cry from what he had seen or felt, or could articulate, on camera. Further, he understood well that if he talked for three hours, he *might* make three minutes on the screen, but that was fine with him. He had other things in his mind, and at stake.

Sitting there, in the shaded room, he wondered at what age did one sense a serious turning of direction, a sudden change of intention (and maybe fortune and momentum too)—certainly not before forty-five, maybe fifty-five, or was it sixty-five these days? Different from Dante-esque views of a midlife turning point. Well, Manny was feeling right now on this edge, like trying as a boy to balance yourself on a thin rail and walking across it . . . Yes, something was stirring in his being . . .

The shooting was a mechanical ordeal. The vertical sheets of extra lighting were too bright and hot upon him, stunning his vulnerable eyes; the crew said they couldn't shift the angle, because of the video picture. Next, the camera people said the jacket or tie didn't show well, so they changed both for him, which irritated Manny; he didn't feel like himself sitting and talking in another's clothes. He chided himself: those were foolish details; forget them. So he went ahead with the two and half hour interview, answering question after question, feeling awkward; and as it proceeded, he continued to admonish himself not to worry about the details, just talk about being a boy and seeing Jackie play, and meeting him outside a few times, getting his autograph, hearing his gravelly voice up close, and seeing his dark probing eyes. (Manny kept quiet about the analogy he later drew with Dickens's Magwitch, the convict, confronting the boy Pip, terrifying him, only to turn out later on to be his secret benefactor . . .) The questions droned on—the questioner amiable—and Manny spoke dutifully, dully, while being reminded to sit upright in his seat . . . and he grew sorry he had agreed to do the whole fucking thing. How boring and brittle was this artificial, staged talking.

But something of interest did happen during the ordeal. He found himself thinking back to Raoul being interrogated for hours, maybe for days, from 1945 to 1947, under a bright bulb or blinding light; and he had a sense of the pressure, the relentless pressure. To the camera he was saying what an outsider Jackie was, an outsider/insider—a black outsider to society and to white baseball, but an insider in baseball, a brilliant base-stealing outlaw in the game it-self. Privately, he was transferring the outlaw image to RW in his relation to proper Swedish society and his proper family—to the neutral Swedes, the con-servative Lutherans, the rich self-protective family. Raoul had come from all that, but he had broken away and chosen a tougher, more difficult, path. (He had his grandfather's counsel, as Jackie had Mr. Rickey's.) A choice that left him alone, unprotected, betrayed.

At the end of the interview, when the director and producer asked him how it felt, Manny replied, "Oh, it was of interest . . . made me think."

"Well, we thought you did really well—though we didn't get that reference to a Mr. Wallenberg?—and of course we don't know how much of the whole thing will get in."

Manny, surprised, said, of course he understood, and it didn't really matter. He didn't add that what did matter was his private offscreen reflection on the association between his boyhood game-hero and his adult life-hero . . .

He kept these revelations private, in the huge black Denali SUV that sped him back to LaGuardia, and in the little propeller airplane that lifted him up to Lebanon, New Hampshire, and in the days following . . .

A week later he drove back up to Sweden, Maine, for another of his son's con-certs; a trip that went across New Hampshire and into the same vast reaches of rural Maine, decorated occasionally with tacky towns and roadside motels, and suddenly opening out to great expanses of green countryside, where the sky was large and the mountains loomed, and you felt a touch of Montana . . . His son's trio played Debussy, in a small rough-hewed cabin, for a dozen par-ents. The music was riveting; the boy played with his firm intonation and usual panache. Afterward, a parent whispered, "Was that your son on the cello? The other two were good, but he was something else."

Manny soon was taking his "something else" for another special dinner in Bridgeton, and he felt his vulnerable soul salved by the music, the boy.

He asked Josh, over his surf and turf, how he liked chamber music.

"Oh, it's great, Dad, but my favorite is still orchestral. I love a big orchestra and the music written for it." He chewed fast, eating with gusto. "I can't wait for GYBSO camp to start! Hey, Dad, this is really good; you should try some!" He looked up and casually added, "And, oh yeah, I wrote another section of my Wallenberg Suite."

"Wow," Manny exclaimed, caressing the boy's cheek. "I'm really getting rewarded on this visit! Debussy *and* Wallenberg."

An hour later, in the cabin studio, he listened to the additional several minutes of the composition, a melody of sorrowful sounds and strong vibrato. "You've really been working!" he told the boy, who beamed.

The question remained whether Wallenberg lived on beyond 1947, in another prison like Vladimir, or else in some Gulag site, like a camp in Perm or Vörkuta, or even a psychiatric hospital. There were hundreds of "sightings" of RW out there, post-1947, the date of his official death (a "myocardial infarct on July 17, 1947," declared the Soviets), by Russian, German, Hungarian, Polish political prisoners. Either it was RW or someone who appeared very similar, some elderly ill Scandanavian, who had been in a camp or hospital for many years. Could it have been possible? Sure, possible. The case remained open for years, with many unanswered questions and many places cited by a variety of apparent witnesses. For example, he knew—from the work of the historian S. Berger of the Swedish-Russian Working Group—that an elderly Swede was witnessed in 1960, in solitary confinement in Korpus 2 of Vladimir Prison, by two former employees, Varvara Ivanovna Larina and Aleksandr Timofeiyevich Kukin; and in 1970, by Josyp Terelya, a former prisoner, also in Korpus 2 of Vladimir. Moreover, if Raoul was alive after 1947, he would most likely have become a secret prisoner in isolation, and such prisoners were assigned either a false identity or a number. Convicted prisoners 14, 16, 17, 18, 19, and 20 were sentenced by Special Tribunal (OSO) between the spring of 1947 and May 1948. In what isolation prisons were they placed after their departure from Moscow, and who were they?

At home, Manny conjectured a scene of the once-young, dark-haired Raoul now a much older man, maybe a emaciated gray-haired prisoner, worn down, wearied, and ill. (Or was it tuberculosis, with that cough?) Gellerman imagined him as observed by one of the apparent witnesses, a guard/attendant:

He sat in a chair, a blanket over his legs, a white scraggly beard covering up a good part of his face. I brought him his dinner daily, a piece of bread dipped in a soup gruel, on occasion a piece of dog meat, and watched him work his jaw excessively. His one true pleasure came from the dry Swedish bread, "Knäckebröd," which I smuggled to him, once a month, courtesy of bribery and a secret benefactor. This reminded him of home and his Stockholm youth, he explained, in the basic Russian he had learned through the years. In the spring, when it was often chilly, he would sit either in the sun with my help or, if it was gray as usual, near the one stove in the large dormitory room, where ten other prisoners lived. They didn't bother him much, and every few years a political prisoner came who talked with him, in German. His speech gradually became slurred, and he coughed regularly.

On rare occasions he had a visitor, an agent from Moscow, who asked how he was doing, and whether he wished to confess anything; whether he wanted to change his mind and offer any information about the long-ago past, so that he might spend his last remaining years—or months?—with his friends or family back in Sweden. These agents, either from the KGB or SMERSH (counterintelligence), always informed him, I would hear, that nobody on the outside had asked for him, not yet. Not after all these thirty-odd years. But maybe soon? When the agents visited, it was often in pairs; one would press him to talk—after all, he was an old man now and it didn't matter—and the other would say something new about Stockholm, where he had just visited. (Of course, he was lying, and everyone knew it.) The first agent would ask him about his contacts with the rich Jews of Budapest, or about his special work for the American OSS. Though it was many decades later, they still did their onerous work, still pressed the old man. They came around maybe twice a year or so.

In response, he always shook his head steadily, said very little, but occasionally asked for a little medicine, some fresh meat or vegetables, and a real doctor. (He spoke in German, which one agent usually knew, and in his simple Russian.) They laughed and said, of course, help was on the way. They would be arriving quite soon, here in Perm, in the middle of nowhere, just another few months, hold on. From teasing they turned serious, "But if you tell us the truth about Budapest, and where you have kept hidden all those old paintings and Jew jewelry all these years, then a doctor can be found. And you will see Sweden again."

Once he trusted me, he asked to see a Swedish newspaper, if I could bring one, and every few months I managed to, through a Moscow friend who asked a foreign office assistant. I would bring a newspaper, like *Dagens Nyheter*, and also some architecture magazines. (I recall an old *Arkitektur*, and *Forum*, which he pored over carefully.) Oh, yes, I remember something else he wished for, a photograph of the Stockholm city library, the "stadsbibliotek," by the architect Asplund. (I wrote down these names.) Sometimes he would sit and draw sketches on rough sheets of paper for an addition to that oddly shaped building, a sort of top hat housing a circular library, his reading room in childhood, and asked me to save them for him. How strange! But I put them in an old burlap feed bag and set it in the small animal shelter. A mistake.

Many of the prisoners were beaten, almost by habit, by the more veteran guards, when they had little to do, but mostly he was left alone, a tottering sick old man. Once, however, early in maybe 1972, I did see a guard hitting him, for no reason or other, and I interceded, bribing the brute. His eyes were astonished, and he had a bloody mouth—nothing serious. I aided him. That's when he started to believe in me. You see, he had been transferred from Vladimir Prison to this hellhole in the Urals, where there was no accountability whatsoever. Just the concrete blocks, the prisoners, the guards. Well, actually, for a few years he did have a friend in there, a general in the Soviet Army, a Ukranian from Khartov who had been a hero in the Great War, but who had spoken out afterward against the injustices of his superior; he was warned, but again protested about the Russian's brutality and stupidity, so he was sentenced to six years in Perm. This General, Artunian, was civilized, and he and the old man hit it off, and for several years they were friendly, before the general was released.

But most of the time my Swedish old man was a man alone, forlorn in a foreign country and penal colony, gradually getting sicker, coughing, a thin bag of bones, until one day he didn't awake in the morning. I think this was as late as 1981 or '82, and that was the end of him. When they took him away, no one named him on the death certificate, of course; he was simply prisoner number 71392. That's the way it went, you see—nameless in prison, nameless in death. I missed him. Truly. And when I went to find that burlap bag, it had feed in it; when I checked with the guard, he said he had tossed those papers into the incinerator; some fool had filled a good feed bag with that paper nonsense!

That's what I remember; that's what I told the investigating commission in 1991 that asked me to tell what I might have known about a Swedish prisoner in Perm. He was there, all right, I can swear to that.

Gellerman, exhausted, got up and wandered through the long house to the kitchen, to make himself a coffee. He felt as though he had been the pained witness, the narrating guard. He checked the plants and saw they needed water. He filled a small pitcher and watered three plants. (The twenty-five-year-old towering avocado, started by his ex-wife from a pit, was scraping the ceiling, but leaning over like a leafy Tower of Pisa.) When the coffee was ready, he took it back to his study and reread his scene. Manny thought it conveyed basic facts, based on what he knew about Perm and Wallenberg—if RW had survived beyond Lybianka and Vladimir. With those more than fifty witness "sightings," the survival was a possibility, and Manny chose Perm because he had met, in Moscow, the son of the real Ukranian general from Khartov who had been imprisoned there for standing up to authority. If RW had survived the despair, the loneliness, the determination of the old RW—had he captured it adequately?—stood in contrast to the heinous moral delinquency of the W. family and the Stockholm government. What a state of rotten Swedish affairs! Who in innocent America could understand such moral and physical geography, such years of Soviet ruin and Swedish decay? . . .

The cheery town of Hanover was like a little domestic park, with one commercial main street and adjoining roads of suburban homes, and well-behaved citizens, a site to view for the anthropologists (or any wild animals), to examine and muse over. As Gellerman performed his errands at one of the four banks and the redbrick post office, passing the overpolite pedestrians, he thought how important it was to keep in his mind the rougher geography and fate of Raoul. So in his mind he created a montage, superimposing the dark streets of Budapest and the concrete fortresses of Lybianka and Vladimir Prisons over this dainty dollhouse town of neat streets, small shops, boutiques, and banks. Over the tidy sidewalks and cheery shoppers, he placed the burly Slavic types, the gloomy Hungarians, the choppy streets. Quite a feat of his imagination, if he kept it up. But he felt it was necessary, a kind of backup storage unit of the imagination, akin to backing up your a disk. Gulag camps over white Georgian buildings, patrolling secret police over patrolling meter maids.

Could he keep Wallenberg firmly in place in this very polite topography, Manny wondered, walking over to Rosey Jekes coffee shop?

Over coffee he opened his laptop, and, via his airport card, there appeared the words of the lady from Budapest:

> *Dear Professor,*
> *I have worked hard to gather all my materials and have them ready for you. I am almost done, and I want to know when you are returning? Have you made a date yet? Budapest is hot, but out here in the countryside, it is much cooler. Of course, we can work here, where there is space and quiet.*
> *Z.*

He shook his head, drank his coffee, and considered matters. Here in the dingy basement coffee shop, downstairs from the clothing shop with the same name, Manny observed a round black table with a group from the Tuck School of Business, their voices loud, discussing a business policy paper; and at another, a tall gentleman of sixty with whom he had once had a sharp political argument, when the ex-*New Yorker* began lauding Reagan as the greatest modern president. It never failed to surprise Manny when a Jew was an arch conservative; but after Podhoretz and his betrayal of the liberal *Commentary*, anything was possible.

Here in the middle of nowhere, he knew he had to answer the lady, feeling reluctance but also a certain inevitable pull, like an RW magnet drawing him. So he wrote her:

> *Yes, my new friend, I shall be booking my ticket soon, so gather your wits and papers and I will gather my resolve. You see, summertime in New Hampshire—I always feel a bit lazy, seduced by the weather, like some Monarch butterfly hanging around and waiting for the milkweed stalks to appear, before it takes off for Mexico.*
> *Manny G*

He drank up, not minding the absurdity of his metaphor, and trekked to the tennis courts to practice his serve, before his match arrived in twenty minutes. He never warmed up enough, and usually paid for it early on in the first set.

After a competitive match, of split sets, 4–6 and 6–3, he took a shower and checked his e-mail from the college. Surprisingly, he opened a note from a stranger in Sweden:

> *I said too much to you, Professor, in my Stockholm meeting, and have been exiled to a tiny branch of the bank, in a remote town. If I say a word more, I will lose my job entirely. I have a family and cannot afford any free exchange. May I therefore wish you luck in pursuing your goal, of finding out what really happened to RW and why it was never investigated properly in the Swedish media. Is it a true mystery, or is it a true cover up?*
> *Peter Magnusson (pseudonym)*

Gellerman, astonished, reread the message, absorbing the news. Now *Magnuson* had been warned, just as he had warned Manny.

He walked over to the inn, bought a *New York Times*, and settled to read in the formal lounge, where he felt hidden out of view in a corner wing chair.

The front page had its usual column on the Iraq war, with a new suicide bombing in a market in Baghdad, killing sixty Iraqis and five more American soldiers. This had become the daily fare, more or less, and the American total was now close to three thousand. As for the Iraqis, was it two hundred thousand or more? Who could tell? In another column, a feature story on the new Asian gangs in big cities like LA and NY, and their taking on the Latino gangs. The number of deaths had risen sharply in the past year. Manny read a few more pieces, then turned to the Arts section, where there was a huge review on *The Sopranos*, and a particularly violent episode. Death and violence were not only in the air; they saturated the climate. Wherever you went—in the streets, in the media, or in classroom subjects—violence was hot, so much so that you took it for granted, maybe even valued it, hungered for it, like some sort of instant high sugar food. Consider the native movies, the advertisements, the vast print dedicated to *The Sopranos*. Was this the America of Thoreau, Emerson, and Whitman? Or was it the America of the Wild West and the slaughtering of the Indians, updated with our wars, our gangs, our HBO shows?

He got up and took a walk around the back to Lebanon Street, and down toward the large stone Catholic Church on the corner, where he stopped and looked in and saw the priest talking to a few parishioners. He recalled a couple of favorite Graham Greene stories about Catholicism: "The Hint of an Explanation," "The Basement Room." He walked up the narrow street, turned the corner at the hidden hostel, and ambled past the town library; then, he went back up onto Main Street, crossed over and walked past the Foodstop Gas Station, and made his way down and up School Street, nodding hello to a passing stranger. In a half mile or so, he marched up the hill to his favorite site, a small obscure park, kept hidden by shrubs and trees, on the right (northern) side. A park that no one but occasional dog owners set foot in. He sat on a wooden bench, serenaded by the chirping birds, smelling the freshly cut grass, and focused on his European plan. Which was what? Well, at least he had researched some handwriting specialists in Boston and the Cape. A good start.

CHAPTER 15

A few days later Manny attended a college talk on randomness by an old friend from Jerusalem, and Maya put on a good show, in the large auditorium, to about 150 students. Apart from talking freely from notes, she used a variety of video charts and graphs—no PowerPoint, thank god—and played clever games with the audience, showing how it was the predictable patterns that they were looking for and expecting, for answers to many things. Through an examination of World War II war codes and code breakers, charts with numbers on them, and various multiple choice questions, Maya pushed forward, with wit and intelligence, explaining to the attentive audience how much they were subject to expected patterns of behavior. And how they therefore imagined things that weren't really there. The best example was the idea of "hot streaks" in basketball, studied by the psychologist Amos Twersky, which proved that there was no such thing as hot streaks, but rather, just the ordinary shooting percentages over the course of the game. Manny, a hot-streak set-shot artist as a high school player, smiled at that. But he did appreciate the value and independence of the truly random, in nature and human nature, that she was emphasizing.

Sitting there, in the modern Filene Auditorium, its hard woods lit softly by indirect lighting, Manny felt the Easy Life pour through and over him, like light rain from a sun shower blessing him, as he listened to the question and answer period and the chatter. Academic life was the soft green oasis in the midst of the dark topography of the Iraq war, Sudan genocide, African famine, Guantanamo torture, Russian assassination, immigration border battles— those terrible woes of the world which were exciting to argue and read about, fret over and forget, here on this remote college isle. Why ever retire, when this life meant a permanent ongoing retirement, in wireless pastel rooms and softly lit air-conditioned auditoriums amidst innocent students and civilized profs? And engulfed by the latest Macs and great books, available for a year at a time.

Afterward, body rested, mind refreshed, he congratulated Maya, made a date to see her later, and walked outside in the warm sunshine.

Later in the afternoon, at the bar in the inn, he had a beer with his cynical colleague, the lively European historian, Tom Jameson.

"Here's the question," Manny said. "This may be—no, probably is—a wild goose chase, returning to see the mad lady over there. But there is something about her fantasy, or her *devotion to her fantasy*, that is intriguing, though I don't know what it is. So I shouldn't go, right?"

The ruddy-faced fellow replied, "So you should go, precisely for the reasons you give. That you are intrigued, but you don't know by what; and also, that you are aware of her possible fantasy. Otherwise," he smiled, "you will stay around here, play tennis, vacation in Maine, do your routine, and miss all the fun of the hunt, even if it leads . . . nowhere."

"So I should go for the fun of the hunt?" Manny smiled.

"You will always wonder if it could have led somewhere. Now you get both, a possible answer to your question, or a closing down of that path. And don't forget, crazy people can lead you to doors that you wouldn't get to with reasonable people. And in a case like this, of unsolved mysteries, holes everywhere, reason will only get you so far. Believe me, I know about that. Besides, you get a free trip to an exotic country. Any good wines over there these days?"

While Manny talked about the Tokaj dry white wine, his thoughts stayed with his colleague's words about crazy versus sane.

"Are you going to publish a book or an article about this?"

Manny shrugged his shoulders.

"Well, you'll need to; don't do all this work for nothing. And by the way, what about that Swedish warning? Did that lead anywhere?"

"No, not in the end. Except that the fellow wrote to tell me he'd been banished from the Enskilda Bank in Stockholm."

"Really?" His friend fixed him. "You sure he wasn't playing you?"

Manny nodded. "Could be. Though I don't know why."

"For the sake of playing an American; these days that's a great sport, all around the world," Tom drained his glass, "when they are not shooting you."

Budapest in late August was hot, not quite like New York with its humidity, but hot enough. Fortunately, he was whisked away to a little village down the Danube about forty-five minutes from the city, called Kismaros. Hardly a village, just one general place, with a bar and an outdoor eating patio. She took him to her surprisingly comfortable house up a small hillside, and, over tea, ushered him into a large living room with a rectangular wooden table in the center. There, she had laid out piles of papers in careful order.

Is this what it had come to, he wondered, sheaves of papers from a weird woman about a probable (or improbable) fantasy life of hers, in some remote village in Hungary? And making sense out of these piles was supposed to be his task? Who was the crazier one, she or he? . . .

Beaming, she said, "It is not done yet, you see," and she pointed to several bulky cartons over by the windows, "but it is a start."

"Yes, it is a start."

"We will have to arrange regular working hours—do you prefer mornings, with an afternoon break, or mornings sleeping late and work during afternoon hours?"

More wild words. He walked around the modest living room, with the simple 1940s upholstered chairs and a stuffed divan, and the odd smells . . .

"Well, we can look into that, yes. How often do you come here? And does Dora come here too?"

She took two steps closer to him, her face animated. "So you do like Dora? Yes, she is wonderful. So unlike me,"—she giggled—"in every way!"

Manny smiled at the humor. (Was it humor?) "How long have you had this place? It looks very well lived in."

"Do you like it? Americans are used to so much comfort; I didn't think you would think much of it. It was mother and father's, used for retreats . . . escapes."

Digesting that, he gazed at books in the windowed bookcase. Histories, geographies, classics like Gibbon and Spengler; literature of Schiller and Goethe, novels (Márai, Móricz, and Kosztolányi, Steinbeck and Hemingway, Selma Lagerlöf and Sigrid Undset), even plays by Strindberg, Lessing, and Ibsen—a real collection.

"You approve?" she asked, over his shoulder.

"Well, it's certainly various."

"What do you mean?"

"Diverse, many different kinds."

"Yes, they were readers, and so am I." She smiled. "The world is different now, of course."

"Of course."

"So we will start on Monday. Tomorrow I have a surprise for you, back in town."

"A surprise? What is it?"

"But it wouldn't be a surprise then, would it? Come, I will get you a drink; white wine perhaps? And while I warm up dinner, already cooked, you can read my preface, or introduction, yes?"

Caught unawares, he accepted the folder, and was led over into the wing chair, where he sat and opened the folder. Amusing, for sure, he figured.

Momentarily, he was brought a glass of the dry wine, with a wedge of cheese on a cracker. She smiled and said, "I have had my pages translated for you, of course."

Birds twittered; Manny read:

It has been my fate to have my life intertwined with history, and I will try to tell my tale with as much accuracy as my memory and my notes allow. Mine has been an unusual story, in many ways, and I can only hope that I will do it full justice. My father was Raoul Wallenberg, the notable Swedish diplomat, and my mother was Klara Esther Frank, another noble soul from Budapest. Few people knew of their union, or of me, their sole child. Their story has never been told before. I hope I have the skills, and the courage, to tell it well.

Two people I wish to thank in advance here. First, my daughter, Dora, a psychologist, who has always helped me with her support and faith. The second is the professor of history from Dartmouth College, in New Hampshire, America, Emmanuel Gellerman, a wise and generous professional who has guided me in my narrative . . .

Manny looked up, not amused but amazed, at this premature expression of gratitude in her manuscript. Why? Why had she proceeded this way?

This memoir has been a labor of twenty-five years of gratitude and memory, for an unusual person and family, and also to give some light on a dark period in history. The Cold War contributed strongly to the suffering of my family and the death of my father, and I hope my tale will contribute to understanding that history from a personal point of view. (I want to add that is why, in part, I chose Prof. Gellerman as my guide here, as he is a specialist in that period of history.)

Now, before I begin the story as I—

She interrupted his reading with a gleaming smile, standing before him. "Dinner is ready, and it is best while hot, if you don't mind."

Dazed and even stunned, he got up and was led to the round wooden table in the next room, the table set with a linen tablecloth. He sat and faced the bowl of soup.

"I made it without too much hot paprika, so please don't worry!"

He carefully tried the first spoonful, a sort of gazpacho. "It's tasty."

"I am so glad!"

He tasted his soup, debating his words, and raising his appraisal of her ingenuity.

"Is the translation suitable?"

Slowly he nodded. "Yes, it is fine." He broke a piece of bread, took another few spoonfuls. "But why did you already insert my name in the text? At this very early stage? I don't understand the need for—"

She stopped him, by handing over a sheet of paper across the table.

He shook his head. And read the note. It was an e-mail printout, with a Yale University Press return address, and he perused the body, a single paragraph:

> Yes, we are very interested in your project, Ms. Wallenberg; it sounds promising indeed. We certainly hope that the writing will be equal to the great subject. And I am delighted that you have secured the services of Prof. E. Gellerman to help you here; I have looked up his work online and in our library, and he is a very credible historian. As soon as you can get me a proposal and a sample chapter, we will send you a contract. Do you have a date yet for the delivery of the manuscript?

It was signed by the editor in chief, Jason Margolis.

Gellerman read it over three times, to try to digest the full import. He scratched his beard, stood up, and went to the window looking out at the green hillside and the birds landing at the bird feeder. "Swallows?" he asked?

"Ah, let me see. But it is Dora who is the bird expert."

Presently she was standing by his side, her white blouse brushing his shoulder, and they gazed at the hungry birds. "Yes, perhaps swallows."

They stood for a moment, looking at the happy birds eating and chattering. The twilight was filtering the yellow light with a yellow-green beauty.

"You like it here?" she asked, smiling at him.

He took a breath. "It's the countryside, and I feel at home in it, yes."

"I am glad."

He waited, and presently she asked him to return to the table for the dinner.

She served him the roast chicken dish, with kasha varnikas and carrots, and he watched her perform the simple tasks with careful skill. Clearly, he understood now, she was also skilled at the more complicated tasks, and with planning as well.

"Would you like some music?" she chirped.

"No need, thanks. I can hear the birds."

She smiled.

He ate a bite of chicken, with the old-fashioned ribbons of kasha noodles, and took a carrot too. Sweet. He drank some wine. She was waiting for his verdict, and he said, "Very tasty." To which she nodded happily.

"Why and how did you choose Yale to write to?"

"Oh," she beamed, "I learned they have a special series devoted to Jewish questions."

"I see," he said, seeing little, understanding less, but knowing this was a sly, formidable madwoman, not simply a freakish nutcase. And if tomorrow was a surprise, what was this, here tonight? An early reward? Or an early warning?

That night he slept fitfully, alert at every noise, wondering if he could possibly be locked away there, kidnapped in some Edgar Allen Poe thriller . . .

The next afternoon they were back on the train, chugging back to town. At Zsuzsanna's apartment, she excused herself and refashioned herself, dressing up in a rather formal suit when she reemerged from her room. When it became clear that they were going out, he nodded and asked where? She put her finger to her lips, silencing his request, and ushered him outside. Soon they were waiting by a tram stop, chatting, and next they were on the tram itself, number 7, zigzagging in and around the town. The heat was sticky, twilight had arrived, and he hoped they would reach their destination soon.

In twenty minutes they alighted, taking care with the sharp steps of the tram. She led him to a small old building, just around the corner from the large celebrated synagogue. Taking his hand, she led him through a long dark corridor and into a plain room—"the real shul," she beamed—where a small group of participants was waiting, mostly older souls. A slender rabbi wearing a blue suit and gray tie welcomed them graciously. Soon a few others filed in, totaling maybe a dozen altogether, and they got ready for the service.

Manny followed the others in removing his shoes; candles were lit, and everyone sat on the floor. Along with a yarmulke, Manny was handed a slender prayer book for the Tishah B'Av service, which was printed in both English and Hebrew. The room was squarish and simple, reminding Manny of the Brownsville basement where he had learned Jewish history and language some fifty years ago in a Sholem Aleichem Bund school; the atmosphere was plain too, except for the flickering lights of the candles. How strange! he thought.

The rabbi spoke in Hungarian but directed Gellerman to the appropriate page and asked if he would read a section, in Hebrew or English. Manny nodded.

As the rabbi began his low chanting. Manny read to himself:

Tisha B'Av, the Ninth Day of Av, is the day on which the Jewish people recall the catastrophes which it has suffered and which have influenced its life and character. The historical events which Jewish tradition has associated most closely with Tisha

B'Av have been the destruction of the First Temple of Jerusalem in 586 BCE and the destruction of the Second Temple in 70 CE—events which were fateful in their consequences.

Because of the destruction of the First Temple the Jews went into exile for the first time—and the awareness of galut remained a constant in the subsequent life of the people. With the destruction of the Second Temple, the Jews lost their independence, were scattered to the four corners of the world, and began their career as an "eternal minority."

Manny was nudged by Zsuzsanna, and he looked up to see the Rabbi asking him to lead off the reading, a graceful courtesy amidst the group sitting around him, like old Indians at a camp fire. So Manny began, in English, in a neutral voice, chapter 1 of the Book of Lamentations:

How desolate lies Jerusalem that was once full of people! She that was once a power among nations is now like a forlorn widow! She who was once a princess among people is now a vassal!

Tears upon her cheeks, she weeps pitifully in the night; of all of her allies there is none to comfort her; all her friends have betrayed her and have become her enemies.

Judah is gone into exile; she dwells upon the nations in poverty and servitude; she finds no peace. On the narrow roads, her pursuers overtook her.

The atmosphere was of quiet and spareness; and the long-ago written words, and the sniffling of Zsuzsanna beside him, worked a surprising sense of uncertainty into Gellerman; he paused. Restraining his tension, he started up again:

The highways to Zion mourn; none come to assemble for the festival; all the gates of her cities are desolate. Her priests despair and her maidens are grieved. Ah, bitter is Jerusalem's lot.

Her foes now rule, her enemies prosper; for the Lord has punished her for her manifold transgressions; her young people are led into captivity before the foe . . .

Gellerman concluded his page-long portion; his friend Zsuzsa sobbed lightly; the group was quietly waiting. Privately he wiped his brow. Though he had read poetry aloud, always in the same neutral voice, the stuff had never really affected him as this selection did.

Next came a yarmulked octogenarian reading in Hebrew, and the hour of reading from the Book of Lamentations ensued. Just as moving as the text of loss and mourning was the intense emotion triggered in his friend, sitting alongside him on the floor; Zsuzsa cried and shook all the way through, though trying to restrain it. As much as Gellerman admired the ongoing rhythmic chant, he had little idea that a text would affect her that way; she used a small white handkerchief constantly at her eyes and nose, but at an angle, away from the sight of the others. Oh, the Jews had lost much, much, and seemed to memorialize and remember each and every blow. Suffering was displayed, honored. The Book of Lamentations was direct, evocative, monstrous in its news, its powerful history urgent and consuming. Near the end of the dark hour, Manny found himself caught up in the grim memory, and his head ached. Probably the plain room, the old Jews, and the simple ceremony contributed to his disorder, he felt.

The hour ended with the Aleinu prayer recited. Zsuzsanna stood and chanted, and he followed her.

Walking out afterward into the soft night air, Manny remarked to his friend that he had never realized how much this holiday of collective remembrance meant to her.

She shook her head. "My father, that's what it means to me. My father! In this room, where he once recited the Lamentations with my mother; it's terrible, terrible! I remember and honor him, and what I've lost. Can you imagine?!" She walked unsteady for a dozen steps or so, and suddenly she began shaking, and nearly fell, sagging onto a black iron fence bordering a park, where she began shaking violently, and crying, hugging herself in paroxysms of pain and torment.

Gellerman was so startled that for a few seconds he stood his ground, stunned, before moving to help her, holding her around, clasping her for the next four or five minutes, holding her to his chest and rocking her for comfort. It was maddening, and bewildering.

Her disturbing performance, especially after the hour and a half in that room of ancient despair, shook his equilibrium and easy assumptions about what was going on and *even how to read her*. He must give her more delicate sympathy, he told himself, and her whole situation too. Obviously she was as frail and stressed as she was obsessed.

Ahead on the main street, the cars darted back and forth, along with the circling yellow trams, and this simple reality flashed for a moment to his overheated brain like some sort of children's toy game, played out here in the night of Budapest. He helped his newfound patient up onto the trolley, and held her hand all the way back to her apartment, where he made sure she was home safe, and then he bid her adieu, saying he would call later.

■

Budapest at night did possess that toy-like quality, he concluded, at least here walking across the Liberty Bridge toward the Gellert Hotel and Palace Hill. Lit up at night, the series of four bridges crossing the Danube made for a pretty sight, with the big white Elisabeth Bridge just up the river to the right, along with the occasional boat gliding down river. You could see the parliament buildings festooned with light in the soft black night. Manny was reminded of his first trek, as a teenage boy, across the Brooklyn Bridge toward the skyline of Manhattan, and feeling the sense of transport to a new world. Now, walking toward the hills of Buda, he thought what a new territory of strangeness this current situation presented, the way the adventure kept taking turns this way and that, so that apparent fact merged with subtle fantasy and sure assumption was toppled by new event. Just ahead, up here in the first district, was where Raoul and his legation had operated, where Vilmos would have the Studebaker ready for him to hop in at a moment's notice, to race to an urgent rescue point.

Meanwhile, the roller coaster ride of the emotions roared on, taking neutral Manny up and down with sudden turns and twists. This was not Dartmouth predictability, or a professional historian's usual journey in foreign turf; this was something else. But what?

He had a quick drink at the hotel and then walked back across the bridge, where he took a tram back to the Oktagon station area and his rented apartment.

In the morning a phone call came from Dora, who explained that Mom had to go to a doctor's appointment, so would he join her for breakfast at a café, and perhaps a walk in the Margaret Island?

Only slightly surprised, Manny accepted, and soon was meeting up with Dora in the New York Café, not far from his place. Was this to be the pattern, a fantastic night with the strange mother, and then a consoling visit from the dutiful, practical daughter? To calm him down?

"This seems like a repeat of how we met last time," he observed.

She smiled lightly. Brown curly hair, white blouse, trim figure, the same lovely young face with the small upturned nose.

Dora sipped tea and nibbled at a roll, while he ate a full breakfast of eggs and toast. They—mostly he—made small chat. Her small cheeks had just a touch of pink blush, whenever he said something slightly unusual, and her shyness was made more attractive by her occasional laugh.

Presently, they took the number 4 tram over the Margaret Bridge, and walked the few hundred yards to Margaret Island, festive in the summer. They walked in the sun, rented a bicycle cart for two, sat on a bench at the far end of the island.

"So," he asked, "what are you here for this time?"

"Please be careful in looking through the papers of Mother," she began. "She has spent a long time collecting them, as you may know. And they are very, very private; even I have not seen them." She looked at him. "What I want so say is this: Please judge the papers, and her, with much care."

"Of course."

"I am not sure if she understands what they may mean, or 'represent.'"

"What? What do you mean?"

A boy of six wandered over and stared. Dora touched the boy's cheek and said something in Hungarian. She dug out of her handbag some jellybeans and handed them to the boy, getting the okay from the mother. The boy tasted one. Not smiling or speaking, he tasted another, and Dora touched his face again.

"I think she has never allowed herself to see them in the open, if you understand me. They were always hidden or buried away. So this will be new for her too."

Now she turned to Manny, removed her large dark glasses, and stared from close proximity, asking for a promise of his complicity in *understanding*. Half of her face was covered by her swirling hair.

"You always seem to be protecting her," he noted, "and wanting me to protect her too."

"Maybe she needs it."

"Why do you say this?"

She paused, in deliberation with herself. "Sometimes I think she is not sure of herself, of who she is exactly."

He took this in and waited. The wind blew softly, mussing her hair more.

"You mean she has multiple personalities?"

"No, not that." She smiled. "Here, let me show you an old card of introduction of hers." She took out from her shoulder purse a business card. It read: "Zsuzsanna Frank, Medium." With a phone number.

He held the card and stared at it, trying to absorb its full meaning.

"I see," he said, seeing nothing. "Well, this is . . . something."

Her brown eyes checked on his understanding. "Mother has achieved many amazing things, I assure you. I have witnessed some for myself. Even when it was dangerous and illegal during the days of Communism, and she was maybe the only non-Gypsy, real medium practicing the art."

He nodded.

"But she has not practiced professionally in a long while, though her services are always in demand. Especially by friends."

He *felt* her strong sincerity, her youthful beauty. "Why did she stop?"

"She stopped years ago because it exhausted her too much. She'd be ill from it. Also, she wanted to devote her energy to focus on her own personal needs, contacts."

Families walked by; two lovers were kissing; ice cream was being hawked.

"Would you like one?" he asked.

"Yes." Searching the fellow's wagon, she chose a vanilla and chocolate swirl cone. "My weakness."

"I am glad to know you have one," he said, and paid.

She pulled down the paper cover and began to lick it.

"Why didn't she, or you, tell me about this before now?"

She shrugged. "It wasn't relevant. All that was years ago, when she did it for a profession."

She was licking the cone all around the edges, with blissful care.

"Tell me, was she able to communicate with her father, after his death?"

After finishing one side, she licked vertically, in a routine. "That you will have to ask her."

He felt the soft wind, the sensuous girl; saw the strollers walking by.

"Do you think she could have *imagined this whole experience* through the eyes of a medium?"

She shot him a look. "You mean as the daughter of the famous man?"

Sensing her accusatory glance, he modulated, "Maybe part of it."

"If you are proposing that my mother is delusional," she retorted, "I reject that. If you are saying that you have doubts about her powers as a medium, I can understand that."

She had a perfect small tongue, he observed, as it darted deftly like a baby snake at the receding cone. And she also made for a perfect intermediary, with her reasoned responses and deft omissions, white blouse and wraparound skirt.

Were they playing him, in unison? Was he a kind of double sucker, one in service to the mom and the other to the daughter?

"I will be careful in how I handle her papers, and her, I promise." *And you too,* he thought.

Gradually, a blossoming smile lighted her small face—that response a clear signal that he understood the ship's fragile journey, and that he would not seek to sabotage it, along with the captain, the mother.

"One last question: Do you believe Mr. Wallenberg was your grandfather?"

Her mouth tightened. She spoke sternly. "I have already answered that question for you. Have you forgotten?"

Yes, she had, and no, he had not forgotten, but he just thought, at the height of this cross-examining section, she might answer it differently.

He tapped her shoulder, a kind of apology, and she relaxed at the touch, and stared at him with her brown eyes.

CHAPTER 16

The papers. He read them in the country-side over a period of three days. He insisted that she be out of the room entirely during his study of these six piles, each of which she had carefully described with a label for purposes of order. She was allowed to bring him a coffee at the beginning, and if he needed anything else, he would go to the kitchen and get it, or ask her. If he had questions, he would also call her over, and she could explain. Having her there, hovering over him, was impossible, he knew. And of course he was dying to ask her whether she had spoken to her father recently.

He sat in the smallish living room, drank his strong coffee, and read.

And what he discovered, or felt, upon a read-through, was that the material broke down into three sections: "Speculations and Inferences" were the nutty hand-scribblings of the madwoman, tiny squiggly penmanship filling the pages with melodramatic and unfounded conclusions; second, "Letters Wife and Daughter," purported to be letters from prison, RW to Zsuzsa and her mother, which Manny read with fifty-percent interest, fifty-percent skepticism; and third, "Fragments from History," which contained several documents and notes from other figures during the historical period. Were the last two categories authentic? He doubted it. What he would have to do, he knew, was to get a handwriting analyst to study a few of the letters, and see when they were written, the quality of the paper, and if possible try to match them up with original RW handwriting, wherever that could be found.

But how to handle the woman here and now, in the country cottage? She hovered in the wings, bringing tea and sandwiches during the days, dinners by evening, waiting with eager anticipation and fervent zeal for him to give the word to start the editing process, not at all to question the materials. This was clear from her general remarks, suggestions for working hours, questions about how much rewriting she would have to do, and the strategic distribution of the overall narrative. Her hairstyle changed every day, one day upswept with a kind of teenage scrunchy, the next done in a French twist. Her attire shifted also, from pretty peasant skirts to out-of-date designer jeans. Zsuzsa seemed permanently flushed with excitement, waiting for the launching of her great project.

"So," he said, as she passed by with her eager glance on the third day, "tell me about this life of being a fortune-teller?"

Stopping in her tracks, she faced him, fiercely. "I have never been a 'fortune teller!' I am not a gypsy!"

He put out his hands to comfort her, "Well, a medium."

"Are you ignorant, Professor? Do you not know the great, the profound, difference?"

Feeling ignorant, he said, "Well, yes, I probably don't."

Her stiffened face relaxed slowly. "Yes, I used to help friends be in touch with loved ones whom they couldn't leave off in their mourning. Is that what you mean?"

He nodded, with sympathy . . . "Oh, I didn't quite understand that. Tell me, why did you stop?"

She shook her head and took an armchair opposite him, across a coffee table. "I had too much personally revolving in my own mind. There was little extra space for others who might have needed my help, my powers."

He drank a local ginger ale. "Do you have such powers?"

She adjusted a cushion behind her, and her eyes narrowed, measuring him. "I won't say I have general powers, only my own qualities."

"What does this entail?"

She smiled. "Are you trying to trap me somehow? 'Reduce' me?"

"Of course not," he immediately responded.

"Well, perhaps you are . . . but . . . Dickens has a short story, whose name I forget—maybe 'The Signal-Man'?—where a man can see a ghost. And obviously in Shakespeare, Hamlet can see the ghost of his father. So there are great writers who do suggest that certain people do have certain powers, wouldn't you admit?"

Clever woman! "Yes, you are right. So please do tell me, what can you see?"

She smiled girlishly. "I would prefer, first, to hear your report on my papers; it has been three days, you realize."

Clever again. He scratched his beard. "Oh, I think there are certain issues that we—"

"Do you mean that we are not yet ready to proceed with our project?"

"There are certain things I would like to check out first."

"Such as?"

Should he delay the moment of truth? "Well, for purposes of historical accuracy, I will need to confirm the authenticity of those letters. That is the first thing."

She smiled, happily it seemed! "And what else?"

"Well, then there are the surrounding documents from the period that I will need to verify, like those notes from Stockholm, say."

To his surprise, she put out her hands to him, palms up, for him to take hold of, and he could do nothing but accept them, out of courtesy. "You are a true historian, and I am grateful for that. That is why I have chosen you for this sacred partnership. Now, can we proceed to our working schedule?"

More than surprised, he was amazed. She wanted to go on, and was accepting his terms! "Well, I am very glad to hear that, really. This will make things . . . smoother, easier."

"Of course." She looked at him, locking him with her gray eyes.

"Now perhaps you can answer my earlier question: What can you *see* with your special . . . qualities?"

Holding his hands still, she stared for a full minute. "There are times when I can visualize my father, hear him, feel him, smell him. Yes, I will acknowledge this."

He breathed hard, listened to the birds, the big clock ticking . . . There were so many areas to ask about and dig into. "And when was the last time? And what did you see or feel?"

"Please, let me explain to you, Emmanuel." (Her use of his first name startled him!) "Do you know the term *Umkehr*?" When he shook his head, she went on. "This is Buber's translation of the Hebrew *t'shuvah* and means return. The noun can be found in the Bible, but not in the sense that it is found commonly in Jewish literature and liturgy. The verb is frequently used in the Bible with the connotations that are relevant here; what is meant is the return to God. You can find examples of this in . . ."—she paused and checked a small notepad—"Isaiah 10:21 and 19:22, Deuteronomy 4:30 and 30:2, and Jeremiah 4:1." She held his hand and looked at him, like a parent with a child. She smiled. "Do you understand yet?"

He shook his head, dumbfounded, transported into a whole new space.

"If you substitute my father for God, you will understand how I have been able to search for him and find him. This *act of return* is what has connected us, through the years. In the Judaic tradition the idea is very simple; at any time a man can return and be accepted by God, one to one. Organized religion has nothing to do with this. And this is how I have been able to reach and touch my father. For my father is God—God to me. *Fahrstay*?"

Exhausted himself, he gently withdrew his hands. "And how often do you speak to Raoul?"

"I cannot tell you this, because it does not happen according to any routine. Our meetings occur at random times and moments, though some of those moments are already filled with high feeling, emotion. For example, when I was collecting these papers, which included Father's letters and memorablia, he came to me, late one night, and offered himself for dialogue; as I explained *you* to him, he understood, and offered his full approval; this was a blessing of sorts for our project. I would not have proceeded with you otherwise."

He listened carefully, trying to make sense of the bizarre reasoning, and saw the breeze shift through curtains of the mullioned window. "Very interesting," he said, wanting to return kindly to the former track. "So you do have 'powers' or 'qualities'—good. Tomorrow, let us go back into town, and I will try to hunt down the experts who can verify our papers here."

She smiled, nodding. "Tell me, please, Emmanuel, do you understand what I have been saying to you?"

"I think so. I hope so."

Her smile turned weary. "I hope so too. Mine is a sacred trust; do you understand this?"

Feeling coerced, he said, "Yes, I do."

"I will feel betrayed if you forget or betray our covenant."

What did this mean? "I will try not to betray you, or our covenant, but I will also do my job, my professional job. After all, that is my role."

She nodded, soberly.

He did not add, as the moment was too charged, that if his professional role contradicted her "sacred trust" and "covenant," he knew which agreement or contract he would have to honor. If it were to turn out, crazily, that there was some wild kernel of truth embedded somehow, somewhere deep in her accounts and papers, he would have secured a special cache, no doubt. One that would put him back on the historian's map, for sure; and one that would excite his full energies too. But the odds of that happening were about as long as discovering another planet.

But then he realized that they just had.

At night, reading in the study—"my father's," she confided—he saw a small photograph of Raoul in the corner alongside one of his grandfather, in two matching oval frames, with an inscription that Manny couldn't make out, in Swedish or German. Manny looked closer and saw a framed note with a quote from Raoul: "A person like me, who is both a Wallenberg and a part Jew, can never be defeated." Manny was taken aback; was this a genuine quote? He knew that Raoul had been a small part Jewish, dating back to a great-great grandfather on his maternal side, named Benedicks, who had converted to

Lutheranism, married a Christian girl, and done well. Manny also knew that Raoul had been proud of his Jewishness—but this proud? He had a thought, an inspiration, and opened his laptop, despite the late hour. He composed a note from Raoul's grandfather, the good Gustaf:

Dear Raoul,

I have received your good letter from Haifa, and am both touched and disturbed by it. I am disturbed because I always wanted you to end up going into something practical, like commerce, and am sad to hear that you think it doesn't suit you after all, for the long run. Especially after Erwin Freund, your boss, an excellent man and Jewish, has written to me how well you have done at his Holland Bank branch, praising you highly and saying you have a real future ahead of you in banking if you wish it. While I have been very satisfied to have you spend your three years in Ann Arbor studying architecture and receiving your diploma there, I always thought you would use that as a stepping stone to move into some form of commercial situation here in Stockholm, if not with your cousins, at least with some other successful firm.

Naturally, I am very touched by your remarks on the Jewish refugees who have been streaming into Palestine, from Europe, through Haifa, and your strong feelings about them. The situation in Germany is growing more desperate, and to have this happen in ultracivilized Germany is most depressing. Once a dictator gains control over the masses, the outcome is tragic. But please, do not get personally involved; concerned, yes, but not involved. The difference is important, Raoul. Would things be easier for you if you moved from the kosher boarding house you are currently living in? I understand your deep sensitivity and sympathy, and even your own personal attachment to your mother's great-great-grandfather, who was part Jewish. But that was a long time ago. It's been a few hundred years since everyone in the family converted, you know, so that your mother grew up Lutheran and thought nothing of it. In these growing dangerous times, lead a prudent personal life, my grandson; no need to take extra risks, personally or politically. (Although I have long admired your high personal principles.)

I have never been hostile to the Jewish people, you understand; on the contrary, I have long appreciated their worth and accomplishments. In every society they have lived, they have enhanced the society. Look, I sent you to my good friend Freund there at the bank in Haifa, because he is a superior banker and good man. And everywhere, always, the Jews have proved to be excellent bankers and leaders in finance. Consider the great banking families of Germany, the

Loebs, the Lehmans, and the Guggenheims; they have been the backbone of high finance in Germany, and will go on doing that. I cannot believe that even this sleazy National Socialism and cheap little dictator will toss out those great banking families. Nonetheless, you be careful. Do not take on extra risk for yourself. Sympathy is one thing, highly commendable; but direct involvement is another, imprudent and problematic. Stay to your course, and accomplish much, but beyond politics, especially in this volatile day and age.

I will only add that your extra sensitivities will probably not go over well with your cousins Jacob and Marcus, who feel little of the Jewish side you have always felt. And if you ever expect to get help from them in your future career, whatever that may be, no matter what you—or I—feel toward them, you should take into account their own sensitivities and preferences.

I look forward to hearing from you and do give my best to Mr. Freund.
Grandfather Gustaf

Manny pulled back, reread the letter, and tried to remember when Grandfather Gustaf died. About 1937? Though it saddened Raoul, it also meant an escape from the loving old tyrant. And it left Raoul on his own, to commit freely to his extra risks and imprudent acts. How would the old man have acted toward Raoul in Budapest 1944–45, once he learned of his intense involvement? . . . Manny thought, or hoped, that Gustaf would have lauded his beloved grandson, while worrying deeply. And certainly the old grandfather would have broken down all private or public walls to try to free him from the Russians.

The next day, he and Z. returned to Budapest, holding Zsuzsa's papers; but her understanding of what he meant by checking on authenticity was not what he had hoped for. First off, she would not let the papers out of her hands or sight. This meant that she would accompany him everywhere. This was itself an embarrassment, he saw, after their first engagement with a handwriting analyst, who insisted that he be able to examine privately, over a period of forty-eight hours, the several letters they had chosen. Zsuzsa laughed derisively and said, "Forty-eight hours? You must be crazy! You can be safely in Vienna by then, and make your fortune, and we would never see you again. I know your type well!"

Manny was shocked. But was her role real, or playacted perfectly? That's what he needed to find out. So he tried another tack, and took her over to the national archives, where they were to examine some of the historical documents from the diplomatic office. Once again she created a huge fuss and semi-hysterical incident. The archivist, a paunchy bespectacled fellow in a frayed suit, brought out a variety of documents for her to sign and get notarized and return with in a few days, and she blew up at him, in Hungarian! Who was this "little man" who thought he could order her and her American professor around? Manny tried to make peace, but it was hopeless, and as they left, Zsuzsa complained bitterly. He understood this was not going to be easy.

"Supposing I take a few of these letters and a few other documents back to the states and find an analyst there who can give us verification?"

She smiled, quite peaceably. "At least *there* we will have competence, without corruption. This is a backward place, you must understand."

All that sounded fine, until he came to understand, later at dinner at Rosenstein's, near the train station, that she meant to accompany him to the US, if he were to take the originals. But chaperoning her was out of the question, he knew. So, what could he do? . . .

At wit's end, he suggested that he make copies of a half dozen or dozen originals, and take those. What did she think?

"Yes, that would be possible. Copies—why not?" She paused. "This food is undercooked. We should have eaten in; my paprika chicken is superior." She smiled impishly. "But while you are here, we may proceed with the start of our work?"

Digesting his food, he felt trapped, and wiped his mouth with the linen napkin. "Well, we could do that, yes, and see how it goes. But I need to finish looking through the materials first, to see where and how to proceed."

A foursome arrived and sat down on the little platform area where they were seated. One couple noticed Zsuzsa, and they came over excitedly to give her a hug and kiss; they exchanged pleasantries, and Manny was introduced, "My American professor friend." The couple returned to their table, and Zsuzsa raised her eyebrows. "Old Communists, now pretending to be liberal! Feh!"

Just as they returned to their own dinner, Dora stood before them, a vision in white!

Mother grinned and hugged her, and Manny stood and held a chair for her. She sat demurely, her face a beacon of innocence in the dour atmosphere.

"Did you eat yet?"

She shook her head. "I don't need much, thank you."

A waiter came by; she ordered a Greek salad with wine and sat quietly.

Mother said, "Good news, we are proceeding to work immediately. Professor Gellerman has agreed!"

Manny barely nodded. He heard some Brits at a nearby table digging into Bush and Blair.

"I have a very strong feeling, Dorottya, about our new partnership. At last I have found a true champion to serve Father, and his memory."

Dora looked over at Manny, her brown eyes fixing him, waiting.

Manny massaged his beard. "Your mother is optimistic. I hope she is correct."

Dora half smiled. "And you?"

"Me? I am always pessimistic, but I am also always foolish. So, anything is possible!"

A moment of puzzling silence, the ladies absorbing that; then Zsuzsa laughed, and her daughter smiled. "You see," proclaimed Mother, clapping her hands, "he is a gentleman of possibilities. What more can we ask for?"

"Yes, a Professor of Possibility," Dora observed, wittily. "That is a good role."

She stared at him, with those shining—demanding?—brown eyes, to see how he was taking her playful mocking. Satisfied, she said in a low voice, "'Anything is possible.' I like that; it is very philosophical."

"Credit to Dostoyevsky, though the new phrasing is mine," Manny explained, breathing in her musk fragrance and pink cheeks, and wondering if indeed the phrase had pertinence here.

The next day, before meeting Zsuzsanna to go to the copy shop, he called the Budapest historian whom he had consulted with in the past, and luckily found him in.

In Borhi's fourth-floor Buda apartment in the third district, Manny proceeded to narrate further—more than he already had told him in the past, via some e-mails—about the madwoman (and/or charlatan or medium), and her wild claims, and her cache of so-called authentic letters, documents, etc.

Lazslo shook his head and said, "Oh, I doubt most of it, as I have told you; but you know, so much of Wallenberg in Budapest and in Moscow is obscure, mysterious, unknown, and even invented, that we can't be sure that her tale is *entirely* fictitious." He shrugged. "I myself have heard many apocryphal stories about him, in relation to the Nazis, the OSS, the Russians, and also his personal relationships of all sorts, so that without hard empirical evidence, we can't prove or disprove such claims. Of course, if we could check some of the papers you speak of, yes, that would help. But if she won't give them up for a day or two, how would you accomplish this?"

"Well, I've tried, but thus far, no success."

He got up, went to his desk, found a name in an address book, and wrote it down on a piece of paper. "Here is a bona fide handwriting analyst, who specializes in old documents and manuscripts. Use my name. I have used him in the past a few times; see if he is still around and what he may require to check the papers. Yes, I believe it will be the originals, for many reasons."

Gellerman thanked him, took the address and phone number, and told him he would keep him informed.

Borhi nodded, and added, "Let me know if anything turns up. All leads should be followed, as you are doing. And really, who knows?" He raised his eyebrows. "Remember, nobody really knows anything about this case, after all these decades, so anything you can come up with will be of great interest."

As Manny departed and entered the small old-fashioned steel elevator, he thought with surprise about how open Borhi was to the possibility of discovering some pay dirt. However, in the elevator cage, as it dropped down, he felt more like a prisoner of the situation than a free man pursuing history.

The next day, Wednesday, at a copy shop, they proceeded to make copies of twelve documents, and as they waited in the tiny shop, Manny realized the folly of this; just as Borhi had cautioned, no serious handwriting analyst could work from mere copies and declare a verdict with any certitude. That was foolish. It came to him that he would have to resort to stealth work, if he wanted to get anywhere . . .

Later, in the apartment, he searched through the *Tribune* for the baseball scores, saw the Red Sox holding up in the dog days of August, and sat down at the large table in the parlor. He shuffled through a pile of papers, then took out a notebook and a pen. He called Zsuzsa in and said, "So, shall we begin? Let me ask you some questions, concerning these letters and other documents, and you can answer as best as your memory serves you . . ."

She smiled, sitting with her hands folded like a prim schoolgirl. "First, I ask you a question, a basic question: You have faith in me, I assume? Or hope?"

Caught off guard, he said, "Well, yes."

"And you are going to check on my papers for reasons of your profession, yes?"

"Yes." He paused. "Naturally."

She nodded, and said, "All right, I understand. But for me, faith is everything, for it means trust, with the body, and the heart, as well as the brain, and that faith is the only path to truth, the deeper truth of seeing things that others cannot see."

He put down his pen, considered her words of prudent self-protection, and sensed that the medium was talking.

"Yes, I suppose what others cannot see, or find; that's what we are searching for."

The teacher nodded to the pupil and said, "I know your suspiciousness; I have felt it, and hope it is only your immediate reflex, not your deeper belief. Perhaps *I* can 'convert' *you*?" She smiled. "May I read these few thoughts to you, from one of your own?" She reached over, took out a small pad, and read: "I am quite willing to believe that a new truth may be supernaturally revealed to a subject when he really asks. But I am sure that in many cases of conversion it is less a new truth than a new power gained over life by a truth always known." She looked up, luminous, having used one of Manny's books to support her view, and perhaps pedagogy. "Your William James wrote those words. A wise man, don't you think?"

If Manny Gellerman ever doubted it, he understood well now that this was one formidable lady, and maybe foe, and that he must not underestimate her. "Yes, a wise man," he repeated her words, but his mind was elsewhere, trying to catch up with his own plans, and the future.

"May I say," he said, "that I didn't realize that you did such quick homework or read so widely?"

At first she observed him sternly, but then she softened, and she laughed. "Oh, not so widely; there is always too little time for reading. But it is my greatest pleasure, apart from remembering and honoring father."

He took a bite from a sweet roll that she had brought, with coffee, and began his questioning of her, wondering, just wondering, if she had managed to feel or intuit his inclination or plan to "borrow" some of her original papers for authenticating.

CHAPTER 17

Driving up on Route 93 from the Boston airport, he had plenty of time to think, rethink, reflect. Above Hookset and before Concord, he crossed over to Route 89 going north, where the cars were few and far between, there were no billboards, and it was practically pitch black, with no highway lamps. He had made this drive hundreds, maybe thousands, of times in his thirty years living up here in the North Country. He drove in a kind of velvety fog, charcoal-smooth and easy, listening to music or encased in his own thoughts. Occasionally, when another car came up from behind, Manny felt it as an intrusion upon his private road, his quiet metaphysical hour.

That his life had been interrupted, or intruded upon, by Wallenberg, was clear enough. For over a year, maybe a year and a half, Raoul, and what had happened to him and why, had come to possess him, almost as much as it possessed the woman he had just left who claimed to be his daughter. While he had seen the mystery, or mysteries, to begin with, and felt he had solved certain of them, others had merely deepened. And as they had deepened they had ripened, it may be said (to himself), to the point where they had taken hold of him, emotionally, so that he now felt very close to that betrayed tragic figure. Oddly enough, he had been right in his early speculations that Raoul was a mix of Jackie (Robinson) and Bartleby (the scrivener): part outlaw, part stranger; two outsiders—like Bartleby, a man of principle, betrayed, abandoned, and left forlorn; like Jackie, proving himself with his great skills (physical), and taking on an extra burden (race). Strange indeed, Gellerman thought, that both these native figures described best how he viewed Raoul, from the inside, emotionally.

Was he going crazy? Perhaps.

He drove, in the clear black night, comforted by the routine radio broadcast of the baseball game, just like childhood evenings . . .

What did "crazy" mean in this present context? Willing to go all out in the face of obstacles, stop signs and detours, in pursuit of his final goal? (Was that Prince of Denmark crazy, seeing and listening to his ghost father and acting as though he were real?) And yet, what was the final goal? Recovering what had happened to Raoul? Recovering—or discovering—who he was? Discovering the culprits responsible for his languishing in prison? Hadn't he answered these questions for himself and concluded that there were criminals besides the Soviets? . . . Yet, if he had his own partial answers, did he wish to reveal them to the world? For example, did he wish to reveal that Raoul was probably gay, and maybe even out of the closet in Budapest? Would the world, and RW's legion of supporters and votaries, really need *or want* to hear that, when the basic issues were political, ethical? . . . Shouldn't he seek to protect Raoul—no matter what the ghost had said to him—and honor the secrecy of his private life?

Now, what about the madwoman/medium of Budapest? (And why did Manny persist in calling her "mad," when she actually seemed, thus far, quite the opposite?) Where and how did she fit in, with her faith and obsession? If—a very large *if*—she had been telling some truth, or a bit of the truth, and Raoul had had a liaison with her mother, was that to be revealed too? Well, she seemed to be writing about just this. For what and whose purposes? . . .

(Did RW also have a liaison elsewhere? With another woman, or a man? . . .)

What more could Manny do? Had he not served Wallenberg sufficiently already with his approximately eighteen months of increasing devotion?

He drove, questions swirling, passing through the blackness like a submarine slipping through dark waters stealthily, every now and then catching sight of red tailgate lights up ahead . . .

The Red Sox put on a rally in the ninth, but lost, and the announcers were putting the best face on it. The Yankees were charging hard to the top. Why not stick to the pennant races, the football season, the academic world, the easy native obsessions with movies, political correctness, celebrities, and the dinner talk about real estate values and Bush bashing?

Work to be done: the small matter of the ongoing witnesses who kept turning up, saying they had spotted RW in some Gulag prison or hospital.

The handling of Zsuzsanna's memoir.

And how about handling Manny? Working on his own book or article? Maybe his Shadow Narrative, or fictional metahistory? His long-term investigation and questions would continue to the end, whereever that end might lead—Budapest, Moscow, Stockholm? . . .

Driving on the fast lane was easiest here, on the four-lane highway, with hardly a car in sight, going or coming; occasionally a New York or Connecticut

car headed up this way, at sixty-five miles an hour or so, and Manny would
cruise by at eighty, his Saab knowing the way by heart and routine. Route 89
North at night was smooth, safe, spacious, an empty road on which to roam
and reflect, to consider one's life and decisions, and if he drove straight up to
Montreal, he'd figure out all his directions and future destinations.

Raoul was there with him; he sensed his past and his presence, a history
alive, a mystery unsolved. Now it began to drizzle, and Manny thought he saw
R's sober reflection in the windshield, challenging him, as the wipers shifted
slowly back and forth, back and forth.

The policeman who stopped him was an older fellow, wearing summer
blues; he checked out Manny's driver's license and registration. "You're lucky
tonight. I'm only going to issue you a warning, but no more eighty-five and
ninety, no matter what time of night. And even if no one is on the road, sir."

Manny, a bit dazed, was grateful for the warning—was it a symbolic warning as well?—and curtailed his speed for the next hour until he hit home.

The next day he felt fired up, and, after breakfast, went to work drafting a
small essay:

In recent years, there's been a small cadre of political and polemical critics who have
tried hard to make Raoul out to be a dirty spy for the Americans, giving the Soviets
a good reason to be very interested in him. RW supposedly worked not merely for
the OSS, but also for a super secret group, known only to the top people around
FDR, called "The Pond." These pundits argue the case that Raoul was in touch with
the British secret service as well, and may have been involved with an arrangement
whereby the Brits would join the Hungarians in going against the Soviets, once the
war was over. (It should be noted that a close aid of RW, Captain Elek Kelecsenyi,
supposedly had ties to KGB agents and probably reported on Raoul.) In addition,
runs the argument, Raoul was able to secure the release of so many Jews precisely
because he was in cahoots with the Nazi high command in Budapest. Thus the Soviets were most keen on detaining and questioning him about the various agents he
might have known, plus the many rich Jewish friends and clients that he worked for.
Consequently, the idea of Raoul acting out of pure intentions was naïve and wrong.

It is worth noting that the leader of the group seeking to erode Raoul's perceived
integrity is himself a Soviet émigré, who, while living comfortably in New York, is a
conspiracy theorist in his heart and mind. This middle-aged fellow, whom I met in
Moscow and whose excessive, relentless essay on the subject is both ideological and
tendentious, has made the case that in fact Raoul was hardly a hero, but rather a
Swedish playboy more concerned about his personal dandy pleasures than the or-

deal of the Jews. If so, Raoul was one playboy who did rather well for the Jews, and we needed more of them!

Why was this effort to degrade Raoul made? And why has this group attacked RW so vengefully, when, to be sure, there was little evidence to back up their assertions, and furthermore, no witnesses to corroborate them? These are perhaps more interesting questions. And why would this push come from an ex-Soviet and a few drive-by American journalists and cheap ex-spies? Was it only the smell of the bucks?

But for a moment, let's say that RW was a spy, working for the Allies while working to save the Jews of Budapest. Considering the context, was this so bad? Look at what the Soviets did to local resistance fighters like Károly Schandl, Lázslo Pap, Louis Klement, who were sent to Vladimir Prison for years! Or Count István Bethlen, who was murdered by Soviet hands in October 1946. Or other Hungarian associates of RW, like Szabö, Szalai, Alapi, who were hunted down by the Soviets and forced to serve long prison terms. Not to forget the strong anti-Semitism of the Soviet troops and leaders. Was it so wrong to work against that huge monstrous machine?

Moreover, the Soviets themselves in all probability did not know whom they had gotten when they captured RW. Although the early facts of his capture are rather nebulous, it's clear that RW himself didn't fully know if he was being taken by the Soviet officials from Debrecen to Moscow as "a guest or a prisoner." There, he was taken to Lybianka Prison, though it still remained unclear if they knew who he was; for it was a few weeks later that Abramov of SMERSH, the counterspy unit, entered the situation to say that he, and not Beria, would run the case. In June and July 1945, in Russia and Hungary, chaos and confusion reigned, with missing souls, dead souls, unknown and undeclared souls, so that knowing who was who was itself a conundrum. With larger national problems of economics and politics on the horizon, and the Cold War already begun, the capture of a single unknown Swede was probably of little importance for the Soviets.

We return to our initial question: Why has the recent squad of political assassins gone after RW and his reputation? Is it because the Soviet sensibility was shaped by a Stalinest thug regime and anti-Communist mindset, which was then enveloped by the new Cold War temperament, wherein conspiracy was in the air everywhere? And within this atmosphere, allies and enemies were practically all the same, all implicated, switching sides periodically, in a No Exit laboratory of liars and betrayers and double agents; and therefore, the idea of a single-minded soul, driven by idealism and a passion for justice and natural sympathy, was not only incongruous but incomprehensible and anathema. The basic principle was simple: everyone in the USSR and East Europe—and the Americans too—in the late forties/early fifties had dirty hands. And now, looking back, the battle-scarred survivors of the Soviet paranoia machine and the Cold War, including those who had been agents themselves of the KGB and other secret agencies, made themselves over into shrewd experts and judges on who was dirty, who was a spy, who was a traitor and double agent; and it turned out, in their absolutist judgment, that ninety-nine percent all of the players were dirty, whether they knew it or not. Conspiracy, spying, betrayal, dark intentions coursed in the blood of this posse of self-appointed vigilantes. Wherever they could, the posse would pursue any renegade or maverick who had not only avoided criminal acts but who had come across as honorable or decent. For one honorable man to exist in that vast sea of crooks, commies, cowards, trimmers, and assassins was as dangerous as the idea of justice itself; and he had to be hunted down and, if dead, his reputation blackened, for if there were no honorable men, then honor itself was out of the question.

Manny stopped for a lunch, grabbed some cottage cheese, nuts, and yogurt, and returned for revision. When he looked up it was twilight. On the horizon lay lines of blue and mauve with cirrus clouds forming amoeba shapes. He felt unsettled, fatigued, as though he had just been digging in smelly muck and mire. Though he had written about the Cold War, he was always amazed at how long it had persisted; and now this new angle, tarnishing the good guys. Had he tried too hard to protect Raoul? No, not at all.

Fresh country air beckoned suddenly, and he went outside in the cool evening, to walk up his forest trail. He might expand the piece and send it to a history journal, or try it over at the *Wall Street Journal*, which had queried him to write something about RW. Walking, he smelled the woodsy air and felt the pleasure of country life, so vividly aromatic after the odors of the Cold War.

He sat on the college green, on a wooden park bench, reading through the papers. The blue sky and warm sun induced the kids to play a variety of games, the boys removing their shirts and the girls wearing tank tops and shorts. An ultimate Frisbee game was being played in one area; in another, a game of six-against-six softball was played; and in a third the kids were spiraling a football. On narrow paths joggers ran with iPods, bicyclists moved along carefully, students tanned themselves on spread blankets. This was a good site in which to regard the letters and documents of Madame Zsuzsanna. In the sun and frolicking green, to probe deeper into the other worlds of dark fantasy and selective memory. By his side was his laptop, wirelessly connected via the college. The spirit of the new technology had invaded every pore of college life.

After consultation, he had sent down to a Boston handwriting analyst six documents and was awaiting the results. Manny nurtured few illusions. Those letters, translated from German by a colleague, were touching documents written by a father to a newly born daughter and her mother from a prison in Moscow; they were composed by someone intelligent and caring, and the impersonator was someone very familiar with Raoul, and no doubt brilliant. As for the official documents, from diplomats to diplomats and to Zsuzsanna's family, they were equally clever and ingenious. Those meticulous copies or frauds were similar to the flawless copies of the great painting masters, where the average art viewer could not tell the difference between the original and the copy. And that's what he expected to hear from the handwriting analyst professional. (He knew that he'd ultimately have to solve the authenticity problem at some point. But for now an honest ambiguity might serve his interest best . . .)

A Frisbee flew near; he leaned down and tossed it back, aiming poorly; he had never gotten the hang of Frisbee tossing or the rules of the game.

He opened his e-mails and, sure enough, some surprises landed upon him on the sunny green. The first e-mail came from Dora in Budapest, asking how the organization and writing was going. Was he ready yet to make working suggestions to Mother? Another missive came from the Swedish mystery banker. "Do not give up your pursuit, Professor. It is a noble cause." Manny smiled, feeling played; but that was okay. Here on the a late summer day, sitting on a bench in this small college town in New Hampshire, he felt beyond grasp of those European hands reaching out for him.

The third e-mail blasted through his complacency. It came from Zsuzsa herself, who said she now had a Hungarian publisher, Corvina, quite interested in making an early arrangement for the book, and they were sure they could also sell it to a large English and American publisher rather soon. "What should we do, my friend? Should we accept this early offer or wait? You see how quickly things can happen! Especially with your name connected to it as well!"

What exactly did she mean by that? Had she forgotten Yale? He put on his sunglasses and felt dizzy. Trying to digest her news, he walked over to the music rooms in the basement of the Hopkins Center, and there met up with his son, in practice room C.

The boy hugged him. "Okay, Dad, sit; here is a surprise for you." He declared this news slowly, melodramatically, "The complete first movement of my Wallenberg Cello Suite."

Sitting on a stool with his cello, he first warmed up and proceeded to play, for six or seven minutes, a piece with dissonant harmonies and strange lovely melodies, a mélange drawn from mid-Beethoven quartets, Mozart, and a touch of Schoenberg. Music that was awkward, potent, harsh, riveting. Using much vibrato, he held notes extra long and played a fast passionate ending!

Manny clapped hard and enthusiastically.

"My allegro maestoso—what do you think?" he smiled widely. "Next comes my poco adagio for the second movement."

Gellerman was rather overwhelmed, by the music, the thought, the playing; he went over and hugged the boy tightly. "Really, it's just terrific! So exciting."

"Yeah, I kinda like how it came out, though it's still a little rough and needs work, of course."

"'Of course'—you little whippersnapper!" Kissed his forehead. "Mr. Wallenberg would have been truly honored, believe me."

"Think so?"

"Know so."

Manny took him for an ice cream at Ben & Jerry's across the street.

The boy said, "It's very hard writing a piece, you know—completely different from playing a piece. I'm not sure if I prefer it."

"You don't have to prefer it at all. Do both or do what you wish. If that's the only movement you ever write, it was great." He wiped some ice cream off the boy's shirt. "By the way, what does 'maestoso' mean?"

"Oh, that means 'grand.'"

Later, at a movie, still feeling the blessing of the boy's composition and grand intention, he reflected on the new serious gambit from Budapest. What had Zsuzsa gotten him into? What had he allowed himself to be seduced and trapped into? . . . A book contract based on materials that were created out of fantasy and clever mischief? Letters invented by a mad, if brilliant, imagination? Manny's name "connected" to it would inevitably mean the loss of professional credibility; "Gellerman's Grand Hoax" would make for great fun in the profession! *That's just what you need, Manny, to finish off your career and life, a little major hoax as a finale.*

In the next few days, he went through his routines with a quiet underlying panic. Walking, reading, taking notes, playing tennis, seeing a few students, watching baseball. He called the handwriting analyst and asked for a verdict by the end of the week. He discovered that the expert, Mr. Blaylock, was on vacation in Cape Cod for two weeks . . . He had tried to be kindly to the Budapest lady and now was on the verge of being destroyed by her, in one way or another. No good deed goes unpunished, he recalled. If he helped her write her so-called memoir, he would be helping her fantasy life come into print, and destroying his reputation. If he signed off the project now, promptly and completely, he would sacrifice the tiny possibility of something real in her past, a point of authenticity or relevance in her biography. And then, might there not be a discovery of some historical importance? One that should be written up by a historian? . . . Fortunately, he had a few weeks of his own "vacation," a respite before he learned for sure what the terms of his decision were to be. Once he heard from the handwriting analyst, resolving that these papers were a fraud—a good or bad fraud—it would be a pure and simple decision. A complete break.

In looking over the letters, he found two groups: the personal letters written to the family, and the others concerned with the political situation. They were written with intelligence and concern, like that of any paterfamilias; and their political acumen was sharp. The effort put into creating this collection was determined. Yet Manny only glanced through it, not going at it seriously, since he knew that in a few weeks the whole escapade would be blown up, and he'd be saying good riddance—and maybe sad riddance too?

But, surprisingly, he came across something else, of different interest and kind: a small booklet, maybe seventy-five pages, written by Zsuzsanna, with drawings, letters, and photographs. It was a kind of child's journal, composed by an adult, and it had a child's charm and appeal. The photographs, pasted intermittently, created a family album, showing Raoul, a little girl (presumably Zsuzsanna) and her own mother. How did this slip in? When was it written? And why hadn't she told Manny about this? . . . One level of conundrum and surprised perplexity always seemed to lead to another here.

Manny asked her those questions in an e-mail. She responded immediately (and he could practically hear her giggle!), "Oh, that. I forgot all about that early project! My first memoir! Did I really leave that with you?"

Of course, by now Manny understood that she did nothing by mistake; with Zsuzsa, nothing was accidental.

Sitting in his living room, with his laptop open and ready, he looked out at the shorn meadow and composed another scene:

June 1947; Raoul in Lybianka Prison

Daniel P., the interrogator, entered the room, nodded to his associate, who left the room, and sat down opposite Wallenberg, now a much wearier prisoner than when he arrived.

"How are you, Raoul? Any more sketches?" Daniel smiled sympathetically, speaking German. A short wiry man, carrying a small brown leather briefcase.

Raoul shook his head.

"Your last ones were quite a while ago, three months or so. I would be happy to see any new ones, you know."

Raoul nodded.

Daniel paused and offered Raoul a cigarette. "Lucky Strikes," he said.

Raoul took it and allowed Daniel to light it for him.

"Raoul, I am worried. You don't look so healthy anymore. This is a troubling development."

Raoul inhaled and exhaled, slowly.

"I think you need to face the situation with reality; it is important." He leaned forward across the table. "You know now, they are never going to rescue you. It's been almost two years, Raoul. You will stay here forever. And perish here. Your family and country, both have abandoned you."

Raoul stared at his close adversary.

"Is this the way you want to spend your last years, my friend? Please don't even contemplate such a fate!"

Raoul smoked, and dropped an ash into a bucket.

"Your face, it is getting . . . hollow in the eyes and cheeks, and I know why; not merely the prison food, but also the lack of hope; I understand this. And I sympathize, believe me."

Raoul looked at him, rather forlorn.

"Do you have anything to say now, regarding any of the questions I have been asking? After these two years, isn't it time to yield a little, and explain yourself more? Talk about your friends in Budapest?"

Wallenberg smoked and said, "I could use another sketch pad, if you don't mind. And some shading pencils."

Daniel jotted down a note in his book.

"Anything else?"

"Have I any mail? Diplomatic or personal?"

The interrogator shook his head slowly. "Not since the note I showed you, what, six months ago? Your colleague doesn't seem to have written you again—not out of lack of interest, I am sure, but probably thinking . . . who knows?"

Raoul said, "If I could get a piece of meat once in a while, I would be happier."

Daniel made a note. Looking up, he signaled to the standing guard, who departed.

He leaned forward once again and spoke in a whisper. "You must listen to me now, Raoul, and listen carefully. I know I am your interrogator, your co-handler; but I am also your ally. Your friend. The date is approaching—I don't know when—when they will make a decision about you, and it won't go well if they have nothing to show for it, after these two years. Do you understand what I am saying to you?"

Raoul put out his cigarette butt and smiled, almost wryly. "I think I understand you, yes."

"I have recently gotten several signals about this matter, and I am anxious. I do not say this to you as a strategy to provoke you into talking, believe me now. I say this to you as one who has gotten to know you, and know you well, better than anyone in these past couple of years, and I admire you and am fond of you."

Raoul nodded. "I believe you, Daniel, and I thank you for your . . . sympathies."

"Raoul, do you not want to see again your favorite old places, the Bergius Botanic Garden for orchids, the Court Theater for Strindberg and Ibsen at Drottningholm Palace, or the Fjaderhomarna islets for your sailing lessons? Do you remember your youthful pleasures sailing in the archipelago?"

Raoul smiled, clasped his hands. "You do do your homework, and always have, Daniel. You are very resourceful, no doubt."

"But I am not speaking idly here, of what you are missing." He spoke even lower. "I am not speaking of merely recovering your life, but of *surviving* your life! That is what I am saying to you, warning you!"

Raoul narrowed his eyes and looked tired. "Why this . . . sudden passion? Please, it's not like you, Daniel."

Daniel pulled back, lit a cigarette, gave another one to Wallenberg.

"Raoul, you are the prisoner; I am the interrogator. But it might as well be reversed. What I mean by this is that we are in this together. You and me. If I lose you, I lose a strong part of me as well. Do you understand?"

Raoul smoked, and blew the smoke aside. "You are getting too deep for me, too . . . existential perhaps?"

"Yes, maybe I am, but I want to, now, here. It is getting late, very late, and the clock is ticking near midnight. Won't you save yourself?"

Raoul leaned in, interested. "Do you mean save you as well?"

"How do you mean this?"

"Will they do harm to you if you have come up with nothing from me?"

Daniel's eyes widened. "Yes, I see—you are worried now about me, and my fortune!" He nodded. "I understand and admire you my friend. No, I am fine, and believe I will be fine. It is *you* I am worried about."

Daniel peered at his prisoner across the table, three and a half feet away.

"Good, I am glad about that." He paused. "Also, Daniel, if I can get any fresh vegetables in the soup, apart from any meat, that will be an aid. A piece of cabbage perhaps? Or a nice turnip? Just something to go with the potato"—and he nearly smiled—"the perpetual potato."

Daniel nodded and jotted down the new requests, as he had jotted them down for months and passed them along, with few results.

Now he reached down into his small leather briefcase and brought out a folder and a small mirror. "Raoul, I want to show you something. Do you recognize this man?" He held up a few photographs. And waited, while Wallenberg gazed. "And here, please, look at yourself." He held up the small mirror. "You see, my friend, what has happened, don't you? The wrinkles, the coloring . . . what this place has done to you? Here is all the evidence you need to convince yourself about what is happening!"

Raoul said, "I am sure you too have aged in two years, don't you think?"

"Touché," said the interrogator. "But there is a difference, between what Time has done to us, and what Lybianka has done to you. Listen, man, you need hope, real hope, and you haven't got much left! And I am worried!" He stood up, a wiry little fox of a man, and marched back and forth, before taking his seat again. "Anything, give me anything—a few names, a Swiss bank account, a basement or attic where the Jews have hidden some artworks? . . ."

Gesturing permission, Raoul stood up and walked to the wall, about a dozen feet away. Oddly, he stood there, arms folded, against the cement blocks.

"For god sakes, man, turn around! Don't allow yourself any self-pity—not now, it's too late for that."

Slowly, against his will, a wounded creature in a drab gray uniform, he turned back toward the room, toward his interrogator, and said, "You know, a fresh cucumber would be a bit of heaven. If you can manage just that."

Daniel sat back in his chair. "I will do my best, Wallenberg. And I will try to get Kaminski not to cross-examine you today; I see you are quite wearied, and maybe some rest will settle you somewhat."

Raoul walked back to the table and sat back down. "I have never asked you this, Daniel, and you don't have to answer me if you don't wish."

The little interrogator looked at him, baffled.

"You are Jewish, aren't you?"

Daniel looked at him in quiet amazement. "Jewish?" He shook his head. "Wallenberg, religion doesn't count in the life of comrades. We are Soviet communists, without any religion."

"I know that view. But your parents gave birth to you as a Jewish boy, didn't they? Your mother and/or father were Jewish, weren't they?"

"Why would you ask such a question?"

Raoul stared at him, at this clever little man with whom he had been dealing and negotiating for the past few years, and who had exhibited, today, an apparent true concern for his life. Raoul understood the pain of these people, the pain and the wound, even of these proud comrades, who believed they lived by secular faith while living with deliberate and cultivated amnesia. He had seen and known many of them in Budapest, and he understood.

"Oh, I was just wondering. Please, don't forget the fresh cucumber, yes?"

Daniel P., at first furious, took a few breaths, relaxed his face, and responded, "Yes, I shall try."

Manny leaned back, rather exhausted, and reflected over where he had gone in the little scene? . . . Why had he pursued this last direction, for example? . . . Would Raoul have played that card? For what purpose? . . . Because Daniel had shown some compassion? (Or was it, to shift to the real, because of Manny's own live interview with the aged Daniel P.? . . .) It was curious how, in trying to discover a possible truth, the "imagined" had taken the historian to unexpected territory. Would the interrogator really have "warned" his prisoner that if he didn't speak up soon, say something of relevance, that his end was near? (Actually, Raoul was probably murdered a month later, in July 1947, probably by lethal injection, after Stalin, in June, had ruled out assassination by shooting.) And did it have a kernel of truthfulness that the two had become, like caged creatures set together for a long while, crossover intimates? Where one felt the emotions of the other as much as those of one's own self, so that at moments the two selves were like one, or were like blood brothers? . . . Was this in part why the real Daniel P.—whom he had luckily interviewed in Moscow—never again admitted a word, not to KGB or to family, in the next fifty years, about what had gone on between them?

CHAPTER 18

Where did he stand now? he wondered the next day, riding his bicycle along the river. The late sun glinted off the Connecticut, and he wore his shade visor over his helmet. A Martian with a beard he appeared. He rode the bicycle leisurely, a good pace for mulling things over. Clearly, just now he was in limbo, waiting to hear from the writing analyst, waiting to figure out what his next step should be. But was there another step? Or were all the steps used up now? What did he have in mind, if the word came through as expected and he cut himself free once and for all from Lady Z. of Budapest? What could he do for RW then—call out to him from across the great boundary as the medium did? Join her in the calling?

The river ran smooth and bending, some angles as smooth as glass. Maybe he should have gone out for a canoe trip with Jack. But Jack was still back in Arizona until the fall term in September. He'd have to write him and see how he was doing. And make sure that he got back here to finish up his degree.

Had Manny been right in his interpretations, personal and professional, for Raoul? Of course, he might wander the globe and search out more witnesses who claimed to have seen an elderly sick Swede in later years. It would be a long wandering, with more bizarre tales, half true perhaps, half made up. And more books would appear, speculations disguised as semi-facts, semi-fictions called biographies. (All future biographies, he projected, would have more pages for apparently new information, but would remain essentially repeats of the past, a life with the mysteries intact.)

As far as Zsuzsanna and her helpers were concerned, they had done brilliant and even heroic work—created a large oeuvre, which, even if a fraud, was fantastic in its construction. Like some giant Lego creation, done by a genius eight-year-old. Little wonder that she was unique: she had built a house of cards upon a foundation of faith. So much *stuff* she had collected, to match her storeroom of faith and obsession. She had *imagined* an entire life story, fabricated a detailed biography, out of her obsession with Raoul. Methodically, she had filled in the openings, gaps, holes, with manufactured letters, photos, documents, memories. An impressive, audacious accomplishment.

What next? He pedaled upward, in the twilight, toward Lyme Road. Suddenly, he pulled up short, as there stood in the road a huge animal, and as he crept closer, really slowly, he saw that it was a moose, staring at him with big liquid eyes. Manny stopped fifteen or twenty feet away and looked at the huge odd creature with the fantastic wide antlers and long face and drooping neck. The mysterious creature observed him carefully. Manny stood by his bicycle, waiting quietly—a standoff, scary, thrilling. Here in the fading light on the small country road, there was mystery, bewilderment. On both sides? Manny waited, and the moose, satisfied there was no threat, walked on spindly legs across the road and back up into the thick woods . . . Manny, still stunned, sat down on the grassy bank. What an odd minute or two. Beauty and mystery, suddenly appearing in the midst of an ordinary summer day . . .

Was the meeting a sign? Signaling what? . . . An ESP from the Budapest medium? Or from someone farther out? . . . A moose sighting was a rare event, especially up close, and he had to take it for what it was. Presently, he was pedaling back toward his car, on clear Route 10. But the experience stayed, the moment of connection between himself and the strange animal a resonant moment.

He sought to refocus his thoughts on RW and the current limbo . . .

In the coffee shop, his historian colleague, Tom, commented, "Whatever it is, it is. But I'm afraid I see a lose-lose situation for you in this. If your expert rules that the material is a fraud, then you will have to back out, gracefully, and will have wasted your time altogether. Too bad, eh? Now, if he were to say that there is a possibility that some of this stuff may be authentic, what do you do? Spend the rest of your years trying to help her write this thing? Or do you try to write your own book, based on her materials? This may not be legal, or moral. So, you are about to be in a bind." He smiled, like a player who had just checkmated his opponent.

Manny considered this. "I don't know," he responded, "my interest is in the man himself, what happened to him, and why. No matter how this particular situation unfolds, that will remain my aim."

The smile was wiped away. "You might recall, you do have a career to think of. And you've spent a good long time on this. Charity work and philanthropy are one thing, but your discipline is another."

Manny nodded. "Thanks for the reminder. You do make a point."

The colleague leaned back in the straight chair. "If I can help hold up the limb you are out on, let me know."

Manny half smiled, "I will remember to."

From the *Wall Street Journal* reporter came an e-mail, asking if he had news about RW, perhaps from a Hungarian source. And did he in fact uncover and interview in Moscow the original KGB interrogator of 1947? Was there a book in the making, Professor, with all this news? Did he care to share it with the reporter? Amazed and anxious, Manny wrote back and said he had no news, and would let the reporter know if anything were to emerge. And he wondered, How in the world? . . .

The report came back in the first week of September from the Boston analyst. Mr. Blaylock wrote:

> *It is unfortunate, Prof. Gellerman, that I cannot report anything defi-*
> *nite to you, one way or the other, based on the materials you have sup-*
> *plied me with. Both handwriting specimens being copies of originals, I*
> *would not venture to give an expert opinion. Without the original sheets*
> *of handwriting of Mr. Wallenberg, it is impossible to make a clear and*
> *firm determination. Yes, they look the same, on the surface; but we do*
> *not deal in surfaces, I am afraid, when we offer our professional opinion.*
> *Should you come up with more verifiable materials, i.e., the originals, we*
> *will be glad to revisit the issue.*

The good thing about the once-over was that the bill was only $350. It also gave him some more time to explore.

So much for being a good boy and not stealing the original pages from Zsuzsanna's collection—it never paid to be "a good boy" in those situations, did it?—though without the Wallenberg originals from the several museums and the family archive, they wouldn't have done much good.

So, he was back to square one. In a never-ending limbo, it seemed . . .

The Swedish-Russian Working Group was begun in 1991 and continued until 2001, when it ceased; its mission had been to find out what happened to Wallenberg, and it was composed of historians, diplomats, and other interested professionals from Sweden, America, and Russia. (Previously, from 1989 to 1991, there had existed the International Commission on the Fate of RW, led by Guy von Dardel, his step-brother.) The Working Group did research, conducted interviews, met with Soviet and Swedish officials—and came up with very little in their decade of existence. They put out several long papers detailing Soviet lies and deceit, Swedish tepidness and cowardice, family passivity, ephemeral witness sightings, but nothing of substance that was new about Raoul. No hard evidence of how he was caught or died, or if he had lived on; no discovery of the "lost" Wallenberg file in Lybianka; no serious diplomatic revelations. The Working Group continued to encounter Russian stonewalling of the issue, and Swedish fear and callous temerity about pressing the case with the Russians. Altogether, the original history from the late 1940s and the recent history from the Working Group's era had revealed embarrassing, even venal, activity by the Swedes, and the Russians' brutal track record. In sixty years, there had been nothing new in solving the deep mysteries surrounding RW.

So he had good reason, Manny informed himself, to become a detective in pursuit of the case, and the real Raoul.

In 2000, Alexander Yakovlev, head of a Russian presidential commission that investigated the case, acknowledged that Wallenberg had been shot and killed. (He had not died of a heart attack, the previous Gromyko line.) Yakovlev said that an ex-KGB secret police chief, Vladimir Kryuchkov, had informed him in a private conversation that RW had been executed at the KGB Lybianka Prison in Moscow. (The only problem here, Manny knew, was that Stalin had issued an edict, in June 1947, forbidding any killing by shooting.) To close down that avenue of denial and stonewalling, another official, Andrei Artizov, offered, "Unfortunately, all materials relating to the case have been destroyed." Very convenient. However, in all probability—according to Nikita Petrov, a KGB expert—the true Wallenberg file lay buried in the infamous basement of Lybianka, beyond the reach of historians, diplomats, politicians, and even most KGB/FSB officials.

Strangely, all of the above suggested to Manny the ending of *Bartleby the Scrivener*, in which the scrivener dies forlorn in the Tombs Prison of New York. The narrator, his old boss, "betrayed" the scrivener by abandoning him when he became an embarrassment. Yet Bartleby sought only to stay in his office with him. Later, when the narrator sees the dead scrivener at the Tombs and discovers that Bartleby had been a subordinate clerk in the Dead Letters Office at Washington, the narrator regrets deeply his abandonment. Manny decided he was not going to imitate that conventional lawyer and abandon the Wallenberg he was getting to know, ghost or man. The novella ends, "Ah, Bartleby! Ah, humanity!" Manny would substitute his own charge, "Ah, Wallenberg! Ah, humanity!" and stand by him, in whatever way that he could. But what did that mean? Or how might that play out? . . .

A new missive arrived from Zsuzsanna, right on cue, after a week of silence:

Professor G., you mustn't leave me. Not now after I have put my full trust in you, opened myself up to you, and offered you my papers, and a full commitment. It will not be fair of you. I will suffer greatly. I need you as a partner in my project to tell the truth about my father, once and for all, and not allow the spiteful enemies and deceivers to fill the void, and ruin his reputation. You will be his savior, as well as mine. And if you should need any papers from me to confirm their truthfulness, I am ready to turn those over to you. But please, don't abandon me!"
    Your friend, and partner, Zsuzsanna

Gellerman, who simply hadn't known what to write her and therefore had stayed silent, was now rewarded for his silence. He would receive some original pages for the handwriting analyst to check on and check out, at last.

Summer was ending, and autumn approaching, and Manny was nearing . . . what? A resolution?

He walked around the tidy town and familiar campus, played some tennis and ping-pong, visited with his son between music camps, tried to clear his head of all unnecessary matters. (But what was *necessary*?) He listened to music, classical (Bach, Schubert, and the Vienna Phil. playing Mozart—son's suggestion) and jazz (Miles Davis's *Kind of Blue*, Ellington's "Mood Indigo" and "Solitude," and Sarah Vaughan). He drove on country roads up through Lyme, Orford, Thetford, and felt pleased by the narrow dirt roads, the thick overhangs of foliage and the dappled sunlight, the green hillsides and low mountains, the privacy and pristine clarity in these New Hampshire and Vermont towns. On this late summer trek to no particular destination, he considered his own quest, specific but open-ended, a destination without a name. Did one journey mirror the other? Not really. But if he took pleasure in the one, couldn't he take solace in the other? . . .

So was it a journey without end—or, maybe a journey on the installment plan? . . .

He called Jack in Hopi and asked how he was doing.

"Well, not too bad, but not so good either," he said. "Family problems."

Manny quickly understood. "You mean you're uncertain about coming back for the term?"

"Yeah, I guess so. But don't worry, Professor; if I miss out on this term, I'll make it up in the spring!"

"Really?" Manny knew better. "Well, I'd like to see you come back now and finish up, and start on the thesis, Jack. The writing you can do back home."

A pause, and Manny realized that Jack was under pressure, maybe even pressure right there in the room.

"Well, I'll give it my best shot," Jack said, feebly.

"Is it the money? I can try to get you some more funding, Jack. Should I?"

"Nah, you've done enough already."

"I can loan you some, no problem."

"Nah, you've been great, Manny."

"So it's the family; they don't want to let you go, huh?"

"Something like that. I can understand them, you know. Arwitha has two kids to take care of, plus her job . . . my parents; it's not easy without me around . . ."

Manny nodded; it didn't matter that Jack had only one term of classes left; the family wasn't interested in the long run. Manny knew that if Jack returned, it would only come about if he went, coerced them, and pulled him back.

"Well, you still have a month to get things straightened out, Jack."

"Yeah," Jack said, "that's right. Maybe things'll turn around. Let's see."

"Sure, let's see."

"Hey, Professor, don't you worry over me, okay? I'll make it through the . . . situation here."

Manny felt tugged, but it was not in Arizona that he found himself; it was in Sweden, at a gathering of experts on the state of RW studies. At the University of Uppsala, he sat on the dais at a table of six panelists, waiting for his turn to speak. The invitation had come from a professor there who said he understood that Gellerman had access to possible exciting new information concerning Wallenberg, and they would welcome his attendance at the conference. Ambivalent about accepting, Manny nevertheless decided on going, not really sure about what he was going to say. Even on the plane going over, he wasn't sure which of two talks he would deliver.

Now, as he sat at the table listening to the diplomat, the historian, the newspaper journalist speak, he felt his heart beating strongly, as much out of indecision as anything else. The lines of the discussion, before an auditorium filled with about five hundred students, teachers, citizens, repeated the old saws: early Swedish diplomatic incompetence, Soviet secrecy and deceit, the witness sightings through the years, and the need to go forward and keep searching. For twenty minutes each of them gave an opening speech, while Manny shuffled his two packets of notes like two hands of poker cards, one with his interpretation of Raoul's personal nature, helping to enhance his outlaw status, and the other, his notes concerning Zsuzsanna's crazy tale . . . He stared well into the back of the auditorium, seeing a clock of some sort and a blinking red light, probably a video recording.

The moderator, Professor Bergston, turned to Gellerman, introduced him, and everyone's attention turned his way.

Manny gave a low-key preamble to his main thread, citing his entry into the Wallenberg story via his graduate student's thesis, his pursuit of research in Budapest, and his coming upon a Hungarian woman who claimed to be part of the Wallenberg family, indeed his daughter. "Of course, it is a speculative story, farfetched, and perhaps entirely fabricated and fanciful, but it must be checked out, and I have been in the midst of trying to ascertain its veracity for the past year or so, and checking on a whole pile of materials. Because of the nature of the claims and, also, to protect the privacy of the lady, I cannot go into the particulars of the case. But I am hopeful of coming to a conclusion, some sort of verifiable result, sometime soon, probably in the next few months."

There was much buzzing in the audience and a stirring on the stage, and immediately hands shot up to ask questions.

Gellerman did his best to answer the questions with vague responses and nonanswers, all in the "service" of protecting the privacy of the mystery lady; but what was eminently clear, during the Q and A session, was that he had become the controversial star of the event. And when the session came to a close an hour later, he was surrounded by a crowd of scholars, diplomats, journalists, and ordinary citizens. Far from elated, Manny felt nervous, cornered, semi-shocked, like a jungle animal who has been brought in from the wilderness to become a celebrity cheetah or panda in a big city zoo, his long-time status of obscurity suddenly pierced and transformed into something else.

What had he gotten himself into? he wondered, as the circle of people around him did not seem to lessen, but grew.

"Mr. Gellerman, can you give an interview to my newspaper, *Svenska Dagbladet?* Swedish citizens will be most interested," asked a bespectacled blonde with a vertical journalist pad.

"What do you think the Wallenberg family here in Stockholm will think of this news, if it turns out to be true?" inquired a small, middle-aged, goateed gentleman carrying a leather satchel.

"Professor, can you tell us how you are handling the materials you have been given, and are so secretively guarding?" This, from the suave historian from the panel. "Do we not deserve to hear a full report about these materials?"

A fiftyish woman wearing a traveler's jacket with many pockets and carrying a camera, asked, "Does the Budapest lady not want to come to Sweden and present herself and tell her own story? Have you asked her this? Please, here is my card. I would love to do a documentary about her."

"You have raised some serious issues here, and I believe the diplomatic corps needs to have a thorough interview with you, Professor," advised a tall rather stern gentleman, handing him a card. "Shall we have a car pick you up at 9 a.m. tomorrow?"

Overwhelmed, dazzled, and exhausted, Manny was finally bailed out by the host, the Uppsala professor, who broke through the huge circling posse and escorted his guest out of the auditorium.

"You created quite a ruckus in there," the young professor said outside, with an American accent. "This is what Wallenberg fans and followers have been waiting for for years, a break in the no-news category."

Manny loosened his tie and shirt collar. "But I hope I made it very clear that this is *not* news yet, but just some sort of . . . research work-in-progress."

The young man smiled his crooked-toothed smile. "At least the rumor of news was true, and you fulfilled it. That's why you were invited."

Manny nodded, bewildered about how to take that, and all of it.

"I hope I haven't created false hope."

"You've created hope; that is enough, even plenty."

"You're American?"

"Yes, I am, but a transplant for over fifteen years. I teach here and have done work on Wallenberg myself. It's a fascinating case, one that embarrasses the state and confuses the citizenry."

They drove to the hotel where Manny was staying.

"So, I will see you about 7:30 for drinks and dinner, yes?"

"Yes, thanks. I'll try for a nap before that, so I won't answer the phone."

At the desk, there were already three envelopes with messages waiting for him. When he got up to his room, the red button was lit up on the message machine, and when he played it, there were seven messages: three from journalists, two from the media, one from the Ministry for Foreign Affairs, and another from a private caller.

Manny undressed, took a shower and felt lighter, then lay down after calling the front desk and asking them to defer all calls until he came down or called later.

What had he gotten himself into? That was the $64,000 question. He had come over here on a lark almost, maybe to test the waters, but really, he suspected, because he wanted some attention for his long-private investigation and steady devotion. Well, he was getting it, wasn't he? In spades. The bright northern light filtered through the blinds, and he took out his eyemask; it would be light most of the night. At least he'd be safe through the dinner and evening, he believed. Who would have dreamed that taking the crazy lady fifty-percent seriously or, rather, humoring her—and himself—would lead to this? . . . What was it, after all? An event. Whose meanings would only emerge later on, he figured, maybe beginning tomorrow.

What interested Manny, as his mind continued to rev, was how different reality was out here, away from books, from academics, from theories and research. You could publish serious papers and complex essays in learned journals; but once you made a public claim, out in the big world, the world was all over you, wanting more, *more*. Was this good for his pursuit? Was this what he wanted? Or was this what the Budapest lady wanted, all along? Some glare and publicity, her eight minutes of fame? Yes, some fame; that's what worried him, a lot. He was unused to this and afraid to confront it. (Especially because of the nature of his evidence, or nonevidence.)

Yet, reflecting on it, hadn't he served her purposes perfectly? Hadn't she—and maybe the daughter too—played him exquisitely? . . .

But now, ironically, was she and her fantasy serving him well too? . . . At least temporarily? Was her fantastical play and narrative now providing him a certain power in the real world, here? . . . But to do what with? he wondered.

Was this a tipping moment for him and his career too?

The dinner food was excellent, and the surrounding chat for the most part was polite. Lots of North Sea herrings—ah, too bad his father wasn't alive still!—and salmon and cream sauces, and superb ice wine. Along with diffident Swedish probes at the table, collectively playing the proper host and not pushing or confronting their guest. Gellerman nodded, ate, and said little, and allowed the other panelists to dominate the discussion. When questioned directly, once or twice, with pointed questions, he put them off easily, with a casual answer about the continuing research of his project. No one protested; in fact, he was openly appreciated for his researcher's restraint. ("Even though you are already trending like crazy on the Internet!")

Just before they departed for the evening, his host, Prof. Sonnanstine, suggested an early breakfast and trip to the airport, if he wanted to escape any of the diplomatic "cars" or further journalistic inquiries just now. "Yes, I think that will be very helpful," said Manny, and they agreed to meet at 7:30 a.m. in the hotel restaurant.

Back in his room, he felt easier, and, alone, watched a television melodrama. Actually, it was the American *Law and Order*. He lay back and . . . suddenly felt inspired. He straightened up, got out of bed, went to the small wooden desk with his trusty Apple laptop, and composed:

Early July 1947; Lybianka Prison, Moscow

A weary Daniel P. entered the conference room, where Raoul W. already was sitting on the other side of the table. Daniel dismissed the guard.

"I have come to say good-bye to you, my friend," Daniel said. "My time with you has come to an end, I am sorry to say."

Raoul looked up, startled. "What?"

Daniel shook his small head. "I am removed from your case."

"But why?!"

He shrugged. "Maybe because we have produced together nothing, you and me."

"You think this?" Raoul paused and reflected, "Yes, it makes a certain sense."

Daniel nodded.

"You say 'maybe.' Can there be another reason?"

Daniel breathed deeply. He narrowed his eyes and stared at Raoul.

"Do speak up. What other reason are you thinking is possible?"

Daniel got up, walked to the wall, lit a cigarette, came back and handed it to Raoul, and then lit one for himself. He sat back down.

"Maybe they are removing me now because . . . because . . . they think the case is over? . . ."

"How do you mean?"

"You understand . . . these are mere suppositions . . . maybe the case is over, because the problem is about to be over."

Raoul smoked and shook his head, not understanding.

Facing Raoul steadily, he said, " 'Where there's a man, there's a problem,' is a favorite saying of Field Marshall Stalin."

Raoul leaned back now and said, "So, where there's no man, there's no problem."

"Yes."

Wallenberg gestured, stood up, and took his stroll to the cement wall, maybe fifteen feet away, where he stood by the radiator pipes. Inhaled and exhaled. Waved the smoke away with his hands.

"There are worse sayings, I imagine," said Raoul, with a rueful wit.

Daniel acknowledged it with a small nod, and reached up to turn off the light bulb. He took out a pocket flashlight, while Raul stood at the wall.

"Do you know when 'the problem' will be eliminated?" asked Wallenberg. Daniel said no.

"But you are officially off the case, my case, today?"

"Yes, today is my last day with you."

Raoul considered this. "Unless I say something of profound interest, perhaps?"

Daniel looked over at him. "Oh, I have not even thought of such a thing."

Raoul wandered back to the table.

"Here is a small packet for you." Daniel set on the table a narrow box of two shading pencils, along with a magnifying glass. "This magnifier has been a personal favorite for a good number of years, and I have found it very useful when studying maps or precise lines. It may come in useful for your remaining work."

"How thoughtful." Raoul lifted the two small objects and studied each separately. "'Remaining work.' I like the sound of that. I will have to hurry then . . . Thank you, I am touched; this magnifier will be useful, especially with these new pencils."

They paused and smoked, the cigarette ends flashing red in the semi-darkness.

"I am very sorry," said Daniel.

"Yes, so am I. About not seeing you anymore."

Daniel nodded.

"I have looked forward to our little chats. Our regular visits."

Daniel nodded. "Yes, we have grown used to each other."

Again, a silence fell, while each, the prisoner and the interrogator, reflected on matters, on the whole two years perhaps, in the familiar windowless room with the two straightbacked chairs, the wooden benches, and the concrete walls.

"It is very useful when the light goes out now and then," observed Raoul, smoking a new cigarette. "And we can be more private for a few minutes."

Daniel smoked, and offered, "Are there any letters or notes you may want to give me? I can see if I can get them through. Or perhaps a drawing or two?"

Raoul rubbed the sides of his cheek. "That is a thought, isn't it? A drawing for a friend or family member. Maybe a sketch for my old Professor Slusser at Ann Arbor." He smiled broadly. "He would appreciate that I kept up the practice, in different locales."

The small interrogator stood up, ran his hand through his hair, and put out his hand. Wallenberg stood and took it.

"I wish you well."

"You have been . . . kindly to me, and I am grateful for that."

"I am sorry I couldn't do more, for both of us, actually. This also goes for your important people in Stockholm. It might have ended . . . differently."

Raoul gave a little rueful smile. "Not all things have to end well, at least not in an obvious way. Perhaps it is best this way."

"Perhaps . . ." Daniel paused, trying to think of a final appropriate word. "The Jews will remember you."

Raoul stared at him through the dim grayness.

"Others too, perhaps. But the Jews for sure." He reached up, pulled on the light.

"Well, even all this may end up differently, in memory," Raoul opined, almost peacefully.

Finished, Gellerman leaned back now. Was there too much melodrama here, he wondered? Melodrama was inevitable. But was this excessive? Morcoever, was Daniel capable of pronouncing those last lines about the Jews? That was a question. (Maybe that was a self-revelation?) Also, would Daniel have committed himself this way, risked himself, in such a farewell visit? . . . (Or was he actually setting up RW in case he wanted, at the last minute, to confess a few things?) Judging from the real-life visit that Manny had had with Daniel, he very well might have. In 1991, when the KGB called Daniel in to question him about the case, promising him no consequences no matter what occurred, Daniel said he knew nothing, remembered nothing. Had he been guilty in any way? . . . And if Daniel's son knew nothing about his affairs, as he claimed, then had Daniel been especially prudent there? Still, how much of the friendship was based upon something beyond endurance, beyond the two years of being locked together? Or was that enough? . . .

Manny had another impulse, and wrote a coda:

Back in his cell, Raoul smoked and paced his eight steps and back. *So it is all over. Good enough. No more falses hopes, no more fantasies of last minute reprieves. I leave that for Dostoyevsky. For me, I will do my last sketches, do my exercises, focus my mind. Perhaps write a note or two, and try to slip them through to Daniel. It may be easier this way, actually, without the tiny speck of hope that one day my cousins will come through finally and bail me out, or that the Swedish government will get pricked and show courage, or that the Americans will create something of an opening. Really, only the Americans might have whipped up a surprise, but now it is too late. Well, Grandfather, I am glad you are gone now and won't have to hear of this ignominious end for me. You don't deserve that, sir. You had such high expectations for me. And you, dear Mother, you will not know about it for some years, I am sure. Good. So, I am ready for the problem to be eliminated, Tovarishch Stalin.*

In the morning Manny was up early and met his host for the 7:30 breakfast, and, skipping the messages, he was out of the hotel by 8:20 and departed for the airport. The fellow said, "I will let them all know that you have much research to get back to, plus teaching, and you will be in touch when you can."

"That's just about right. Thanks."

He almost made it too, but at the airport, he was caught up by two members of the journalistic corps, a man and woman team. "Professor, please, can you say a few words about the nature of the Wallenberg family in Budapest? We have been shocked, you may say, to hear about this revelation, which is so important and exciting for all Swedes to know about."

Manny faced the brown-haired woman holding a pad. "How did you find out about this news, by the way?"

The young man said, "We got a surprise e-mail from Budapest, actually, a few weeks ago."

"Yes, that's right. That is why you were invited to the conference, I believe."

Of course, what a dummy! Manny scolded himself. She had taken matters into her own crafty hands!

"Well," he responded, "just as I said last night, it remains to be seen how authentic this 'family' is. This is what I am investigating now, and therefore it would be premature to comment on it."

"Aren't you being ultraconservative, sir?"

"And playing the academic research card too strongly?"

Gellerman smiled. "Your English is sophisticated, maybe even more so than the English of some of our own journalists."

They smiled politely and waited, one with a tiny recorder, the other with the pad.

"Let let me have your e-mail address," Manny said, "and when I know something, you shall be the first to know, okay?"

The woman produced a professional card and gave it to Manny. Boel Andersson, *Dagens Nyheter.* "We would prefer to do a feature story, you understand, for the Sunday magazine."

"And we can come over to you in New Hampshire, if that is more convenient."

"Well, thanks. Now I have your addresses and phone number, and I will be in touch."

"Please understand, Professor Gellerman, the story of Raoul Wallenberg is the story of the Swedish people, both of its sides, the bravery and the cowardice."

"His story is a metaphor for the Swedish soul, Professor, and how that has been corrupted through the years."

What handsome rhetoric, he thought, slipping away. In the Scandinavian Airlines jet, he smiled at Zsuzsanna's shrewedness, her tactics. So he had been set up, all along the way, by the Puppeteer in Budapest—not a bizarre or mad woman but a supreme puppet master, who was pulling all his strings and watchings him dance! And now the entire state of Sweden would be in a state of high alert, high excitement, to learn more!

And he, Gellerman, obscure professor, was now her chosen pointman to the world, and maybe the world's point man to her! Brilliant!

He tried to read an airline magazine, figuring things out and pondering the future . . . The Wallenberg scene of his last days in Lybianka still lingered in his mind, where Raoul is warned and released by his interrogator. In real life Raoul had been left alone, abandoned by all, so why shouldn't Manny stay with him in the imagined life? And he remain moved by the scene still, at 35,000 feet . . . In the magazine he flipped through a piece on the Abba: The Museum, another on sailing in the archipelego, and a third on a new department story created with fancy architecture. In another world, it might have been Raoul designing this store and other assorted buildings in his Stockholm . . .

Opening his laptop, he saw a new note from Zsuzsanna in Budapest:

How are you, my friend? What is new with you and our project? Have you started to work on the organization yet? I know that aspect may be my fatal flaw. Meanwhile, I have been reading two books of great fascination, I and Thou by Martin Buber and Gershom Scholem's On the Kabbalah and Its Symbolism. Do you know these valuable texts? You have to reread them to fully derive their meanings. For example, here are lines from Buber, which I think relate strongly to my father: "But what if a man's mission requires him to know only his association with his cause and no relation to any You, no present encounter with any You, so that everything around him becomes It and subservient to his cause? How about the I-saying of Napoleon? Wasn't that legitimate? Is this a phenomenon of experiencing and using no person?" Buber then goes on to show how Nap. never knew "the dimension of the you." You can see, Professor,

the true value of my mother for my father, how she became his personal
You so that his cause, to save the Jews, was not merely an It? I am prob-
ably putting this badly, but you understand what I am getting at, yes?"
*   faithfully yrs, Zsuzsa*

The stewardess asked him if he wished a drink, and he asked for a ginger
ale. She proceeded to find one and pour it in a cup for him. Manny reread the
note, once again surprised by her detour. Naturally, she knew he had just attended this conference, and probably what had occurred, but was slyly waiting
for him to announce any news. In the meantime, a little *luftmenschen* learning.
Face it, Manny, the Chessmaster from Budapest was two steps ahead of you, no
matter how hard you tried to catch up. He wrote back:

*   On my way home to NH from Stockholm, where I attended a confer-*
ence on the fate of RW. I think I was able to contribute a few words of
scholarly appreciation, when someone mentioned the rumor of a possible
family in Budapest. As soon as I am home again in my woods, I will have
the time to evaluate your papers.
*   Your friend, MG*

There was also another e-mail from a *New York Times* reporter, asking
about the recent news emanating from the conference. Manny didn't answer
that one. He set the empty cup on the corner of his tray, put on his eyeshade,
and dozed off.

CHAPTER 19

Back home at the college there was a stir, and he discovered that he had become a sort of mini-celebrity while he was away. A note on the Internet, a newsy revelation from the conference that used his name, had ignited the buzz. This was a whole new experience for Manny, who for fifteen or twenty years had been a marginal player. His boss, the amiable Irish dynamo, called him up, asked him to lunch, and insisted that he give a faculty talk on his powerful research. Even the dean of faculty dropped him a note. The chair of the former Swedish-Russian Working Group invited him to attend a special meeting, excited to hear of his discoveries (especially the Pagliansky meeting). And the Swedish Embassy in DC called and invited him down for a luncheon discussion. Meanwhile, the handwriting analyst called and asked if he had gotten any of the original papers yet for him to examine?

His head swirling, his thoughts revving, Manny was grateful to be diverted by the boy's return from summer music camps and his needs for the new school year. Helping him, along with his mother, get prepared with fall items (new backpack, sneakers) grounded Manny for the week, and he was satisfied. "Dad, is it true, you've made a real discovery in the Wallenberg case?" What could Manny say, but "Maybe. It's too early to tell." The boy retorted, "Robby saw your name on Yahoo! Trending! That's awesome!" The Internet would lift you, or doom you, or both.

He felt so ambivalent, so anxious, so unsure about what to do, how to act, that he didn't—didn't answer the expert, didn't write the Budapest lady (asking for the originals), didn't respond to the Working Group or Embassy. In a state of paralysis, he waited for a sign, a signal, to pull him free.

An e-mail arrived from Jack. "It's best if I really do skip the next few quarters, Professor G., and shoot for the spring quarter. I hope you won't be too disappointed. Don't worry, sir, I'll try really hard to make it back."

No surprise for Manny, but it disconcerted him. He understood what it meant, and he could either leave it alone and let it run its course, or he could intervene, as in a drug intervention. Jack was good and smart; Manny felt a connection, and he didn't want him to fall away into a lost wilderness.

He prepared for his talk, to be given in a circular hall in the Rockefeller social science building, holding maybe 150. The crucial thing was the strategy of the talk: what to tell, what to omit, whom to thank and pay homage to.

September distracted Manny with memories. It filled him with longings, or energized his old longings . . . for his sons when they were little: the older son who read R. L. Stevenson and Kipling at age six or seven and understood all the motives and plots, while beginning to write his own small artful stories; and the younger son who played his one-quarter-sized cello in the living room at age five; for his Russian father, who would speak tenderly in his native language to Manny at six, taught him chess, took him on Sundays uptown to the Fourteenth Street Stanley Theater in Manhattan to see Russian movies and eat dinner (homemade borscht with potato or sour cream and a well-done brisket of beef) on Second Avenue with other émigrés; for his sports-splashed youth, playing baseball in Lincoln Terrace Park, (pink Spaldeen) handball and softball at the PS 189 schoolyard, or ring-a-levio in his Brownsville/East Flatbush neighborhood, near the El at East 98th Street . . . And now, this curious longing for Raoul, the abandoned prisoner in Lybianka, or Gulag . . . Weird how Wallenberg had penetrated his consciousness so deeply . . .

The talk would be "safer" if written out as an essay and read aloud, where he could carefully edit the words and monitor the fault lines; but it would be easier and richer, though more dangerous, from notes . . . Which to choose? The dilemma was what to leave in, what to omit and stay away from entirely? . . . He sensed there would be a big crowd, larger than the usual narrow academic one because of the subject and his new renown.

Indeed, the crowd was overflowing, with standees on the sides and in the back. After a dramatic introduction by his flashy boss, he stepped behind the podium before the eager audience—judging from the ovation—and tried to speak neutrally, seeking to deflate the high expectations of the moment:

"I want first to thank my former graduate student, Angela Roberts, who first came to me to discuss a possible thesis, did some useful research on Mr. Wallenberg, and wrote a good one. That thesis rekindled my interest in the subject, leading to my pursuit of new field research and investigation. Secondly, I want to thank Richard Mackie, my chair and colleague, who has always given me great support, no matter how far afield I go, in my research wanderings. And believe me, they can be far afield . . . [laughter]

The chief thing to remember, when talking about Mr. Wallenberg and his fate, is how many true mysteries are associated with him; and how few have been solved through the sixty plus years since his disapparance. Has there been another figure of such prominence who has vanished so thoroughly, both in fact and in history? One whose identity has proven so difficult for historians and biographers to pin down? Maybe, but if so, not many . . ."

Manny took a drink of water and breathed deeply, trying to relax and focus on how he wanted to proceed, and what tracks to avoid . . . "First, let me lay out the mysteries of the man and his work that have arisen through the years; and second, offer a few clues on those mysteries; and third, suggest a few opinions if not outright conclusions . . ." As he spoke, from his notes on a Steno Book spiral pad, it was easy enough to cover the first: the uncertainty of the actual death of Raoul, the curious languishing for two years in the Soviet prisons, the apparent passivity of the Wallenberg family, and the incompetence and cowardice of the Swedish diplomatic core and government. (He mentioned the post-1947 witnesses who had cited seeing old man Raoul in various Gulag sites.) Next came the overview of the man himself: his background and training, including his three years at Ann Arbor, which seemed to astonish everyone. With dexterity, Manny described Wallenberg's character: the fortitude, the humor, the early and ever-present rebelliousness against authority (as when, in his early officer training days, he stood up for justice), the ability to handle himself cooly in a jam (as he did during the holdup outside Chicago). Now, with about ten minutes left in the hour, Manny had to race through the modern history of the investigation, with few results from RW's own Swedish family (step-father Fredrik von Dardel and half sister Nina Lagergren), the Swedish-Russian Working Group. Finally, the recent discovery of the *possible* Hungarian family of Raoul, now under his current research and probing. Yes, he figured, with the audience clapping, he had gotten through it, protecting Raoul, protecting himself.

The questions came, and the first several were easy enough; but then one came about this recent strange family. "Who were they? How did the professor come upon them?" Here he resorted to the historian's shield of privacy and protection for the family. "Until I can firmly deduce the authenticity of the papers I have received and make a true judgment on them, I don't think it is fair to reveal any details or sources. Of course, I have consulted with the family members and they concur with me on this." There, he had used Madame Zsuzsa against herself, for once. The follow-up question pushed this logic farther. "Does this account for the fact, or impact upon it, that Mr. Wallenberg did not marry that we know of?"

"Yes, that is a very good question, and you have provided your own answer," he responded. "It will indeed impact upon that question, *if* the papers prove to be authentic, and not mere . . . wish-fulfillment, perhaps."

"In your estimation, Professor, was there any truth to the later witness sightings?"

"So far as I can tell, mistaken persons and wishful projections of one sort or another. Still no hard evidence."

"And what about the charge that he was indeed working for the Americans, gathering names and data to use for the OSS against the Russians?"

"Again, no real evidence for that; Wallenberg had little truck with the Nazis or the Arrow Cross; he in fact despised them, but he needed them in his work to save Jews."

"One last question, over there."

"Was he a real hero in your mind?"

Manny considered his final answer. "Yes, but I would call him a tragic hero, one who didn't start out trying to be a hero, but conditions thrust that role upon him; and then he was doomed, because of the confluence of circumstances, to an awful fate, a slow perishing in a Soviet prison."

The crowd surrounded him, and he understood that while he had protected Raoul—no mention of his possible gay status—Zsuzsa had protected him, at the same time that she had propelled him to this higher level of authority and expertise. And soon, in return, wouldn't he have to protect her, and her fantasy, for everyone's sake? A thrilling, or chilling thought . . .

At the dinner at the inn afterward, he was pushed on several counts by colleagues, but Manny shook his head and offered a crafty smile, one of pretend power and deep knowledge, and asked for more red wine.

There was a letter from Zsuzsa in his e-mail box:

> *My Dear Professor,*
> *I sense that you are in a state of dilemma, of perplexity, and therefore offer you this wisdom, from Mr. Fitz James Stephen, as quoted by your Mr. William James at the end of his splendid essay "The Will To Believe," which I hope you will read.*
> *"What do you think of yourself? What do you think of the world? . . . These are questions with which all must deal as it seems good to them. They are riddles of the Sphinx, and in some way or other we must deal* with them . . . In all important transactions of life we have to take a leap in the dark . . . *(my italics). If we decide to leave the riddles unan-*

swered, that is a choice; if we waver in our answer, that, too, is a choice;
but whatever choice we make, we make it at our peril . . .
  "*We stand on a mountain pass in the midst of whirling snow and*
blinding mist, through which we get glimpses now and then of paths
which may be deceptive. If we stand still we shall be frozen to death. If
we take the wrong road we shall be dashed to pieces. We do not certainly
know whether there is any right one. What must we do? 'Be strong and of
good courage.' Act for the best, hope for the best, and take what comes . . .
If death ends all, we cannot meet death better."
  A leap in the dark, Emmanuel?
  Yours, Zsuzsa

Was the woman clever, or was she way more than clever, as well as dangerous? You gave her a book gift, and she used it to challenge you! Who was helping her choose those passages? Was it little, sly, devilish Dora? The daughter
was quiet and smart, and maybe, beneath her innocent surface, knew just what
was going on.
  Another e-mail came from the eminent Hungarian congressman in Cali-
fornia:

  Dear Professor Gellerman,
    It has come to my attention that you have come upon a family or sur-
  rogate family of Raoul Wallenberg in Budapest. As you probably know,
  my parents were saved by the great man, and my wife too, and therefore
  it is of urgent interest to me what you have discovered. Please let me
  know as soon as you are able to, and I will be much appreciative. I am
  pleased to help you in any way.
    Frankly, I always felt there was more to this tragic and bewildering
  case than the Russians, or Swedes, have let on.
    Respectfully yours,
    The Hon. Tom Lantos

Things were heating up for sure. Clearly now, there was more to the case
than all those professionals and diplomats knew or imagined, only her name
was Zsuzsanna.
  Manny had to get away from all of it, and also he had a chore to take care
of, so, in a week, he was on his way to Arizona. He he had answered both letters
with polite and appropriate responses, promising reports soon on any and all
progress. On the lengthy flight, with stops in Chicago and Phoenix, he was

glad to have brought along the folder of papers projected as Lady Z.'s memoir. Waiting in airports seemed the perfect place for reading such stuff (or mush?).

Of course, it wasn't mush, as much as musings, memories, magical history, millenial thinking, memorabilia. How strange! Not uninteresting either. With accounts of places in the countryside outside Budapest during the war, where Jewish families went to hide. Many letters, diary entries, newspaper clippings, letters from Raoul to the family and the daughter, and from the mother to diplomats, statesmen, the Wallenbergs. A mass of materials, assembled by a shrewd magician and probably assisted by a top-notch researcher, or team. Well, he'd sit on it and wait. No need to rush to judgment, especially one that could topple him back into obscurity, and probably comedy.

In Phoenix, Gellerman rented a car and drove up through Flagstaff, through Winslow, and on to Hopi land, a small rectangle set in the midst of the much larger territory of the Navajo reservation. He had been at the reservation once before, years ago; but once he stepped outside, he recalled immediately the simmering heat, the arid fields, the sense of desolation. (He recalled too several lines from RW's Ann Arbor notebook, and his desire to see/study the region for its architecture.) He drove up to the Second Mesa, where he would meet Jack, after a call. At the modern Hopi Cultural Center, a surprising series of interconnected adobe buildings housing a hotel and a commercial store, he parked and walked inside. There was Jack, immediately coming up to greet him warmly.

Giving Manny a bear hug, he said, "Good to see you, Prof!"

"You too, Jack, you too."

"C'mon, let's get over to the house, where we have some lunch." His face had grown darker, leaner, in such a short time.

With Jack directing, they drove out on the single two-lane road, passing isolated small houses, run-down and shack-like with giant antennas or new satellite dishes on the rooftops. The landscape was hilly, gray, and bare, with two mountains looming nearby. Jack explained again the tragic history of the tribe, which had been reduced by smallpox at the turn of the century, and by the marauding Navajos, who had raided and pillaged them again and again. "It's not the white man who was my boogeyman when I grew up, you know, but the Navajo and his greed and deceit. They stole all the great land from us, and left us with this. And we're still fighting them through the legal system, but once Senator Goldwater died, we didn't really have a champion to fight for us. But I told you all this, right?"

"Well, maybe some years ago, yes. But I always need a refresher course."

At the small house three kids were shooting hoops in the yard. Jack introduced his two sons, teenage boys, dark, with big eyes and good smiles.

"Do you have a favorite team?" Manny asked.

"Phoenix, of course!" they shouted in unison. "Steve Nash!"

Jack shook his head. "My Celtics are too damn bad right now, wrong generation to have raised them!"

Inside the dwelling, in the small kitchen, Jack's wife, Arwitha, had prepared sandwiches, with salad and bottled water. She was a small dark woman, with jet black hair and narrow dark eyes. Manny shook her hand. A television was running in the adjoining room.

With his wife leaving to do errands, Jack hosted their lunch, and soon they began the discussion of relevance, how to bring Jack back to school.

"Look, as I said, if it's a question of the money for travel, and even to bring your family, we can try—"

Jack shook his head, stopping Manny. "No, sir, it's more than that, really. It's my mom and dad too; they count on me in more ways than one. Maybe you'll meet them and see." He crossed his arms. "It's a kinda different culture here than back east; the old folks here really rely on their children to take care of them; they don't go off to assisted living or nursing homes or things like that. They die at home here. And the kids, like me, care for them."

"I understand," Manny countered, seeing a framed photo of JFK on the wall, "but you've got to understand too—finishing your graduate degree will help you seriously, and it can be completed in a few more terms. You'll then be eligible to be the principal of the high school you've talked about, or even go on for a PhD as you've sometimes joked about. In the meantime, you can come back here every few months for a visit; we can arrange that."

His arms crossed, grinning softly, Jack said, "You know, Professor, I really appreciate the time you've taken to come all the way out here, just trying to persuade me. Let me think on it for a few days, okay? And you can have your own room too, for your work, for the few days here, like I mentioned. And maybe, at the end of the day, I'll drive you around and show you the sights if you won't be too bored. Not much grass or water around these parts!"

"The room would be useful, and yes, maybe later in the day, we can see some sights."

Jack stood up, lean in his jeans, and Manny too, less lean.

Outside in the warm dry September day, Jack spoke to the kids for a minute, citing chores ("Pick up them eggs!"), and told Manny to follow him.

Jack jumped into his Ford Ranger pickup and rumbled away, with Manny on his heels in his rented white Impala. They drove down the rickety road, past an isolated ramshackle house with old people sitting on the porch, who waved at Jack. It was a moonscape area up on this mesa, with an occasional patch of green, where corn was high and plentiful. The ride was potholed and bumpy, but Jack drove along like it was a highway. Manny took it easier. This arid, strange landscape was a long way from green New England and its smooth roads, fertile earth, and picture-postcard campus town.

In twenty minutes they were parked by a modest modern building, one floor, with an awning and a sign: "Hopi Artifacts For Sale." Inside, he followed Jack to meet his niece, LuEllen, a young woman reading *Glamour,* at the front counter. In a glass showcase behind her, there were shelves of Hopi jewelry, leather pieces, and colorful kachina dolls of all sizes.

Escorting Manny inside to the adjoining room, Jack introduced him to his Aunt Linda—"her American name," he said smiling, touching her shoulder—a short dark woman in her fifties, working at a workbench, painting dolls meticulously. She smiled and explained how she couldn't shake hands properly. "You see, she doesn't have time for small talk!"

Jack took Manny by the arm, and walked him through a plank door to the other half of the studio, which had a sort of workbench/desk with a high chair. "You can work here, Professor, and there's a chair for reading as well. And you can use the cot for naps if you wish! Not the prettiest, but it'll do, right?"

Manny was charmed by the makeshift studio space, and said, sure, this was just right for a little work. "I'll get my papers and laptop from the car. And do a little of my own homework."

Jack grinned widely. "I thought you'd like the place. And Euella, or Linda, she's a mouse, never peeps a word or listens to loud music, any of that stuff. A good person and a good artist too. Also, there's a little fridge out in the front, and you're welcome to use it, Mr. G."

Manny tapped his friend's arm, went to the car, got his stuff, and was helped by Jack back to his side of the studio.

"All right, thanks, now you know what you have to do this weekend," advised Manny. "Reflect on the things I've said to you, your long-term future, okay? Ask me any questions. Let's try to come up with a pragmatic solution."

Jack nodded. "A perfect place for decoding Mr. Wallenberg, right?" he teased Manny. "Your own private kiva! Anyway, I'll see you about six, when I pick you up, okay? We can have a ride and some evening chow with the family. Good luck today!"

"You too."

Left alone, he sat in the wooden armchair—a crude version of a Morris chair, with wide arms—the upholstery torn, the wood splintered—and picked up his files of Lady Z.'s papers and his own notes. The room's walls had small symbols painted on them: a curlicue, captioned, "oraibi"; another of a hand

and a sideways *S*, "Chaco Canyon," and one of an angled seesaw with circles at the ends, and a narrow snake-like creature shimmering up alongside. Manny would have to ask Jack what these little designs meant and who had done them? The space itself was a spare rectangle, shabby but decent, a few pieces of furniture, including a bookcase with books. Resisting those, he sat back and realized it could be easier to focus here than in NH, without routines or college responsibilities, friends or students; maybe a serendipitous weekend after all?

He started looking through the notes and realized how much he missed his radios, to surround his boring background. He got up, quietly knocked on the door, and, excusing himself for interrupting Euella, asked if a radio on low would bother her. She shook her head.

"Do you happen to have one around?"

She nodded, called out to her daughter, and asked her to bring in the little portable radio. The girl, on the sullen side, went and did her small task.

Back in his space, he turned on the old Emerson, searched the dials, found only pop and country music on AM and FM, and settled on the latter. A case for Sirius Satellite Radio, or at least a CD music box. Well, if he returned some time and stayed on, he would bring one with him. Just like crazy Manny—he told himself—to skip Europe, skip the Caribbean, and return to this desolate, haunted land . . .

So, with Sugarland singing, he started reading his madwoman's pages . . .

He was about twenty minutes into reading, or rereading, the materials when he opened his laptop to check contacts—Jack had told him of the new Wi-Fi connection for the store out front—and he found two new messages of interest, one from his Washington, DC, historian friend. She wrote to alert him that a Russian historian, Arkady V., was claiming, in an essay or book, that the KGB interrogator Daniel P. was perhaps present at the death of Wallenberg. Was this true? she asked. Manny, amazed, didn't really know, but wasn't sure he believed it. He wrote back and asked her to let him know when "something tangible" turned up. Yet her note, and the claim, brought back to him the last scene he had created, Daniel P.'s late good-bye to Raoul, and he realized how ironic that would have been, if the Russian historian's claim had real evidence behind it. Manny would have to wait and see, and check it out . . . But imagine if Daniel had been there, witnessing it . . .

He pondered the new gambit put out there, and it revealed to him the full power of the new Internet world: here, on a southwestern mesa on a remote reservation, one didn't need a real library for research and information, a necessity in the old days; one could sit here and do work through the virtual world. Especially if one knew what one was searching for. (Just now, for example, he googled KGB and found a brand new site created by the Lithuanians! A handsome site, too, presenting the whole KGB structure in East Europe beginning in the 1940s.). This new world might have surprised Aldous Huxley too.

Here, in the shabby partitioned studio, he felt okay, semi-real, up to par; cut off and not cut off from modern civilization; alone, and yet surrounded by these ancient pre-Western Americans; engulfed by the curious little symbolic drawings on the walls, and protected in the background by one special friend who provided the local hospitality. Things could be worse, far worse.

The second message came from somewhere in Finland: "My understanding, Professor, from your website, is that you hunt for the whereabouts of Mr. Raoul Wallenberg. Let me tell you I was in a cell with him, in Lefortovo Prison, cell 151, after Willi Roedl left. Then he was sent to the Gulag, somewhere in the Urals. Maybe you find someone who was there with him? Keep me on your list, please."

On my list? My website? Manny was baffled, shocked; and, of course, he understood. Yes, naturally, Lady Z. had "creatively" set it up, helping him out.

Later, in Jack's pickup, he sat in the shotgun seat, and bumped along the rutted dirt road as his student drove up these narrow winding roads, taking them high up to Old Oraibi on Third Mesa. Slowing down as they headed into the village of a dozen at the far edge of the mesa, Jack pointed to a handwritten sign and grinned. It read: "This village is offlimits to whites because you have broken our rules. You are no longer welcome here." Jack tapped him playfully on the shoulder. "Take it easy, I'll get you through," he kidded, or half kidded. "You're with me now."

"Hey, thanks, but you know, I like to go where I am not invited, been doing that all my life."

Jack smiled. "We'll pay a brief visit to some relatives of mine."

Presently, they were driving on the dirt road of the small village, sitting on the precipice of the mesa. This stark countryside was different from any that Manny had ever seen.

But his mind was drifting to the wiry KGB interrogator and his prisoner, what had happened, and how Manny had imagined it.

"Why create a village in so extreme a neighborhood?" Jack answered his own question. "Because the Spanish conquistadors, when they came, couldn't conquer them—too steep to get up here from the other side of those cliffs."

During the visit with Jack's elderly relatives in a small adobe house, in the small spare kitchen with the photo of Barry Goldwater on the wall, Manny was wondering about that last meeting between Daniel P. and Raoul. At the end of the visit, the relatives gave him a book written by their uncle, *Sun Chief: The*

Autobiography of a Hopi Indian. He thanked them and accepted the paper-back.

The old man held up his hand. "I'm too old now to read small print. But you read that and tell me or Jack what you think, whether it's understandable to someone outside of the tribe."

For Manny this was like an old Jew giving "The Rise of David Levinsky" to a foreign Gentile to read. "I'll do that."

They drove back down, more slowly, and Manny soaked up the bizarre mountaintop landscape and isolated clumps of small houses, and tried to think of what sort of architectural sketches Raoul might have drawn for his Michigan professor. What a strange country this was, Manny thought, right here on the other, far side of America.

They had dinner at Jack's house; he chatted politely with the kids and quiet wife, and, when it got late-ish, about nine, Jack surprised him by taking him down to the Hopi Cultural Center, where he had secured a room for him at the hotel.

A small, cozy, clean room. "It's quiet, you'll get a good night's rest here."

"Hey, I could have slept in the studio, on the cot."

"Nah, this is more 'civilized.'" Jack beamed. "The studio is for working on your book. And here's your bag."

"You've thought of everything."

"Almost."

He faced Jack, nodded, thanked him, and added, "I'm here to take you back to school, you realize."

"Yeah, my very own bounty hunter. Gellerman for DeNiro."

"Never thought of it that way, but why not?"

Jack nodded. "You get some good sleep now."

"And you think of what you have to do."

"It may take a while. You may have to stay longer than the weekend."

"Well, I've brought my work."

"That's the spirit. But you gotta finish up your project; we're all waiting." Jack punched Manny's shoulder playfully. "Maybe especially Raoul?"

When he closed the door, Manny washed up, sat on the bed, and replayed the day, the Jack advice. He took out the gift book and read in different sections. An interesting Hopi life, especially from an anthropological point of view, with unusual aspects of daily life, like the roles of man and woman . . . Certainly it would upset some current fashionable positions. How would the contemporary moralists handle it: Native American ways versus current political correctness?

Manny had an impulse to open his laptop, but it was over at the studio.

Could he walk there and find it in the dark night? He knew it was up the road a bit; he had a flashlight, and it wasn't exactly downtown Detroit; coyotes weren't going to mug him. Wearing a light windbreaker, he walked outside into the soft cool air, a pleasant wave. The walk from the driveway to the road was brief. A full moon was up, and though it went in and out of the clouds, it lit his way well enough, with the flashlight doing the rest. There were no cars, only the sounds of the whispering wind and stray calls in the night. Periodically, when the clouds allowed, he saw the blinking stars, and he tried to identify the constellations, sighting the Big Dipper and the North Star, and even finding Cassiopeia. Seeing the W-shape from a different angle out here, he strained his neck around to catch the full W. Those billions of stars, those sparkling shapes and designs, reassured him. His sneakers crunched on the gravelly path. If he kept up his pace, he figured it couldn't be more than fifteen minutes, and if he felt lost, he'd turn around.

He hadn't been alone this way, in nature, in the moonlit darkness, since he was a seventeen-year-old boy sailing on Norwegian ships and, as a "dekksgut," serving on the graveyard shift as the lookout. Standing on the bow from 11 p.m. to 6 a.m., facing the rolling Atlantic, he'd stand for an hour with the blue-black sea crashing beneath him and the black night above, waiting and watching to sight the first lights of any ship headed toward them. If he saw one, he'd clang the loud metal bell, one, two, or three times, depending on the approaching ship's direction, to alert his partner three stages above in the pilot's cabin on the bridge, so he could turn the ship ten degrees starboard. Back in his seventeen-year-old sea-youth, he had experienced an early sense of the solitariness of man in the world, a perception of the physical beauty of the natural world. Now, near fifty years later, in the September night walking out on this high desert plateau, he felt a return of those youthful emotions and perceptions, the same sense of solitude and stark beauty.

When the moon passed behind the clouds, he thought it best to keep the flashlight on, and his silver metal whistle in his other hand. You never knew when a coyote would become a pack, or turn into a wolf, he figured, walking on. In the bracing night air, before the stars, Manny felt somehow on the right track in his long search for Raoul. He wasn't quite sure what that meant, but whatever its destination or meaning, he felt it as a journey worth continuing, worth interpreting.

Lo and behold, after twenty minutes or so he came upon the studio building and was gratified—as though he had undertaken a vast adventure, not a mile walk in the empty night. When he tried the back door, on his side of the studio, he found it open still, a bit of luck. Though he hated to turn on the light, he had to, to find the wired laptop. He sat down, opened it up, waited for the dialup, and read first a few messages.

Another message from a foreign destination, Pecs, Hungary.

> *I believe I stay for a period with Mr. Wallenberg in a Soviet psychiatric hospital in north of Russia. Near Vörkuta. He was great much older, and rumored they were examining experiments on him. He was weak, and sick. To me he always a gentleman. We play chess once, I recall. If you need further my help, I here for you to speak with.*
> *Ferencz Patyi*

Gellerman wondered, How long will this go on? Or is this just the beginning? Now, armed with a new public website, was he open territory for all the new (old) witnesses, those pursuing wish fulfillment, with selective memory, with dementia? Get ready, my friend, they are coming at you, full steam ahead!

Another message, from the department secretary, asked how many students he was ready to admit into his fall term's seminar, History and the Novel? More than fifteen, or not? It was getting crowded.

Suddenly Manny felt the pressure in his chest of having to teach in three weeks or so . . . He was not in a mood for that.

A third message came from his infamous lady in Budapest: "Prof. Gellerman, where are you? I have not heard from you in several weeks. Write and tell me how things are—. How deep have you progressed with my papers? Have you started the formal writing yet?"

Yes, she had a point; well, he'd drop her a note tomorrow.

When he turned around, there was the familiar gentleman sitting in the upholstered chair, wearing an open-necked shirt and jacket, hat in his lap. The face was sober, narrow, familiar.

Startled, Manny said, "You? What are you doing here?"

"The better question is, what are *you* doing here?" the fellow paused and turned his hat. "Haven't you had enough?"

Manny shook his head slowly, bewildered.

"You have pursued this diligently, with intelligence and with dedication, but isn't it time to give it up now? And get back to living your own life?"

Manny didn't know what to say. "I don't know . . ."

"Well, I do. You have taken this as far as you can. Look, here you are, at a lonely edge of the world, far from Moscow, Budapest, Stockholm archives, still searching . . . As your friends would counsel, enough is enough. You have been . . . tried and true in this pursuit."

Gellerman smiled at the use of the idiom. "Is that what you came here for, to tell me to give it all up?"

The fellow fiddled with his hat and leaned forward. "Would you propose a different reason?"

Manny said, "Maybe to answer some questions, or to reveal some truths?"

The stoic gentleman studied the wall with the Hopi designs, drawings, shapes. "They were very inventive, weren't they? In symbolic nonwhite ways. My professor in Ann Arbor, Dr. Slusser, suggested that I travel here, spend some time with Hopi and Zuni, and observe Southwest architecture, the materials, like burnt adobe, and the manners. So I always wanted to visit and observe, and while in Arizona visit Frank Lloyd Wright's Taliesin West. Later on, I even made a few preliminary sketches for a desert project—just right for a Swede," he said dryly.

Manny admired the allusion to the old professor and his own aspiration.

"But you," the visitor narrowly smiled, "You seem to know the territory and to value it highly." He reflected. "Maybe I should have come down this way, and designed a place to return to, after my Budapest duties? . . . In any case, Emmanuel, you have been nothing less than valiant, as I said, but it is probably time to leave it go."

"And let history take its course?"

The gentleman smiled ruefully.

"May I ask you," Manny gambited, "did you have a family in Budapest?"

The Swede stared. "Do you think I have arrived here to answer such . . . esoteric questions?" he shook his head. "My mission is simply *to relieve you of yours. Of pursuing the odd case.* What happened to me, *happened.* It is not a handsome story. For it to end—without resolution, without answers—that is a suitable ending, I would think."

"Ironically, you speak as if I am a burden upon you, rather than the other way round."

A generous smile. "You have a clever way of putting matters. But there is no need anymore. The facts speak for themselves, the absences and mysteries speak also. So, what else is left? . . . Interpretations? They will go on and on. And will resolve little."

"But supposing they blacken you, tarnish what you did? Who you are?"

"Oh," he said, adjusting the band of the hat, "that is the nature of things, don't you think, when it comes to human beings? And maybe historians?" He laughed a little. "Besides I can bear all that, I assure you."

"Well, maybe I can't."

They faced each other, in the small spare studio, and Manny felt the oddness of that new request. What was he to do now? . . .

"I will take into consideration what you are asking of me and try somehow to find a response."

"Good."

The gentleman stood up, lifting his obscure backpack, and Manny joined him.

Manny said, "Too bad you don't have your old Studebaker outside, huh?"

This warmed Raoul, who nodded in agreement. "Absolutely. Along with Vilmos to drive us, perhaps."

Manny turned away for a second, hearing the beeping on his laptop of a new message, and when he turned back, RW was gone, vanished, just like that. Manny opened the door and peered out into the darkness, adjusting his eyes, staring, searching for a clue, but there was no sign of him. Manny stood there, transfixed, hearing the wind and the eerie calls from the mountains. Jackals?

He began to walk back, but now the treeless landscape, dark shapes, and eerie cries were much less scary than on the adventurous trek out. As for the little occurrence inside, why and how did the stranger know he was there? . . . Who had summoned him here? No matter now. Manny knew he had many things to consider, so he'd get up early and attend to them—simple and complicated things.

Back inside the hotel room, he was conscious of the sharp differences between the bewitching studio and the cozy familiar room. Here he could remember clearly why he came in the first place, to retrieve his AWOL student, and bring him back for his schoolwork and degree. To that simple task he'd devote himself more fully in the next day or two . . .

As for the deeper journey, he couldn't let that go; it had hooked him, he knew. (Was Mr. Wallenberg worried that he was getting closer to the—or a— truth?)

CHAPTER 20

Back in the classroom two weeks later, he felt on home ground again, like someone sitting back in his favorite automobile or in his position on the field. Here with his fifteen students ready to become educated, a few even devoted, he handed out his reading list and outlined the course:

"So we are going to study the intersection of history and literature, and where and how history is best served through the lens of literary works. In no particular order, we'll read *Homage to Catalonia* by George Orwell, a work of literary journalism about the Spanish Civil War. Another classic, *Man's Fate* by André Malraux, is a fictional portrait of the Chinese Communist Revolution. Closer to home, we'll read *The Book of Daniel* by E. L. Doctorow, a novel about the Cold War in America and the Rosenbergs. While there are many good books about World War II, I've chosen two first-class novels, *History: A Novel* by the Italian writer Elsa Morante, and *Life and Fate* by the Russian Vassily Grossman; the former is well known, the latter, obscure. For a work imagining political revolution in South America, let's do Joseph Conrad's *Nostromo*. And for a modern view of that history, Gabriel Márquez's *One Hundred Years of Solitude*. Later, if we have the time, we'll try *Rebellion in the Backlands*, by da Cunha, a Brazilian journalist who wrote what I think is the greatest South American novel."

He paused and shuffled in his book bag, to ready his private manuscript. "To explore Nazi history, we'll read *The Tin Drum* by Günther Grass, and the lesser known *To the Unknown Hero* by Hans Nossack, about a young man writing a doctoral thesis in history."

Knowing smiles. He went on.

"And we might try the hybrid works by W. G. Sebald, reflections upon World War II, which mingle fiction with history—maybe *Austerlitz*. Among works on the Holocaust, let's look at *An Interrupted Life: The Diaries of Etty*

Hillesum, and two great autobiographical fictions, *This Way for the Gas, Ladies and Gentlemen* by Tadeusz Borowski, and *A Scrap of Time and Other Stories* by Ida Fink. Of course, one of the memoirs of Primo Levi. That should give us enough to start with."

That remark got the class laughing. "Obviously, we will choose *from among* those works, and not read all of them." He paused, fiddled with pages.

"But first, I want to begin the course with a problem in basic historiography, namely how to examine sources, study the various materials, and consider how they get developed and transformed into an actual book. In other words, *you* are going to be the historian here, not just the student. So for the first few weeks let's look at this updated source book for the trials of the Rosenbergs and the Alger Hiss/Whittaker Chambers trial, and how they emerged into the history books, and the notable novel I cited above. This will be interesting. But maybe more exciting, and more exacting, will be this"—and here Manny raised high the manuscript from his tote bag—"a bunch of collected papers by a woman in Budapest who claims that she is the daughter of Raoul Wallenberg, the Swedish diplomat." He paused. "Anyone know the name? Who he was?"

A few hands went up, and he called on a student, a European who uttered a few sentences about Raoul. "Good," Manny nodded, and went on.

"It's not all that long, maybe 150 pages in sum. But it will be like digging into an original archive of historical material. As I said, you'll play the historian. And alongside that, I will have you read some of the essays and maybe a few select books written about the subject, Wallenberg. What you and I will be examining are the notes and letters for a memoir written by this private lady, the self-proclaimed daughter of that Swedish hero who saved Jews in Budapest. *If these papers are real, they will change the way we look at Wallenberg, and you graduate students will be engaged in making history.*" He paused, for emphasis. "We will read the materials, explore ways to verify their authenticity, and finally try to determine their ultimate historical value. Is this a collection of papers of major significance? Or is it a minor contribution to the subject? Or hardly even that? Perhaps a few of you will try to put all this together here, into a publishable form. It could be an end-of-term project for one or two of you. Start with a long paper, and turn it into something more extended for a thesis or monograph?"

The class buzzed and took notes. Several questions were posed. And while he answered, Manny understood that now, while he was doing as Raoul had suggested—getting back to his own life—he was also continuing with his own preference, keeping up his long pursuit. No, he would not abandon Raoul—

not abandon him as Bartleby's former boss had abandoned that lonely scriv-ener—he would pursue Raoul in the classroom, with his students. And in writing. Further, via his newly "discovered" website, he'd keep up with RW's wish-fulfillment "followers" and "would-be witnesses" who buzzed him from all corners of the world, weekly, monthly. Yes, Raoul would stay with him, stay in his daily life, in teaching, e-mailing, and maybe even in occasional private conversations.

As for the Medium in Budapest? He had written her, and "spun" the situation for her, calling it "rather exciting." He was giving the materials over to his class to sort out, examine, study, for developing the memoir, and after that, he would work on it along with the lady herself. Her "devotion" to her father would be respected, and they both could observe how intelligent readers react to the materials . . .

To his amazement, Zsuzsa agreed to this unforseen "new situation," and said she was willing to leave the matter in his hands. When was he returning to Budapest? He was able to explain, with sound logic, in a few months, after his course was over. She accepted that too, and added, innocently, that she could even visit the class, if he wished? (Was she not brilliant?!)

And then: "There is a chance that Dora will come to visit you, after her conference at The New School. You will be happy to host her, yes?"

To this bright news, he responded, "Of course." Only later, he wondered what he had said yes to. . . .

From the Holocaust Museum in Washington, DC, he received an invitation from a historian who wondered if he could come down and talk to him about the new Wallenberg materials he was working on. Calling the discovery "very noteworthy indeed," Professor Shapiro also suggested that, after their meeting, he would try to set up a panel discussion on the full possiblities and value of Manny's "groundbreaking new work."

Suddenly, via Lady Z.'s "Let's Pretend" pages, and vision, he was catapulting onto the world map of Wallenberg scholars in no uncertain terms. From Sweden again, from Moscow, London, and Budapest, he received invitations to address one or another institution, or committee, to discuss his new findings. Not to mention media like the BBC, CNN, NPR, two major Swedish TV stations. For now, he held off, keeping them at arm's distance, but not entirely away.

What a bizarre mask he felt himself wearing, part truth, part illusion, part fraud, and he didn't quite know how to escape it. Did he want to? . . . After all, for now he had his class to teach, and he might learn from them, as he always did from the brightest few, what they thought of the "collected papers." And he could take it from there, go wherever, and develop what he might think fitting . . . Now here was coming little Dora, visiting. *Why? . . . As an honored guest or a cunning spy?* . . . (Like Raoul wondering if he was taken as a prisoner or a guest to Moscow.)

His son cheerleaded his new mini-celebrity status, saying, "Dad, you must go on all the shows, accept all the lectures!" His luminous face and hazel eyes beamed with pride. "You deserve it!"

Surprisingly, in his new limbo status, Manny felt relaxed enough, in paradoxically out-of-control cruise control. Things were so daffy, so baffling, he felt there was no way he could unscramble everything, or resolve anything. Yet the fact of the new attention being devoted to RW in various countries and sites, that was healthy enough, for now anyway. All the old facts of his desperate situation were being dug up, and there was even talk of putting new pressure on Putin to have the FSB dig up that lost file from the basement of Lybianka and allow real discovery . . . Maybe something really honorable would emerge from the deceptive situation after all? . . . Further, if he had to play this hide and seek game in order to protect certain private truths about the real RW—while offering to the world the family version of RW—well, why not? . . .

Jack came by his office one late morning, his hair in a ponytail, bearing his backpack, and Manny suggested they have coffee.

So they proceeded to the backstreet coffee shop Rosey Jekes, and sat in that quiet space with small wrought iron tables.

"I never thought I'd be back here, Professor, I'll tell you that."

"How does it feel?"

"Pretty good, actually. But it's because of you; you're 'the man.'"

"Oh, I didn't do that much, did I?"

"You did what you had to do, man! You showed up *on my territory*, you stayed around, you met the whole family, and they then all agreed that, yeah, you really did care, and you really wanted me back! And therefore I should go back and finish up!"

Manny stirred his coffee and overheard a Tuck School group, busy planning.

"You know, they don't invite too many whites to the Walpi snake dance!" He smiled. "But my uncle and aunt, they said you were maybe the most honorable white man to come to Oraibi since Mischa Titiev arrived in the early thirties!"

Who was that? Manny wondered, embarrassed. "How's the thesis going?"

"Oh, well, I'm just getting into the real writing, you know, where you don't know how it's going. It's not easy getting focused again after the months off!"

"I know what you mean."

"And I'm still unsure how I feel about General Crook, his role in the betrayal, after all this time. I keep going back and forth."

"Well, you'll figure it out as you write it."

"Yeah, I know, you always say that! Hey, how's Wallenberg coming?"

Manny reflected. "Not too bad."

"Any new 'revelations?'"

"Just some . . . false positives," he smiled, "as they say about my PSA exam."

"What's that?"

"A medical exam for old guys like me. No worries for you yet."

"Hey, I know what you need, a Hopi prophecy man, you know? Someone who can go to the mountaintop and have a special Vision! Yeah, I'll introduce you to an old one next time you come around."

"Yes, you do that," he said, and listened to the coffee machine hissing a latte. A Hopi vision about Wallenberg—yes, that would do the trick, and add to the mix.

Jack lifted his backpack onto his lap, and removed an item in white wrapping. "This is for you, a little present from the family."

"Hey, you didn't have to bring me anything."

"I didn't, Professor; *they* did, especially my aunt, you know, the lady on the other side of the studio from you."

He set down on the table the package, which, when unwrapped, turned out to be two kachina dolls. One was about ten inches, the other maybe sixteen inches high; brightly painted, richly detailed, with black squares for eyes and feathers on their heads and tails. They were mounted firmly on thin platforms of wood.

"Those are real eagle feathers," Jack explained. He leaned forward to whisper, "Even though that may be illegal, you know!"

"Well, thanks; and thank the family. I'll put them on a shelf where I can view them daily."

"They might bring you real luck!"

Smiling, Manny said, "I will count on that."

Later, at home, he set the two Hopi dolls in his study, on a bookshelf in front of books. Colorful, strange, forceful, they looked like two odd sentries on guard. Against what, protecting what? Should Manny shrink and paint himself and climb up there with them, and look colorful and strange? . . .

In a few hours, he picked up his son—meeting his mother halfway—and brought him outside for a cookout dinner. When the boy asked about the trip to the Southwest and was shown the kachina dolls, he smiled widely. "Dad, they're great! Can you get me a pair next time you go?"

Manny laughed. "Sure, next time I go. What will you do with them?"

He thought a second. "Put them on my shelf overlooking my music!"

After dinner, the boy went to the cello in the living room, sat down, fixed the end pin. "Here, Dad, the final section of the Wallenberg Suite. It's pretty short. Ready?"

Surprised, Manny sat on the couch and observed the boy tuning the strings. Concentrating, he was already a little pro at thirteen.

The music proceeded for five to six minutes, a mingling of the mournful and the lyrical, maybe some Schubert with Mozart, part harmonious, part haunting, with lots of stacked chords. Every now and then he looked up, checking to see if Dad was listening attentively. Oh, he was, for sure! Those several minutes seemed like a lifetime for this adagio section, as Manny tried to peer through the music to the boy composing, and contemplate what he wanted to express through it. While the boy played, his mouth forming, as it had from childhood, that small O of concentration, Manny followed the lightning-quick fingering of the strings, the position of the right hand for bowing, the occasional pizzicato. Manny wondered, Which aspect of Raoul was the boy reaching for? With the windows at his back, the tall avocado plant at his side, and fields behind him, the boy looked like a figure in an interior painting (Vermeer?). He finished off with several harsh dissonant chords, however, which forged a frightening sound!

Silence, and a wide sweep of his bow; a gleaming smile emerged, and he took out his handkerchief to wipe his perspiration.

"That's really special." Manny clapped. "And so interesting. That ending, where'd you get that from?"

The boy nodded. "I took it from Shostakovich, his own funeral quartet that he wrote for Rostropovich. Did you recognize it?"

Manny shook his head. "Tell me, was there a particular aspect of Wallenberg you were trying to capture, or express?"

The boy reflected, still wiping his face with his handkerchief. "Oh, his courage, and then his terrible downfall."

"Well, *I felt that*. Strongly. And maybe, somewhere, *he* felt it too."

The boy looked at him, puzzled. "You think so, somehow?"

"Why not? Stranger things have happened."

The boy shook his head. "It's really *very hard* to compose—I think I'll stick to playing after I revise this."

Manny gave him a tight hug and soon was driving him back to town to his mother's place, and school the next day. "You did a great job! When you're finished with the revising, you have to make a recording of it for me, okay?"

"Sure. But that may not be for a while, you know."

"Of course. When you're ready, take your time. Bye sonnyboy!"

Manny, walking back to the lounge of the inn, felt a stirring, sat down with his laptop, and recalled a remark made by Raoul in an early letter to his grandfather, about how studying in Michigan for three years had confirmed his idea that America was different from the Old World, and how the experience had changed and deepened him in many ways.

Now, in his out-of-the way corner, Manny composed:

Sitting in a curved row in the lecture hall, Raoul savored the modern space, and savored more *the way* the class was taught. Not a monologue lecture with occasional slides, as in Sweden, but a lecture that was often broken up by the give and take of student questions and comments.

Like just now, as Professor Slusser was lecturing about Louis Sullivan and his first skyscrapers, second-year student John Hermansky raised his hand and asked, "But don't we have to look at and question the full context of these skyscrapers? I mean, sir, the fact that they interrupt and supplant regular residential neighborhoods—well, shouldn't the architect have to consider this?"

Slusser nodded, and replied, "I think you do have a point. But there is also the question of the commission itself, and therefore it is up to the individual architect."

"You mean," John countered, "whether he is commercial minded or aesthetic?"

"Hey, come on," put in Jacob Trottier, from across the aisle, "can't the architect be both? After all, most of us are going to have families and mouths to feed. Mr. Sullivan was not exactly a capitalist pig monster, you know."

The class laughed.

"By the way," put in Ted Smith, "can't a cluster of skyscrapers constitute a whole new neighborhood, like now on the Chicago skyline? For example—"

Prof. Slusser silenced him with his hand, saying, yes, the architect had to consider the whole neighborhood context; and yes, the skyscraper "neighborhood" was also an interesting topic, but that that was a discussion for later on. For now, he wanted to move to the transition from Louis Sullivan to Frank Lloyd Wright, his disciple. As the tall professor with the monotone voice spoke, Raoul felt again the rich pleasure of the open discussion and debate, which could go on at length and even get heated. Raoul promised himself to overcome his natural reticence and European restraint and join the class discussion one day . . . That democratic student-prof question and answer and rebuttal was so different from the Swedish lecture hall, he knew, where the atmosphere was imperial—the professor ruling his empire with dogmatic voice and rigid ideas, while student silence was *de rigueur*.

As Professor Slusser began talking about the "prairie style" of both architects, Sullivan and Wright, showing slides, Raoul's mind suddenly grasped something. He began to jot down notes, on a graph-paper pad, for a grand idea, based on the slides and prairie style. He admired the long horizontal lines, open interior spaces, flat-pitched roofs, and he briefly sketched out a house; and he decided, right then, on his thesis: a plan for a grouping of such houses—maybe a half dozen on a single street in a suburb of Stockholm, like Lindingö, near the river, where right now there existed only a scattering of conventional homes. Naming it the Lindingö Project, he would do a formal design for the cluster and write a long introductory essay, with individual notes for the different residences, marked by small variations. Our suburbs need artful simplicity and variation, he thought, but also economic planning and the most modern materials of wood and glass. First he'd visit a Wright residence, naturally. He couldn't wait to tell Grandfather about his sudden inspiration.

"Mr. Wallenberg, have you been with us?" asked the Professor, amused. "Or have I so enchanted you that you are off dreaming?"

The buzzer rang, interrupting the professor, who nodded and called it a day.

"Hey, Wallflower, come join us for a beer!" said John H. "You're always going off on your own. C'mon!"

Two students teasingly lifted him up and escorted him out of the lecture room, where they were joined by four others. Soon, they were hustling Raoul into a large jalopy, Ted saying, "We need to give you a nickname; what do you think?"

Tim jumped in, "How about "The European?"

"Or," suggested Jake, "The Swede!"

"God, no, let's be inventive," said Hermansky "Let's see . . ."

"I have it!" said Phil Roberts, "We've known you for nearly a year now, and no one knows anything about you, so, you are hereby annointed Mystery Man."

The sardine-squeezed gang of six cheered!

Raoul, uncomfortable, found himself saying, "Is that really a nickname?"

"Well, it will do till a better one comes along!"

Raoul relented, smiled, and allowed the joking to proceed. As the Plymouth careened along through the leafy streets of the charming college town, Raoul thought how surprising these colleagues were, all this good-natured kidding masking their true talent and intelligence. And maybe Hermansky was right; maybe he was the Mystery Man—to himself as well. Well, for now, he'd have his beer with the fellows, and then, later, sit in the library and work on a serious sketch for his bold thesis inspiration.

Phil Roberts meanwhile continued to hold him by the arm, and Raoul wondered about the friendships of these Americans—how loose they were, how loose and easy, so very different from his own more formal Stockholm culture.

Phil turned and smiled broadly, sitting in his lap, saying, "You see, Mystery Man, you can rest easy with us, your secrets will always be safe with us."

Gellerman pulled himself back up from the scene and reread it. Did it catch the youthful but complex spirit of Raoul—his appealing quest for learning and understanding in the New World, but also his uncertainty? While the little portrait captured certain traits, like shyness, propriety, collegiality, did it reach deeper into his personality? Maybe *there, at the end, with Phil so close?* When Raoul wrote to his grandfather that America was changing him, did that include a freeing of his inner self and desires, which were taboo in Stockholm? Or was Manny reaching out too far? Perhaps. But for now, he let it be. The Wallenberg with whom he had recently chatted on the Hopi Res deserved a replay of his spirited youth, his comic spirit, and his rebel's stance, but also his complex character. If he imagined a scene based on his interview with Olaf Selling, would more emerge?

An elderly couple stopped and asked Manny for a direction on the campus. Manny took them outside the inn and pointed out the small redbrick Hood Museum, down the street a few hundred yards. The gentleman thanked him and turned away. But as he did, Manny realized the man reminded him of someone: Daniel Pagliansky in Moscow, with the thin wisps of hair flying, the small wiry frame, the lively brown eyes. And right there Manny stopped, suspended briefly, for he suddenly felt he *understood* something, or rather, understood that he had *failed* to see something. How naïve, of course!

He returned inside to his obscure corner, opened the laptop, and composed:

Late July 1947; Lybianka Prison, Moscow

Raoul was led into a Medical Lab 272 by two guards and set down on a metal armchair. The square room was lit by several unshaded bulbs and a standing lamp, and it contained two large glass medical cabinets, an examination table, a wash basin, several chairs. Presently, a bespectacled doctor wearing a white medical coat walked in, nodded, and examined a file at the green file cabinet. Two minutes later the doctor was followed in by two KGB agents, wearing full uniform, including large military hats. Raoul at first barely recognized his interrogator friend, since he looked so different, dressed formally in his military uniform of olive and red.

Raoul looked at him, and Daniel looked back, and nodded very slowly. No words were exchanged.

The doctor read through his file, turned to the two agents, and had them sit down on two chairs by the far white wall.

He gestured for Raoul to move up to the examination table and remove his shoes. Raoul got up, removed his shoes, and sat at the front edge of the narrow table covered with a sheet.

The room smelled of sulphuric acid and other chemicals.

Raoul said, "Daniel. Good to see you came, to say a real good-bye to me."

Daniel took off his large officer's hat and nodded.

The doctor motioned to the prison guards, who came alongside Raoul, each on a side, and each gripped an arm. The doctor returned from the medicine cabinet with an ammo box container of bandages, small vials, and an injection needle.

"Do you wish to say anything?" he asked Raoul.

Raoul shook his head slowly but firmly.

"We have your confession sheet for you; would you like to sign it?"

Raoul shook his head.

"No matter, we will sign it for you. An enemy of the state doesn't have to sign for himself." The doctor walked close to Raoul, nodded to the tall guard, who gripped the right arm. Carefully he filled the needle with a grayish liquid.

Daniel and his associate agent stood up, holding their hats.

Suddenly, in a small but distinct voice, Raoul spoke: "Daniel, wouldn't you like to do the honor?"

The doctor looked strangely at Raoul and then over to Daniel, who stood small and stoic; no one was very amused.

Returning to the business at hand, the doctor searched for a prominent vein, found one, and injected the needle. The doctor waited, along with the guards, for maybe twenty seconds, with Raoul looking straight ahead, before he lost consciousness; at the doctor's nod, the guards laid him down on the narrow bed. The doctor leaned over, opened his eyelids, and checked his pulse.

Turning to the KGB agents, he said, "Which one of you will sign the death certificate?"

Daniel and his associate looked at each other, hesitated, before Daniel came forward and scribbled his name.

The doctor, adjusting his spectacles, proceeded to sign his name. He said, "Sign again here."

Daniel signed a second sheet.

The two guards rolled in a gurney, lifted the body onto it, and waited for one of the certificates to be attached to the gurney. The doctor put the second sheet into the file.

"Case number 4581 is now officially closed, comrades."

The two agents put their hats on, nodded, and filed out, while the doctor stayed. He began cleaning up, tossing out the empty vial, cleaning the needle, and washing his hands. He organized his medicine cabinet and locked it. He put the certificate into the manilla folder, wrote something on it, and set the folder in the iron basket on top of the cabinet.

Finally, looking about, satisfied, he closed the lights, stepped to the door, and exited.

Manny felt depleted, melancholic. He sat in the wing chair in the formal lounge, entranced, while well-dressed guests and students paraded through, chatting. His throat was dry. Had the scene *really* happened? Here, now, the scene of Last Betrayal seemed right, in keeping with Soviet ways and KGB tactics. Why hadn't he thought of it before? Because, he figured, he had been thinking like an American scholar, not like a Soviet comrade. He tried to console himself with the thought that this scene was imaginary only, right? No hard evidence for it! . . . Still, he felt awful.

"Thank you," said the elderly man, suddenly reappearing with his wife, "but the Hood Museum is closing now. We will try tomorrow."

Manny, taken from his depths, looked up, and for a moment swore he saw Daniel right there—the bony structure, the wispy white hair, the alert eyes.

Manny nodded, "Oh, I see. Well, yes, try tomorrow."

Who had sent the fellow? This montage of lives, which Manny had experienced before, proved a revelation. The accidental meeting was a sign, yes. *His imagined character of a minute ago was revealing to him the real one whom he had visited in Moscow.* A historian's irony? Or history's irony? . . . The cycle was now complete: RW was abandoned by family, state, and friendly interrogator. Manny saw now how in his earlier scenes he had been a naïve romantic. But now, he felt more the realist . . . For now he understood—it made perfect sense—why the real Daniel P. had never told his son or wife, or spoken to anyone else, even when it could have benefitted him, anything concerning RW and his dealings with him. Nor did he acknowledge anything to the KGB when they interviewed him in 1991 and offered him complete immunity. Silence became his signature, for family, state, and history. To be a KGB operative was one thing—involving institutional perfidy—but to be a personal betrayer on top of that, added a new layer of evil.

Standing up, Manny heard in his mind the last sounds of his son's finale, those harsh dissonant melodies that Shostakovich had dedicated to Rostropovich, to be played at the composer's funeral.

CHAPTER 21

The apparent "downfall" of Manny didn't occur for another few weeks, in October, when the leaves were falling, the colors were changing, football had begun, and the baseball playoffs were heating up. But there was little time to enjoy the foliage and sporting fun for Manny. It happened this way. In Budapest the Medium lady couldn't—or wouldn't—restrain herself and take a chance on missing out on her several minutes of fame and glory. So she managed to leak a story to a Hungarian journalist about *her so-called identity,* and which "famous professor" was editing her papers in America. The rest happened fast, furious, and was not so pretty. Newspaper services from around the world picked up the story, printed first in the Budapest magazine *HVG,* and it spread like rumor-wildfire to all sorts of media, starting with the likes of the *International Herald Tribune,* the *Wall Street Journal,* and the *New York Times,* and going on to *Dygens Nyheter* and the *Huffington Post.* Was YouTube next? Manny was phoned, faxed, beeped, wired, e-mailed, texted, confronted. How were the lady's papers proceeding? When would the memoir be finished? Who was the publisher? (Several New York publishers, plus Yale and Chicago, had expressed immediate interest.) Conveniently, a few inquired whether her revelations were accurate.

When CNN and the BBC called and asked for interviews, and Tom Lantos and the Swedish-Russian Working Group chipped in to ask for and demand answers, what was he to say?

In the next few weeks, there were surprise meetings, journalists, lawyers, interviewers, a detective, scholars, lawyers. His life quickly became a circus; he was followed around by a new group every day on the quiet Ivy League campus. One day he was ambushed inside his classroom by that journalist from Uppsala, who now, with her camera/sound man, sought to film him in class, as part of the process of making a documentary about him; the fifteen graduate students grew very excited, and Manny, very nervous; naturally, he turned them away, to the dismay of the students.

Manny understood, of course, that he was about to be blown out of the water any day, by the clever Budapest lady, so he had one of two choices: expose her himself, or let her make a mockery of herself, and shrewdly try to remove himself from her and the field of combat by seeking to create distance from her.

In the meantime, daughter Dora showed up on his doorstep, after her New York conference, coming up to see the real New England in the fall and to be hosted by Manny. Good timing? Or good scheming? ("Mom hopes to follow me here one day, if you give her an invitation." The petite young woman smiled, after setting down her small valise inside the kitchen of his large farmhouse.)

When the chair of his department called him in, Manny imagined the worst: direct questions about the authenticity of the papers and the date of publication of the memoir.

"You've given us more publicity than our department has ever had," he laughed robustly. "This will help us, within the university, for raising our profile and for getting us more funding."

Manny nodded.

"What sort of woman is this? How'd you come upon her in the first place?"

"Actually, my student Angela first mentioned her to me," Manny said. He explained the evolution from the thesis and described the lady, "She's unusual, let's say that. Rather bohemian in her thinking, her ways."

"I would imagine so, after that life! Well, you've done a great job!" He leaned forward and said, in a lower voice, "There are several alumni groups that really would like to hear about all this. Can I get you to address them?"

What could Manny say, now, before any exposure explosion, but "Sure."

"Great, I'll set it up and let you know. This is very productive for the department, puts us on another level of importance." He lowered his voice for delivering crucial verdicts: "This is important for you too, Manny. I was worrying about you . . . This brings you back up, just what you need for a comeback!"

Later, at home in the countryside, he set out two wine glasses for Dora and himself, and sat in the living room, waiting. The giant avocado plant needed serious tending and pruning, its branches reaching up to the ceiling and out wildly into the room. The twenty-five-year-old plant was holding its own, though looking strange, its branches lunging every which way.

"Hello," she said, entering, wearing a white blouse and flowered skirt. "I really like your house."

"Here, this is for you." He stood and gave her a glass of white wine.

"Thank you. And here, this is for you, from Mother."

She handed him a small package, tied with a ribbon, and sat down.

He opened the simple wrapping to find a small cardboard box. He opened it and took out a note and a worn leather pouch, three inches by four, heavy with a weight inside, and tiny eroded writing on it. The note read: "Please accept this gift from me and my father, a present given him by a Jewish survivor in Budapest. My father used it as a paperweight on his desk and was very fond of it. I hope you will be too." It was signed, "Your friend, Zsuzsanna."

He lifted the little (terra-cotta?) paperweight, feeling it, and passed it to Dora, sitting alongside.

She lifted it, raising her eyebrows mischevously, and said, "You are becoming like one of the family!"

He looked at her. "Is that good or bad?"

She sipped her wine. "Good, I hope!"

He drank his wine, observing the surprise present, and the young woman, suddenly here, with her beautiful face, in his living room. What did it mean? What was he supposed to do with her? . . . Was she a plant from the mother?

"How long are you here for?"

"Oh, just a few days." She smiled. "I won't be a bother to you, I promise. Mom said I should pay a visit and see the leaves."

Was this young Hungarian beauty really a family link to the great ghost of a man he had been pursuing these past few years?

"Yes, the leaves," he repeated. "Maybe we can climb Mount Cardigan this weekend, so you can get a wide view of their colors turning."

She nodded, her brown eyes fixing him.

Manny had many questions to put to her, but not now; and he wasn't sure that she could answer them. He stood up and went to the avocado plant, seeing that a few dead leaves had fallen, and retrieved them. "I suppose you want to know how your mom's papers are coming along?"

She shook her head. "No. That is between you and her."

"Yes, that is true. Well, *we* should consider dinner, shouldn't we?"

In the ensuing few days, Manny *felt* the young woman's presence and tried to imagine her mother really being the daughter of Wallenberg, rather than the obsessive RW-cult fanatic he believed her to be. Did it really matter, however? he wondered, climbing the 3,200-foot mountain with his young guest. Wasn't Zsuzsa's long obsession enough, deserving enough in itself? As he glanced at the trim Budapest daughter, with her backpack and hiking shoes, take the steady ascent like a small mountain goat while he climbed like an old goat, he tried to ponder what it all meant, what the real fallout would be, and when? . . . They were ascending now above the tree line, onto a stretch of granite ledge and big boulders. From here they could view the top of the mountain and the forest ranger lookout hut, jutting out high on its wooden stilts. Windy here; he took out his light windbreaker from his pack. The energetic young woman eyed him every so often, nodded or half smiled, didn't speak much, and looked easy, comfortable.

At the top they had a 360-degree view of the topography below, mostly forest with some open fields and dark-blue lakes and little white houses dotting the woodsy landscape. If you peered closely, you spotted the periodic clusters of the small villages, and even, if you looked through the binoculars, you could sight selected places, like his house and land or the college library steeple. Dora paid the expected compliments—"almost like Machu Picchu, where I climbed once." There was sweat on her pink flushed face. Radiant herself, she appreciated the visual beauty, and stealthily he sought any resemblance to RW . . . Why couldn't he simply accept the situation as young Dora apparently did? If it happened that she was Raoul's secret granddaughter, it happened, and if not, not. (Could he ever ask her to take a DNA test? But without Raoul's corpse, how could they confirm a match?) She seemed easy about accepting such ambiguity. Why not Manny?

They drank their bottled waters, viewed the spacious vista. "I like your New England," she acknowledged, and he responded, "I like your Budapest." A pair of hikers came by and said hello. On top of the mountain, closer to the clouds, he sensed a curious responsibility for this young person. For her not being damaged by the mother's delusions and derangement. Or his folly? Naturally, he kept this feeling to himself, and pointed out the few sights he knew: the beginning hills of the White Mountains, like Smarts, and the great stony Whites, with the 'baddest' weather in New England." Pointing, he explained, "Right there on top of that one, Mount Washington, the wind regularly blows at fifty or sixty miles an hour in winter. A foolish hiker gets lost there every winter." She nodded, her small chin forward, and asked defiantly, "Are you going to test me?" He retorted, "Absolutely. As soon as we get back." Actually, he thought he should test her, but not about mountains.

When they did get home in two hours, he found in his e-mail box another witness sighting, this from a Russian immigrant residing in Rehovot, Israel, a retired physicist who claimed he had seen the "old sick diplomat" at a Gulag camp near the Urals, and would be happy to talk with Professor Gellerman. Manny jotted down the name and a phone number. After a shower, he met up with Dora in the kitchen, and they planned a dinner. "I cook; it's my turn," she said. The dinner was good too, a roast chicken in a pan with carrots, potatoes, and onions; and the talk concerned her work in children's therapy. He kept waiting for the questions to come about her mother's "manuscript," but they never did. A smart and discreet young woman.

The next day in class, he spoke to the students about their progress thus far in the mother's memoir papers. He mentioned to them again the Sacco and Venzetti source book of primary source materials, *Commonwealth v. Sacco and Vanzetti*, which included trial transcripts, newspaper articles, letters to the editors of the time, a repercussion section. So now he asked the class if they would like to work on that Wallenberg source book. "Using perhaps as a basis the Hungarian lady's letters, notes, newspaper clippings, and photographs. What do you think?"

Kevin said, "That's cool, really cool, sir. Do you think we might be able to publish it?" A growing buzz and affirmation ensued.

"Why not? It would make a very useful source book, especially with so many still unanswered questions, and we could also include some of the research findings of the Swedish-Russian Working Group, plus some of Raoul's own Budapest reports and letters. Those should be in there too."

The class sounded its approval.

"Let's do some homework, round up a few other source books to go along with the Sacco and Venzetti model," he advised, as the students tapped keys on their laptops. "There's that one about the Rosenbergs that I mentioned."

Manny sensed that he was now paying the healthiest homage to Raoul, keeping him alive in the classroom, in the young minds; and in his own life of research. Raoul needed to be remembered; the memory of his deeds, and his abandonment, needed to be put up there, on the big American, maybe European, radar screen. (Even if this were to be a sanitized Raoul, for new-era political purposes.) Yes, there would be more beeps and signaling on his website from the "witnesses" around the world and, who knows, one might come through—like the physicist?—with new words of authentic memory and suggestive illumination.

Jesse raised her hand, "If we do a good enough job, maybe we could send a copy over to Moscow and see what the current Russians think or want to do."

"There's an idea," Manny took up, only half humorously. "We send Putin a Wallenberg source book as a gift, marking off a section of blank pages for him to fill in a missing file."

The class went on and deliberated, and then returned to the work coming up, the Doctorow novel, and some of the original sources from that era.

After class, he went to the office to pick up a few items, and the cordial secretary handed him a Registered Letter from Sweden. ("I signed for it, sir.") Heart beating. Manny opened it and found a formal letter from Danowsky and

Partners, Attorneys at Law in Stockholm, stating that, on behalf of the Wallenberg family, a legal suit was being filed in the Swedish courts for "unproven and perfidious allegations staining the name of their late family member Raoul Wallenberg, concerning an illegitimate Hungarian family and living daughter in Budapest." Manny nodded to the wondering secretary, signaling all was fine, and wandered out and across the campus green. In the autumn twilight, he walked over to the inn, entered the restaurant, and at the bar ordered a scotch. If the Enskilda Wallenbergs were excited by the "news" of a possible family in Budapest, what would happen when and if his projected book was published, with its imagined charged scenes and conclusions about the brothers? (Not to mention a memoir by Lady Z.) That might *incite*, not merely *excite*, the Wallenberg boys even more!

He made a mental note to call up his legal buddy in New York, smart and able Marty Goldmark, who was as passionate about legal combat as he was about the First Amendment. He'd have great fun arguing in a Stockholm courtroom, and winning—and wouldn't he? The tough Jewish bulldog going after the cool Swedes!

"So you've really hit the news, huh?" asked his worldly colleague, Tom Jameson, sidling into a barstool. "Your ship has come in, at long last. Here, I'm buying this next one!" and he called over the bartender. "Will you even be talking to deck boys like us, who are here to swab the decks and clean the latrines? I doubt it. Out there in the big world, the stakes are different, and the players too. And you're a player now!"

Manny was quietly astonished at what Tom was saying. "Oh, I don't think I'll be making many changes just yet."

"Yes, that's the spirit, saying the right words! Do remember those words for just a few seconds, when the CNN makeup crew is applying the finishing touches for your appearance, okay?"

Manny smiled and nodded, and went on to the second drink. He barely heard the ribbing and sniping of the next half hour by his cynical pal.

"Kidding aside, my new Frederick Turner, *you might be making real history out of all this, right*?"

Manny smiled, absorbing the humor, and reflected on that phrase. Maybe the fellow was onto something more than what he was saying?

Later, at the house, while Dora was making her farewell dinner for them— she was leaving in the morning—he remembered the "making history" phrase, and recalled a line from the great Thomas Macaulay. In his study he searched his notebook and found it, never having understood it until now: "History, at least in its state of ideal perfection, is a compound of poetry and philosophy" (from *Hallam's History,* 1828). Manny would add to that compound the qualities of imagination and fiction. He'd try to make his history filled with that extra-rich compound.

Over a dinner of veal paprika, they listened to Sarah Vaughan, drank a pinot noir, and chatted about autumn here. Dora looked sparkling in her own handmade knitted vest and blouse.

"So you might tell Mom that my graduate class is now studying her papers along with me, and they may indeed create a new and fantastic source book."

She took small forkfuls of food, and eyed him. "You should report to Mom directly, I think. How do you like the veal? Too strong?"

"Tasty!" he said. "And how do you like New Hampshire? A bit dull, yes?"

"Oh, I can get used to dull places like this—mountains, lakes, a small university and museum nearby."

"Not quite the new-world America that Europeans hear about."

She twirled a bite. "I like the way you live, actually. Maybe I'll even return, *if I am invited back.*"

A pause of surprise. "It's a date," Manny offered, and then, reflecting, put out a pawn gambit: "Maybe next time we can drive out to Ann Arbor and see where your grandfather went to graduate school."

She ate slowly, chewing each bite carefully. She eyed him with her small brown eyes, considering how to judge those words.

"Where is Ann Arbor?"

"In Michigan."

She nodded. Ate. Eyed him. Smiled slowly. "Next time I think I will make it a little spicier."

"And see how much I can take, right?"

She laughed. And mocked him. "*Right.*"

Later he wondered about her real view of things—her mother and her obsession, her own beliefs and understanding, Manny and his interaction with her mother, and even Manny and herself. In the night shadows of his bedroom, he conjectured how extraordinary it might be if indeed Raoul's real granddaughter was sleeping a few rooms away! He got out of bed, searched for the anthology on the shelf, and turned to the poems of Emily Dickenson. He found the one: "Much madness is divinest sense / To a discerning eye . . ." The principle was beautiful, but what about the reality? Did he have—and could he hold onto, in the light of day—such a "discerning eye"? Was it possible, just there, a few rooms over? . . .

The next morning, at breakfast, he had a four-and-a-half-minute boiled egg, bagel, and coffee, and made for Dora her buttered toast and tea.

"Please take some of this homemade jam, made by my ex-student," he said, handing over the raspberry preserve, and adding, almost casually, "and please tell me how your mother became so knowledgeable about Jewish things, biblical references, etc."

She nibbled at her toast, raised her brown eyes to face him squarely, sipped her tea, contemplating the question and the questioner. For nearly a minute she examined both and finally said, "Well, I will tell you something, because I believe that you are sincerely trying to help her. Mother was a Catholic growing up, like many Hungarian Jews during the war who were in hiding from the Nazis and Arrow Cross. She never knew that she was Jewish, I believe. Only later, in the late sixties I think, did she convert to Judaism, after she heard a visiting rabbi who came to the Great Synagogue from Israel, who tried to call back those who had been raised Catholic for purposes of survival. When she did return, she threw herself into study, working for two years with a learned rabbi, studying and reading everything she could." She paused, observed his reaction, took another bite of her toast. "That's what I know." Pause. "Yes, this jam is very good."

Scooping egg from the shell, he eyed her. "Did Mom tell you to tell me what you just said?"

Her lips and face tightened. "Do you mean am I her messenger? No. She never gives me instructions, *on anything*." She looked at him sternly. "Is that why you think I came up here to visit you?"

He had hurt and offended her, and he shook his head. "My question was no more than what it was: a question, not an accusation. Please understand that."

After a moment, her face relented, and she nodded slowly.

"But that does explain her rather full knowledge of the subject."

She stared at him, then her wristwatch.

"Yes, we better get going; the airport is about an hour and a half away."

The drive down was uneventful, a return to easy cordiality. He kept his thoughts and questions to himself, like why had she in fact come up, and what more did she know that she had not yet told him. Instead, he drank in her youthful beauty. At the airport, he gave her a proper hug and warm kiss on both cheeks, and she returned them, looking up at him. The connection was real, but ambiguous, and they both left it at that. When he said he'd e-mail her, she said, "I'd like that." She added, with a smile, "And more of that jam."

He returned to the college, and felt better, safer, on home turf. Here he could think rationally, address the wild issues and challenges as they came blowing his way, assess his gains and losses, and take the measure of where he stood. He read his pact with himself this way: if he had become part of the obsession, a misfit piece rather than a solver of the puzzle, so be it. His Wallenberg mission was now set on higher, riskier ground, and if that meant he was a man possessed, a man of "much madness," so be it. Even here, walking on the sparkling oval green framed by the white steepled library at one end and the red-bricked inn at the other, ambling amidst this Ivy college order and sanity while feeling "secretly possessed," this was fine. This was a state of mind, a spiritual feeling, that he was content to live with, like a religious devotee, no matter the challenges, tests, pressures, sure to come. (*And if little Dora returned for more jam, did that also mean more secrets to be revealed?*)

He found himself wandering over to the library, and then, before going upstairs to work, walked down to the basement. There, he was immediately enfulfed by Orozco's giant murals, with their stylized figures (and colors) marching through the long history of Mexico, from the Aztecs to the Revolution. These daunting murals were painted on the high walls of the near-empty reading room. Students hardly studied here anymore, once the new library addition opened with its bright fluorescence and computer-oriented space. Slowly Manny walked around, as though parading at the grand Bolshoi Theater ballroom at intermission, following along the historical depictions (*Departure of Quetzalcoatl, Gods of the Modern World*), taken aback once again by the violent imagination, the crazed stylized figures, the waves of flaring reds and blacks, the anti-Christ and anticapitalist images. Here, underground, existed a different world from the one above in the library or on campus—a space of deeper truths, darker confrontations. (Like RW's life?) This special underground world had been created in the 1930s by the talented Communist painter—his politics outraged the college administration and the townpeople of the time—and here it remained, a mostly-empty library room mural, visited primarily by tourists, foreigners, art specialists.

Manny, as he strolled, felt the strangeness, the incongruity, within himself: this absorption of a radical view and defiant sense of reality. Fondly he recalled again his graduate days in Madison with that gutsy professorial gang of Curti, Mossi, Williams, Hazeltine, Goldberg; and their pursuit of the dark truths behind the carefully prepared façade of American history. Were Manny a painter, he'd be tempted to try a mural of Wallenberg and the events of his life, from Stockholm youth to Ann Arbor architecture school, Budapest safe houses to Lybianka imprisonment, to possible Gulag camps. A narrative of defiance, risk taking, cool heroics, persistence, betrayal, and secret private life. Despite family, despite state, despite religious tradition, despite establishment morality, it would depict a fight for personal freedom of his own soul—and body? But how would you paint that? . . . Switching back to the current mural, Manny realized he felt at home down here, in this underground of fiery vision and fierce truth.

A librarian called out from the reserve books desk, "Professor Gellerman, did you want to reserve any books for your class this term?"

Manny stopped in his reverie, looked over. "Thanks, John, I'm all set."

Yes, he thought, switching tracks, he did have a mural to paint, but it was called a history, a history to write—and to account for. In the land of Winnebagos and Catalinas, pop songs and formulaic films, iPods and feelgood pills, academic piety and national venality, Manny would keep the Wallenberg memory and man alive and well, in some small corner, through his bit of hard spade work.

Standing at the doorway, taking in one last view of the mural, the professor was now suddenly accompanied by a familiar figure framed in a dark suit, fedora hat.

The gentleman shook his head slightly and stared, a stare of disbelief and sobriety, skepticism and forlornness. The look read, "Still at it, here too?"

Manny did a double take, but nodded, appreciating the solitary, if begrudging, support.

Outside, presently, the air had turned seasonally cooler, and it washed over him refreshingly as he walked up the little hill toward his office. He had a class to prepare and much private work to do.

"Keep the Aspidistra flying" Manny told himself, repeating, for no reason, George Orwell's sign-off call at the end of his essays to buck up his fellow citizens in London who were enduring the Nazi blitz bombing. Well, maybe Manny could find some native flower of signature cheer for his own good spirits, when and if the legal and critical attacks started coming.

But for now, he felt okay; he accepted it all—the figures in his imagination, the delusions of the medium, the calls of the remote witnesses, the antics of the critics and lawyers ready to pounce. He embraced the present day of autumnal glory and the sunny innocence of the passing students. Yes, come one, come all, he thought, so long as the Swedish gentleman, his private sidekick from history, stayed around, alongside, checking in peridocially to chide and caution. With that secret sharer in his life now, for all seasons, Gellerman felt ready, a new self in the making, a revised history waiting to be written.

CHAPTER 22

Manny sat stiffly in the wooden armchair on the high platform in the Stockholm Tingsrätt District Court. Even though it was just passed 11 a.m. and he had only been sitting here forty-five minutes, he began to perspire. The questions were the same ones asked yesterday, and just as relentless. He could feel the sweat twirl around his shirt collar, and he didn't know how long he could go on with this steady Swedish torture. And this was only a preliminary hearing, for cause for a full trial! Every now and then he'd nod to his defense attorney; but when the taciturn fellow tried to help him by raising an objection, the judge always seemed to rule against him.

The Armani-suited interrogator, a lawyer from the firm of Danowsky and Partners, persisted, in good English, with the same repeated queries:

"Where have you first found the lady and family in question?"

"Did you check out thoroughly their credibility? How so?"

"Does the professor have documentation that could prove her claims? Or your own claims, in your defamatory essay and public statements?"

"Professor Gellerman, why hasn't this Budapest lady shown up at this preliminary hearing, if she has nothing to hide, and why haven't you, Professor, insisted that she be present now?"

"Please tell the court, are you able now to verify her cache of letters from her supposed father, which the Hungarian lady has claimed to be 'authentic, and held in her possession for years?'"

"Why did you deliberately choose to follow up your oral presentation at the University of Uppsala in the spring with your winter essay in *American Scholar* on the subject, *If you are still not sure of documentation and substantiation?*"

"Does the professor have some personal secret agenda for wanting to defame the Wallenberg family, its noble history, its present family members, and its high professional name? Please think carefully before you answer."

As Manny listened to these questions over and over, he loosened his collar (furtively) and sought to answer as best he could, repeating his own standard statements, which were rather weak generalizations:

"The lady in question, Mrs. Zsuzsanna Wallenberg, was invited by me to come here, but she adamantly refused, declaring such legal battles and defenses have nothing to do with her and her family. In fact, she says that they are a Swedish attack on her integrity and honor.

Well, as I've said before, more than a few times, I have been in the midst of trying to authenticate both the woman's words and also the value of her private collection of letters and memorablia . . . I have had to check this out carefully, with several experts, including international ones, all of which takes time, much time.

Look, my article in *American Scholar* was as much about the nature of historiography, the writing of history, as it was about the Wallenberg case in itself. I could easily have published something for a much wider audience, something in the *Wall Street Journal* or the *New York Times Magazine,* if I had wanted easy fame and money from my project here.

I have tried to act as a historian, but also as an on-the-ground investigator, because of the many mysteries and vast gaps in the case of Raoul Wallenberg. And what I have learned and claimed has been based on my evidence and investigation, not on a preconceived political theory or personal agenda. Moreover, I have tried to be very clear in making distinctions between my speculative opinions and those based on hard, if occasionally circumstantial, evidence, such as what occurred just after the war for the Wallenberg business and banking interests, including its relationship with America and the allies . . ."

While Manny delivered those answers to the courtroom and judge and a scattering of spectators, including journalists, he berated himself again for having published his essay in a public magazine and not in a professional journal. If it had been placed in a historian's obscure journal, no publicity would have come from it, and he wouldn't be sitting here now, in a Swedish courtroom, pinned like a New England butterfly and grilled! In his "New Uncertainties, New Proposals," he had talked about the old Wallenberg problems: How and when did Raoul die? Did he outlive his Lybianka days? Why hadn't he been exchanged or bribed out of the Russian prisons? But it also brought into play Manny's new findings, new directions, and options: the suggestion of Raoul's gay inclinations and its ramifications; the Wallenberg family's post–World War II jam-up with the FBI, when Enskilda Bank was put on their blacklist; their harmful if not criminal passivity during the two years of Raoul's imprisonment; the Budapest lady's claim of a Wallenberg daughter and grandaughter still living.

As the prosecuting lawyer continued his relentless press, asking him if he knew what the laws of character defamation were in Sweden, Manny gazed out beyond the beautiful wood panels of the courtoom to focus on an oblong of the gray sky emerging through the mullioned window. And he couldn't help recall sitting within the green oval of his campus, lazy and easy, watching the students stroll or jog by. Oh, how far away was that green zone of academic ease! And having not one friend here, or colleague, made the ordeal all the worse. Later, when he returned alone to his bed-and-breakfast, on a side street, it seemed bleaker than any prison.

Was this his final punishment for trying to get at the truth, or truths, and not taking heed of the several Warning and Stop signals along the way?

His legal advisor had said, "If you drop the pursuit of the book now, and make an apology for any unwarranted statements, the Wallenberg family is willing to drop this suit."

What a mistake to have come here in the first place—to sign a book contract! Why had he done this? Tempted by the sensational if minor celebrityhood? By the modest money? How foolish! And he knew the lady of Budapest would have no part of defending herself or "rescuing" him here.

He twirled a rubber band in his hand as the prosecutor repeated another query: "Do you have some secret vendetta against the Wallenberg family, Professor? Does the personal attack have anything to do with the downward spiral of your career and the need to prop it up sensationally?"

He smiled weakly. "No personal agenda, Mr. Svenson, I assure you."

The questions continued on until the break for lunch, when Manny, eating his open-faced sardine sandwich in the restaurant across the street, wondered how he had gotten into this new particular pickle. And how he would get out of it? . . .

"Excuse me, may I sit down for a moment?"

A ponytailed dirty-blonde-haired woman in dark glasses was hovering near him; he seemed to recognize her from somewhere.

"Yes, it is I, from Uppsala, you remember?" She removed her sunglasses. "Boel Andersson, the journalist and documentary maker."

He smiled, "Oh, yes, sure, please do sit."

"I am glad to see you again, although not glad for you in this situation perhaps. But you see, this is good for me—I mean, for the film I am making about you, this situation." The waitress came, and Boel ordered a coffee. "They are bullies—everyone knows that—but here, this bullying is out in the open, where people can see it. And I am filming it, as much as I can—the courtroom, their attorneys, you. I get a bit of it inside the courtroom, until they stop me. But it will all be in the documentary about the case, and I am quite sure I can get it onto Swedish TV, the cultural channel. The exposing of the Wallenbergs will be available for all to see, and it will not be suppressed by them."

He nodded, not fully following what all this meant.

She faced him openly, a pale-faced look of confidence and reflection, asking how much could he, Manny Gellerman, hold up under all the pressure?

"Don't worry, Professor, it will turn out in your favor, I believe. The citizens here are on your side, trying to find the answers to what happened to Raoul. He has become a kind of folk hero to the people here, and you have now become his . . . benefactor?"

Manny took off his wire-rim glasses, wet the lenses, and dried them delicately with a cotton napkin. The noun she had used reverberated in his memory, and he thought again of Magwitch, Pip's benefactor. "Well, I am flattered," he offered.

"And we are most grateful"—she took his hand—"for all your effort and determination. We have waited for over sixty years, you know, to move forward somewhere, *to something*." Her smile was warm, displaying tobacco-stained teeth. "There is a strong current of sentiment in your favor, and my documentary will make that stronger."

He eyed the lady, who reminded him of one of Bergman's movie blondes, and he nodded for no reason.

"Therefore, in a way it may be said this pretrial is a blessing, since it brings new attention to the old problems. And all Swedes know that if the Wallenbergs are angry, it is because they are not getting their way, and are very defensive and afraid! So you may suffer a bit, for a while, but stay assured that in the end it will all come out on the positive side for you and our cause."

Drinking his water, he pondered that statement. Glancing at his watch, he stood up and said, "Well, thank you for coming over. I must get back to my 'bit of suffering' just now, but maybe we can have a dinner later if you are free?"

"Yes, why not? Here is my card with my mobile number."

He put the card in his jacket pocked, nodded a good-bye, and walked out into the cool sober street, where the wind had picked up and was making the small Swedish flag, hung on the court building, flutter sharply. Replaying Boel's words, he told himself to be hopeful, that this afternoon and tomorrow of being grilled and tortured was only a temporary state of affairs.

The police guard at the door nodded to him knowingly, as though he were welcoming a regular client to this judicial site.

CHAPTER 23

He sat quietly, cozy in his armchair in the small, well-fitted cell, reading *Jenny* by Sigrid Undset, found on the bookshelf. Hardly a prison cell—it was more like a comfortable library cubicle, with two shelves of books, a trundle bed, a reading chair, a mirror, and a small vanity by the toilet. Plus, he had a small radio, tuned in to classical and jazz stations. And the food was pretty good too: fish dishes with cream sauces, open-faced sandwiches, a variety of cheeses and fresh salads. A prisoner could live here on a long-term basis and not do badly, Gellerman thought, crunching a biscuit with his afternoon tea. Being jailed in Stockholm may have had more perks than renting apartments in many cities.

The irony was to be found, for Manny, in the contrast between his comfortable Swedish open prison in Aby, Sweden, and Raoul's incarceration in Soviet Lybianka. A bit different, the conditions. Of course, the imprisonment was for different reasons; Gellerman's was for personal libel, while the latter's was for being Raoul Wallenberg. Yet, there was a serendipitous affinity between their physical settings, Manny winding up here *precisely because of his search for Raoul.* The affinity was not missed on Manny, who pondered his fate in this relaxed space. His fate: weeks or months here, or longer? It was unclear now, while he stayed stubborn and debated his options. Also, he had another convenience here: the Wi-Fi access, for two hours daily, to the Internet and his e-mail, via a jail computer. So perhaps, all told, he had scored a peculiar sort of victory in his refusal to give in, offer an apology, and remove the allegations.

Of course, he had heard from the lady in Budapest a few days after his incarceration: "I read in the newspapers of your predicament and am wishing to help you. This is simply silly. I will come to Stockholm and meet with you and we can discuss the situation with the judge and then decide what is best. Yes?" Typical enough, as she was always appearing suddenly on the case, a Johnny-on-the-spot, a Master of the Mysterious. Manny didn't quite know how to answer her. Let her come and talk to the judge? Why not? Or would she see to it, somehow, that he'd be a resident here for some years?!

On the other hand, maybe she'd get him set free, set him loose?

But did he want to get loose?

Curiously enough, he suddenly heard the introduction for NPR International and the familiar voices of the two hosts, the soothing Asian woman and the savvy Jewish gentleman. A bliss, or a curse, to hear NPR here? Both, probably. The usual radio talk about what to do about the recession, and soon, the standard three minutes on Afghanistan; for how many years will they torture the news (and serious listeners) with their carefully diced-up three- to four-minute segments, from wars to recessions to "summer reading" to vacations and pop culture? Everything was flattened out to the same value, same denominator. Well, the voices signified home, the familiar, nonetheless. He went back to Undset's *Jenny*, the radical Swedish freethinker who belonged to no club or ideology, just lived a life on her own, an independent soul in Paris in the 1920s. A fine portrait of an unconventional individualist way ahead of her time . . .

Later, he was outside in the June cloudy weather for his afternoon hour of stretching his legs, mini-jogging around the small courtyard, wondering whether to ask for a sail on the Archipelago. This comfortable jail continued to surprise him with its versatile conveniences and considerations.

When he got back to his cell, he found a few notes from his sons, asking what the hell was going on? When was he getting out and coming home, or should they come over and see what was really happening? He wrote a note to each, saying how things were progressing on the legal front, and everything would be worked out soon enough.

The two lawyers arrived at 3 p.m., and they spoke in the conference room.

"The terms remain simple," explained Sven Jorgensen, the plaintiff's chief lawyer. "Simply offer a public retraction and apology in one of the large Swedish newspapers, and give the Wallenbergs authorization to review your final book manuscript. Immediately, all will be forgotten, and you can go home swiftly."

Manny stared at the fellow and crossed his legs.

"Are you ready, Professor?"

Manny shook his head and couldn't resist saying, " 'I would prefer not to.' "

"Prefer not to, what?"

"Offer a retraction or apology."

"Why not?"

"I wrote the truth, as I know it. So I will put it into the book as well."

Jorgensen held up his silver ballpoint. "But is it so important to you to get your 'truth' across, here in a foreign land, that you would sit in jail over it?"

Manny considered that. "I guess so."

"That is very divisive and unfortunate."

"Unfortunate for me, sir."

"Yes. Unfortunate and inconvenient. Don't you have a life you want to rejoin?"

Manny scratched at his beard. (Needed a trimming.) He peered over the shoulders of the lawyer to the portrait of a king on the wall, a poker face of cool imperturbability, and recalled the 1945 indifference of the Swedish government. As for the Wallenberg family and their role in the deadly game, well, he had written his views on that. Both players, family and government, had seen to Raoul's grim fate in Moscow right here, in Stockholm. Maybe Manny's place was here, too, after all? . . .

"You are silent, Professor Gellerman. Don't you want to rejoin your life?"

"This may be my life, sir. Right here . . . waiting."

"Waiting? Waiting for what?"

Manny contemplated, viewing the lawyer's blue eyes. "I am not sure just yet."

Sven Jorgensen shook his head, spoke words to the second lawyer, shuffled his papers together into the portfolio, and stood.

"You may be here a long time, my friend."

"I understand."

"I hope you do; but for now, good day. I will report your response to the plaintiffs and, should you change your mind, you will let us know."

Manny stood, watched them depart, and was escorted back to his small cell.

Later, while reading, he was visited by his shadow friend, the slender gentleman who still traveled with his hat (and backpack). Only this time it was the fellow's old Anthony Eden hat, the silk-trimmed black-felt Homburg from his Stockholm days. He stood at the brick wall, facing Manny sidwways.

"You said you were waiting to the lawyers—for what, may I ask?" Wallenberg said. "Do you yourself know?"

"I suppose . . . for . . . justice to be done."

Raoul laughed lightly. "You will wait a long time then."

"I have time."

"While lying about here, in a jail? No, my friend, you have been loyal, you have pushed far, but you have better things to do with your life, I know."

Manny smiled. "I didn't realize you knew which duties or obligations were, or should be, highest in my list of priorities."

"I don't, but I do know that sitting here, waiting, will not serve your cause." He felt the silk brim of his hat. "*Even if that cause happens to be me.*"

Manny took that in, sitting on his trundle bed. He observed Raoul's dark narrow face, the thinning scalp, the purposeful stare of the sharp brown eyes.

"Maybe you are right."

Mr. Wallenberg nodded. "Maybe so."

"So you believe I can serve you better on the outside, then?"

"Serve yourself better, I mean to say. Besides, what sort of justice do you think you can get for me? A redemption? A retraction? An apology?"

"Well," Manny started, thinking of several apologies to begin with, but said, "A revised history. A verification of what went wrong, who did you in."

He shook his head. "No need for sentimental excuses for history. I helped do myself in, somehow, I am sure, and the Russians helped me out, that's all."

"You are being too honorable."

"I don't think so."

"And your family helped you out. And the king and his government 'helped you out' also, significantly."

He shrugged, took out a cigarette, lighted it, inhaled and exhaled.

Manny eyed the fellow and wished he recalled the right Shakespeare lines to describe the restrained nobility, the higher soul, of this fellow.

"I will confess one thing to you," said Raoul, smoking, "I have enjoyed your company, our brief chats, your unusual concern."

"The feeling is mutual, Mr. Wallenberg, I assure you."

He inhaled and rejoined, "You will do well to get out of here, I believe, and do your work on the outside. I remind you, you should call me Raoul."

"I will, in the future, definitely." He added, "I believe we have become friends through this . . . long ordeal."

Raoul stared. "Yes, friends, odd friends," he paused, and smiled wryly, "long-distance friends, to be sure."

"Yes," countered Manny, "long-distance friends. Maybe they are the best in certain situations?"

"Perhaps you are right," said the reflective, lean fellow. "Well before I say good-bye for now, I will confess there is one other matter," he added, reflecting. "I do actually know a few things, a few things of some significance, to add to my entire case, and maybe you and I can work on them together, here. We would need to gather the evidence, you might say, and decide then the best way of bringing it out." A surprise smile. "Now that I see that you really are determined, stubborn, and really serious. Probably too much for your own good, it seems."

Manny removed his glasses, scratched at the beard, stared up at the fellow and his odd words. *Two years, and now, only now, Raoul believed he was "really serious"?*

The gentleman leaned forward, and half whispered, in the silent cell, "I lived on," and he gazed at his long-time shadow friend.

Manny stared at the grave expression and felt his own heart beating at the words and the meaning of the revelation. Finally, he said, *"Lived on? Where? For how long?* How did you—"

"That is why we need you to get out," Mr. Wallenberg smiled triumphantly, "and begin the search, the new search."

"But how and where—"

Mr. Wallenberg tipped his hat and added, "It is fitting, don't you think, that you, a Jew, *should be helping me now?"* He nodded, "And myself, a sort of ghost, accepting aid from a private ghostwriter?" He smiled and exited.

Manny, still in shock over the revelation a moment ago, sat there for a while on his cot, trying to take it all in. What was going on? Was he batty, or more whole than ever?

Then, suddenly renewed in spirit by the new direction, he stood up to call the warden, to see about his release, to explore his new mission . . . He called, "Guard!"

Here in elegant Stockholm, he would situate his base of operations for a while. And probe the austere, masked city with more hands-on investigation, especially with his ghost of a friend around so much, revisiting—and haunting?—his old home ground. Maybe the two of them together, one living, one a live-in specter, could indeed work to dig up new old evidence, discover something newly relevant, either here in this stealthy town in a secret diplomatic note, or family letter, or in KGB/FSB files, or in a new surprise . . . Gellerman felt in his gut something stirring, sure now that they were forming a unique partnership, a kind of metaphysical detective agency, in pursuing the elusive truths of this sixty-plus-year-old cold case of murderous indifference and moral corruption. "Guard!"

The guard came by and informed him of his lawyer's appearance, and Manny adjusted his shirt and jacket, alert, refreshed. He would have to get out, but on terms different from the plaintiff's lawyer's demand. *Fitting, that a Jew should be helping Raoul now.* And that he the historian should now evolve into a ghostwriter. . . . Should he speak to the judge directly? Or call in his American lawyer friend? Whatever. But outside, he'd be able to work hands-on to gather significant documents, alongside his guiding shadow, who had much experience in this old town and knowledge in avoiding predators, just in case Manny himself became too hot to handle. *He lived on, really? Where? How? For how long? Did the Mystery Lady from Budapest have anything to do with that?*

Meanwhile, over pickled herring (in cream sauce) and Swedish schnapps in the smaller conference room, with a framed photo on the wall of Björn Borg hitting a two-handed backhand with a wooden racket, and another of the king, Manny discussed with Advokat Sonnerup the various options he had for returning to the orderly streets and his newfound (collaborative) work. Yes, he'd work a compromise out, now that he knew from his lawyer that the other side, the Wallenberg family, wanted one too, as it was getting embarrassed and slammed more and more in the daily media.

While waiting for his release, he sat in his cell and took up a favorite book he had brought along, Bernard DeVoto's "The Course of Empire," which he admired for the passion and the sweeping narrative, a book which always relaxed him.

At the same time he understood, or sensed, that he was pushing farther his imaginative projection, and hoped that it was taking him in the right direction; and yet not taking him too far out, like sailing in the Archipelago with his friend and finding themselves drifting into the Baltic Sea.

CHAPTER 24

The cordial guard, Lovah, came over while he was reading, and announced that he had a visitor from abroad. He looked up, surprised, and was led into the small conference room, where he found, sitting at the long table, Dora. She was dressed in a blue wool cardigan sweater and green blouse, looking about fifteen.

He sat down across from her and shook his head slightly.

"Hello," she said.

He nodded. "You've cut your hair."

Half smiling, she said, "Twice, since I've seen you last."

"Yes, it's been a while. How's your mother?"

"Fine. Worried about you."

He paused. "Did she send you here?"

She shook her head. "No, she wouldn't, and I wouldn't listen."

He nodded.

"So you came on your own? I am flattered."

She smiled her small crooked-toothed smile.

"How long will you stay here?" she asked.

"Oh, not much longer, I don't think."

She fixed him, concerned. "Where will you go then? Do you have plans?"

"I don't think so, not firm ones."

"Then will you return to Budapest?"

He half smiled. "It's a thought."

She paused. "I would like that."

He wondered, What did she mean? "You know that I have more work to do, and it may take me to different places, like Moscow or here in Stockholm. And—"

"But Budapest surely is one of those places, yes?"

"Yes," he conceded. "It is one of those places."

She fingered the large collar on her blouse. "Do you think I can help you?"

He removed his glasses and wiped them with a tissue.

"Well, that is an interesting proposition. Let me think on it."

She nodded.

"Do you offer this for Mr. Wallenberg's sake, yours, or your mother's?"

She smiled. "You forgot the professor's sake."

Yes, he had. "You are good, and brave, to come here independently and get involved this way and even offer me this. Thank you."

"But you haven't accepted me yet." She smiled. "Or have you?"

Oh, how clever and wily were the perfectly innocent! That much he knew, for sure. "You will have to do a bit of traveling, and taking notes, and keeping your eyes open and ears alert."

She smiled broadly, her looks rather dazzling.

"You may not even like some of the things you hear, or see."

"I am not a child, you know," she retorted sternly. "You mustn't treat me as one."

He took that in. "All right, accepted."

"Good." She softened. "Now, is there an immediate task?"

Impressed, he said, "Well, not really"—but then he thought of something. "I understand that Mr. Wallenberg may have lived on, beyond his supposed death in Lybianka Prison. Can we find out more about this?"

She took out a journalist's notebook and jotted a note with her left hand.

"You came prepared, I see."

A light smile, still note-taking. "Any more details, Professor?"

How ironic, that this young Budapest beauty—perhaps, on the long-distance chance, Raoul's granddaughter—was now agreeing to work to find the grand old man's whereabouts. Was she doing this for him, or for Manny? *(Or did the ghost himself send her?)*

He put that question to her, soft-toned.

She eyed him carefully. "I am working for you, Professor. And if we discover useful new facts about Mr. Wallenberg, that will be good, very good."

"Yes, this is true."

She stared at him, mustering force. "I am serving you, sir, not any wild dream or vision."

He understood, and thanked her.

"I will get to work, Professor Gellerman—"

"Please, call me Manny."

"All right, I will get to work and report back tomorrow or the next day." She paused, looking at him. "Professor."

She stood up, took her wool coat from the wall hook, smiled curtly, and left.

In his room, he considered matters, looked through some recent documents online, and wondered if indeed Wallenberg himself had sent her as his living emissary. How clever that would be!

Two days later he found himself sitting in the small kosher café/restaurant in Budapest, the same shabby one in the Jewish Quarter where he had first met the lady a few years ago. (He told Dora to meet him later, after his meeting with her mother.) Zsuzsanna looked the same: oval pale face with smooth skin, and hair tied up in a bun, looking like a young teenager. She greeted him with a warm smile.

"You have missed our Event while you were over in Stockholm."

"Yes, the séance; your daughter told me."

"But something important has perhaps resulted, as I told you on the phone, which I have waited to pursue with you personally."

"Thank you."

She stood up, tucked her cashmere shawl around her, and took him by the hand. "Come, it is a short walk from here, please."

She walked with him down the long narrow street toward the Great Synagogue, holding his hand firmly.

"Spring will be here soon. You remember this, yes?"

"Of course."

"Lots of excitement since I last saw you, Emmanuel."

"Yes, although I myself have been away from it all for a few weeks."

"I have heard." She giggled and her eyes twinkled.

She marched them down Dob utca, nodding to several people and giving a Yiddish greeting, gripping his hand. Just before the Holocaust sculpture garden with the metal tree of remembrance at the back of the Great Synagogue, she steered him into the old wooden doorway of the dilapidated old Shul.

"And this perhaps you remember too?"

He nodded, recalling, surprised.

They walked inside, down the long decrepit corridor, passing an old Jew in a fedora, moving to the other shul rooms in back, where they had sat for the Tisha B'Av ceremony a few years before.

What was going on? he wondered. Yet another of Lady Z's "revelations"?

In the drab, modest library room, she took out a spiral notepad from her pocket and found her notes. Then she motioned for him to follow her along the musty bookshelves, where, with reading spectacles, she fingered the Dewey decimal numbers on the book spines, searching them according to her notes.

What was this? he wondered. Jewish Raiders searching for the Lost Ark?

She led him along, finally stopping at a rickety shelf of history books; she set down her large handbag and took out a row of a half-dozen books, and then, strangely, she stretched in vain to reach behind to the empty space.

"Please, you can help?"

She pointed to the vacated space on the bookshelf, and he reached up and inside, bewildered, but quickly felt something. He lifted it out and handed it to her.

She smiled blissfully at the long brown envelope, blew dust from it, and wiped it with her hand. Reading the words on the face, she nodded and handed it to Manny.

"There you are, Professor, directly from my father to you."

He stared at her, astonished, and accepted the missive, wondering what the hell she was talking about. Crazy, as usual?!

"To Whom It May Concern," was written in cursive on the outside, and inside was the handwritten letter, on some crinkly old airmail paper.

Manny shook his head, baffled, sat down at the end of the long wooden table in the center of the room, and the Lady Zsuzsanna followed him, sitting across. She clasped her hands together like a little girl waiting for the teacher to direct the lesson.

Privately, Manny read the letter, handwritten in pencil, reasonably legible:

My Last Thoughts

I have been living in Labor Camp 701 in Vörkuta region for these past dozen or so years, making the best of the worst. I have benefited from the fortunate luck of owning a small Chagall painting in Budapest bank vault—due to an elderly Jewish couple, with no relatives, deported to Auschwitz—so my guards have been persuaded to allow me certain privileges, like sneaking out this letter.

Grandfather did the right thing, choosing to send me to America to study architecture, believing correctly I would learn many other things while I lived in Ann Arbor. Those three years were the best of my young adulthood, and the memories have sustained me here, in Lybianka and in the Gulag. I can still close my eyes and be sitting in Lorch Hall with Prof. Slusser.

My 18 months in Budapest were the most challenging, and vital. They provided life at its highest intensity, and forced me to live in the moment. A true education. My days in the Swedish diplomatic delegation were aided by brave friends like Per Anger and Lars Berg. But no one could have dreamed of a more trusted comrade and valuable friend than my driver, Vilmos Langfelder, whose dire fate I have been responsible for. I still see him vividly, in our Studebaker, urging me to hurry! Forgive me, Vilmos, if you suffered at the end. And to the many Jews whom I was lucky enough to protect in my Safe Houses until they were able to escape, you were my salvation as much as I was yours.

Reflecting on my Stockholm family, I am sure that Marcus and Jacob would have done better, if they were in a less pressured situation. Guy van Dardel and my half sister Nina were exemplary. Yes, our ambassador at the time did not help them or me much, but Soviet Russia was not an easy country to deal with. I know this personally. As for Daniel P., my interrogator who betrayed me, it was my own naivete. Now, regarding those very close to me in Budapest, the less said the better, since the KGB has great big ears, and they never forget, never let go. But you mustn't forget me, as I have never forgotten you.

How does one survive? In "bits and pieces," as my friend in Michigan used to say. If you can find someone to play some chess with, on the makeshift board, you are lucky. If you get a potato in your soup, or a vegetable, you are doing well. If you can get new socks and "bushlati" every year or so, you are lucky. Also a thin mattress made of straw and sawdust to put on top of the concrete slab made for tolerable sleep. These favors are in exchange for the right bribe—my "vziatka," was a Swiss bank account, a good arrangement for both sides, the prisoner and his guards, and the warden. Naturally they expect you to die here of one or another causes, malnutrition and freezing among them. I have suffered from frostbite, TB, emphysema, arthritis, and a steady hacking cough. But the guard has managed to get me some aid on occasion, even a doctor's visit and a few aspirins every so often. (Not too often.) One lives by habits if not hopes. A grand pleasure has been the two books smuggled in, which I read again and again, Jack London's short stories and the first half of Copperfield by Dickens. Boyhood nature in one, and boyhood in London in the other; these always boost my spirits.

Mine was not a kindly fate, one could say; but on the other hand, it was a truly lived life, offering big challenges and affording a few personal victories. Had I stayed in Stockholm and entered the family business, I would have been more comfortable but not terribly challenged. Or felt so needed and useful. So, adding all things up, I am grateful. Even satisfied.
RW

When Manny looked up, his heart beating hard, he saw her sitting there watching him, her shrewd cat-like eyes belied by a shy smile.

An old Jew wandered in and picked up a Sidur from the table. He looked at them and left. The room smelled of age and mustiness. Manny held the two pages in his hands, scratching his lower lip with his teeth.

"Naturally, I will want to see if I can get this handwriting analyzed here, and see what to make out of this. Or, I could send it abroad to my analyst in the Boston area?"

Zsuzsanna spoke softly. "You must do what you must do, Professor. You have been a doubter for so long now; I expected this. Please, may I read this letter?"

He slid it across the table to her.

She put on her spectacles and began reading, slowly.

But now, to his amazement, he found something else in the envelope, a small dog-eared black and white photograph. Brittle with age and faded badly, it showed an older man with a narrow face and goatee, in profile, playing a game of chess with another prisoner. Could it really be RW? Manny couldn't actually tell. On the back, was printed, "Vörkuta, 1962." He felt a bit dizzy.

She wiped her eyes with a handkerchief, "So now, Emmanuel, what is your decision, a final step in the puzzle so we begin serious work, or yet another delay tactic?"

He bit his lip. "You are a very determined woman, Zsuzsanna, and I respect you a great deal. But I . . . I really don't know what to make of this. I shall have to—"

"Please." She stood up and slid the letter back into the envelope, and reached her hand out for the photograph.

"Do you recognize him in this photo?"

She looked at it closely, wearing her spectacles, and nodded. "Poor father!" She sunk down, her head in her hands.

Gently, he said, "If you give me the original, I can have it looked over carefully, and we can begin our work."

She smiled, weirdly. "All will be taken care of, in due time. The important thing is, Professor, that we have communicated with him and found his words and direction accurate." She shook her head. "And now we have new evidence of how he ended."

She started to pack up.

He asked if he could help her with anything.

She shook her head, now rather distant.

They retraced their steps to the outside. Gray and cool.

"I must go now," she said.

"So, when shall we meet?" he asked, "I'd like to make a copy of the letter and the photograph. As soon as possible would be best."

She thought a moment. "Yes, tomorrow morning at nine, at the Central Café," she offered. "You have not yet said what you think of this . . . news?"

"Well, I must digest it, of course. And verify it. But thank you, and I will see you in the morning."

He kissed her cheek, and they departed.

That night in his small hotel he e-mailed several friends about finding the right handwriting specialists, both in Budapest and in Stockholm. Also, he called Dora, telling her of the strange news and arranging a meeting. He wrote to his expert friend, the historian Berger, telling her too. He tried to tamp down his excitement by going out and taking a walk along Andrássy Avenue, which pleased him with its old-world shabby charm. He slept well, feeling, curiously enough, a burden being lifted from his shoulders. Of course, he knew he was jumping the gun, but . . .

At 8:45 a.m. he was seated at the large Central Café, ordering his juice, rolls, and coffee, and waiting. The square marble table and stiff wooden chair suited him.

At 9 a.m. he was drinking his coffee and peering up to see some of the famous artists and writers of Hungary of yesteryear staring down at him from the walls.

At about 9:20 a woman appeared, wearing the *Scheitel* (wig) and demeanor of the religious, and asked if he was Gellerman, the American professor. She handed him a note in an envelope and excused herself:

> *Dear Emmanuel,*
> *I was very disappointed in your response yesterday to a true mitzvah. You treated it with your usual American skepticism, while I was much overwhelmed. Imagine, a real letter from my father, and you act with disbelief and mistrust! I am sorry, Professor, but I have to take a little time off now, to decide if I wish to work with you any longer. You have disturbed, maybe destroyed, my belief in you. Please do not try to reach me, as you will not be able to. When I am ready to see you again, I will let you or my daughter know. Believe me, for you to act as you did, when I was ready for us to celebrate, was a big damage to my feelings, and my memory.*
> *Zsuzsanna Frank Wallenberg*

Manny sat there, in shock, at what had occurred. He saw the customers walking to and fro, heard the clattering sounds of dishes and silverware, barely heard the waiter asking if he wanted more coffee, and he nodded.

It had all happened so fast! Had he truly misplayed his hand? Had he missed the chance of a lifetime? Was he totally reasonable in his doubt, but stupid and insensitive in his wording to her yesterday? His eyes grew blurry, his chest heaved.

"Professor, are you alright? Sir?"

Dora was suddenly sitting at the table, wearing a simple cardigan and looking at him with her beautiful youthful face.

He shook his head and told her what had occurred. "The letter even spoke about 'those very close to him in Budapest,' or words like that. Of course, it could easily have been made up, but . . . who knows? . . ."

She ordered tea from the waiter.

She shrugged. "My mother is up and down, moody, you know that. She is very sensitive. Easily offended. I think she will come around, though it may take some time. But we have time, don't we?"

He sipped coffee, looked at the trusting girl, wondered if he did have time, and smiled wanly. "I don't really know what to believe, actually."

"I understand that, sir." She put her hand on his, for the first time. "If it was a genuine letter, she will let you have it, I think. It's too important for her not to."

"I am not clear any longer about what is genuine and what is not."

She smiled. "That is true; sometimes it is hard to tell. In people too."

"You should call me Manny, while we are waiting for her."

Dora nodded dutifully, accepting the porcelain teacup and saucer set on the table. "Where should we wait, do you think?

He gazed at her and tried to focus on the question.

She smiled softly, "Budapest? Stockholm? New Hampshire?"

"How about Vörkuta—do you think they've opened it up yet to foreigners?"

She raised her eyebrows, wondering if he was serious.

He looked up, and saw through the big windows, and figured, for now, this new piece of "evidence" was as good as any in the giant RW conundrum. And maybe Vörkuta was the right place to start the next leg of the hunt?

"Come, let's walk down by the river and see what we think."

Gellerman paid the bill, and they went outside and walked across the traffic to the old law library, and down toward the Elisabeth Bridge. They walked along the river—she had taken his arm—like a couple strolling. The air was cool and windy. They walked on, and on.

What to do now? he wondered.

They came to the Parliament area and the Margaret Bridge, and a small area that was set with a striking memorial on the river embankment at the edge of the Danube—a stark grouping of a dozen or so bronze shoes, a testament to the Jews who were shot by the Arrow Cross and tossed into the river.

The bronze shoes stopped Manny.

He thought of the brave soul who had saved so many but who remained such a personal mystery. How much had Gellerman entered into it, shed light on it?

"Imagine if that letter was real," he said aloud. "In any case, either way, he was quite grand—either as your grandfather or as a grand illusion or mystery."

She looked up at him. "And you are perhaps grand, for searching for him the way you have been and continue to do."

"Well, he's become a friend, actually, a friend who comes and goes, sometimes with advice, sometimes with cautions. I've become his invisible shadow, you could say." He smiled. "Or he mine."

They stood a while looking at the roiling river, with the Margaret Bridge nearby, at the randomly set shoes symbolizing the dumped, murdered Jews. Manny peered at the hilly area of Buda across the river; and beyond, above the hills, he saw a configuration of cumulous clouds, forming architectural shapes in slow motion. He was reminded of a Wallenberg sketch in a notebook, and they created in him a kind of dense music, which resonated mysteriously. Without thinking, he took the young woman's hand—this Dora who may or may not have been related to his heroic friend, and who stood alongside him and stared silently.

And now he began to feel something, some motion within that mirrored the wind outside, and he tried to discern its meaning. Here, beside the choppy blue-gray river, not far from the bronze shoes of memory, he began to understand, or *feel*, what Zsuzsanna was furious about—his lack of faith in *her* Wallenberg. Why of course. In truth there were several Raouls, some imagined, some real. *For didn't all complex souls require several selves and demand multiple interpretations?* Wasn't *his* Wallenberg just as mysterious, just as much a matter of faith, speculation, as hers? Hadn't he created *his Wallenberg, his living ghost*, through his own deepening faith, based on his knowledge of the evidence at hand? He half-smiled. In fact, the same means were often, maybe inevitably, used in the writing of history, when crucial facts were missing and one interpreted—or even unconsciously invented—based on a collection of other, circumstantial facts. So why shouldn't Manny should give credence to Madame Z's version of the family Wallenberg, as strange as it might seem, with its mystical reasoning, its medium's sightings, callings? Deliverance could be reached along very different paths. The clouds shifted, a bit of dusk light escaping through the edges.

"Yes, we have work to do," he offered, "but I feel promising vibrations."

The young woman looked up at him and squeezed his hand, in concert.

About the Author

Alan Lelchuk, novelist, professor, and editor, was born in Brooklyn in 1938. He received his BA in world literature from Brooklyn College in 1960 and his PhD in English literature from Stanford University in 1965. He is the author of seven novels: *American Mischief, Miriam at Thirty-four, Shrinking: The Beginning of My Own Ending, Miriam in Her Forties, Brooklyn Boy, Playing the Game,* and *Ziff: A Life?* For young adults he wrote a memoir, *On Home Ground.* His short fiction has appeared in such magazines as *The Transatlantic Review, The Atlantic, and Partisan Review.*

Lelchuk has taught at Brandeis University, Amherst College, and, since 1985, Dartmouth College. He has been the recipient of numerous awards and honors, such as Guggenheim and Fulbright awards, and visiting professorships and writer-in-residence appointments in the US, Israel, Germany, Hungary, Italy, and Russia.

He served as associate editor (with Philip Rahv) of *Modern Occasions*, and was a cofounder of Steerforth Press. He co-edited *8 Great Hebrew Short Novels* in English.

Alan Lelchuk lives in the countryside of New Hampshire, and has two grown sons.